SATURDAY CITY

SATURDAY CITY

❖❖

Jan Webster

St. Martin's Press
New York

Library of Congress Catalog Card Number: 78-21203

ISBN 0-312-69974-3

For Lyn and Stephen, with love

FAMILY TREE AT 1880

Robin Balfour
|

Kate Kilgour
m. Findlay Flemin

Jack Kilgour
m. Clemmie Macnaughton
|

Sandia, George, Andrew,
Mabel (dec.), Kitty, Alisdair

Duncan
m. Josie Daly
|
Carlie

Jean
m. Pat McGahey
|
John, Samuel, Jakey,
Peter, Brian, Terence

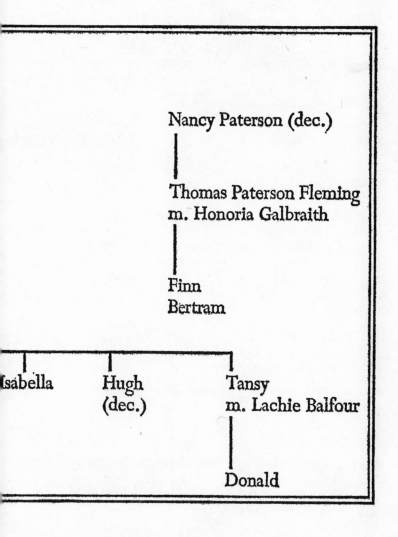

Nancy Paterson (dec.)

Thomas Paterson Fleming
m. Honoria Galbraith

Finn
Bertram

Isabella   Hugh   Tansy
                  (dec.)   m. Lachie Balfour

                                Donald

SATURDAY CITY

PART
ONE

◆

Chapter One

The two girls sat in the horse tram going along Glasgow's
Sauchiehall Street. The open upper deck was draughty, damp
from recent rain, and whisky fumes reached them from the
seat behind, where a drunk man sang morosely into his
gingery beard.

Sandia Kilgour, torn as always between her desire to
expand experience and her wish to be a meek, obedient
daughter, already regretted being drawn into this Saturday-
night adventure by her friend Kirsten Mackenzie. The conflict showed in the whitened knuckles of the hand grasping
the brass rail in front of her, the rigid posture of the slender
neck and the way dismay followed eager involvement
moment by moment in the expressive, wide-set blue eyes,
like fleeting clouds obscuring a watery but persistent sun.

Her mother believed she was at Kirsten's home near the
university, stitching nightgowns for the poor under the
benevolent eye of the professor and his hospitable English
wife. Some kind of judgment was upon her, she was sure.
Maybe death from fright and remorse as the tram lurched
and shambled through the throng of Saturday-evening

9

shoppers. Or it was possible God and her parents had something else up their sleeves.

Kirsten, by contrast, seemed totally at ease. She was never bothered by vague, ill-defined reservations about behaviour. English people seemed to possess this sang-froid and Kirsten was half-English, of course, her craggy Highland father having brought home a dark-haired, educated bride from some Nonconformist eyrie near Manchester.

'We'll save Argyle Street for last,' said Kirsten now, 'as it's the best.'

'But it's rough there,' Sandia demurred. Sauchiehall Street would be altogether safer and more salubrious, she felt. But Argyle Street was the real hub of the city, where everyone went : football supporters, bargain hunters, street musicians, pavement artists, second-hand booksellers and sharp-eyed shoppers buying everything from new suits to chipped crockery and broken biscuits. Part of her wanted to go there every bit as badly as Kirsten; the other part was consumed with holy terror at the very thought.

At Renfield Street Kirsten pushed her friend before her down the tram stairs. Gasping on the pavement, Sandia said faintly, 'I think, Kirsten, I'll just go back home now.' But Kirsten took her firmly by the arm.

'You are you,' she said forcefully. 'It is a free country, under the Queen. Your parents do not own you, you know.' At this seditious statement, Sandia looked paler than ever, but now she was actually among the cheerful Saturday crowds, recklessness took over. A jig played by a street musician made her treacherous feet do a joyful little shuffle. Kirsten felt her shift of mood immediately and said encouragingly, 'After all, my dear Sandia, we *are* grown-up. You are seventeen and I am eighteen. Surely we are old enough to look after ourselves?'

'Your parents are different,' Sandia pointed out. Dr Mackenzie was quite alarming in the way he kept speaking of women getting the vote and his wife positively encouraged girls to have a point of view, an attitude which sometimes embarrassed Sandia as at home she had to behave with much greater decorum.

If her parents only knew the half of the things discussed in the Mackenzie household! For example, Mrs Mackenzie was sometimes heard to declare: 'It is not enough for women just to have babies.' She had even insisted that there were ways people could employ to *prevent* having children, and Kirsten had blithely offered Sandia a book called *The Fruits of Philosophy*, about something called birth control, which had been the subject a few years before of a notorious prosecution by the courts. She said her parents had encouraged her to read it and Sandia could borrow it to study if she wished.

Sandia had refused, of course. Ever since Kirsten had told her what she alleged happened between men and women when they married, she had felt it was probably wrong for them to go on being friends. Sandia doubted if Kirsten could in fact be correct. Was it not much more feasible that people – well, simply embraced and kissed and that from such spiritual union something vague and cloud-like turned from vapour into matter and so into an infant? But then again, she had once been sure Heaven was a physical place with tables, chairs and sofas that you ascended to through white fluffy clouds and blue skies, and God a physical presence like her late grandfather Findlay Fleming, and neither tenet seemed probable any longer, so she could be wrong about babies too. If only her mother did not look so pink and confused and evasive when she asked for facts!

Sandia had not broken the friendship, however. She had gone on listening in horrified but fascinated silence while Kirsten pointed out that this birth control thing was necessary because the population was getting so out of hand – more so in Glasgow than anywhere else in Britain – that some extremists were advocating that all babies after the third in poor families should be killed.

When Sandia's disgust had broken through in protest Kirsten had rounded on her fiercely. 'Have you seen the East End slums? Babies die anyway from malnutrition and neglect. Mothers do get past caring. Open your eyes, Sandia, dear. Surely if families were limited to two or three, life would be worth living for those poor child-bearing machines, for that is what they are?'

Very often Sandia said nothing. She knew that Kirsten's experience of the world was much wider than her own. When the City of Glasgow Bank had failed two years ago, in 1878, leaving a fearful trail of misery and bankruptcies, the Mackenzie family had been tireless in organizing soup, bread, coal and money for the unemployed during that cruel, hard winter, which had seen degradation piled on misery when the shipyard workers came out on a long, embittered strike. Although the two girls had not known each other then, a dreadful consciousness of what it was like to be destitute and hungry had entered Kirsten's mind and even now she told Sandia tales of death and hunger at that time which kept the younger girl awake at night, combing her conscience as to whether prayers and the odd bundle of worn-out clothes were enough.

But in the main Sandia accepted calmly enough that she and her friend lived in different worlds — Kirsten's free-thinking, outrageous and advanced; her own stable, kirk-bound and restricted. She could then listen to her friend's more advanced ideas without being a party to them.

Kirsten's vivacity made all her other friends colourless by comparison, that was the trouble. That was why she was on this ill-considered outing, even now trembling from time to time at her own temerity.

'My mother would have one of her turns if she knew,' she moaned to Kirsten.

'Your mother uses her turns, as you call them, to her own ends,' replied Kirsten. 'She is quite spoiled with servants — and you are one of them.'

Sandia's mouth beaked open in protest, but as often happened, nothing came out. Some rebellious depth in her acknowledged a grain at least of truth in what Kirsten said, but allowances had to be made for Mama since Mabel's death. Sandia missed Mabel, too, perhaps more achingly than any of them, for they had been closest in age, but she did not admit it to anyone, even Kirsten. Her dead sister's face came back to her now, sharp, freckled and admonitory, as it had been in life, and annoyed that she had been the one to Pass On, when they had shared the same fever.

Now Mama put most of her love on to Alisdair, Sandia thought. Glancing at a mechanical bear being made to dance along the gutter, she thought how much Alisdair would have enjoyed this outing. He was a very responsive little boy, bright and loving. She felt Mama kept him at her side too much, in those fussy ringlets and dresses, protesting he was delicate when he was simply made too much of. She should not criticize Mama, of course, but being with Kirsten always seemed to embolden her.

When Kirsten suggested they go to Mr Stuart Cranston's Tea-rooms in Queen Street to have some refreshment, Sandia assented with an almost pleasurable leap of terror. The tea-rooms had only been in existence a few years and were the first of their kind in the world, so Kirsten assured her. They were surely intended for such as they, who did not want to enter the grim, businessmen's restaurants and would never entertain the notion of going inside a public-house.

They stood outside the tea-rooms reading Mr Cranston's announcement: 'A sample cup of 4s. Kaisow with sugar and cream, for twopence – bread and cakes extra: served in the sample room.'

Sandia peered over the lace curtains and saw that the tea-room was small but crowded. Throwing caution to the wind, she followed Kirsten inside and sat elbow to elbow with other Saturday shoppers. It was fun to observe and be observed. She knew they made a striking pair, Kirsten in her green cloth dress with its kilted frills and a white feather in her bonnet, she in her brown velvet walking dress, her second-best but still her favourite, with its pretty mussel-shell buttons.

She knew also she was quite pretty in a wholesome, fresh-faced way, taking after her Grannie Kate, they said, with her fine complexion and fair hair; a foil for Kirsten's dark vivacity. The strange thing was that if you analysed Kirsten's features, took them one by one, there was no way they could add up to beauty. Her brow was too narrow, her nose too aquiline, her chin too short. Yet she had something that made heads turn, that made total strangers look at her and smile as though they'd known her all their lives. And her hair was beautiful, a mass of dark, auburn-highlighted curls and tendrils, so thick Sandia feared it must sap her strength, as her mother maintained was the case with very luxuriant tresses.

Kirsten gave her a small conspiratorial smile and whispered, 'Mr Cranston is a great tea expert, you know. He was with Joseph Tetley, where they called him "the wizard of the leaf", and he's a coffee-taster, too!'

As they gave their order, Sandia could feel the eyes of a pink-faced, handsome youth at a nearby table constantly upon her. She had never seen such thick, light brown hair nor a gaze so desperate yet honest.

Kirsten jogged her arm. 'Someone is looking at you,' she said archly.

'It is more probably you,' Sandia countered. But she felt a tide of excitement rush through her, making her so mindlessly happy she scarcely gave a fig for decorum.

'No, it's you,' Kirsten insisted generously. She began to giggle, a small, irresistible sound. 'He's just spilled some tea down his waistcoat! See what you've done to him!'

Sandia could not look for embarrassment. But as she and Kirsten threaded their way back to the street, she glimpsed the young man's confusion and pity tilted her mouth in a faint smile.

Her doubts about the expedition had disappeared completely. It was like coming alive. All she could think of was that she was in Glasgow on a Saturday night, as she had so often dreamed. Glasgow, the Second City of the Empire, throbbing with a brash and dangerous life, like the engines of the great steel-boilered ships which carried her name throughout the world in these eighteen-eighties! Her father liked to repeat some of the street names like a litany: Union Street, Jamaica Street, Virginia Street, St Vincent Street, Nile

Street and Wellington Street. Many of them had come about through Glasgow's commerce with the West Indies and American colonies, in the rich old days of the tobacco barons. But how could even these days compare with now?

The light-headed excitement lasted as she and Kirsten strolled along Buchanan Street to the Arcade, a roofed-in promenade with a multiplicity of little shops which led through to Argyle Street. Sandia declared her head was beginning to spin from seeing so much in one afternoon.

'You know, it is very interesting,' said Kirsten, as they passed the Clan Tartan Warehouse. 'People used to barter for goods in the warehouses. Papa says that the politician Campbell-Bannerman's family – drapers, of course – were the first firm to have fixed cash prices. But bartering sounds more fun!'

Sandia nodded. What with gawping at the stiff poses in the photographic studios, and drawing Kirsten's amused attention to an advertisement for an 'electric and magnetic self-adjusting' cure for practically any illness, including Indecision and Palpitations of the Heart, she was in a receptive, happy daze of enjoyment.

But later, walking along Argyle Street, clinging desperately to Kirsten's arm, she began to be less euphoric. Here were the really poor that Kirsten was always talking about, obtruding like sores on the city's bustling, confident surface. Among the sharp-eyed, decent folk making one penny go the length of two, and the Saturday sports with money to burn, were the atrocious, scabby beggars, the barefoot, dirty children with runny eyes and noses, the quiet, waxen babies, carried like shrunken dolls in filthy shawls round the mothers' bodies, and men so drunk and helpless they fell in heaps in the gutter, grimacing and groaning and sometimes passing into oblivious sleep.

The noise was beginning to make her head ache when Kirsten suddenly dragged her off-course and into St Enoch Square, where a few people were struggling with packages towards the station that took passengers down the south-west coast to places like Girvan and Stranraer. In the cobbled street near the station, some soapbox orator was gathering a lively and fairly substantial crowd around him. Sandia had had enough. If Kirsten got interested in what this man was saying, they could be there for hours. And Sandia's courage was on the ebb again, sapped by sore feet and the start of a throbbing headache.

'Please, do let's get the tram home, Kirsten,' she begged, but her friend turned an upbraiding face towards her, saying, 'Shh! It's the reason I've come. I've heard him before – and he's marvellous.'

'*I* don't want to hear him,' Sandia protested, near to tears. Suddenly she was thinking longingly of the quiet life they had all lived at Greenock, before Papa became involved in ship refrigeration and they had had to move recently to Glasgow's West End. She really was not up to Kirsten's sophistication. And the rough, contentious types already shouting at the speaker, heckling him constantly, made her fear for their safety. A number were Irish, she judged. You could tell by the wary stance they took up on the edge of the crowd. Maybe just arrived that day at the Broomielaw. Papa said they could come for fourpence now, from Belfast, and what with the Poles and Italians and Jews, and all those folk from the Western Isles, they were making Glasgow more like New York every day, Papa said. And he should know, for he'd sailed to New York many times, first sail-and-steam as a boy stowaway, but latterly in style in the big steel ships, at the captain's wheel.

A drably-dressed woman walked through the crowd, handing out pamphlets. Sandia took one silently and looked distractedly at the heading: 'Dounhead Miners' Union Asks For Your Support.'

Below were several paragraphs setting out the grounds for the miners' complaints against the coal-owners. They claimed that wages were being reduced and the men's demand for controlled output and stable wages ignored. The pamphlet called for strike action in the Lanarkshire coalfields, and the nationalization of the mines, the railways and land as well.

Something filtered through Sandia's agitated brain then, as

she stood next to Kirsten in the heaving, shouting crowd, baptized now by a little light evening rain. The heading on the pamphlet said Dounhead. That could really mean only one thing. Her father's family came from there and his half-brother Duncan Fleming was the agent for the Dounhead Miners' Union. She looked again at the woman who had handed her the pamphlet and realized that she was, in fact, her Aunt Josie. The start of the rain and the fact that Sandia's head had been drooping dispiritedly when the pamphlet was handed over had prevented each from recognizing the other. And the bearded man on the rostrum was her Uncle Duncan, categorized by her mother as an agitator but by her father as a good, unselfish man.

She had met them both a short time ago at her little cousin Donald's christening. That was what came of belonging to such a big family – you had uncles at either end of the social scale. The baby's father was Lachie Balfour, one of the coal-owners Duncan was in the process of castigating. (It was only her redoubtable Grannie Kate who held them all together on occasions like the christening.)

But it was her own position now that filled her with utter panic. If Duncan or Josie saw her, they would surely tell her parents. The delights of the tea-room and shop windows were forgotten as she tugged frantically at Kirsten's arm. 'That's my uncle up there. We *must* go. I don't feel well. Please, Kirsten. Please.'

Her friend simply did not hear her. Her eyes were fastened on Duncan Fleming, her face straining to hear every word he said. He certainly had a compelling demagogic style, his right hand stabbing the points of his argument home, his left raised in exhortation, sometimes both arms held wide as though to embrace the motley horde before him. A dark-haired, thin-faced man, handsome as a poet.

But something he was saying now was stirring the crowd to anger. Sandia listened in spite of herself.

'I appeal now to our Irish brothers among us. Don't let them use you as blackleg labour in the pits. I know well enough the circumstances that bring you here, the desperate bad harvest, the fact that thousands of your fellow country-men are without a roof over their heads, evicted because they are expected to pay rents when they have no money, no jobs – and yes, I know well enough the job the politicians have done in Ireland. But the way to a better day is through the brotherhood of labour . . .'

'Send the bloody Fenians back where they came from,' shouted a dark-browed man in the crowd, hoarsely.

'We've as much right here as you,' bellowed a red-faced man next to him. 'We need work – '

'Ask him about the murderers in New York,' screamed a woman. She turned dramatically to the Irishman, and what looked like a pound of sausages for Sunday's dinner, wrapped in string and brown paper, fell to the ground in her agitation. 'Do you deny the Fenians go there for money for guns and bombs to kill the people here?'

'You and your like,' shouted the Irishman imperturbably, 'came to our country and trampled it under your feet.' If you're so keen to keep us, then you can't object when we come here. We're only returning the compliment.'

'Oh God, why did we come here?' Sandia groaned, as scuffles broke out in the crowd. Kirsten had her in an iron grip and would not let her move away. Eventually, how-ever, the scuffling and shouting subsided. The Irishman spat and walked away in search of a drink and the woman who had challenged him picked up her battered sausages and, hat askew, continued her shopping. Duncan changed tack and was now talking about political aspirations in a general way, and, sensing a cooling-off, one or two more hotheads in the crowd drifted away.

Sandia wondered if she dared catch a tram home on her own. She felt very inadequate and feeble compared to Kirsten, but then all kinds of arguments were daily meat and drink to the Mackenzie family. Sandia, for example, was perfectly happy to attend the Free Kirk with her parents as she had always done, but Kirsten had joined the Evangelical Union, because she argued that Christ had died for the whole of humanity, not for a small elect as the

Calvinist Free Kirk believed. This made her think the poor were her equals, even the scabbiest beggar rattling a tin mug in the gutter. Sandia simply couldn't see how that could be. It was just more of Kirsten's outrageous nonsense and, really, after this escapade maybe she should indeed finish with Kirsten and go back to embroidering samplers and discussing novels with her quieter friend, Mirren Hood.

'Oh please, no!' she pleaded inwardly, as she heard her uncle call now for the vote for women as well as agricultural workers. There would be no getting Kirsten away now! In desperation, she saw Kirsten put up her arm and call in that commanding voice she got from her professor father, 'You are right, brother. We shall never have justice for women until we give them the same power as men to judge the greedy and the drunken among those who rule over us.'

It was frightening. The mob who had been concentrating on Duncan Fleming turned now almost as one to stare unbelievingly at this well-dressed female with her cultured tones who had dared to infiltrate their Saturday-evening meeting-place. Hoarse laughter and jeers were turned on Kirsten, with much gratuitous advice about where she should take herself. Sandia coloured as she heard swear-words used, and pulled her skirts away in time to avoid a gob of spit aimed in derision at her friend.

'Give the young woman a chance,' Duncan Fleming was challenging, but suddenly Kirsten and Sandia were being jostled and pushed and a red-faced woman was attacking Kirsten with her umbrella. Kirsten pushed her away and that was the signal for another wave of aggression from the crowd. Fists and voices were raised and it was all Sandia could do to keep her feet. Her hat was knocked askew and a jarring thump landed on her back, knocking the sobbing breath out of her.

Just as suddenly her uncle was beside them, urging them away from the cobbled square as fast as he could move them.

'Sandia,' he breathed urgently, 'what are you doing here?'

'Don't tell Mama,' she pleaded.

He rushed her on and as a tram slowed down near them,

propelled both girls on to its platform.

'It's going the wrong way,' sobbed Sandia.

When he had bought three tickets, Duncan looked at both girls almost genially.

'We had to get away from the mob. It gets like that sometimes,' he said. 'Introduce your friend, Sandia.'

'Miss Mackenzie, meet my uncle,' said Sandia briefly, still half-sobbing in her agitation. 'Oh, Uncle, please don't tell Mama or Papa.'

'That isn't my intention. My intention is to get you safely home.'

'And what about Aunt Josie?' cried the girl wildly. 'What will they do to her, back there?'

'She can handle any crowd,' said Duncan easily. 'She's with union friends who are taking her on to a temperance meeting.'

Kirsten had said nothing, content with observing Duncan closely as the tram swung and swayed through the busy, darkening street, where gas jets and paraffin lamps were being lit in shops and houses. The turn of events, though surprising, was entirely to her liking. Her pale face, too irregular and small-chinned for beauty, but wonderfully mobile and expressive, had taken on a rapt and dedicated air.

'We get off here,' Duncan ordered, when the tram had lumbered the length of Argyle Street. Skilfully he began to lead them up side streets and along cobbled alleyways with the purpose of getting them back to Sauchiehall Street and so on their way home.

At last he stood in the shadows at the end of the terrace in the West End until the door of his brother's imposing house opened to swallow the breathless and fast-repenting Sandia into its roomy depths. He had no wish to meet with his half-brother tonight, or, more especially, to justify his presence to the plump, self-indulgent Clemmie, his sister-in-law.

Sighing as one half of his mission was completed, he turned to take Kirsten safely back to her home at Gilmorehill. Against the pale night sky, delicate and translucent after the rain, he could already see the imposing spires of the university itself.

Kirsten gave him a dazzling smile.

'I have heard you before, you know. Once at an open-air meeting at Glasgow Green and once at a temperance rally.'

'So you're temperance-minded?'

'Of course. Not that I think drink is the only problem. It's so much more than that.'

She looked at him a little shyly, wanting to say more, yet thrown into confusion every time her gaze met those dark, intelligent eyes.

When they reached her parents' commodious apartments on the ground floor of a red sandstone building, she said hesitantly, 'I don't know if I can ask you in. My parents are out. At a dinner given by Sir William Thomson at the university.'

'The Atlantic cable man?' asked Duncan, interested in spite of himself.

Kirsten nodded. 'The great professor of natural philosophy himself.'

'He regards war as barbarism.'

'And do you?'

'Certainly. What else? I believe in the brotherhood of man.'

She said on a low, concerned note, 'You do look weary. Come in anyway and I'll make you some tea.'

He didn't argue. He was beginning to realize how long it was since last he'd eaten. And the money he'd used for the tram fares had been the last he'd had in his pockets. He sat in the huge parlour before a dying fire while Kirsten made for the kitchen after informing him it was the maid's night off. First she had lit two lamps and he was able to take in the florid magnificence of the white velvet mantel-valance, with its paintings of orange blossom and maidenhair fern, its green silk fringe and carved wooden balls fastened to the fringe for good measure.

The mantelpiece itself was loaded with enormous amber vases, silver-framed photographs, conch shells and candlesticks. Another time the vain show would have irritated him; tonight he was for the moment too tired and too comfortable to care.

Kirsten brought in a tray with soda scones, ham and cheese as well as tea.

'Eat up,' she begged.

'Just a cup of tea,' he said politely.

'You can leave your working-class scruples behind here,' she advised him, teasing. 'When we're hungry here, we eat.' As though to demonstrate, she cut a hunk of cheese and sank her teeth into it. 'We're a very radical family.'

He laughed and took a buttered scone.

'You look younger when you laugh.'

'I'm hardly Methuselah.'

'I didn't say you were,' she responded, blushing. 'But do you eat enough?' She blurted the question out. 'You should take care of your health. You have a job to do.' He was very thin; his moleskin trousers and rough jacket hung on his angular frame as though on a scarecrow.

'Aye, well,' he said, warmed by her concern, 'I eat when the occasion arises. But empty bellies are commonplace where I come from. And there'll be more, when the strike starts.'

'There's to be another strike? I heard Macdonald is against it.'

'Aye, but Keir Hardie's for it and he's got the Hamilton men behind him. It'll spread throughout the coalfield.'

'Who's Keir Hardie?'

'A coming man. A young agitator the bosses would like to get rid of. He's got a strong style of oratory.'

'But Macdonald has the advantage of being an MP.'

'Parliament has watered him down, as it always will so long as our men go in under the Liberal banner. The men see their wages being whittled away and they think the Lanarkshire Miners' Union started by Macdonald is letting them down, so they're joining the breakaway unions.'

'Where do you stand?'

'Somewhere between Macdonald and Hardie,' he humoured

her. It was no time to be going into the rough complexities of coal-mining politics. She was, after all, no more than a girl, and he began to feel the lack of propriety in the pair of them sitting there chatting, almost as though they'd known each other all their lives.

'Let me help,' said Kirsten impulsively. 'You have no idea how I long to be involved. I have my temperance work and my poor visiting, but it is all so – so puerile.'

'What could you do?' he asked, with patient good nature.

'I could run a soup kitchen. I could distribute warm clothing – ' She broke off, looking red-faced and a little embarrassed. 'No, that's not enough. I want to be involved at a proper political level, with a labour section of the Liberals whose concern will be with working men and women.'

'I can see your heart is in the right place.' He smiled to soften the somewhat patronizing comment. 'I'm not turning down your offer of help. But this struggle at Dounhead, as you know, is about more than charitable soup. It's about extending the franchise and it's about the right to work and be paid a decent wage. It's about keeping blacklegs out of the pits – Poles from the pogroms or starving Irish who are only compounding their own misery by accepting too little.'

To his consternation he saw she was nearly in tears. She said, as evenly as she could, 'Why does no one take me seriously?'

'But I do!'

'No. You don't really. I can see it in your face. But women have to get involved. They *must*. I have two brothers who are doctors and one a scientific sort and I never have any difficulty keeping up with them mentally. Yet even Father, who agrees with me in theory, still half-wants to keep me at home, embroidering. No one thinks a woman should or can command.'

'But that's all changing,' he said gently. Smiling, he put a hand to her eye and lifted away a tear. The hand was rough, grimy from Glasgow's soot, and she drew a quivering breath at his touch. 'I'm not sure I agree with you, anyway, about women not commanding. I know plenty of Scots households where the woman wears the breeks. My own wife works as hard at politicking as I do, and I have a sister, Isa, a doctor in the mission field in Africa. So don't let's have any more talk about feeble women. It's your life. You can do what you want with it.'

'Yes.' She nodded soberly. 'But what real advance can women make, till they get the vote? You *are* in favour of that, aren't you?'

'What else?' he replied lightly. 'And I want it for farm labourers who live in outlying districts. We're lucky to have it in Dounhead, since it's a town, if a small enough one. But it's an invidious situation when men who work the soil can't vote.'

'Gladstone is no help,' she said fiercely. 'He talks about joining the Women's Liberal Association so that in time we may *earn* the vote. But we shouldn't have to earn it. It should be ours by right.'

He grinned. 'Aye. He knows he can't be seen supporting the women outright. He wouldn't remain Prime Minister for long, if he did.'

She changed tack. 'Father's half-agreed to let me try for Cambridge – women can go there now, you know – but perhaps I should stay in Glasgow and work for the suffrage.'

'I think you could do a lot, if you put your mind to it.'

She clapped her hands together.

'How marvellous to meet a kindred spirit! Do you think the unions will come out for us eventually? That would rattle Gladstone's composure.'

He laughed. 'If all the ladies were like yourself, he wouldn't have a leg to stand on.'

They smiled at each other, like conspirators. He thought she was an uncommonly bonnie young woman, with her rich, tumbling hair and sparkling animation. To his ironic amusement, he could feel the old Adam stir in him, making him feel about seventeen again. It was warm, he was fed: was there harm in staying a little longer? She'd be about eighteen or twenty, he'd guessed, and he was thirty-three.

24

An old married man. It seemed irrelevant for the moment, though he knew it would not be the moment he put his foot outside the door.

He lay back in his chair and said encouragingly, 'You should think about going to the university. I could have gone once, you know – that was in the old days, before they built this great new pile at Gilmorehill in 1871.'

She nodded, laying her head on her arm which was outstretched along the back of the sofa and gazing at him contentedly. She looks like a painting by Dante Gabriel Rossetti, he thought, with a sophistication beyond her years. He was stirred and excited and amused by her and it made him talkative.

'I remember once passing the Old College and hearing the "angry bell", as they called it. The students were tearing along like mad, for the doors were closed whenever the bell stopped, and nobody else allowed in. It was a foggy afternoon, I remember; the gas jets were on all day long and the air was almost yellow. I thought of all the good Scots brains that had sat there – '

'My father for one. He came from the Isle of Skye on a bursary, living off oatmeal and herring – '

'And your father's friend Sir William Thomson for another, matriculating at the age of ten with his brother James, and winning all the prizes, because they were decided by the students' votes in those days, but he would have won them anyhow.'

'My brothers all copied Sir William.' She smiled. 'And so did I. We all used to carry a green notebook about with us, as he still does, in a gamekeeper's pocket, so that he may go ahead with his calculations at any time.'

'So you would like to do something scientific?'

She blushed. 'I don't know. My father says I have a tolerably good mind – I can understand the various theories concerning electricity and magnetism and heat, and I shall explain to you how Sir William's mirror-galvanometer works on the trans-Atlantic cable, if you like!'

He smiled at her merriment.

'But I am too much a woman to work in abstractions. There are plenty of technical advances being made here in Glasgow without me! What about you? What would you have studied?'

'I don't know. Language, maybe. Literature. But I was tied then as now to the colliers' rows. You have to choose what you'll do in this life, and stick to it. Remember that!'

'Oh yes. I shall never forget it. With me, it is the women's vote.'

Duncan put down his cup. He had drunk three cups of tea, and eaten well, and he felt warmed through to his marrow. It was with reluctance that he stood up to go, looking round at the rest of the richly-furnished room with a mixture of distaste and interest. In his mind, he suddenly saw Josie waiting about for him, her face pinched, stamping her thin-soled boots to keep warm.

Suddenly uneasy and guilty about the warmth and comfort he had enjoyed, he said formally, 'I thank you for your hospitality, lass.'

'I wish we could have talked some more,' she said impetuously. 'Could I come to Dounhead some time, do you think? Meet your wife?'

He was suddenly at a loss for an answer. Josie was sociable, hospitable towards those in need, but she could be rude and aggressive towards people she felt to be overprivileged. His pause registered and she said quickly, 'I'm sorry. I presume too much.'

'No,' he protested. It was important somehow to make her understand. 'It's just that folks in the Rows don't have all this – ' he waved his arm to indicate the room, the books, the comfort – 'and they can be forthright if they think they're being patronized.'

'It was never in my mind to patronize.' Her face went pale with hurt.

'No. I know that. But you have to admit there is a gap, a gulf, between the likes of you and the likes of me.'

'I find no difficulty at all in talking to you,' she protested. 'In fact, you are the only person who has ever understood

26

how I feel about the vote. I had thought we could be friends.'

Her directness excited him. Josie was suspicious of articulate people, but with this girl he felt he could open his mind. He was seduced by the idea of talking to her. There were so many things surfacing even now in his mind, things he had had to keep to himself for so long, because so few understood what he meant.

He made the decision. 'Yes, come out to Dounhead. See what it's like in the miners' Rows. It'll be a good Radical education for you!'

They smiled like conspirators. 'Yes,' she agreed. 'I'll do that.'

Captain Jack Kilgour put an arm round his wife's shoulders and ushered her gently in the direction of the office door.

It wasn't that he didn't enjoy those occasions when, on one of her shopping trips, she chose to rest for five minutes away from the horse traffic in his quiet sanctum.

It was just that he had so much else on his mind this morning and her annoyance over Sandia, their eldest, was something that could wait till he got home.

'I wouldn't have minded so much,' Clemmie mourned persistently, one hand on the door handle, 'but to hear it from Mrs Farquharson Reid herself. Our Sandia coming out of Cranston's Tea-rooms on a Saturday, and all these men in there. "You don't own me, Mama." That's what she said to me, Jack. My own daughter!'

'I'll speak to her,' Jack promised. 'Why don't you buy yourself a new bonnet, since you are here in town?'

'No, Jack. Bonnets are far from my mind. Get your clerk to fetch me a cab, if you would.'

The Captain kissed his wife's cheek and watched as she sailed like a little brigantine through the front hall of his lately-acquired company premises. She was too solicitous of all the family welfare. Sandia might have stepped out of line, but he was secretly glad to see her show a little spirit.

Not that he felt anything but the most tender concern for Clemmie. They were two halves of the same being and when she had one of her nervous headaches or unspecified weak turns, he was filled with a cold ache of terror that he should ever be asked to go on without her. It had been pleasant to see her in town instead of, as more frequently seemed to be the case, retired to her couch or bed for a lightly-steamed fish dinner or a quiet hour with the *Lady's Companion*.

So much of what they had been through in their early life came back to haunt him. Her marriage to someone else because he had not been able to give up the sea for her. Their defiance of accepted morality when she had found out her mistake. Sandia's birth out of wedlock. And the time the three of them had come near to perishing on the old wooden hulk, the *Chancellor*, which had burned like a brand in the cusp of the waves. The shame and humiliation of her divorce, although that first marriage had never been consummated. All these had taken their toll on Clemmie's strength, and Mabel's death, too, had been a cruel blow, although it was a rare family indeed that did not lose a child in infancy or later.

The determination to care for Clemmie, never to see her or their children in want, was what strengthened Jack's resolution as he waited now for his next visitor. There would be no more poor furnished rooms in Gourock, as when Sandia was a baby. Now there was the big house in Ashley Terrace, furnished from Wylie and Lochhead as Clemmie wanted it, staffed with maids and heated with best coal. And that's how it would remain.

His mouth set in a grim line. He had not found the transition from sailor to businessman an easy one, but he was sure he was on to a good thing with ship refrigeration, which would soon mean the whole of the British Isles could be fed on cheap beef and mutton brought from New Zealand and Australia at twenty degrees below freezing point. Just the same, after the bank scare of a few years ago, he didn't want all his eggs in one basket. He had to diversify. Diversification could mean a summer villa down the river, his own yacht, Clemmie indulged in clothes and jewellery. Scots-American syndicates were nothing new, after all. He rattled his knuckles against the glass case that held a model of the first ship he had ever sailed, the *Titania*, sail and steam, and waited for Joe O'Rourke to be shown in.

'Jack Kilgour! Cap'n Jack!' The little Irishman, dressed in brown hat, suit and Ulster, gold rings gleaming, danced across the expanse of Brussels carpet with a hand extended and pulled Jack into a bear-like embrace.

'It's grand to see you.' Jack sat the visitor down with a generous whisky in a glass of Edinburgh crystal and beamed at him with genuine affection.

'D'you know, the older I get the more I value old friends?' declared Joe. 'I told the new wife – she's an expensive one, that, I may tell you, Jack – I told her: Jack Kilgour and me have been friends since we were both knee-high to a grasshopper. D'you think about the old days in New York, the way I do, Cap'n? The time you stowed away from Greenock. Brave as a lion you must have been. How old were you? Ten? Eleven?'

'Maybe twelve.'

'You took half my newspapers and sold them for me. And I took you home to my poor sisters, both long since dead, God rest their souls. A life of adventure you've had, Jack my lad.'

'No doubt,' said Jack, more quietly. 'Who would have thought then you'd have risen to a fortune, Joe? And I don't forget what you did for me. Gave me my ship when I thought I'd never sail the seas again. When Clemmie and I thought we hadn't a friend in the world.'

'A roller-coaster,' said Joe. 'That's what life is, Jack. I've been up and I've been down and now I'm going up again.' He swallowed his second glass of whisky, took off his jacket to reveal a jewel-encrusted gold watch and chain and said with genial purpose, 'Let's get down to business, then.'

Jack moved the papers in front of him and said without further preamble: 'These New York companies, Joe. You can vouch for every one of them?'

'Certainly.'

'Some you're involved with, some not?'

29

'Right.'

'As things are, it seems to me that you're expecting too large a proportion of money to come from this side of the Atlantic.'

'Nothing so unusual about that,' Joe argued. 'Glasgow's where the money is, America presents the opportunity. Lumber, mining, railways, land reclamation, building, agriculture.'

'You come here,' said Jack severely, 'because you know you'll raise money at a lower rate than anywhere in America.'

'Right.' Joe's gold tooth glinted as he smiled. 'But we can even things up a bit if you can get your brother Paterson to come in.'

Jack looked at his friend speculatively. He wondered how far the whole operation had been set up by Joe to bring in Boston-based Paterson.

'You know my brother could buy and sell everyone on your list?'

'I know that. He's railroad, isn't he?'

'He's the shrewdest man I know, and he's my own brother. Or rather, half-brother. But he's not coming into this till he knows more of the Glasgow end.'

'You persuaded him to come over?'

'Yes. He's bringing his wife and their two boys. Clemmie doesn't know it yet, but she's going to have to set up the hospitality.'

'His wife is Scottish?'

'From Dounhead. Daughter of our minister, that our mother was once housekeeper to.'

Joe's gratification was obvious. 'I tell you, Jack, we're going to be all right in our old age, you and me. You think you're well off now? Just you wait!' He drew his face into a more sober expression and asked with assumed nonchalance, 'Hard man, is he? Paterson?'

'Went out there just after the Civil War,' Jack replied. 'Crossed the plains in the first steam trains. Saw off Indians and buffalo. Nothing he didn't know about designing locomotives. He had a genius for it.' His face softened. 'I remember him as a ragged-arsed wee laddie in the Rows, asking me to draw an engine for him with a stick in the dust! He was my step-father's love-child, you know, that my mother brought up as her own.'

'Since he's from Boston, but was born in Dounhead, why don't we call our syndicate the Boston-Dounhead Trust?' suggested Joe. 'He'll appreciate the tribute.'

'No doubt,' said Jack drily.

Their business completed for the day, he took Joe down in the direction of the Broomielaw for a sight of the water and the ships, and then for a solid meal in one of the businessmen's restaurants. The small Irish-American was visibly impressed by the stir and bustle of the city.

'Gee, it's as good as New York,' he admitted.

'Funny,' said Jack, 'that's what one of the newspapers called it the other day: "Little New York." Glasgow folk feel close to America, you know. I suppose it's all the ships that have sailed from here to there, and back again, in the last forty years.'

When Jack broke the news to Clemmie that Paterson and Honoria were coming, with the boys, the whole family went into a tizzy of excitement.

'Jack,' said Clemmie, 'I shall want new curtains, all through the house. And gowns, for myself and the girls. I expect Honoria will be very à la mode.'

He noticed she had forgotten all about Sandia's misdemeanour. When he asked where his eldest was, the others chorused that she was in her room.

Sandia was pleasurably aware of the stir in the house, but she had other things on her mind. Staring into the heavy oval mirror of her dressing-table, she bit her lips to make them red and pinched her cheeks to heighten their colour.

She *must* see the young man in the tea-rooms again. She would go into a decline if she didn't. It was as though his bold, innocent glance had fallen like a stone into the quiet pool of her life, sending out endless and disturbing ripples.

Chapter Two

Lachie Balfour stepped down from his gig at the pithead of Dounhead Colliery and lightly tethered the little black horse, which looked round greedily for its feed-bag. It was growing dark as he walked across to his office and all along the rows of miners' cottages he could see candlelight and firelight sending soft pools of light into the dusk.

He stopped for a moment, caught up, entranced. He would have liked to paint the Rows now. In this evening moment, blurred and shadowy, they were mysterious, almost beautiful, and at this distance there was no smell from middens, no screech of fretting babies or shouts from distracted mothers. When he'd been left the pit by his grandfather, he had had no feeling for it. Nor was there much now. But he could feel that gut-response, that pull at the emotions, which preceded the wish to paint a picture, and at the same time the powerful, obscure anger that he was not free to do what he wished to do.

He stubbed his toe, feeling his way across the office to light the gas, and swore with a vehemence out of proportion to the mild pain. Waiting for Duncan Fleming, he lightly sketched the scene he would like to have painted. How could he achieve that blue – fathomless, like melting into chaos, that was the moment before night? And then the colours of firelight and lamps and candles, delicate blobs of white and yellow and orange. The whole frail and evanescent, like a wisp of smoke or a moth winging into the twilight.

'Aye, you wanted me?' It was Duncan, clattering into the office in his muddy, tackety boots after a sharp unceremonious knock at the half-open door.

'I wanted you,' Lachie affirmed sourly. 'You could have

scraped your boots.' There were times when he was well enough disposed towards his wife's brother, but this was not one of them. How different they were! His wife, Tansy, with her light, careful, artificial voice guarding each consonant, her ability to convince county and aristocracy alike that she was one of them; and this pig-headed, stubborn, proletarian rabble-rouser, with his show of learning and assertive, wide-legged straddle, as if daring anyone to try and push him – or his ideas – over.

Tansy wanted the good things in life for herself. She admitted this with a disarming frankness. But Duncan wanted to turn the universe upside down, start again and arrange everything differently. Duncan wanted to play God.

Well, Lachie had shown him where he got off once already, beating him in the elections. He was prepared to take him on again, but the whole thing was a bore of crashing proportions. He sighed, gritting his teeth at the loss of a rare inspiration. The picture he wanted to paint sat in his mind.

'That's good.' Duncan approved the drawing.

Lachie drew it away.

'We're not here to discuss my drawings. Can I not get you to see sense?'

Duncan strode about the room in the insistent, awkward boots.

'It's not a question of getting me to see anything. The feeling has been building up in the men for a long time. If they decide to strike, I can't stop them.'

'Nor do you want to.'

'Nor do I want to.'

'This damn' Keir Hardie,' said Lachie. 'He sees himself as the saviour of the masses. Does he know the misery he brings on the men's families when he brings them out on strike? It's all right for him up there on the platform, carried away by the sound of his own voice.'

Duncan looked down at Lachie disbelievingly.

'You refuse to see it, don't you? The Lanarkshire pits have an accident record that will damn you and the other coal-owners to hell. How many men perished in that Blantyre pit? Two hundred. Not a week passes but some poor bastard gets his back broken or his face smo'ored in slack. You talk about misery – '

'I've improved our safety record.' Lachie was stony-faced. Never far from the surface of his mind was the death of his father-in-law, Findlay Fleming, when he'd tried to rescue men trapped in a fall-in.

'Aye.' Duncan surveyed him grimly. He was remembering, too. 'You've learned a thing or two there, Lachie. But you talk as though you were extending some kind of privilege. "Right, men, you crawl on your hands and knees from dawn till dusk, swallow the black dust till your inside's as black as your breeches, and I tell you what I'll do, men: I'll make sure the bloody roof doesn't cave in and break your backs. Can't say fairer than that, can I?" ' Duncan's satire was savage, his mimicry of Lachie's polished accent woundingly accurate.

He went on in the same lacerating tones: ' "So you fancy an eight-hour day, men, do you? What would you do with the time left on your hands? Sleep? Dig your gardens? Walk up the hill behind the pit and listen to the larks? Let me tell you, larks aren't for the likes of you. Nor books. Nor politics." '

'Cut it out.' Lachie's voice sought to deflect argument.

'No, I won't cut it out.' Duncan's fist crashed on Lachie's desk and he sat himself down with a heavy, deliberate thump on the chair opposite. 'You asked me here to do something I'll never do: break faith with these men in the Rows down there.'

'I did no such thing,' Lachie remonstrated. 'I asked you to come because, despite our differences, we can still talk to each other. You're a rational being, I hope. You don't shout obscenities, like some. Even at this late hour, I want to stop a strike that will hurt everybody. I don't want blacklegs in my pit. I'd much rather have my regular men down there.'

'Then do something about restricting output. Don't cut their wages so you can sell cheaper and cheaper coal.'

'I'll sell no coal at all, if I don't cut prices.'

'You're timid, man,' said Duncan. Lachie's face flushed at the contempt in his voice. 'You could talk a bit of sense into the other masters. You've more humanity than some. But you're frightened to show it. Aren't you?'

Lachie said angrily, 'I'm wasting my time. You'll not see sense.'

Duncan gazed at him levelly. 'You married my sister. Tansy never made any secret of the fact that she wanted to go up in the world. She wanted soft hands and servants. But it doesn't mean her brother is a boss's man. My demands are the same as Keir Hardie's. Reasonable demands.'

Lachie held the pencil he'd used for the drawing between taut knuckles.

'I've never victimized a man in my pit, no matter what his views. They have a week's holiday. I've spent thousands making it the safest pit in Scotland.' He looked at Duncan bleakly. 'But it all comes back to old Findlay dying down there, doesn't it? You've never forgiven me for that.'

'No,' Duncan said. 'If he hadn't been foolhardy, he could have got himself out. I don't hold it against you.'

'Then why the bitterness?' Lachie's tone was conciliatory. 'Whatever happens over the strike, let you and I keep up a communication, for Tansy's sake.' He rose, opened a corner cupboard behind him, and began to pour out two small tots of whisky.

'Not for me. You know I'm temperance.'

'That small amount wouldn't hurt a baby.'

Duncan ignored the whisky and the rationalization.

'I'll tell you why the bitterness,' he said consideringly. 'I'll try to make you understand, although your fancy education has so far removed you from the people you live among that it'll be difficult.'

'I know you envy me that education. Tansy says so.'

'Ha! Envy you? I consider myself better read and better educated than you are. I've done it for myself –'

'Narrow! Hidebound! True pupil of McChoakumchild. You use knowledge like a battering-ram –'

Duncan sat back in something like amazement.

'What else have we got? As a nation? Only our brains.'

'And they're all exportable, man. Go down to the Broomielaw and you'll see him, the Wandering Scot, setting out for the ends of Empire, his sums and his catechism tied up in a kerchief. Maybe you should join the exodus.'

Duncan burst out in appreciative laughter, disarmed at last.

'All right. I haven't had the benefit of your cosmopolitan education. Your grandfather's money took you abroad, opened your mind to painting and music and literature. Do you see, man, thanks to that, you have a freedom the rest of us will never know?'

'I don't follow.'

'The rest of us struggle up towards the light. We know there's a big, wide world beyond the parish pump. Dimly, dimly we sense it. But we can't feed the spirit or the mind because the body is always hungry. Or tired. Or, in the case of women, broken open giving birth to children.'

'You sentimentalize, you know. Most of them down there just want a full belly. Their eyes are closed to finer things.'

Duncan said with a contained anger, 'Right. We'll settle for full bellies to start with. But don't think because a man has no soles to his boots he can't respond to beauty. Whether it's nature, or pictures, or poetry.'

There was a genuine note of affection in Lachie's voice. 'I think it's a shame, brother-in-law, that you never got away from the Dounhead muck-heap. You're the only civilizing influence in this parish. I wish you'd talk the men out of this strike. The masters have agreed a hard line is necessary. No matter how long it lasts, you can't win. Go back to your men and tell them that. Make sure they understand it.'

Duncan made a quick, almost dancing movement towards him, and although Lachie ducked away, he dragged him by the shoulders to the office window.

'See that end house there? In the third Row? Poor wee light, isn't it? They don't run much to candles or paraffin. Willie Macarthur lives there, with Jessie and their bairns. How many? Too many, probably. But they do their best for them. On a pound a week.'

He looked into Lachie's face and grinned without pleasure. 'Go back to your fellow masters and tell them Willie Macarthur is striking for a stable wage. Willie Macarthur wants to nationalize the pits. Willie Macarthur thinks *he's* going to win. Make sure they understand *that*.'

'Why can't I go to Dounhead?' Kirsten persisted.

Her father sipped appreciatively at the hot barley broth in front of him, making little smacking noises with his lips. 'This is good,' he told his wife. 'A fine, strong flavour.'

'Why, Father?'

Dr Mackenzie turned his deceptively mild blue eyes in Kirsten's direction.

'Because I've said so.'

'But that is no reason at all. That is totally without logic. You can't bring me up to think for myself and then turn round and dictate to me – '

'I fear you have an inflated and romantic notion of what a coal strike is all about – '

'He is merely pointing out, dear,' said Mrs Mackenzie, 'that you know nothing of the hardships out there. Tempers can be inflamed when a strike breaks out. They may even call in the Hussars. There'll be fights and drunkenness.'

'Father only pays lip-service to the notion that women should be emancipated,' argued Kirsten. 'What if I decided I wanted to be a missionary? I have thought about it, you know. Would you let me go to Africa?'

'The case does not arise.'

'You couldn't stop me. It would make a mockery of all your Christian beliefs. In what way are the poor of Dounhead different from the African natives?'

'And in what way are you fitted to help either?'

'I can run a soup kitchen.' Despite herself, Kirsten's eyes filled with tears of aggravation. 'I should be working with Sandia's aunt and uncle. They are good people.'

'We only have your word for it. We have not met them.'

Kirsten got up and put her arms around her father's neck.

'Please. Let me go. I want to live my life.'

He gazed into that soft, unmoulded, intelligent face. He had always held that the female intellect had been too much subsumed by the domestic and trivial, but all sorts of fatherly and protective instincts rose in him now, wanting to guard this beloved sprig from the hurts of the world. It was no help at all that she merely wished to carry out his own theories.

Made angry by his fear for her, he said, 'You'll get no blessing from me if you go.'

She patted his greying hair. 'I'm going, just the same.'

An hour later Kirsten took the horse tram to the Central Station. She was calm and had managed to put her father's anger behind her. Strangely, it had been her mother who had reassured her, with a kiss and the quiet declaration that she would be all right so long as she remembered her Bible and common sense.

In the tram she sat next to a grubby child with bare feet and a tear-stained, dirty face. The child drew her tattered, smelly rags towards herself, not to contaminate the lady.

'Don't you go to school?' Kirsten asked her gently.

'I work. I wind bobbins,' replied the girl. 'But I'm not working today for I'm going to see my mother in the infirmary.'

Further questioning elicited that the mother had probably been carved up in a street brawl. Kirsten gave the child a shilling. She was symptomatic of everything that was wrong with Glasgow – the casual brutality, squalid slums, child exploitation in the sweat shops. Yet symptomatic of its tough spirit, too, as she got off the tram ahead of Kirsten and ran off, spinning the coin joyfully through the air.

It was Josie who opened the door to Kirsten when she at last reached the cottage in the Dounhead Rows. A hot and dusty Josie, engaged in cleaning out the coal range, whose eyes widened at the sight of the neat, blue-clad figure on the doorstep, bearing a carpet-bag and asking in a clear, well-modulated voice if she were Mrs Fleming.

'I am,' said Josie shortly. 'What's your business, Mistress?'

'Miss,' Kirsten corrected her. 'Miss Kirsten Mackenzie.'
She held out her hand. 'Your husband said I could visit you.
I want to help – '

'So it's you?' Duncan appeared in his shirt-sleeves behind
Josie, a pen stuck behind one ear and his hair on end. 'Come
in, lass.' He turned to Josie and explained. 'She's from
Glasgow. Wants female suffrage, same as you.' He grinned,
not put out by Josie's accusatory stare. 'I told her we could
show her what politics are all about.' Now the grin was
turned on Kirsten. 'I never thought you'd have the nerve
to come.'

Kirsten looked round the kitchen with a curiosity not
untinged with revulsion. The table was piled with unwashed
crockery and scraps of food left over from meals, except
for one clear corner where Duncan had obviously been
working on a speech. In a wooden cradle near the recessed
bed, a baby was stirring from sleep. Baby and other garments
littered the chairs, while a dusty sideboard held an amazing
clutter of magazines, books, papers, china and food.

'You could stir it with a spurtle,' Duncan admitted cheerfully. 'Josie whisks round once a week with a broom. If she
has the time.'

The baby, Carlie, let out an ear-splitting scream, and Josie
picked her up and nursed her as the visitor took a hastily-
cleared chair on the opposite side of the table from Duncan.

'Well,' said Kirsten nervously. 'Here I am. What can I do
to help?'

Josie half-turned away from her and put the baby to the
breast. At fourteen months, Carlie would have been weaned
but for an attack of measles.

'I'm still not clear what brings you here,' Josie said
ungraciously.

'This is the lass who was with Sandia,' said Duncan. 'She
wants to see for herself why pitmen in Lanarkshire are talking about a strike.' He smiled at Kirsten a shade uncomfortably.

'What is it to her?'

'I want to *help*,' Kirsten intervened. 'I'm tired of being

39

the sort of Christian who never gets her hands dirty, Mrs Fleming. I want to get involved in politics. But maybe you think women have no right to put their noses in.'

'I never said that,' said Josie sharply. 'My man will tell you I'm a believer in women's rights.'

Kirsten beamed at her. 'Then we can be friends.'

Josie sniffed. 'You'd have been better to stay in Glasgow. The Rows are no place for the likes of you.'

'I can think of no better.'

'The Rows are not your fancy West End drawing-room, where you can discuss the poor with your pinkie held out over your cups of China tea.'

Duncan laughed to soften the harshness of Josie's words.

'How old is the baby?' asked Kirsten, ignoring the jibe. Carlie gave up her feed and turned an interested gaze on the newcomer.

'Fourteen months.'

'Would she come to me, do you think?'

'No,' answered Josie triumphantly. 'She's just had the measles, and she's grizzley.' She hugged the baby possessively, watching Duncan with a certain smirking irony as he tried unsuccessfully to tidy the table.

'You must be tired from nursing her,' said Kirsten sympathetically. She rose and competently cleared the table, piling up the crockery for washing. She took off her braided jacket and removed her hat, taking a little blue feather from it to amuse the baby.

To Josie she said intently, 'You have made my point for me. It's time I got away from the talk and involved with deeds. Can't you see?'

'Just so long as you know what you're letting yourself in for.'

'That's that, then,' said Kirsten relievedly. She added, 'If I can have something with which to cover my skirt, I can tidy up.' Josie pointed to a piece of rough sacking behind the door, her look indicating that if Kirsten were soft enough to get her hands dirty, she was welcome to get on with it. While Josie nursed the whimpering baby and Duncan tried again with his speech, Kirsten systematically swept and dusted and in an hour had transformed the room. By then, Josie had nodded off before the fire, loss of sleep from the baby's illness finally catching up with her.

Kirsten was acutely aware of Duncan, even though he wrote steadily without raising his head. At last he threw down his pen and gave her a long, considering look. She felt her clean, well-made clothes and the memory of her comfortable, well-run home like an affront, at that moment.

'I'm glad I came,' she asserted, almost as though he'd asked the question.

She made some tea, poured it into freshly-washed cups and produced some tea-bread from her bag to go with it. She felt the urge to scratch under the waistband of her skirt. Still, what were a few flea-bites? She was well and truly launched on the long road ahead.

Duncan hurried through the gate at his mother's grey-stone cottage, sending the silly hens scurrying through the cabbages in a squawking crescendo of panic. Kate's face was at the parlour window, peering a little short-sightedly to see who was coming.

She fancies she looks like Queen Victoria in that little lace cap, her son thought indulgently. She was tranquil in her widowhood, tending her hens and her garden. When he remembered the hard times in the Rows, the periods of his father's drinking, he was glad for her.

'Maw, I can't stop. There's a strike meeting in Summerton's Field.' He kissed her hastily. 'I want a favour of you. Can you put up a visitor from Glasgow, a very respectable young woman? She'd be no trouble at all to you.'

Kate had given sleeping accommodation in the past to Duncan's political friends, trade union leaders, co-operative members and once, even, a Member of Parliament. But a woman was something new.

She looked closely at her son's expression, but it registered nothing but a slight impatience.

'What sort of a young woman?'

'A professor's daughter, sympathetic to the cause. Now this strike's dragged on, she wants to help Josie run the soup kitchen. She's a born organizer – '

'All right, she can come,' Kate agreed. 'Are you putting up someone else in your own front room?'

'Might be,' said Duncan evasively. Realizing, as always, that there was no point in telling his mother less than the truth, he admitted, 'She and Josie get on well enough. But they are two strong wills – '

'Say no more,' beamed Kate. She quite liked the sound of the professor's daughter.

Duncan set off at a run for Summerton's Field, which was in fact little more than a rough piece of stony ground which the local farmer had allowed to pass by default into public use. It was near the river and a favourite spot for children to go paddling, swimming or guddling for baggy-minnows in the summer.

Keir Hardie had promised to make a fleeting visit to rally the strikers. He was running into trouble at the Hamilton pits, mainly because he appeared to have dug too deeply into union funds, but he would still be a draw here. It seemed to Duncan that the entire population of the Rows had turned up, and half the remaining village as well.

He struggled panting towards the co-operative float that was to be the platform and on which stood a harmonium which Josie had spirited away from the new co-operative hall. Kirsten was seated before the harmonium, playing soft chords and harmonies that floated out over the summer air. It could have been a gala, a festival, and the children seemed to be treating it as such, playing games among themselves. But the women hugging shawls and gossiping were drawn-faced and anxious. The strike was into its fourth week and they had been serving up tatties for dinner long enough. No wonder they called it the Tattie Strike! Although they had been away from the coal-face for a month, the men still wore lines of coal-dust round their eyes and on their hands.

Duncan gathered up the attention of the crowd.

'Brothers and sisters, let us sing together.' He and Josie

and Kirsten had agonized over the choice of hymns, wanting them to be as broad-based and near-secular as possible.

With Kirsten pounding away at the harmonium, it was impossible for the crowd not to join in. After the first hymn, Josie dragged a young miner with a fine voice up on to the platform to sing 'Jerusalem'. Even the children stopped playing to listen to him. Duncan looked around the daisy-strewn field, at the scarecrow, raggedy crowd that inhabited it. The contrast between nature's graces and human deprivation choked the words in his throat.

'Brothers and sisters,' he began his speech, 'we are not giving in, are we? We are hungry. We have nothing to put in our cooking-pots. No coal for our fires. No boots for our children. But we are not giving in, are we?

'We know if we give in, one day it will all have to start again. Unity now means a stable wage. It means the eight-hour shift is coming nearer – '

Down the edge of the field to a mixture of cheers and cat-calls came Keir Hardie, the young miners' leader from Hamilton who, some said, was going to end up in Parliament.

He disappeared when he had made his speech, and it was Josie who now took over, giving out details about the free soup and clothing which she and Kirsten had been organizing.

Suddenly Duncan became aware of a disturbance at the far end of the field. Ribald shouts and jeers went up from the men as Lachie, with Tansy by his side, rode his gig to the edge of the crowd and stood up in it. The crowd rapidly surrounded him and Duncan had no option but to join them, with Josie and Kirsten.

' – no victimization . . . strike has gone on long enough . . . wives and children who suffer . . .' Duncan could only catch part of Lachie's words. But his bold intention was clear enough. And Tansy sat up there, straight-backed and grave of face, in a yellow dress, giving him her tacit support.

Somebody picked up a turf and threw it. It sailed over the little horse's head and landed on Tansy's lap, sending scurries of dried mud down the beautiful frock. It was followed by another, and another. The horse showed the whites of its eyes, rearing up in terror and alarm. Grim-faced, Lachie gave up the battle, took up the reins and forced his way back out of the field. Children followed the gig a short way down the road, more from mischief than malice.

Ivy Thompson, one of the more voluble wives from the Rows, turned from shouting insults after Lachie to confront Duncan and his party.

'What's she doing here?' she demanded, jerking her head in the direction of the departing Tansy. 'She needn't put on her airs and graces with us. We know she's from the Rows.'

'I can remember her when she had snotters at her nose,' cried a woman called Nettie Boyle spitefully.

'And a bare backside,' said another.

'I suppose,' said Nettie Boyle to Duncan, 'she sees that you lot are all right for meat and victuals.'

'No, that's not true,' said Duncan quietly.

The woman shook a skinny fist in his face. 'Get away home! We've had enough of you and your damned Hardies. Get the men back to work!'

Duncan said in the same quiet, reasonable voice, 'Are you running out of victuals at home, Nettie?'

There was no colour in her distraught face. Two lanky, greasy strands of hair framed it and skimpy tears ran down it, almost as though they, too, had run out of supply.

'We've got nothing. We've got nowhere to turn.'

'I'll see Josie brings you down something tonight,' he promised. Nettie wiped the tears away with the end of her shawl. Trailing out of the field, her children followed her like so many tattered, dispirited ducklings.

Josie and Kirsten were quiet all the way home. Josie had retrieved Carlie from under a hedge where she had been sleeping, and Duncan carried the still unconscious infant slung over one shoulder, like a plaid.

'So that was Keir Hardie?' said Kirsten at last.

'At least,' said Josie, 'he spared us the story of the Glasgow baker.'

44

'What story was that?'

'About working for a baker when he was nine and getting the sack and a fortnight's wages cancelled because he was a few minutes late. He was frightened to go home. All he had as he wandered about in the rain for hours was a morning roll he had stuck down inside his semmit.

'When he did get home, his mother had had another bairn and the starving family shared the roll.'

'What a terrible story!' said Kirsten, stone-faced.

'I know, I know,' confessed Josie. 'It's just that I've heard it all before, and we could all produce tales to match it.'

'Josie,' said Kirsten sternly, 'I believe you have the makings of a cynic. Did you not think his reference to the men working "seventy fathoms from the daisies" very moving and poetic?'

'No. I'll stick to empty bellies and bare feet,' said Josie. 'That's moving enough for me. Hardie's brought the men out, but Hardie'll not fill their weans' stomachs. It's the wives who have to do that.'

'But Duncan is behind the strike, too.'

'Aye, well, Duncan's not always right,' said Josie, with an enigmatic glance at her husband. 'Men get carried away by their principles. I think the iron-masters and coal-owners can break this strike, for they can still get blacklegs to work for them regardless.'

They had reached the cottage in the Rows and Josie took the baby from Duncan and laid her in her cradle, while Duncan stirred the fire to life and Kirsten took the kettle outside to the pump to fill it.

'So you think we should throw in the towel?' Duncan asked Josie angrily, while Kirsten was out of earshot.

'I never said that.'

'You're *weakening*.'

'Not me. But these poor women are. They're starving. And you promised that Nettie Boyle I would take something down to her tonight. Where am I to find it?'

'We can spare something.'

'We've always got to "spare something". I've "spared

something" till the cupboard's bare.'

Kirsten came in with the kettle and heard the last words. As she pushed the vessel down on the coals to boil, her eyes were bright with determination.

'I'll go up the farm after dark and steal some turnips. That's what you said you did when you were little, Josie, isn't it, and there were times like these?'

Duncan laughed.

'You can't do that. Not someone like you.'

'Can't I? I'll take a bucket and a sack and get some coal while I'm about it.'

'Where'll you get the coal?' he humoured her.

'Off the bing. Off the wagons at the pithead.'

'You'll get pinched for stealing.'

'I'm only taking what belongs to the Rows. It isn't like stealing. Not real stealing.'

Josie was going round the room, making up a small packet of tea, taking a heel of bread out of the bread tin, gathering a few potatoes together and scraping dripping from a dish. She counted some lumps of coal carefully from the bucket at the fireside into an older, more battered bucket.

'I'll take these down to Nettie.' She was soon back, looking happier, and shared the unsweetened tea with Duncan and Kirsten. It had little white lumps floating on top. The milk had gone off. There was nothing to eat with the tea.

Kirsten rose resolutely when she'd finished and said, 'I'm off, then. Where's that sack you had? And the bucket?'

Josie glared at her.

'Don't play at being poor. It isn't a game.'

'Aren't you coming with me?'

'Not me. He can go if he likes.' She jerked her head towards Duncan.

'Will you come?'

'What's the matter? Feared of the dark?'

She didn't answer him. White-faced, she stomped off down the back of the Rows. It was a moonless night, the dark soft and warm, like a furry animal. Everyone was in bed; there wasn't a lamp or candle still burning. Ahead lay the small mountain of earthworks the pit had regurgitated: the bing. Small areas where spontaneous combustion had occurred glowed in the dark with a sinister appeal. She knew barefoot children scrabbling for coal there had been burned and scarred. She would have to be careful.

The soft thud of boots sounded behind her and Duncan's voice said in her ear, 'She says to come with you. I'd rather be in my bed.'

Relief flowed through her. But she was still a little angry at his lack of practicality and she walked on, saying nothing, stumbling over stones and ridges in the dark. The pink saugh growing at the foot of the bing brushed her skirts as she climbed. He came behind her, slithering, grunting annoyance.

'Where do we begin?' he demanded.

Her sharp eyes had picked out where the children scavenged, near a spot where the bing alternately smoked and smouldered. There was a little light from the smouldering and her eyes had grown more used to the dark. And fingers could become amazingly skilled at telling slate from stone and stone from coal. The sack began to fill up and even Duncan became absorbed by the task and contributed handfuls of small, but burnable, lumps.

At last, her bad temper evaporated, Kirsten straightened. She turned and looked at the night all around her. A sense of its mystery, combined with a memory of its childhood terrors, assailed her. She said, almost to herself, 'How beautiful is night.'

'Southey, isn't it?' said Duncan, by her side. ' "No mist obscures, nor cloud . . ." I've forgotten the rest.' They scuttered carefully down the bing side, braking by turning their feet sideways, carrying the heavy sack between them. Kirsten could just make out the shadow of the wagons on their banking leading from the pit. They were loaded with coal, ready for transporting in the morning. Blackleg coal.

'Leave it,' Duncan advised her.

She rattled the bucket. 'I won't take much. Just a few good lumps. They will never be missed.' She jumped up on the wagon buffers, felt about under the tarpaulins for lumps she could grasp, and heaved them down to the track where Duncan stood. Meekly he stowed them in bucket and sack. She jumped down again, dusting her hands with sighs of satisfaction.

'Now for the turnips.'

'Leave them,' he advised again.

But on the way home they had to pass the turnip field and she struggled through a hole in the hedge, returning with an armful of hard, rooty vegetables. She was filled with a heady sense of accomplishment.

'What did you say about getting me a Radical education?' she challenged Duncan. He began to chuckle, and she joined in. Between laughter and the weight of their burdens, they had to stop for breath. They could scarcely see each other in the pitch black. But when hands touched or breath landed on a cheek, each was very aware of the other's presence.

Chapter Three

Kirsten struggled up from sleep to the sound of a teaspoon being rattled noisily against a cup. It was old Mrs Fleming's way of telling her it was time she was up. She peered from the womb-like security of the recessed bed and saw that her hostess, having risen from a twin bed next to hers, was tucking into a fresh, boiled egg while the yolk ran, deliciously tempting, on to a piece of toasted soda scone.

Kirsten dressed hurriedly and joined Kate at the table. There was a boiled egg for her, too, the first that week. 'You can't run the cutter for everybody in Dounhead, without something inside you,' said Kate. 'So eat up.'

The girl had grown to enjoy these morning tête-à-têtes with Duncan's mother. They were like an oasis of gracious comfort in days filled with making soup in the big wash-house boilers, ladling it out to longer and longer queues, and then setting out to cadge bones, meat, barley, vegetables from any source that could spare them for next day. The soup was the only thing that kept the strike going. That, and the potatoes that were so plentifully harvested that year.

'I think Josie's looking worn out,' said Kate now. 'This strike has taken more out of her than anybody, I think.'

'Why do you say that?' queried Kirsten.

'Because she gives away more than anybody else,' said Kate. 'She would give her very life for Duncan and what Duncan believes is right.'

Kirsten could think of nothing to say. She felt a little hurt and aggrieved that Kate had not paid tribute to her own sacrifices. Not that she had not made them gladly, but —

'Josie wasn't the lass he picked for a wife,' Kate was confiding now. 'There was Lilias, the daughter of our minister, the Reverend Galbraith, and Duncan's heart was always set on her. But she died, and Josie just stepped in and said she would take him on.'

Kate was not looking at her directly and the realization grew on Kirsten that she was trying to deliver some subtle kind of warning. Kirsten made a nervous movement of denial. She knocked the knife from her plate and picked it up, staring at Kate red-faced and deeply perturbed.

The older woman put out a hand and said in tones of great gentleness: 'My man Findlay had an eye for the women. Not after he met me, I'll grant you. At least not as far as I know! I don't know about Duncan. I'm just telling you, he loved Lilias and he got Josie. He might think he's missing something. But he's wed to Josie. And I think a lot of her.' She smiled. 'And of you.'

Kirsten went blundering down the Rows later to see Duncan and Josie, her mind caught up in a nexus of emotions she could not untangle. Surely it was obvious to everyone that the one thing that had brought her out to Dounhead was the strike and the wish to help the poor? Surely no one had done more, not even Josie? She had scrubbed vegetables till her fingers were rough and dyed. She had gone scrambling on her hands and knees for coal. But then the memory of that night, out in the dark, alone with Duncan, came back to reproach her with its intimacy and laughter.

She was already quiet and thoughtful when she lifted the latch on the cottage door and went in. Duncan's back was to her and he did not turn round. Combing the baby's hair, Josie looked up and said tonelessly, 'It's over, then. The men are going back.'

Kirsten cried then, scalding quick tears of rage and disappointment. 'We can't give in,' she wept. 'Not after six weeks. It'll all just have to be fought for another day.' She looked round the cluttered, untidy room that had become like home to her and grasped at the recollection of recent days when she had been needed and useful as never before in her life. She felt a terrible hollowness then at the thought of going back to those big, spacious rooms near the university.

Josie was looking at her drily. 'It's not whether "we" or "you" give in,' she admonished. 'It's the folk in the Rows. And they've had enough of the Tattie Strike. There's to be a meeting with Lachie Balfour at the pithead this evening.'

'Can I come?' Kirsten asked Duncan quickly.

He shook his head. She was about to argue, when he said firmly, 'The men wouldn't stand for it. They'd chuck you out. It's not politics now, after all. It's a matter of getting back to work.'

The baby, Carlie, sensing drama among the grown-ups, threw her little tin mug and feeding tube down on the hearth with a clatter, staggered to her feet and announced with beguiling aplomb, 'Me good girl.' For once, nobody heard or smiled. Her father went about the house for the rest of the day with a dark and silent face.

Kirsten stayed with Josie while Duncan was at the meeting. They sat in the kitchen with a glimmer of light from the fire. There was no paraffin for the lamp. Kirsten talked about her theories for a better deal for women, while Josie told her tales about the women she knew in the Rows: women kept down by too frequent childbirth, abused by drunken husbands, defeated in the constant struggle towards 'respectability'.

Kirsten was on the point of leaving to spend her last night at Kate's cottage when there was a commotion farther down the Row. At first it was shouts and scuffling feet and then lights swayed outside the window and the door crashed open.

Duncan held a lantern aloft as four men carried an inert figure into the room.

'What's happened?' cried Josie.

'It's Lachie.' Duncan pushed the lantern into her hand and pantomimed that she should hold it up while they brought Lachie in to the chair by the fire. Kirsten screamed as she saw that a great gaping wound on Lachie's forehead was pouring blood.

'It was big Dan Miller,' said Duncan. 'Lost his head and started a fight with the blacklegs. Lachie got between them and he got this blow with a pick-handle that was meant for somebody else.' His grim face looked down at the stricken man. 'I've sent for the doctor and for Tansy. We couldn't take him home to Dounhead House till he's had attention.'

'Lay him on the floor,' ordered Josie. Somehow her hands were full of bed-linen, which she was tearing into strips. She made a pad and, bringing the edges of the wound together, applied it. Kirsten covered Lachie with a blanket.

Nettie Boyle came to the door with an armful of firewood someone had given her. 'Take it,' she urged Josie. 'You'll need to boil a kettle.' Someone else brought candles. They stood around outside the door, anxious faces peering in. A few doors down, Dan Miller was giving his muddled version of the incident to anyone who would listen, while his wife nursed their youngest in a shawl and upbraided him in a constant, keening shriek. 'I told you to keep out of trouble. Where did you get the drink?'

Tansy arrived, driving herself in the gig, and the crowd outside the door parted respectfully to let her in. She fell on her knees beside Lachie, seeing the blood everywhere and his dreadful pallor. She looked up at Duncan and said with a deadly calm, 'You did this.'

Josie raised her up, sat her in a chair and put a cup of tea into her hands. 'Lachie got between two men in a fight. The blow was never meant for him.'

'Is he dead?' Tansy looked at her fearfully. Somehow she had always liked and trusted Josie. The relationship went back to their childhood and had not been affected by their difference in station.

Josie shook her head.

'No, no. Of course not.' It sounded more encouraging than she felt. 'The doctor will be here soon.'

'Why doesn't he move?' moaned Tansy. She fell to her knees once more, picking up an unresistant hand. 'Oh, my Lachie. Don't leave me. Lachie, do you hear?'

'Get away to your beds.' It was the stentorian voice of Dr Pettigrew, ordering the crowd away from the door. He came into the kitchen, hauled Tansy unceremoniously to her feet and indicated that she should be taken into the front room.

'He can't be moved from here tonight,' he told Duncan, when he had examined Lachie. 'He's very weak from loss of blood. Can he be taken into your front room?' Duncan nodded.

Tansy had recovered her composure. She came into the kitchen now and asked the doctor quietly, 'How bad is he?'

'Bad enough!'

'Will he die?'

He glared at her with his hardened, professional expression.

'Who am I to say? Ask the brute who did it. Ask the Lord.' Relenting, he added, 'He has a strong constitution. Thank God for that.'

The night passed in a strange, nightmare blur of sensations for everyone concerned. Kirsten made tea at intervals while Josie helped the doctor, and Kate, who had hurried from her cottage at the news, sat with her arms round Tansy, just as she had done when she was a child. Sometimes a head would nod in sleep, a figure stir as cramp attacked a limb.

When dawn was streaking the sky, Pettigrew put his head round the door and beckoned Tansy. She went into the room and saw that Lachie had regained consciousness. His mouth stretched weakly in a parody of a smile.

Tansy Balfour rubbed glycerine and rosewater into her hands, briefly admiring their pallor and softness. Before going in to see her husband, she had changed into his favourite dress, the peacock blue with its kilted frills and the foam of lace at the neck. She touched her piled mass of brown hair without approval – it seemed to have lost some of its natural curl in all these days and weeks of worry.

Lifting the lines of her face into a smile, she carried the *Glasgow Herald* into the invalid's bedroom. Safely installed in his own home, with his own nurses, Lachie was making a slow recovery. But it had been touch and go. For a week he had hovered on the borderline between life and death.

53

He had changed mentally, in some subtle way she could not define but which was tied up somehow with his attitude towards her. Almost as though he blamed her for what had happened. She came from the Rows, didn't she? He was harsh and autocratic with her, blaming her if there was the slightest hitch or error in his daily routine.

Pettigrew had advised patience, saying that the blow had been so severe that she might well find Lachie changed in temperament. It was lucky he was not paralysed. Keep him cheerful, he had admonished. It was not always easy.

'There is a most ridiculous advertisement here,' she said now, tapping the paper. 'It says "Vessel Lost, Stolen or Strayed". It seems that some man called Walker chartered a ship called the *Ferret*, loaded her with coal, wine and groceries, took on a crew of runners – and then sailed from the Clyde and has not been heard of again!'

She watched him closely to see if there was a glimmer of interest, then went on with determined cheerfulness:

'Glasgow is full of theories about the *Ferret*. A ship can't just disappear. Some say it could have gone down in the Bay of Biscay, but sailors discount that. British consulates all over the world have been asked to keep an eye open for it. I think it must be a sort of pirate ship, don't you, up to all sorts of no good!'

'I am not greatly interested,' Lachie averred.

Tansy sat down on his bed and took his hand in hers.

'Will it interest you, then, to know that Clemmie and Jack are planning a splendid reception for Paterson and Honoria, with all sorts of Glasgow luminaries, and the whole family are invited, too?'

'You mean Duncan and Josie as well?'

'They're family, aren't they?'

'Duncan and Paterson don't hit it off. You told me so yourself.'

'That was as children. They are different now.'

'I have a theory. We don't change as we get older, just become more ourselves.'

She touched his face tenderly, glad to see him more animated.

'My mother will be coming. And Honoria's father, the minister.'

'I won't be going. I won't be well enough.'

'Of course you will. The doctor says all you need now is rest and care, and something to interest you.'

He threw the paper to the foot of the bed in a petulant gesture.

'Have you heard how things are at the pit?'

'All's quiet. There's rumblings through in Ayrshire, but no troubles here.'

He stared straight ahead of him, with that rather fixed intensity she had come to fear. He was still deathly pale, his strong, aquiline features blurred and distorted by illness and the body that had made such skilful love to her collapsed in on itself, folded round a skeletal frame. She held down a hysterical terror, a fear that nothing could ever restore him to her as he had been.

'Darling.' There was longing and despair in her voice. She leaned forward and kissed him, feeling her body stir with need for him. She leaned her head lightly on his chest, waiting for him to give some sign of reciprocal feeling.

'We're getting out of it,' he said above her head.

Without lifting her head, she waited, going cold with apprehension.

'We're getting out of the pit. I'm selling my shares. We're going away from here.'

'Oh, no.' She sat up straight, looking at him with total disbelief.

'They nearly killed me this time, wife. You know that, don't you? It's the second time they've had a go at me. You remember that night before I was elected, when they left me for dead in the snow? There's coal-masters who keep union men out of their pits altogether, and employ children, and pay no attention to safety. I've made sure mine is a safe pit, ever since your father died down there, and I don't

55

victimize men for their views. But they have it in for me.'

'It was an accident this time,' she answered stonily. 'Miller never meant to strike you.'

'Miller was too drunk to know what he was doing. They're scum, Tansy. Duncan can say what he likes.'

'If you give in to the roughnecks and blackguards, I shall not be able to look up to you,' she said hardly.

He got up. His legs were like spindles, so thin they could scarcely support him, and yet the sight of him tottering about in his night-shirt was so tragi-comic she gave a nervous laugh.

'I'm giving up the Commons, too.'

'You can't.' She was aghast.

'I am indifferent as to what happens to these people. I am going to paint. Isa once said it was what I should stick to, and she was right.'

'Pity you didn't marry Isa.'

'Maybe it is.'

She gave a little cry of genuine pain. 'What's happening to us, Lachie? I've tried to be a good wife to you.' He had collapsed into his wing armchair, and she folded a thick blanket round his legs and poured him some water to sip.

'This.' He put both hands to his head, holding it as though it were some frail, inanimate object. 'I've been down some strange pathways in my mind since this. And now it's as though I'm here on different terms.'

'What about the baby? What about little Donald? You're talking about throwing away his inheritance.'

He laughed, as though humouring her. 'All we inherit is our skin. He'll have to take his chance with the rest.'

She was angry then, quietly but deeply angry. She would not talk to him any more. She called his nurse to get him back into bed and stalked off downstairs. In the hall, the baby's maid was placing him in his baby carriage. She was the first in Dounhead to own such an object, but the fact gave her no pleasure today. The baby smiled and stretched to catch her attention, but she scarcely saw him.

Even the vases of hothouse flowers in her favourite

Lavender Room, where everything – carpets, curtains, walls and furnishings – was in shades of mauve, lavender or purple, failed to distract her. As did Miss Sillars, the pale, spinsterly dressmaker, who called later to discuss her dress for the Glasgow reception.

She threw aside samples of satin and silk, tarlatan and grosgrain, plaid and muslin. She saw it all slipping away from her and her life which had been so straightforward and indulgent change at a stroke into hideous nightmare.

The next day she was wheeling the baby in his carriage in the drive of Dounhead House when her brother Duncan came towards her.

She was cool. 'I hear you're going to Clemmie and Jack's jamboree. I hope you and Josie will have something decent to wear.'

He ignored this. 'Is Lachie all right? He's sent for me.'

'Sent for you?' She couldn't be sure she had heard him properly.

'Sent word down with the groom. He wants to see me urgently.'

She remained where she was, wheeling the baby in the sunlight, while Duncan went up to the invalid's room.

'Come in.' Lachie was swaddled in a quilted velvet dressing-gown and a scarlet blanket. Although the day was warm, a banked fire gave out an intense heat.

'How are you?' asked Duncan.

'Delicate,' replied Lachie, waving a frail hand. 'Delicate. But I've not asked you here to discuss my health. Sit down.'

He seemed to savour the impatience in Duncan's face, but at last he said, 'I'm giving them up. Pit and Parliament. What have you to say to that?'

'You can't mean it.'

'I do. I thought you'd be pleased. You can fight the Dounhead seat again, can't you? This time you might win.'

'It gives me no pleasure to hear you talk like this. You'll soon be well, man –'

'What would you say if I asked you to run the pit as a co-operative?'

57

'I wouldn't know what to say.'

'Are you telling me capital and labour can't work together?' Duncan hesitated. 'Well, are you?'

'I don't know what to say, Lachie.' Duncan walked to the window, staring at the well-kept grounds. 'You can't go making big decisions, decisions that will affect Tansy and the boy, until you're well and strong again. You know me better than to think I would take advantage of a man when he's down.'

Lachie stared into the fire. For several minutes neither man spoke. Then in what was much more like his normal tones, Lachie said, 'I don't want the responsibility of running men's lives. I never have. I'd be prepared to take a smaller share of the profits, in exchange for a nominal position at the pit. Or I might sell out completely.'

'No.' The word rapped out like a pistol shot from the open door. Tansy stood there, her face pale. She strode towards Lachie, breathless and shaking with a mixture of anger and contempt.

'Have you taken leave of your senses? Or are you doing this to spite me? Yesterday you told me the colliers were scum. Today you're offering to let them run the pit.' She turned on Duncan. 'You're not listening to him, are you? Carry a word of this to the Rows and I'll never forgive you. He doesn't know what he's saying – '

'It's all right.' Duncan calmed her down. 'All Lachie is doing is trying to re-order his life a little. Nothing's been decided. I wouldn't let him make a decision like this till he was stronger, in any case.'

It was as though Tansy didn't hear him. She knelt down in front of Lachie and said very carefully, as though talking to a child, 'If you're not man enough to run the pit, I'll do it. I'll make the decisions in your name. You can give up the House of Commons, but we're not giving up Dounhead House. I'm not giving up my maids and clothes. Is that clear?'

Duncan said tentatively, 'There could be great changes made at the pit, if Lachie were so inclined.'

She faced him boldly. 'Forget what he said. We're hanging on to the pit, and our money. I've no wish to end up back in the Rows.'

Duncan shrugged. 'It's you and Lachie for it. I don't want to get involved in family arguments.'

Tansy looked as though she were about to launch into another tirade, but something in her husband's face pulled her up short. She drew a juddering breath instead and said to him, 'I'm sorry, Lachie. Maybe I've said things I shouldn't. But we're in this together. I won't let you give up.'

He looked past her to Duncan. 'I don't care what happens. A little socialist experiment might have been quite amusing. But I just want rest. Leave me.'

Later, when Tansy tiptoed past his room in case he was sleeping, she saw that he had got his nurse to fetch his paints and easel. He was seated by the window, absorbed and busy. But she could not bring herself to go and talk. He was too much of a stranger.

The cobbles on the quay at Greenock were slippery with rain and a heavy, rain-soaked mist hung over the Clyde. The piper in full regalia, purple-faced from the whisky drunk to keep out the cold, coaxed a wild tune from his bagpipes as he marched resolutely up and down.

On the big ship angling its way into the harbour the sound that could scarcely be classed as music but was something more primal and direct was heard by the passengers, astounding even the sophisticated by its power to constrict the throat and draw tears to the eyes.

Those who had tried America and found it too much for them, and those coming back to close dying eyes, and those who had made a dollar or two and could not wait to impress the folks at home with fancy fashions and even fancier stories, piled down the gangway into the cold and mist as into the embrace of a chilly mother.

Paterson was one of those bewildered by the strength of his feelings for the old country as he and Honoria led the excited children, Finn and Bertram, on to dry land at last.

The boys had got a shade out of hand on the crossing, which had at times been pretty rough.

'This is your parents' native land,' Honoria was impressing on them now. The children obediently tried to see what they could of Bonnie Scotland through the mist, but mostly it was other passengers clamouring for their luggage, and farther up the quay this strange, hairy figure in a tartan skirt emitting sounds of alarming ferocity.

Paterson's eyes met Honoria's in a look that was both triumphant and relieved. Contrast this arrival, the look said, with our departure as newly-weds all those years ago, rich in nothing but hope.

'Paterson! Honoria!' There was no mistaking the burly, bearded figure of Jack bearing down on them, with Clemmie puffing just a little behind. Paterson felt his arm being pumped up and down with such enthusiasm that he feared it would come out of its socket, while Honoria was pulled into a fur-filled, violet-scented embrace by Clemmie and the two boys kissed and hugged till they went scarlet with wriggling embarrassment.

'I've arranged dinner at the Inveraray Hotel,' said Jack, shepherding the others through the crush to a hired cab. On the way through the darkling streets, Clemmie was aware of the richness of Honoria's clothes, the fine, deep furs, gold jewellery and entrancingly fashionable hat with its bold, shaded feathers. Paterson, too, wore a checked greatcoat that spoke wealth and position and the ebony stick that aided his limp had an impressive top of beaten gold.

But she felt, in all conscience, that she and Jack matched their relatives in sober, well-chosen elegance. She warmed, with a thrill of pleasure, to the excitement and cosmopolitan tone that their transatlantic visitors were bringing into their lives.

Rich plates of mutton broth followed by salmon and meat soon dispelled the marrow-chilling cold of the afternoon, and after the meal in the hotel the ladies took up position before a roaring fire in the guests' parlour, while the boys read or played and the two men got down to discussion with a glass of whisky before them.

'Well, young 'un,' said Jack easily, 'you haven't changed all that much.' The narrow, blond head still had that sharp, distinctive tilt, though Paterson had grown a luxuriant moustache to counteract a slight thinning at the temples.

'I've changed in here.' Paterson thumped his chest. 'I've hardened, Jack. I've had no option. I learned my credo on the railways, and you don't survive there unless you've a stone for a heart.'

Jack smiled to show he didn't believe him, but Paterson persisted. 'They don't call America the melting-pot for nothing. There's no kid-glove treatment for anyone, worker or boss. It's all get on, get on – "the survival of the fittest". That's how Carnegie got to be where he is.'

'It seems to agree with you.'

Paterson hesitated. For a moment, his face looked tired and defenceless, but he was soon off again, speaking in a low, persuasive voice, as though trying to convince Jack of something.

'I've got where I am by my own efforts and that's what I believe in. Laissez-faire, that's what they call it, isn't it? Let the Government keep law and order and look after defence, but for the rest, let every man look out for himself.'

'No compulsory education?'

'Positively no. No labour regulations. Let people rise from the bottom of the heap, as Honny and I had to do. You'll never know what we went through at the beginning, Jack.'

Jack smiled mischievously.

'I can't wait for you and Duncan to meet.'

Paterson's face clouded. 'Is he still one of those rogue unionists?'

'He's getting to be a big labour man now. He's just helped organize a strike in the Lanarkshire pits.'

'By God!' cried Paterson, getting excited, 'we know how to deal with the likes of those in the States. We've had the state forces out to them, and the company police.'

'There's doubtless times when they have justice on their side,' said Jack judiciously.

'You've heard of the Molly Maguires?' Paterson demanded. 'A secret miners' union which went after the employers and the managers? They were still spreading murder and mayhem through the anthracite pits in Pennsylvania when I first went there in the 'sixties. I saw a man die from the cleaving they gave him. They finished me with union men, for good.'

'The unions are becoming more respectable here. Duncan's a man of conviction, not of impulse. I hope for Mother's sake you two will keep away from each other's throats.'

'Aye, well,' said Paterson moodily. 'We never did see eye to eye. He fancied Honoria, you know. I had to fight him for her.'

Jack's recollection was that, if anything, it was Honoria who had taken a girlish fancy to Duncan, but surely it didn't greatly matter now. He saw that Paterson's struggle to the top had been paid for in a certain amount of nervous strain. His fingers drummed a constant tattoo on the arm of his chair.

'This friend of yours, Joe O'Rourke.' Paterson briskly changed the subject. 'I've had him checked out by my agents in New York.'

'I thought you might.'

'If I thought he was in any way involved with Tammany Hall in New York, the deal would not go through.'

'But Joe's straight,' Jack protested. He looked alarmed.

'Relax.' Paterson permitted himself a smile. 'Joe's straight, all right. Some of his connections have been involved in bribes from contractors, protection money from criminals, that sort of thing. That's how the powerful buy the votes of the poor, these days.'

'But Joe has no political ambitions.'

'No, but some of his friends have. A little judicious weeding out of the New York end of the trust may well be necessary.'

Jack felt a stab of unease. The trouble with business was the endless permutation of risks. Still, the mood today should be light and celebratory. They would postpone any further talk of business. Paterson caught his eye and gave a half-ashamed grin.

'We should be talking family, not business.'

The ladies were bearing down on them with the children in tow.

'It is time to catch the Glasgow train,' said Clemmie. 'These two dear wee boys want to meet their cousins.'

Sandia tripped along the road towards the Mackenzies' apartments near the university with a mixture of emotions. It was good to be out in the sharp frosty air, wearing her new fur-trimmed jacket with its caped sleeves and peplum and the dear little hat to match.

On the other hand, not having seen her friend Kirsten for some time, she had a secret to impart. And part of her wanted to hug it close for just a little longer. You couldn't, however, keep secrets from such an observant friend as Kirsten. She was bound to notice something different about Sandia's demeanour.

Sandia inhaled the sharp cold air gratefully. No denying, it was a relief to be away from the constant clacking between her mother and her Aunt Honoria about the coming reception and dance, each one trying to put the other down with recollections of great occasions attended. And then there were Finn and Bertram asserting that everything in America was bigger and better, and Uncle Paterson and Papa niggling over the guest list with their interminable qualifications.

It was Uncle Paterson who was responsible for her present mission. The guests, mainly the big business names of the city with whom her father was increasingly involved, should be augmented, according to Paterson, by a few more academic and kirk luminaries. 'Town and gown, Jack,' he cried. 'You want the balance of town and gown.' Her father was always gentle and amenable as far as Uncle Paterson was concerned, as though he were still the lame little half-brother who needed looking after. Sandia liked this in her father: she thought it showed a magnanimous nature.

The Mackenzies were late names on the list, which was why Sandia was now bearing the invitation towards her friends personally. Kirsten was invited, too, and with a spurt of pride that was less than commendable, she conceded, Sandia looked forward to besting her friend when it came to ball gowns, for her own was exceedingly pretty, pink silk and muslin with rosebuds and lovers' knots caught up in the bustle.

As it happened, she did not have to walk all the way to the university. Approaching the herbalist's, where her mother had asked her to stop, she met Kirsten, who had just been buying some fennel for her father's indigestion.

They hugged each other, cold cheek to cold cheek, and Kirsten cried delightedly, 'Why, Sandia, I have been meaning to call. It has been far too long since I saw you – '

'I was coming to visit you.' Sandia held up the invitation. 'This is to ask you and your parents to a reception my parents are giving. Do say you'll come! It's going to be very grand – music, dancing, carriages at midnight.'

'Oh, I hope it may be possible!' Kirsten said warmly. 'But, look, we have so much to talk about. Let's walk in the West End Park for a little first.'

Sandia hesitated momentarily. Her face reddened. Then she agreed. 'Why not? First let me pick up some skullcap from the herbalist for Mama's headaches, and oil of cloves in case the children have the toothache.' She was quickly in and out of the herbalist's store, for despite the imposing red, green and amber bottles in the tiny windows, the shop was full of strange odours and the herbalist, old Mrs Hunter, disconcertingly witch-like in her dusty black, with her ragged-tooth smile and warty, filthy hands.

Sandia took her right hand from its cosy muff and pushed it through Kirsten's arm as they strolled companionably towards the park.

'You know I've been helping your uncle in the Tattie Strike?' demanded Kirsten. 'Oh, Sandia, he is such a splendid man. I admire him more than anyone I know.'

Something in her tone made Sandia look at her sharply.

She thought the reference to the Tattie Strike a little vulgar, but she let it pass.

'He has such fire and enthusiasm,' Kirsten bubbled. 'You don't know how bad things were during the strike, Sandia. But he never loses faith. He really cares about helping his fellow men – '

'I am surprised your parents let you go,' said Sandia tartly. Often recently she had compared Kirsten's freedom with her own lack of it.

'They trust me,' Kirsten said.

'Then perhaps you should not speak so warmly of my uncle,' Sandia said impetuously.

'Whatever do you mean?' Kirsten's face was scarlet.

Sandia had not realized she would bring forth such a reaction. 'Oh, I didn't mean anything.'

'Oh yes, you did.'

'Please don't let's argue. I have something I want to tell you – '

'No, we must settle this first. Do you think I am – well, taken up with your uncle? Because it's really not so. It is just that he is quite exceptionally interesting – '

'And good-looking,' returned Sandia. Then she relented a little, seeing how miserable and crestfallen Kirsten was looking. She wanted her in a more cheerful frame of mind before imparting the secret.

'I am sure you are not the sort of girl to flirt with married men,' she assured her friend. 'You would much rather argue about theology or magnetism or votes for women.' She patted Kirsten's hand but Kirsten continued to look put out and on the verge of tears.

Sandia, however, could wait no longer. 'I've got something terribly important to tell you,' she burst out. 'Do you remember the young man we saw that night in Cranston's Tea-rooms? Well, I've met him again and his name is Alexander Peel. Dandy for short.'

Kirsten gave her unwilling attention.

'I had been shopping for Mama one day and a package fell from my basket. He picked it up and came after me and we – we spoke. He said he hadn't forgotten me and, Kirsten, we've been meeting most afternoons, here in the park. I'm hoping to see him now, this very afternoon.'

Kirsten managed the glimmer of an amused smile. 'You're a dark horse. Do your parents know?'

'Of course not. We haven't been properly introduced, so how can I tell them? We were wondering, Dandy and I, if we could say you had introduced us? He's a student at the university, you see. He's from Belfast, and wants to be a shipping engineer.' She was breathing fast, her face animated. How could she convey to Kirsten his big, blond presence and easy masculinity? There was a kind of swooning response in her that frightened her.

'You may say it if you like,' said Kirsten. 'It is better you take him home than continue to meet in secret.' As she would have to do, were she and Duncan . . . She said abruptly: 'I must go now, Sandia. Please thank your parents for the invitation.'

Sandia quickly forgot about her friend, deciding she would puzzle over Kirsten's somewhat moody attitude later. Meanwhile, she wanted to be open to the delicious probabality of seeing Dandy at any moment. Her skirts trailed through the frost-rimed leaves, making small crackling sounds. She felt cold but wonderfully, almost painfully, happy and alive.

'For madam.' Dandy jumped from behind a rhododendron bush, producing a crumpled bunch of violets from his coat pocket with a flourish. His sandy-lashed blue eyes smiled down at her. She wanted to touch his cold face but a sense of decorum stopped her hand half-way to the gesture.

That was the trouble. With Dandy she scarcely knew the meaning of decorum. He caught her hand and for a little she didn't care who saw. It was bliss to feel her fingers caught up in the snug wool warmth of his mittens. She wanted to run about like a child, to be chased and caught, to be kissed by him. She wanted to behave in a most unseemly and irresponsible fashion. She must have taken leave of her senses.

'Sandia!' He pulled her towards the shrubbery. 'I have to

66

kiss you. No one will see us here!'

It was sweet and alarming and joyous and frightening and she could not stop. When he pulled her down on to a bench she went straight into his arms again. He was crushing her, lifting her skirt, touching her knee. But for her hose and bloomers, he would have touched skin. She drew away from him in sudden terror of sin.

'Sorry.' He did not look a bit sorry. He looked pink and lost and frightened and nearly as bewildered as she was. She said gently, 'I've asked my friend Kirsten to tell the parents she has introduced us. She had agreed.'

'Now I can take you out properly. If they agree.' He looked so pleased she had to turn away from him for a moment. He hooked her face around with his finger.

'I want you for mine, Sandia. Hear me?'

She felt a sudden rush and crush of emotion. She had a momentary wild desire to get up and run back to the nursery, to the easy, domesticated tasks of brushing hair and tying sashes and pleasing Mama.

But Dandy was looking at her so lovingly and longingly that she cast herself adrift from all doubts, and like a brave, inexperienced swimmer, set out from the shores of childhood, determined not to look back, if she could help it.

Chapter Four

'Mr and Mrs Duncan Fleming,' intoned the superior person in a red coat and satin breeches. At the entrance to the large parlour stood Clemmie and Jack, receiving their guests, and beyond them, Honoria and Paterson, waiting to shake hands as they were introduced.

Clemmie's smile was strained as her Dounhead in-laws came forward. It was too bad of Jack not to have insisted they wore formal dress, like everybody else, especially when she had offered one of her own old gowns to Josie. She saw Josie's gaze alight with a satirical gleam on her own gown and then Honoria's – the one a deep plum red with black lace décolletage, the other ice-blue taffeta set off by Honoria's magnificent diamond and sapphire pendant.

Josie wore a cheap-looking brooch at the high neck of her black dress (which at least she had brushed, for a change) and her only other concession to the occasion was the care she had taken with her red hair, which she had set off with a Spanish comb. Her smile glimmered at Clemmie's cool greeting, but Duncan, coming up behind, shook Clemmie's hand warmly and placed a kiss on her cheek. His clothes looked cheap and coarse compared to the dark suitings around him, but Clemmie conceded he had a natural dignity and presence that helped one to overlook his dress.

The house in Ashley Terrace had never looked better. The maids had coaxed the rich colours from the Brussels carpets with stiff brushes and vinegar-and-water spongings. They had steamed the velvet curtains into fresh lushness and polished brass door handles and window fitments till they glittered like the sun. The dining-hall had been set out with snowy napery, decorated with fern and carnations, set with twice-polished silver and fluted china. In their flowery alcove, the

ensemble which would provide music for dancing enter-
tained the arriving guests with light airs from the Continent.

Into this gracious and animated scene crowded the jowly
bankers and their alert, assessing wives, the shipping magnates, wealthy drapers, sharp-eyed lawyers, trenchant clerics
and scholars, eligible sons and flirtatious daughters of
Glasgow's *haut monde*.

Banished to bed, the younger members of the household
scuttered recklessly from their rooms at intervals to peer
through the banisters, down through the prismatic glitter
of the chandeliers at the tinkling, chattering, awesome
kaleidoscope underneath. It wasn't fair, Kitty told her cousin
Finn, that Sandia only should be allowed to attend. When
her mother sent for Alisdair to be carried down for five
minutes, to be petted and kissed all over his golden ringlets,
she sobbed vehement tears into her cambric nightgown.

Although she had a considerable domestic staff in her new
domain, Clemmie had required extra help for the occasion,
and down in the kitchen Tansy's cook, Mrs Batters from
Dounhead, glowered dourly at the uppity ways of Clemmie's
cook, Mrs Jessup. The little kitchen and scullery maids, half-
silly with excitement, nipped and pinched at the lavish food
whenever they got the chance and hid away treasures in odd
corners for future sustenance. Which was why there were
ashets of ham and tongue in the laundry cupboard and fruit-
cake wrapped in a napkin all but stopping the pendulum
of the kitchen clock.

Clemmie had decided that six courses would be enough,
but afterwards, in case anyone should complain of hunger
pangs, cake-stands piled with baker's delicacies would be
on hand. The men, especially, often liked to finish off a meal
with something like gingerbread with butter.

Other rooms on the ground floor had been opened up and
transformed, so that the men could retire for their port and
cigars while the ladies repaired the ravages of mutton juice
or Atholl brose to their chins and décolletages.

Before Jack began on the real business of the evening,
which was to get Paterson involved in telling as many people

as possible about the potential of their Dounhead-Boston Trust, he pulled Duncan to one side.

'You're going to contest the Dounhead election?' he enquired. 'Then I can introduce you to a man who will do your cause no harm at all.' He indicated a well-known Glasgow Liberal politician. 'He's a friend of Henry Campbell-Bannerman, the Financial Secretary to the War Office. Get him behind you and you've a fair chance of getting the Liberal nomination.

'I don't know that I want it,' Duncan said.

'But you've just said – '

'I said I would stand for the seat Lachie has vacated. But I'm thinking of going in as Independent Labour.'

'That's foolhardy, man.'

'It might be premature,' said Duncan good-humouredly, 'but don't call it foolhardy. I haven't decided yet, so maybe it would be as well to meet your Liberal friend, in case I decide to sail under his banner.'

Jack grinned. 'We'll make a politician of you yet, man.'

When the music struck up for dancing, the men emerged from their consultations well pleased with deals put in hand. After the first dance with his wife, Jack danced with Josie, whose feet seemed to be happily at one with the music, although her face remained cool and impassive.

'You look a little solemn,' he chided her. 'You weren't hurt by Clemmie's offer of the gown, were you? I tried to explain to her it was a matter of principle with you, not to dress up.'

Josie's mouth relaxed in a slight smile. 'It didn't worry me. All this does. No harm to you, Jack, but I despise most of your friends.'

It was his expression that tightened now.

'They're hard-working people who have earned their rewards.'

'Factory-owners, iron-masters, ship-builders. All these fine feathers on their wives' backs have been purchased at the price of workers' health and lives.'

'Come on, Josie,' Jack argued in a low voice. 'It takes men

of vision to provide the work.'

'I don't deny it. But what's to stop them paying proper living wages? You see that old charlatan over there, talking to Lachie and Tansy? He's a big Glasgow baker, isn't he? It only takes a year or two for him to work his men into the grave.'

'He came up from nothing,' Jack protested. 'It's human nature to compensate for the hard times with a bit of high living.'

'Aye, well,' said Josie, 'all this makes me feel uncomfortable. I belong in the Rows, where folk may not have very much, but will share what they do have.'

It was with something like relief that Jack led his partner back to the family group. He wondered if the fact that Duncan was dancing with the young Mackenzie girl had something to do with Josie's deepening ill-humour.

'Come and sit by me,' said Kate kindly to her daughter-in-law. Josie glared at Dr and Mrs Mackenzie, who were seated on the other side of Kate, talking animatedly with Honoria's father, the old minister, James Galbraith.

'You've the bonniest head of hair in the company, Josie,' said Kate conciliatingly. She leaned over and with a mischievous twinkle added, 'Fine feathers don't always make fine birds,' a statement reinforced by the passage of the baker's ill-favoured daughter in a lumpy galop.

'I only came to please Duncan,' Josie muttered.

'Then don't look as though you mind him dancing with Kirsten,' said Kate very quietly.

Kirsten's gloved hand in Duncan's as they danced was cool. 'I hear you hope to stand for the constituency of Dounhead.' Conscious of Sandia watching them from the sidelines, she kept her voice deliberately light and formal.

Duncan affirmed that this was true. 'I would like to go in under the Labour banner, pure and simple,' he said, 'but the time doesn't seem to be ripe for that.'

She took him over to meet her parents, anxious her father should like him, for he could use his considerable influence among the Liberals to help his adoption as a 'Lib-Lab' candidate, if it came to that. She then joined Sandia on the pale-blue horsehair sofa for a dish of sherry trifle, her demeanour gentle, friendly and decorous. Only Sandia noticed the feverish sparkle in her eyes, and she put that down to the heavy lacing of sherry in the sweet they both enjoyed.

As the evening wore on, the little orchestra became more abandoned, fiddle and percussion alike persuading the staidest of feet into reels and strathspeys, galops and polkas. The bankers' wives were heard to dissolve into girlish giggles; the shipping magnates sailed the perilous musical seas at full rig; in corners and alcoves and on the stairs, unwise confidences escaped from careless lips, maiden daughters behaved with unmaidenly gaiety, and the elderly bakers and drapers stared with maudlin nostalgia into their cups.

Tansy, looking flushed and beautiful and totally in her element, had no shortage of partners. Josie sat beside a pale Lachie, finding a certain rapport in their mutual boredom and disapprobation.

As for Kate, she found herself after a bit sitting quietly with her old friend, the minister James Galbraith. She had not expected him to come, but she had underestimated his wish to please Honoria and make her visit home to Scotland a success in every way.

Nevertheless, he looked a great, craggy eagle thrust into a cage of gaudy parakeets. Smothering a smile, Kate teased him: 'I hadn't thought you would fancy a gathering of this nature, Reverend.'

He was well aware she was twitting him and answered her with great affection: 'I have seen a great open-mindedness come upon the Church in general. And I do not mind this, Kate, for the bedrock of truth is always there, in the Bible. I would wish the Kirk had declared Biblical infallibility, as the Roman Catholics have declared Papal infallibility. But maybe is it better as it is. "In my Father's house are many mansions." '

Kate forbore from putting forward her own opinion, which was that much present-day Christianity was like a piece of elastic, able to be stretched round any moral attitude. She wanted to drink in every detail of this Glasgow scene, to remember the dazzling gowns, the jewels, the cosmopolitan manners. It was very worldly of her, no doubt, and James Galbraith would castigate her if he knew how entranced she was by it all. But it would be good to remember back in the cottage at Dounhead, in the winter when the dark set in early and the only music was the pit horn.

Paterson slipped away from the noise of the dancing to the smoking-room and found Duncan there, pouring himself a small port.

'How's the man?' demanded Duncan genially. 'Is it getting too much for you in there?'

Paterson gazed at him levelly. 'Josie didn't seem to be pleased about you dancing with that young thing.'

'She's a family friend. A clever young woman who might end up in Parliament before me. Nothing more.' Duncan waved a dismissive hand.

'I mind how you used to flirt with Honoria,' said Paterson tartly. 'You seem to have the looks the ladies go for.'

Duncan let out a hoot of merriment.

'I would have thought that with your money, you'd have the edge on me nowadays.' He cuffed the top of Paterson's fair, straight hair. 'Not that you're so bad-looking yourself, for an old man in his thirties.'

At last Paterson relaxed and smiled.

'Jack's kept me at it,' he admitted, seating himself and helping himself to some port too. 'This Dounhead-Boston Trust is getting bigger than I expected. I never thought there was so much money in Glasgow. I've had to put up more on my side, for I want chief say in its disposition.'

'Have you had trouble? Raising the wind, I mean?'

Paterson coloured. 'I've done it,' he said shortly. 'Never mind how.'

'Did O'Rourke help?'

'He did, if you want to know.'

'And he *is* sound?'

Paterson shifted a little uncomfortably. 'As far as I can make out.'

Duncan decided it was none of his business. He found it would be no trouble at all to find a point of argument with his brother, but he recognized his feelings as those left over from irresponsible childhood days, when they had fought simply for the sake of it.

How could he preach the brotherhood of man if he couldn't get on with his own brother? He saw the delicious irony of it and made fresh efforts to be pleasant.

'Those are two fine boys you and Honoria have. Bright and intelligent. That Finn is like you, a born engineer.'

He saw from Paterson's look how closely his brother's thoughts had been following his own. They exchanged grins and Paterson acknowledged, 'Bright enough. There will be more for them in America when they're grown up than there was for you and me as children here.'

'You think the old country's washed up?'

'It stands to reason, Dunc. Look at the pace of emigration. And without wanting to start an argument, it's the best that leave, the best in brains and guts.' He gave Duncan a searching look. 'Why don't you join the trail? I can take you into the business, pay the fares for Josie and the baby to join you. You'll come out to a world you never knew existed – '

Duncan played the theme along indulgently.

'What would I do?'

'You could manage men. From what I hear, you've had plenty of experience.'

'You mean exploit them.'

'No, I don't mean that.'

'I *represent* the colliers. I could come out and start a union for the mineworkers. From all accounts, it's an even harder job out there than here.'

'Damn your unions.' Paterson's eyes flashed. 'They will be the end of independence, the end of the spirit of adventure, as I see it. I'm offering you a job, a proper job. You're the only one in the family, Duncan, who hasn't got on – '

Now it was Duncan's turn to colour with anger.

'What if I don't subscribe to the great god Get On,' he shouted. 'What if I cry "Stop. Think what you're doing to your fellow-men, in the coffin ships and the sweat shops and the filthy stinking hovels they're forced to live in." You damned little Carnegie, you! You think you can make your money regardless and then come here and hand me a sinecure like old Carnegie hands out his public libraries – "Take this, and wheest about the labour I've undercut, the pits I've failed to make safe – " '

'Save your preaching for the converted,' Paterson ground out. 'In America, *any* man can start from scratch and make a living. A good living. America's full of homesteaders, millions of them, exploiting nothing but the plot of land they live on.'

'Well, Scotland's good enough for me,' said Duncan, his anger subsiding. The very thing he had hoped would not happen, had happened. Despite everything, despite his business deals, his obvious wealth, there was something about Paterson that brought out his compassion. He remembered the valiant little boy who had never given in to that limp or that heavy surgical boot. He held out his hand. 'We'll not part in anger?'

Paterson shook his hand reluctantly. 'We'd best get back to the rest,' he muttered ungraciously.

Jack looked up enquiringly as they re-entered the parlour. Carriages had been ordered for midnight and people were beginning to pick up cloaks and overcoats. Jack had been encouraging the men to have one last drink and now he hastily handed a whisky each to Duncan and Paterson.

He looked round the ponderous and ruddy faces of Glasgow's business elite, and raised his own glass: 'A last toast, gentlemen. To the fortunes of the Dounhead-Boston endeavour. May they bring Scotland and America ever closer.'

'To work for the hungry,' said Duncan, holding his glass towards Paterson.

Paterson replied unsmiling, vaunting his own glass higher, almost as though it were a torch : 'To rewards for the brave.'

Josie Fleming climbed the dusty wooden stairs to the *Miners' Clarion* office, remembering the old radical Alf Maclaren who had handed the paper over to Duncan after his defeat the last time he had stood for Parliament. The time Lachie had got in.

She was remembering, too, how Duncan had got her the job with Alf before the old man had retired. And thinking how she still loved this ramshackle place, where she had first learned to turn her angers and resentment into words. Not elegantly, for she had not Duncan's gifts. Painstakingly and awkwardly. But without that outlet, she did not know what would have happened to the burning reformatory zeal inside her. She could have become a street-corner ranter, a vehicle for mockery and jibes, instead of which she had painfully earned for herself some of the dignity that clung to Duncan and all he did and said.

People pretended not to think much of the *Clarion*. It had to be printed on the cheapest paper and sometimes the ink got smudged beyond legibility. Yet when they had grievances they knew the *Clarion* would print them. And two other things helped to keep the paper going. Orders for copies from London, where proliferating socialist societies were beginning to accord Duncan great respect. And printing orders from Dounhead Co-operative Society for such things as soirée tickets and posters for the annual gala.

If Duncan became an MP, she would have to run the *Clarion* on her own. But it wouldn't be the same. Nothing would be the same if he took south. She sat down on a rickety chair, hugging her arms to her stomach as though she had some internal ache.

Was there any chance at all of him standing as an Independent Labour candidate? He had gone to meet other miners' leaders to discuss the possibility and had promised to meet her here and let her know the result. It was what she wanted for him, but he had made it clear the chances were not good.

'Politics is the art of the possible.' He was fond of telling her that. Nor did he like arguing politics on a class basis, as she did. He wanted 'evolutionary radicalism', and when she made a face at his phrase-making he advised her to go and read John Stuart Mill. 'The human race is one and indivisible,' he told her. 'Not one class against another.' She often thought that although he had never been inside a church since the death from diphtheria of Lilias Galbraith, his first love, he was still basically a reforming Christian, and should maybe have been a lay preacher like his father, old Findlay Fleming, had been in his young days.

As for her, she had long turned her back on her own church and as a lapsed Catholic was regarded in the village with a mixture of suspicion and uncertainty. She had long since given up thinking about rewards in Heaven or punishment in Hell. She was obsessed by the need for simple, practical improvements here on earth. Like people not drinking so much. Like babies not sickening after weaning and dying from undernourishment. Like an absence of bad smells, scabs and running noses, consumption and scarlet fever. Like not hearing the sounds of shrieks and weeping when men who had drunk most of their wages came home and battered their wives. Like not seeing men carried up dead from the pit, so black and stiffened with coal dust they were like inanimate matter.

She put a few bits of dry firewood in the office stove and set the kettle above it to boil. Then, strangely drained and tired, she stood by the *Clarion* window, staring through the peeling gilt lettering, waiting for that lift of the heart when Duncan should come in sight.

There he was! There were times when she wished he did not fill up so large a part of her universe. Nerves, fibres, heart, mind, pulsed with a stronger life whenever he was around. And she was not alone in feeling this, she knew. He had a kind of power, an aura. It would be too easy to agree with all he said. Well, she would not do that. She had her own fire, and she would guard its flame as jealously as

77

she guarded his.

Wordlessly, she handed him his mug of cocoa as he came in. He put his cold hands playfully against her cheek, then sank into his chair and rattled his leaky boots against the little fender in front of the stove. Josie threw on some more wood, wiping her hands on her skirts in an absent gesture.

'Well?'

'It has to be the Liberals.'

'Why?' It was a despairing wail.

'We're not organized. The likes of Willie Small, in Lanark, and Bob Smillie, in Hamilton and Larkhall, they do their best, but in the whole of the country I doubt if we have more than two thousand union members. You can't campaign without funds, and we've no funds. I go in as a Lib-Lab, if I go in at all.'

'You'd get support from more than the miners,' said Josie desperately.

'A few land reformers, a handful of contentious Irishmen from Glasgow, maybe three home rulers and a couple of socialists from London,' he said humourously. 'It doesn't add up to a Labour Party. No, I've lost enough time already. If I want the Liberal backing, I've got some hard work to do.'

He saw her face change, tighten with disappointment. He said bracingly, 'You have to face facts, Josie. We're not ready yet to strike out on our own. As a Lib-Lab I could do some spadework. You'll have to be satisfied with that.'

'So what happens next?' Her voice was subdued.

'I'll have to seek the Liberal nomination. Go before their committee. I think Kirsten and her father will be some help there.'

Her expression darkened. She fiddled with the stove, throwing in small pieces of wood, rattling the lid. He said in exasperation, 'What's got into you?'

She denied anything had got into her. But he took her roughly by the shoulders and forced her to face him.

'Josie?'

'It's Kirsten this, and Kirsten that.' She felt physically ugly in her jealousy. 'She'll be only too happy to run your campaign for you, if you're chosen. But it's not votes she's after, it's you, and you're too blind to see it!'

She made a sound that was half-way between a sob and an explosion of rage.

'Do you know what I feel here?' She struck her heart in a dramatic gesture. 'When I see the likes of her looking at you *that* way, and you looking back?'

He took up his defiant orator's straddle.

'I don't know what you're talking about!'

'Aye, but you do.' She was suddenly deflated. She said in a quiet voice, 'Let her come and wash your clothes for you, and cook your dinners, and take off your boots. I've had enough.'

He didn't argue with her. He put his arms around her and held her, presently making rough stroking motions over her hair, till she raised her face to be kissed. He could see the expression on his own face in a cracked and fly-spotted mirror over his desk. It was like a distortion, no one he knew. But Josie knew him. The certainty filled him with a kind of dread, like a sickness. *Kirsten, my bonnie bird*, he thought.

'Come in, man,' said Kirsten's father, Dr Mackenzie, warmly.

The nomination committee was meeting in the ante-room of a large public hall. Kirsten had met Duncan outside. 'Measure every word,' she advised tersely. 'They'll try to catch you out. Remember your trump card – the support you have from the people in Dounhead itself.' He nodded at her calmly enough, but as he went in his mouth was dry.

'What do you think of the Transvaal question?' A burly man on Dr Mackenzie's right threw the first question. 'Do you think Mr Gladstone is right to refuse to return it to the Boers?'

'I think Transvaal should have independence,' said Duncan briefly.

'Tell us some more of your avowed aims,' suggested Dr Mackenzie.

Duncan looked round the gathering. Well-fed, well-clothed, they had an ease and assurance about them that spoke of scant acquaintance with poverty.

'My chief concern is to improve the conditions of the working man, and especially of the miners. To this end I would press in Parliament for the establishment of the eight-hour day – it worked for a time in Fife, you know, so it could work elsewhere. I would like to see a court of arbitration set up to settle labour disputes and we could then have agreed regulations of output according to the requirements of the market.'

'There are those who think your pit unions will be the ruination of the industry,' said a portly red-faced man urbanely.

'I can't see why,' responded Duncan. 'There has to be co-operation between the men who own the pits and the men who work them. I see no reason for conflict between capital and labour and surely organized labour is easier to deal with than wildcat outbursts that arise from frustration through needs not being recognized.'

'Not all your supporters are as reasonable as you are, Mr Fleming,' said the man, and got a sympathetic rumble of laughter.

'Leaving aside your sympathies for the miners, of which we are all aware,' said Dr Mackenzie strategically, 'what other views do you take on matters of public concern?'

'My mother is a Highland woman, and I would be a poor Scot if I did not want a stop put to the clearances that are still oppressing the crofters in the north, and a system of land reform set up that would give the land back to the people. I want the vote for agricultural workers, and for women.'

'Would you support home rule for Scotland?'

'I would, and for Ireland, too.'

There were murmurs of dissent at the latter.

'There are many sides to the Irish question,' said Dr Mackenzie. 'You would agree?'

Duncan nodded. He was well aware that Kirsten's father was steering him in the direction he wanted him to go, and rebellion rose up in him like a black tide.

His voice strengthened as he looked towards Kirsten, remembering and rejecting her rejoinder about measuring words. He wasn't here to measure words but to fight for what he believed in.

'I should make my position clear, gentlemen,' he said. 'The poor in my own county are my chief concern. I want those poor to be represented in Parliament as I do not think they have a voice at present. They can be crushed by the whim of any iron-master or coal-owner, who can answer any argument by taking foreign blackleg labour into the pits. The poor have a right to work, and a right to dignity.

'If they protest when their miserable wages are cut, they are thrown out like slatey coal. These are men with wives and children to clothe and feed. I tell you – if we do not heed the grievances of these poor, then we play into the hands of revolution itself. I am here to tell you: time is short.'

The questioning went on for another half-hour or so, but Duncan knew that by his display of passionate conviction he had lost his chance of nomination. Faces were hardening around him, faces that denied the uneducated poor knew what was good for them. He had let anger take over, and anger was a poor advocate with this audience.

He did not wait to exchange pleasantries at the end, but avoiding Dr Mackenzie's patent disappointment and Kirsten's stricken look strode off to catch a horse-tram. Hardening inside him was the knowledge that his own lack of judgement had caused his failure. He should have presented himself in a more worldly, protean way. He had to learn to be all things to all people. They had wanted somebody who could stand up in Parliament and put his case trenchantly, perhaps even elegantly. He had been the pithead demagogue. It came to him that perhaps he hadn't wanted this nomination, after all. To be going in as anything but a straight Labour man had been too big a hypocrisy to swallow. But that was to rationalize. He had failed, missed his chance. What was he but a blundering idiot?

'Duncan!' He had forgotten all about Kirsten, but now

she came running after him.

'You rubbed them the wrong way.' It was a statement, not an accusation.

'And they me. But I should have kept my head.'

'I'm sorry.'

'Not half as sorry as I am. I found out something today though, Kirsten. I found out I'm not a Liberal. Or even a Lib-Lab. I want a Labour Party of our own here in Scotland.'

'Yes,' she agreed instantly. 'I am with you.'

'Dear Jesus,' he said. 'Have any of them in there been down to the slums here in Glasgow? Have they seen how people live? Police checking out how many adults there are to an apartment, while folk hide up on the roof till they're gone? If a bairn dies, it has to lie in its wooden box on the dresser, with its brothers and sisters playing round it – '

'I know,' she said. She patted his arm tentatively, but the contact made him turn towards her, the passion he had felt for his cause spilling over into that other area, his feelings for her.

'I haven't been able to get you out of my mind,' he said harshly, directly.

Her colour came and went. She said nothing, merely walked beside him, carefully pacing her steps. He could hear her breath coming fast and light.

'Duncan. I have something to tell you.'

'Is it that you feel the same?'

She shook her head. 'I'm going away to university. To Cambridge, as I told you. It's all been arranged by friends of my father.'

He stopped, forcing her to do the same, and stared into a shop window displaying ship's instruments. A light snow had begun.

'It would be the best thing,' he said. 'But I'll miss you.'

'You see, it would be very wrong – '

He turned and looked at her now, relentlessly. The cold had stolen the colour from her face, except for her nose, which was pink. The beauty came and went from that face, part of its attraction.

82

'Aye, it would be wrong.' His hand took hers, holding it so fast she winced. 'As many things are wrong. My Kirsten.'

The snow had begun to fall with that inconsistent, inchoate lightness that always takes by surprise. They put their hands up to it, felt it melt on their faces. She said, with an intense, trembling intimacy, 'You are so poorly clad. You must get a warm coat.'

'I am hardened to the cold,' he said carelessly. He had been denied something, back there in the hall. It was almost like retaliation now, taking her. He pulled her into the shop door. His lips tasted melted snow on hers. She struggled a little, then her lips responded.

'*Kirsten,*' he said. '*My bonnie bird.*'

'Are you sure no one will come?' Kirsten looked out of the tenement window near the Cowcaddens and saw it was still snowing. The room behind her smelled of stale bodies and tobacco and liquor, but Duncan was coaxing a fire in the grate and the small, eager flames suddenly made the place more homely. He looked up at her, with that look compounded of guilt and longing that she was to come to know so well.

'Would I lie to you?' he pleaded. 'Jamie Pullar is away to Manchester for a union meeting. I have the run of this place when I'm in Glasgow.'

'He has no wife nor family?'

'He's a widower. No bairns.' He came over and stood beside her in the gloaming, saying gently, 'We aren't trespassing. He has stayed with me many a time. We're union brothers.' He looked round the shabby room almost with affection. 'This has been where many a campaign has been hammered out. It's a kind of radical headquarters. Pullar is no kind of a domestic animal. He lives for the labouring poor.' He was trying to indicate to her, delicately, that they were not intruding on the sanctity of someone's hearth; that this was an impersonal place. Seeing she still hesitated, he added, 'If you want to leave, bonnie bird, I'll take you down the street to your tram.'

For answer she came over to him and put her arms about him and lifted her face to him. They kissed with a passion that was almost violent, broke off and kissed again. He began to peel off her coat and she took her hat off, and drew the curtains on the thick-falling snow, which was descending as though someone at a window above was emptying a feather bolster.

'Shall I make some tea?' he suggested. He put a blackened kettle on the spirited little fire. She tidied papers on the bare wooden table, automatically, till he dragged her down on to his knee on a rickety chair by the fire. Before he kissed her again, her mind automatically registered the headline on a paper Pullar had left lying on the bed set into his kitchen wall: 'SINGER'S TO START FACTORY IN GLASGOW'. That would be good, she thought. That would bring work. The thought slid away as his arms tightened about her, squeezing her till she had to fight away from him, gasping for breath.

'Kirsten! Look at me.'

Suddenly she could not. With her face averted, she said, 'I don't know what I'm doing here. I shouldn't be here.' She looked at him pitifully. 'I can't help it.' With more vehemence she added, 'It doesn't feel wrong. It feels necessary. As though I have to do it to survive.' She threw herself into his arms. 'Oh, I want to belong to you, Duncan. I love you, I love you.'

He moved her arms down and said harshly, 'I'm the one who should know better. But I'm compelled, too. You're all that matters to me. Right or wrong.'

Her cheeks, her eyes were brilliant, as the fire warmed the room. 'We can't go back now. Can we?'

'You've never been with a man before?'

'Of course not.' She moved away from him, trance-like. Reaching up to a shelf, she brought down two chipped, rough cups and set them on the table. She found the brown teapot and the rusty caddy on the mantelshelf. Extracting two spoonfuls of tea from the scanty hoard, she poured the boiling water over the leaves. Then, as though it were some kind of ceremony, sacrament even, she handed Duncan his tea.

Holding her own cup, but not drinking, she said, 'I am frightened, Duncan. I have read about love, but I am still frightened.'

He took the tea from her. 'Not of me. Dinna be frightened of me.' He kissed her temple gently. 'You can't know love from books. You have to go through love, like fire. Dive into love, like water. I'll take you there. You'll see.'

He unbuttoned her dress, slipped her arms out of the sleeves and as she shivered he kissed her and drew her nearer the fire. She put her hands up under his coarse shirt and vest and felt the tender skin of his body beneath. 'You, too,' she urged boldly and they peeled off clothes till each stood naked, in front of the other, hands on each other's ribs. He had never seen Josie naked in all the years of their marriage.

She kissed his shoulders and his starveling ribs where her hands had rested.

'Don't look at my skinny body,' he said.

'I love it for being skinny. I love you.'

'Aye,' he groaned. He led her over to the set-in bed and there he held her. He was delicate and careful with her, but her passion was a quick teacher. He took her and they reached a climax of loving together, her long wailing cry ricocheting against the firelit walls.

Afterwards she lay back and said in wonder, 'I did not know it would be like that.'

'Nor did I.'

'Oh, Duncan. Come to me again and stay in me. Make us one person.' She placed her slender girl's body on top of him, kissing his face, smiling, laughing. He pulled the grubby blankets about her, rolled her over and still held her. It seemed like a new form of existence for both of them, that if skin peeled away from skin, each half would wither away and die. The wag-at-the-wa' clock ticked away another hour and at last she sat up, aware of the chilling of the room and the minutes slipping away.

85

'I must get home. They will wonder what has happened to me.'

He watched her dress and rose to help her do up the tiny buttons on her bodice. The stuff of her gown was finely woven, soft to the touch, delicately trimmed with silk braid. Reminded of their difference in station, his fingers fumbled and stiffened.

'Are you sorry?' he demanded.

She put a hand up to his cheek and answered him soberly. 'Never. Never, never, never.'

She saw with a terrified joy that the act that had transformed her life had done the same for him. He looked different, younger, more vulnerable. It was as though hardship and disappointment had melted away, leaving a Duncan she had never seen before.

Going down the dark, evil-smelling stairs from Jamie Pullar's single-end, he said in her ear, 'What difference will this make to your going away?'

Down in the cold street, under a yellow street lamp, she looked at him hungrily and said, 'I don't know.'

'I don't want you to go.'

'It isn't for a few weeks yet. We have time to think and talk.'

He put her on her tram to go home, saying almost formally, 'Come to Jamie's again tomorrow. Same time.' Her nod was casual. When she was seated in the tram, she looked out into the slushy street in desperation to see him once more. Their eyes met and he sketched her a salute.

Their affair had a desperate, lunatic intensity about it. Just as he lied to Josie about having to stay in Glasgow on union matters, about living at Jamie Pullar's in order to help him with a mythical report, so she found ways of deceiving her parents with stories about temperance and women's suffrage meetings.

With a disregard for the dangers, they met in tea-rooms, walked arm-in-arm through Glasgow Green, oblivious of the cold. Sat on benches, talking about philosophers. Stood in cold closes or shop doors, talking about her hair, his father, memories, her eyes, wishes, the cold, songs sung in childhood, coal dust in the lungs, summer. Fingers laced. Cold felt in the feet, in tense, importunate bladders. And while Pullar was away, almost always ending up in the dingy apartment up the dank stair, where they burned in the fires of love, and drowned in the seas of love, and came back each time to be reborn and die again.

Sometimes they played games. Walking in Argyle Street, she would pretend to be his wife, choosing from a butcher's cheery window the mutton pies and other delicacies for his tea. Or he might see a ring or gown he wanted for her, or books they might read together.

Each waited for the other to say the words they knew had to come. It was getting more and more difficult to be together. Jamie Pullar returned and his room was no longer available. At home, her parents talked encouragingly of the new friends she would make at Cambridge. She was to have a little special tuition before joining the university itself and no doubt there would be some pleasant socializing. Bright in her mother's eye she saw the hope of a good match, a fine mind to suit her own.

In one of the new tea-rooms one night, sharing frugally in the pre-theatre bustle of high teas, she said the words: 'Help me to go, Duncan.' He had been quiet all evening, guilty because the money that had brought him to meet her should have gone to Josie, for food.

The next time they met, he was grimly smiling and jaunty. 'I've decided,' he said. 'You've to stick to your studies. If you are going to be of use in this world, and you are, you must learn all you can. And I expect you'll meet a nice, upstanding young fellow, and marry him, and give him bairns.'

Her eyes looked as though he had bruised them. 'And do to him what we've done to Josie?' They had been all round and over the topic of Josie, many times. Josie and Carlie. Who would not go away.

Relenting at what her words had done to him in turn, she said with the same terrible jauntiness he had patented: 'If

I've to go away and work, you've to remember what you're in the world for, too. You've to remember what there was, before us.'

'I can't remember,' he said dully.

'Remember the night you enumerated the different kinds of hunger?'

He smiled then. It had been in Jamie Pullar's mankie bed.

'Hunger for beauty, hunger for books, hunger for dignity. Poor folks need their dignity, you said. You have to make sure they get it. In Parliament. One day. You hear me, Duncan?'

He shook his head. 'I hear nothing. I feel nothing.'

She was drawn down into his despair. 'I can't even pray for us any more,' she admitted.

In the end there were no more words. Even touch became unbearable. Her parents were travelling south with her, so there was no question of him seeing her off. They met for the last time three days before.

He had wanted desperately to give her a memento, and had persuaded his mother to let him have a small doeskin edition of Burns's poems, on the pretext that it would be useful for quotations in his writings and speeches.

When he gave it to Kirsten, a paper-thin, dried wild rose fell out from between the pages. 'A Scotch rose!' she exclaimed. 'Look at its brown leaves! They call it the burnet rose.' He picked it up with great care, laying it in her palm. 'Beautiful,' she said, and he agreed, his eyes never leaving her face.

By a strange irony, he was in Glasgow for a genuine union meeting the day of her departure. He could not stay away from the station, but mooned about in the shadows near the London platform, rewarded when he caught a glimpse of her, pale and dreamy, between her parents.

The train was late in leaving. They held it up, as quite often happened, for the great scientist, Sir William Thomson, who was going down to London on important scientific business. Duncan remembered the first night he'd spoken to Kirsten, her jokes about explaining Sir William's mirror-galvanometer to him.

He walked up towards the university afterwards, because it felt like being nearer her there. Sir William's house sparkled with the new, sharp gleam of electric lighting, the first in Scotland.

That was a miracle, wasn't it? Energy jumping from pole to pole. If only he could find such a miracle, that would transport him to the world of talk and ideas she would soon inhabit. Who was there to understand him, now she was gone?

He would go home to Josie. Maybe the time would come when he would feel comfortable with her again, when her cool look would warm and the child would stop looking at him with that wide-eyed, disquieting stare.

He could only think of fires going out in dirty grates, and women coming to their door in smelly shawls for a bit of butter, or an eggcup of tea for their men's snap tin. Warmth and sunshine were draining away in a train going south.

His burnet rose.

PART TWO

♦

Chapter Five

In the Jubilee year 1887, Kate Fleming was seventy and the old minister who had always styled her Kate Kilgour, because that had been her name when she was his housekeeper in Greenock, died. She had been with him when he raised his head to listen to his church bell toll for the last time; then he had fallen back on his pillows with the look of a mighty spirit resigned to obey its Maker, and move on. James Galbraith was buried in the small Dounhead kirkyard, beside his daughter Lilias, and a new young minister, who played golf and told jokes, took his place.

For Kate, there was a void nearly as great as when her husband Findlay had died, and the family realized it. Which was why Tansy was picking her way carefully over the frozen February puddles towards her mother's cottage, with the gift of a gold and seed-pearl locket and an invitation to birthday tea at Dounhead House.

The years since Lachie's resignation from Parliament had changed Tansy greatly. A number of them had been spent with him in Paris and the South of France, mixing with painters who were breaking away from the old traditional ways, and she moved with a stylish freedom and grace that were the outward signs of a loosening of the many inhibitions that had been laid upon her as a child in Scotland.

She was still the old Tansy in regard to fashion, ahead of her time in that her gown was bell-shaped, not bustled, and the sleeves quite daringly wide. Her face, though sometimes sad and reflective, was more often lively, mobile, responsive. Not the customary contained, watchful Scots face, so careful of its dignity. Tansy was cosmopolitan, as at home in the salons of Paris as she was in the little greystone cottage adjoining the Rows that she now approached.

Kate received the locket in its blue velvet box with admonitory cries about extravagance, but she admitted it looked beautiful once Tansy had fastened it round her neck, and her fingers strayed frequently to touch and cherish it. She confessed to having a 'hoast' on her chest and from her rough cough Tansy decreed it would not be wise to go out, and prepared instead a small celebratory tea for the two of them. Kate showed her, with evident pleasure, a long letter from Isa, describing her life at the mission station.

'Nothing from Jean?' She was almost afraid to ask the question. It was many years since Kate's eldest daughter had written home. The busy demands of family life in New Zealand obviously took all her energies. Tansy knew Kate grieved and hoped. She shook her head now, but uttered no criticism. 'It'll be in her mind to write,' she countered gently. But Tansy begged leave to doubt it.

'Where's your Donald?' Kate demanded. She found her seven-year-old grandson and his chatter vastly entertaining, if on occasion tiring.

'I left him playing with Carlie down at Josie's,' said Tansy.

Kate looked at her in some surprise. Josie had not become any more houseproud over the years and the house in the Rows was often in need of a good turn-out and brooming. Tansy acknowledged this now with a rueful smile, but said, 'I felt Josie needed cheering up. She's fond of Donald and he and Carlie get on together. He's teaching her a poem by

Robert Louis Stevenson. You should see her face! She hangs on his every word.'

While Tansy fed the fire and set the table, Kate pondered the unlikely friendship that existed between Tansy and Josie, one a natural autocrat, the other so down-to-earth and uncompromisingly working-class.

'You and Josie get on well,' she volunteered.

Tansy put down the cut-glass jam dish that brought back the bitter-sweet memories of childhood Sunday tea and sank into the rocking-chair on the opposite side of the cosy hearth.

'You know why?' She hooked her chin on her hand, rocking and half-smiling, reflectively. 'We've both had difficult husbands. Josie scarcely sees hers and although mine is sometimes there in body, his mind is always elsewhere.'

'He is generous with you,' Kate said. She had heard the note of bitterness in her daughter's voice and was anxious to be fair to Lachie. 'You have all the nice clothes you want, lass, good food, a life of variety.'

'Oh, yes.' It was as though Tansy shook herself mentally. 'The managers and I have to run the pit between us. He puts in a token appearance at the office, once in a while. But I don't complain. I like meeting his painting friends. They are amusing and different. I sit for them sometimes, and I listen to their confidences. Sometimes I play a little Chopin for them, to soothe them when a picture goes wrong.'

She laughed, to tease a smile from her mother, who was looking solemn.

'The latest thing is we are to take a house on the Isle of Arran for the year. Lachie is there now and will stay painting for some weeks, and his friends will come and go in the summer as they please. They want to practise *plein-air* painting – nature in all its guises. It is quite serious, really. Lachie talks about establishing a "Glasgow School", which will bring in poor young painters who have not been able to study abroad, as he and some of his friends have, and they will be able to criticize each other's work and help each other.'

Kate looked at a print of 'The Light of the World', by Holman Hunt, which hung in a heavy gilt frame beside the dresser. James Galbraith had been doubtful of any literal delineation of Our Lord, but she found it very beautiful and moving.

Tansy followed her gaze and said, 'The Glasgow School won't be anything like that. You see, Maw, the camera could produce a picture like that. It is very exciting, what someone like Lachie can do with colour and composition to make you see more than the camera ever could –' She broke off. She had been about to try and explain about the relation of colour to mass when she remembered all this was doubtless unintelligible outside the ateliers of Glasgow and Paris. 'At any rate,' she finished, 'the Glasgow boys are trying to do something different from the English or even the Edinburgh painters – and influential people in Boston and New York are buying. First commerce, now art, Lachie says. It is the one thing he really cares about.'

She lapsed into thought for a moment, then added, almost as if to herself, 'I have learned not to mind too much, to develop my own tastes and interests. I have tried to tell Josie this, but she's obsessed with Duncan –'

'Aye, well, poor lass,' said Kate, 'she's held down by poverty. Not like you. Duncan gets to London and all over the place on his union business and now it's this new Miners' Federation with all its fighting talk about the eight-hour day. He says it has twenty-five thousand members –'

'It'll just mean more strikes.'

'And more suffering for the likes of Josie and the other wives. You know she scrubs out the butcher's shop – I saw her scattering the sawdust for dirty boots. And she runs the *Clarion*.'

Tansy said sombrely, 'You and I know she doesn't care what she does, Maw. She would wear a sack for a dress, if it would help Duncan. No, it's the old business of his eye for other women – she suffers agonies of jealousy when he's away about the country.'

'His father had an eye for a bonnie lass when he was

93

young,' mused Kate.

'She wonders if he still sees Kirsten Mackenzie. She's convinced they once had an affair, you know.'

'How could he be seeing her? She's in London – '

'And he goes there sometimes. Like last year, when there was all that labour agitation.'

'He'll always come back to Josie.'

'Maybe he shouldn't. Maybe it would be kinder to make a clean break.'

Kate sighed, and poked the fire. She was remembering the time that Findlay had brought home his illegitimate child by Nancy Paterson and handed him to her, and how then she had not been able to reject him, because of the terrible bond of love.

'You have to compromise,' she said softly. She knew there was some rift, some dissonance that she was unable to talk about, in Tansy's life too. Yet surely she had compromised also?

'Maybe,' Tansy said in a whisper. What would her mother say if she knew she, Tansy, had a young lover? Not in the scandalous sense. Hamish Macleish had been content to sit near her feet all that summer at Antibes, ready to fetch and carry, obey her whims. His painting of her had caused much comment later in the Paris salons.

She was suddenly aware of the magisterial tick of the grandfather clock, with the picture of Burns at the plough on it. 'Gracious, Maw, I must fly. Now promise me you'll watch that cough. Have you got some lozenges for it? I'll send the maid down with some beef tea and potted head.'

There were five rows of pit cottages at Dounhead and Tansy had been instrumental in having communal wash-houses built at either end of them the previous year. When Duncan launched into an attack on how little they did to help the colliers, she could point to this amenity she had provided for the colliers' wives.

The women were supposed to use them on a rota system, but there were interminable fights over whose day was which, and one was in progress now as she picked her way over the hard, rutty ground towards Josie's.

From a safe distance, she gazed into the steaming wash-house where one woman was bent over the wooden bine, scrubbing something that looked like a pit shirt. Carefully, and in graded sizes, she had already hung out bed linen, infant clothes and starched aprons, and from the pile at her feet there were still pit socks and coal-grimed underdrawers to come. She was red-faced, hot, in need of her traditional washday dinner of porridge and sour milk, and obviously in no mood to listen to the other woman arguing at the wash-house door.

'I don't care what you say, Tuesday's *my* day for the wash-house key,' this virago was saying. 'You think because your man brings you home all his pay, you're above the likes of me.'

'I can't help it if your man's a drunkard,' cried the washer-woman shrilly, still pounding industriously.

'Away and ask your holy Willie who he takes up the bing for walks,' suggested the onlooker. 'I would rather have a drunkard for a man than a whoremonger.'

Something sodden and soapy from the wash-tub slapped across her face and, squelching about in her clogs on the sloshy wash-house floor, the industrious one screamed with rage: 'I'll send my Willie down to your Tam. He'll knock his big soft head off. And then, by God, I'll start on you –'

The challenger, having achieved the effect of aggravation she had been after, took a clean pair of heels off up the Rows, but was back in a minute bearing a kitchen knife, with which she sawed at the washing-line of her opponent. In a moment, linen, petticoats, aprons all lay in the frosty mud and the washerwoman surveyed her morning's work undone and stood undecided whether to scream, laugh, or weep before she attempted to wrest the knife from her neighbour and murder her with it.

Tansy approached the scene of the incident with fast-beating heart. It would have been easier to walk away, but her conscience would not have let her rest.

'Good morning, ladies,' she said firmly. 'Are you having some trouble, then?'

Their faces were a guilty study. Tansy bent and helped the washerwoman to pick up the muddied items, clucking sympathetically.

'It's Jean – Jeannie Watson, isn't it? How's your man's back?'

The washerwoman straightened up and threw the damp burden from her arms into a wicker clothes-basket. 'Not bad,' she said cautiously.

Tansy turned to the other woman, who was eyeing her dress and cloak with a naked, child-like envy.

'Ivy Thompson? You shouldn't let your temper get the better of you.'

'It was my turn for the wash-house,' Ivy maintained stubbornly. But she knew better than to show disrespect. 'I'll sine these muddy things through for you,' she offered grudgingly, turning towards Jean Watson.

Jean gave it as her opinion that she would not let Ivy wash a dish-rag, and the exchange of insults continued for several more minutes. But the heat was going out of the situation, and dipping into her bag for pennies for the children of both women, now clinging round their mothers' skirts in wide-eyed curiosity, Tansy finally went on her way. Farther down the Rows she could see Auld Francie, the cross-eyed tinker, setting up his brazier for the mending of pots and kettles, and promising the children he would make them tiny shovels if they coaxed their mothers into giving him some coal or firewood. Naughty children! Sometimes they upset the old man's brazier and had him hurling his soldering iron after them with great oaths and imprecations. She smiled, remembering her own childhood in the Rows.

Josie was in the customary domestic muddle. The last of the breakfast porridge was singeing in a pot over the fire. Donald and Carlie had taken ornaments, cushions and other household items of their fancy under the big whitewood table, where they had played an absorbing game of Houses. The beds, set into the wall, had not been made, and the fire smoked because its base was choked with ash. On a hard chair near the door, a girl in a tattered shawl was sobbing out some tale of woe while Josie listened and at the same time tried to cut up the vegetables for some broth.

When Tansy appeared, Josie spoke some comforting words to the girl, pushed some bread and a packet of tea into her hands and eased her out of the door.

'She can't work – she takes fits,' she explained briefly. 'And if that's not enough, some rotten blackguard has given her a wean.'

'Josie, no wonder you never have anything for yourself,' Tansy scolded. 'You'd give the folk around here the eye out of your head.'

Josie shrugged off the compliment. 'You been to the poorhouse like you said you would?'

Tansy nodded. Josie was for ever nagging her into good works. It wasn't that as châtelaine of the Big House she didn't appreciate she had a certain duty towards the poor of the parish. She wanted to help. She'd been poor herself, after all. But Josie wanted to rub her nose in it.

'Did you see these wee lasses of eight and nine scrubbing the floors?' Josie demanded. 'They've nothing to wear but those short-sleeved, low-necked dresses and they go naked to their beds. They've nearly all got bronchitis from the cold and damp.'

Tansy nodded. 'I had a word about that. I've arranged to have some warm material sent down from Glasgow for dresses with sleeves, and they've to have nightdresses or I'll know the reason why.'

'Good.' Josie nodded in approbation. 'The next thing you can tackle is why they shove those poor older lasses out to fend for themselves and their bairns ten days or two weeks after a birth.'

'Josie,' said Tansy patiently, 'these are loose girls and I won't encourage them to have their illegitimate bairns.'

'You'd sooner see the bairns die, then, or the lasses take up with some old man who'll soon give them another?'

'You know that's not what I mean.'

'Then the parish should look after them.'

Tansy sighed. 'All right. I'll see what I can do. But the church folk are very firm against sin.'

Donald stuck his head from under the table and said, 'Mama, we've played some good games.'

Shyly, Carlie, red-haired like her mother, brought forward some wooden spoons wrapped in old bits of cloth and explained, 'This is our family. Three boys and two girls.'

'Carlie was crying sometimes,' said Donald, emerging to stand by his mother's knee. 'She says her head is sore.'

Josie pulled her offspring towards her and felt her brow. 'She's hot,' she said worriedly. 'Are you not well, pet?'

Carlie laid her head on her mother's lap and sniffed a little. 'Not very,' she admitted.

Feeling her own throat go dry, Tansy said, 'See if she has a rash, Josie. I hear there's scarlet fever in Dounhead.'

With fingers that were trembling slightly, Josie parted the child's thick woollen clothing. Across her chest lay a veritable forest of red spots.

'It's sore here, Maw,' said Carlie, pointing to her throat.

Ivy Thompson picked her way carefully down the back of the Rows in the dark. A small boy, whistling to keep the bogey-man away, passed her on the way to fill a bucket at the communal pump.

She rattled the latch at Josie's door and after a short interval Josie appeared, wrapping a shawl about her shoulders against the freezing night air.

'How's the bairn?' demanded Ivy solicitously. A big, quick-tempered Glasgow woman, she was regarded in the Rows as 'gallus', meaning ready for anything, with not too high a rating for dignified behaviour. She was also kind-hearted to a fault.

'No change,' said Josie. 'She's sleeping now and the doctor says that's the best medicine. That's why I can't ask you to come in.'

'Here.' Ivy shoved a tin canister of something hot and liquid into Josie's hands. 'It's chicken broth. Don't ask me where he got the fowl. He says it strayed, but you know what a bloody liar my Tam is.' And Ivy gave a full-bodied roar of laughter. Just as quickly, her face darkened as she laid a confiding hand on Josie's arm.

'Listen, hen. I didn't come just with the soup. Has your man heard about the riots at Blantyre? You knew they were out on strike there? Well, they sent the police in and it was like a bloody war, they say. Now they're sending in the Hussars from Glasgow. And my Tam says they're coming out in sympathy at Dounhead. Can you not get word to your Duncan? The Federation should be doing something, Tam says.'

'The Federation's doing what it can,' said Josie quietly. 'But the coal-owners won't listen. They're out for a show of force. Strike – and in go the blacklegs. It's as though they want to provoke trouble.'

'Aye. I still think you should get hold of Duncan and get him down to the pit,' said Ivy. 'I can smell bad trouble here, so I can.'

Josie closed the door on her neighbour while her mind chased around for an answer on where to find Duncan. A week ago, when the child had taken ill, he had stayed at home for two days. The doctor had agreed that Josie could nurse the child, and anyway the beds at the cottage hospital were already full with victims of this virulent fever that killed so many.

It was not that he didn't love Carlie, Josie assured herself. It was just that as soon as the child seemed even fractionally better, he had been caught up again in this great, unsteady vehicle that was the Scottish Miners' Federation.

The Federation had been set up in October with Keir Hardie as its secretary, and in November Duncan had joined Hardie, William Small from Lanark, Belfast-born Robert Smillie and Chisholm Robertson, the savage Stirling critic of the Lib-Labs, in hammering out an all-out attack on what they saw as the unplanned anarchy of laissez-faire in the pits. They wanted the eight-hour bill and a uniform policy of output restriction. Duncan saw the Federation as the instrument of change he had worked for for six years and now that the miners were thus organized, he campaigned relentlessly for the adoption of the Federation's aims.

He had learned in the past the penalties for lack of organization and now he was as fanatical as Keir Hardie about making the Federation effective. But its task was doubly difficult. Not only were the coal-owners quicker than ever to respond to strikes with a naked show of force; the individual unions and coalfields still had not learned the lesson of unity, but pursued their own parochial demands.

The battle had taken its toll of Duncan's strength. His hair was greying, his lean frame thinner than ever. Because it was second nature to support him, Josie had sent him off to Glasgow on Federation business, while she took full responsibility for nursing Carlie.

She decided in the end there was no way she could get in touch with Duncan that night. In the morning she would find some means of despatching a message to Glasgow.

Carlie in any case took up her attention. The child, hot and fretful, began to wail in a thin, heart-breaking way, and called for her daddy. Josie sponged her hands and face constantly and gave her frequent sips of water. When that did not seem to be enough, she wrapped the thin little frame in a blanket and sat with her on her knee by the fire, rocking her back and forth and singing anything that came into her head:

'Shoo, shaggy,
Ower the glen,
Mammy's pet
And Daddy's hen.'

At midnight, as the fire had burned low and Carlie had at last dropped off to sleep, the latch lifted on the door and Duncan came in. His face was white and exhausted and his clothes sodden with rain.

'It's all right,' he assured Josie. 'They got word to me about the trouble. I've been down there and quietened them down. The night shift's on as usual.'

He eased his cracked boots off with a sigh.

'How's the bairn?' He rose and looked down at his daughter, whose red curls lay damply round her too-rosy, sleeping countenance.

'Don't wake her,' Josie commanded sharply.

'Is there aught to eat?'

She stirred some mutton stew over the embers and he took it from her, with a hunk of bread, and ate hungrily and absently. Josie undressed and climbed into the bed with Carlie. Presently she heard Duncan undress also and ease himself into the other bed. The fire flickered into a last brief glow, sending shadows all round the room. Then all was dark and silent except for the child's troubled breathing.

Josie awoke at daybreak, her first thought for Carlie. The child lay in a deep, restful sleep, her brow cooler, her mouth curved in a smile as though she were dreaming something pleasant.

The knot of tension in Josie's chest dissolved and she moved about the room, kindling the moribund fire, starting the porridge, cutting bread. Thin fingers of rose and gold across a dark-blue bolt of sky painted an inspiring picture beyond the kitchen window. She opened the door and gazed out at the dawning miracle of light, drinking in the silence like music. A scraggy opportunist cat shot in between her feet to see what it could salvage of food and warmth at her hearth.

In the moment of closing the door she heard it. Feet. The hard pounding noise of heavy pit boots.

And then a scream that went on and on, violating the lovely morning. She opened the door again and found herself running wildly, spontaneously, towards the sound. The door of Ivy Thompson's cottage was open and her kitchen seemed full of coal-begrimed figures. They parted as she went in and she saw Ivy's big, cushiony body cast down on a chair, while her head moved back and forward and the powerful, nerve-assaulting noise came from her lungs.

'What happened?' One of the coal-black figures moved a pink tongue round rough lips and said, 'Her Tam. He's down there. He's trapped.'

A voice inside her said sickly, *not again, not another*. But she grasped Ivy's arm strongly and said, 'That's enough, lassie. Don't frighten the bairns.' From the two beds set in the wall, tousled bewildered heads looked out at the scene, eyes rounded in shock and terror.

Deep in sleep though he had been, some instinct that was always alert had roused Duncan, who now appeared, fully dressed, and took over. As the miners who had brought the news to Ivy accompanied him back to the pit, he gleaned from them what had happened.

There had been agitation and argument last night, even after Duncan had talked the night shift into going to work. The vituperation had been particularly bitter between Tam and Wattie Clegg the safety-man, a peaceable soul who was always against striking, no matter what the objective. To show how little he thought of Clegg, Tam had bull-headedly worked a part of the seam that the older man had warned him away from, and the roof had fallen in on his head.

There were men down there already, careless of their own safety, pulling the coal and slurry away with shovels and bare hands where necessary, knowing Tam would have done the same for them.

Duncan joined them, fresh after his sleep, his muscles soon into their old rhythms. In a grim way he acknowledged it was salutary for him to be there: it reminded him of how much there still was to be done.

What was it Hardie had written in the preamble to the Federation's objectives? 'These who own land and capital are the masters of those who toil. Thus Capital, which ought to be the servant of Labour and which is created by Labour, has become master of its creator.'

His spade touched something soft. With a sick premonition, he laid his spade carefully down and called for the others to add their light to his. He felt in the coal with his hands. Something loosened and fell with a soft and sticky thud into his hands. It was Tam Thompson's guts.

No man went on day shift that day. Tam Thompson's rejection of the safety-man's orders was forgotten and the blame for his death was laid elsewhere. The Federation was reviled, the Hussars were dared to come and do their worst, police were jeered by the women and children, and a sick and angry fury lay over Dounhead like Tam Thompson's pall.

It was the day before pay day, the traditional day for poor suppers and the other economies of living hand-to-mouth. The pithead fury spread like boiling jam scum into every house in the village, and men, young and old, tumbled into the streets looking for a focus for their scalded sense of outrage.

Wylie the grocer had his windows broken and his stock pillaged. Stones and bricks were hurled through the colliery-office windows and would have been thrown at the windows of Dounhead House had not the police put a guard on the gates.

When the Hussars came in they were set upon with sticks and clubs and bricks, anything that came to hand. The women came into the streets to scream defiant abuse at them. Miners were spirited away to their cottages to have heads bound and wounds dressed, while their sons who were old enough to take up the cudgel – and some who were not – went out to take their place.

Duncan worked with authorities to abate the violence. When the men would listen, he tried to calm their wild, anarchic mood. They had to accept the fact that the pit was their livelihood.

When it was all over, the fighting and the shouting, they would have to go back to work. Every coal-owner in Lanarkshire knew this. For children had to be fed.

Duncan faced the fact that the Federation was less than useless. The men had no faith in it and the owners treated it with lofty scorn. He was conscious of the fact that he was putting on some kind of mental armour. He, the man who had preached the brotherhood of men, who had wanted Capital and Labour to lie down together, like the lion and the lamb, knew he had to lay aside some of his pacifistic notions from now on.

A lot had changed since that moment in the near-dark when what was left of a man had been held in his hands. But this was a time when he saw the future darkly, and the vision of what he had to do was blurred, elusive and oppressive as nightmare.

'This has been a sorry time for Dounhead.' Dr Pettigrew raised the glass of Madeira to his lips and gazed across the expanse of carpet in the Lavender Room at Tansy. He could see her fingers nervously working at her handkerchief and sought to distract by his reference to the wider scene.

'Nothing but broken heads to see to,' he lamented. 'I've never known anything like it. I hear the Fifeshire miners sent in their support. Their John Weir is a respected figure, a moderate, thinking man. But it makes no difference. The miners know they have to go back on terms of total surrender.'

'They will have to learn how to negotiate with words, not strikes,' said Tansy sharply. 'It may appear very weak and frivolous of me, Doctor, but my chief concern at the moment is my son upstairs.'

The doctor put his glass down on the sofa table and said as reassuringly as he could, 'Scarlatina is not a disease to be taken lightly, as you know. But the children who succumb to it are mostly those who are ill-nourished. Your child is well fed, his nurse is a most capable body and she has my instructions.'

Tansy bit her lip to stem the tears and said anxiously, 'Should I think of getting in a specialist from Glasgow?'

'I doubt he would have more experience of this than I,' the doctor said shortly, 'but you must please yourself. Would you like me to arrange it?'

'Yes, please. The best man there is.'

Distractedly, Tansy climbed the stairs to Donald's bedroom once the doctor had gone. The child was in a troubled sleep and his nurse put her fingers to her lips and persuaded Tansy in a whisper to go to her own room and lie down.

She couldn't settle. Whenever she closed her eyes, the sense of self-reproach seemed to swell in her chest till she felt she must suffocate. If only she hadn't taken Donald to Josie's! Now it seemed that Carlie was over the worst, while with her child, the crisis was still to come.

She had loved him too dearly, that was it, and he was to be taken from her. Why wasn't Lachie there to reassure her? The weather had broken and for two days the steamer had not been able to put in at Arran, so he didn't even know yet that the child was ill.

She heard the front-door bell jangle and hoped it would not be her mother or Josie, come to enquire about Donald. She didn't even want to see them just now. But she heard the maid's protesting voice and then the rapid tread of feet taking the stairs two at a time and the deep rumble of a man's voice saying it was all right, Mrs Balfour would see him.

There was a peremptory knock on her door and it opened before she had time to answer. Hamish Macleish stood there, gazing at her anxiously. Even in her distress, she thought with a spurt of near-mirth that he looked like a *Punch* caricature of a painter. Floppy tie, floppy hair. Those wild, pale-blue and hypnotic eyes. 'Look,' Lachie had once said jokingly, 'he has the typical mad Highlandman's eyes – all that white around the iris.'

'Please go away,' she said now. 'I don't want to see anyone.'

He ignored her words and strode into the room.

'I came, the minute I heard you couldn't get word to Lachie. You shouldn't be on your own. How is Donald now?'

'Poorly.' She bit her lip hard, feeling the tears rush to her eyes at the warmth of his sympathy. The others in the painting brotherhood regarded him as the rough country boy, reared on porridge and oatcakes, bare-bottomed under his kilt, but he had an extreme emotional sensitivity many of the others lacked. And although Lachie teased him about his social uncertainties, the way he embraced new fads and fashions to keep up with the *beau monde*, she knew he thought his work advanced, exceptional, bordering on genius. He had helped Hamish to sell paintings both in Britain and America, in markets where they were in competition with his own. Lachie had his faults. Lack of generosity towards his fellow painters wasn't one of them.

'You shouldn't be here, you know.' There it was, whenever she looked at him. That rush of feeling that wasn't quite maternal, answering the open, defenceless pleading in his eyes. He was so young. And she felt old. When she had asked her mother once, in childhood, how old she was, Kate had said with a smile, 'I'm old as the hills.' That was how she felt now. Old as the hills.

'You could catch the illness yourself,' she told Hamish.

'I had it. When I was ten.'

'Oh, well, I suppose you should sit down.' She was ungracious, abrupt, annoyed that her attention had been taken from Donald.

She went along now to the little boy's room, sending his nurse, young Ina Jamieson from the village, to have a meal and a walk in the fresh air. She fed Donald soup, sponged his hands and face, sang him snippets of music-hall songs till, fretfully, he fell asleep.

'Come on. Your turn to rest and eat now,' said Hamish, when she returned to her room. He had been down to the kitchen and had organized a tray of food. He buttered toast for her, handing her little pieces as though she were a child or a pet dog, fussing over her like a mother.

She smiled in spite of her anxiety, 'Hamish, apart from Lachie, you're the only person I could tolerate just now.'

'He leaves you too much on your own.' His face was pink from the compliment and now deepened to red with the rashness of his statement. 'No, I didn't mean that. It sounds disloyal – '

'You're right,' she said. 'Why dissemble?' She began to cry harshly, putting the backs of her hands up to wipe away the tears. He watched her helplessly for a moment, then offered her a spotless kerchief from his top pocket.

'Don't you and he – make out?'

'I don't know where it all went wrong.' Her face tilted up towards him. 'But it did. We were happy up till that time of the strike, when that man attacked him. He was never the same after it. He shut himself away. In here.' She tapped her temple. 'Only his painting means anything to him now. I am to be given respect, money, even affection, such as you might give a sister.' She shook her head, shakily composed. 'But not love.'

'I've known you weren't happy.' He sat down opposite her, so that he could look into her face. 'It's bothered me. Someone as beautiful and full of life as you, Tansy, but with shadows on your face. I wondered why.'

She looked down at her hands, folded on her lap.

'Have you ever felt you've failed someone?' she asked reflectively. 'I was hard with him, when he gave up his political career and wanted to give up the pit. That was when the bad times began, the closeness changed. And once that closeness goes – ' she moved her hands apart in a gesture of resignation – 'a marriage can quickly fall apart. In its true sense.'

Very matter-of-factly he said, 'You know I love you?'

She shook her head tiredly. 'You only think you do.'

She rose and moved to the window, looking down into the trees in the drive. They were tossing and waving in a stormy wind; their soughing reached her ears like distant seas.

When she turned and looked at Hamish, he seemed a great distance away. She realized then how desperately tired she was and there was another night of Donald's illness approaching, another night of nightmare, fever and delirium.

He grew frailer and frailer, her child. She could hear him crying now and she went running down the corridor to his room, desperate to soothe and save his ebbing strength.

Why wasn't Lachie there? She felt a great, bruising anger against him sweep through her. And although she felt like weeping, this time she did not. It was as though she had passed beyond that, to a harder place.

Chapter Six

Fifteen-year-old Kitty Kilgour skipped along the passage from the kitchen, across the wide hall, and began the climb up the stairs towards her father's first-floor study. At least it was cool in here. Outside, everything broiled and burned in the sun. She pushed the ringlets away from a damp nape, hitching and flapping her skirts to cool her body.

She was furious about having to leave the summer house at Helensburgh to come back to Glasgow in this heat. Watching Father and the boys sail the boat had been such fun. Why did they all have to come back home, pray, just because Sandia wanted the business of her and Dandy settled once and for all? It was Sandia who was upsetting Mama again. That and the heat. Mama had certainly looked very pale and ill as they'd helped her to her room. Alisdair was there now, reading to her. *Little mother's pet*, thought Kitty. Mama was patterning him on those sickly little boys in American novels.

'Go up and tell your father his brother Mr Duncan wants to see him,' Cook had bade her. She had been about to protest that the maids were there to run errands, when something in Cook's face had stopped her. That, and the figure of her uncle sitting on a hard chair by the kitchen door, his cap in his hand, staring straight ahead and not seeing her. 'Go on, Miss Kitty,' Cook had urged. 'This is family matters.'

Jack ushered Duncan into the smaller of the two parlours downstairs. Duncan refused his offer of tea or 'something stronger', saying he had been given a glass of water by the cook.

'What did you come to the back door for?' Jack upbraided him.

Duncan indicated his clothes. The elbows were out of his

jacket and the soles starting to gape on his boots. 'I might have embarrassed Clemmie, coming to the front.'

'Dear God, man,' said Jack, 'you might have let me know things were so bad. I could have helped.'

'That's why I didn't tell you,' responded Duncan, with a glimmer of a smile. 'But I am here to beg something. Six guineas. Six guineas to take me to New York. You'll get it back – '

Jack dismissed the last words with a wave of his hand. His face was red and concerned.

'Are you throwing it all up, then? Getting out? What's to happen to Josie and Carlie?'

'I'll send for them when I can.'

Jack looked down at his half-brother, noting that his hands were so frail they appeared to have no blood in them. His face was cadaverous, his neck so thin a sharp blow could snap it. Without further argument, he rang for the maid and ordered her to bring tea, sandwiches, cake and the whisky decanter. When Duncan had eaten and was looking less like some desperate spectre conjured by the heat, Jack said emotionally, 'You should have come to me sooner. For our mother's sake, if for nothing else. Does the union pay you nothing for all your hard work?'

'When there's nothing in the kitty, I get nothing,' said Duncan. 'The men get behind with their dues.' His voice roughened, and Jack saw with alarm that he was on the verge of shaming tears.

'I'll give you the wherewithal to make a new start,' he said hastily. 'And enough to take Josie and the child with you, too.'

'Six guineas is all I want.' Duncan's voice was hard and Jack knew it was useless to argue.

He took some gold coins from an inner pocket and placed them in front of Duncan, studying him soberly.

'I never thought *you* would emigrate,' he said reflectively. 'Are things so bad, then, that they'll never get better?'

'Who said anything about emigrating? I've got to find temporary means of staying alive. I can't even get work down the pit here. So what option have I? But I'm coming back.'

'What happened to your Miners' Federation?'

'Faded away.' His tone was bitter. 'Like so much else in the past few years. Jack, I've given them the skin off my back and I've achieved nothing. I doubt if I've put one hot dinner in a hungry belly or a pair of boots on a single pair of bare feet.'

'Well . . . it's been a bad time for the whole country,' Jack said. 'If it hadn't been for the Dounhead-Boston Trust, I could have been in deep water myself.'

'It'll continue till the government takes responsibility for unemployment,' said Duncan. 'You know what happened two days ago? You read it? They had the police and the Life Guards laying into the unemployed when they tried to demonstrate in Trafalgar Square. Bloody Sunday, they call it.'

Jack shook his head. 'There's plenty who'll neither work nor want. What do you do with a man who drinks his wages and turns up for work half-cut?' As he saw Duncan about to argue, he held up his hand. 'No, no. I know all about the chemical works with twelve-hour shifts and no meal hour and the dirty attics where girls like Kitty wind bobbins for a pittance – '

'And what about the single-ends that a quarter of Glasgow lives in? Over-crowded? That's an understatement, if ever I heard one. Most of them take in lodgers at that. No wonder nearly a quarter of the babies die before they're a year old – '

'I'm not starting a political argument with you,' said Jack, firmly but with good humour. 'It's too hot and, besides, I've been through all that radical stuff as a lad. I'm for self-help and independence. For folk marrying later, having only the children they can afford. I'm for temperance – like you – although I take a little whisky for my health. And then for a limited amount of government direction to soak up the unemployed.'

Duncan's pale face stretched in a grin. 'We'll make a Possibilist of you yet, man.'

'You'll not stick any of your new-fangled labels on me,' countered Jack. He gave Duncan a long, considering look and then admitted, 'I wouldn't mind seeing a few working-class candidates in the next election. You've heard of this man Champion?'

'H.H.? The one that calls himself a Tory socialist?' Duncan's laugh was genuine.

'Would you not take help from him? He wants working men to confront the Liberals next time.'

Duncan shook his head. 'And be accused of taking Tory gold? I would never live it down.'

'Then maybe America is the best place for you. You'll find no shortage of bosses to fight over there.' Jack's tone was jocular, but his expression serious. 'I could find you some kind of job, if you want to stay here.'

He saw it was better not to press the point, but went on, 'Let me at least give you one of my jackets. One that's too small for me – you'll do me a favour, taking it out of the way.'

'Thanks.'

Jack beamed with relief at having his offer accepted. He put his hand on his half-brother's shoulder and said, 'I've been glad to talk to you. It's taken my mind off Clemmie. The doctor says her heart is bad – '

'I'd no idea.'

'And now we have Sandia wanting to leave home and marry.'

'Is that not the natural state of affairs?'

'Her mother depends on her. To run the house. Keep an eye on the others.'

'But – '

'Her young man's from Belfast. It would mean her living there. Clemmie would see little of her.'

'Do *you* want her to go?'

'I've told her she must decide for herself.'

The quiet opening of the door made both men turn.

'Papa.' Sandia stood in the doorway. 'I'm off now to meet Dandy.' She advanced into the room, hand outstretched.

'Uncle Duncan! Kitty said you were here.' She kissed Duncan's cheek lightly. 'I wish it were not so hot! The *Herald* says it was 149 degrees yesterday at Greenwich!'

'You out-dazzle the sun!' said her uncle warmly. She was wearing a gown of pale-blue voile with mauve bands and rosettes, and the short, embroidered jacket called a zouave. The blue hat trimmed with mauve feathers sat jauntily on her fair hair. Her complexion was flawless.

'Flatterer!' She smiled at him, but a little subduedly.

'Your uncle is going to America,' Jack informed her.

Sandia looked astonished. 'I somehow never thought of you as the sort of person who would leave Scotland. I mean, with your politics and such – '

'Scotland has nothing for me at the moment.'

Her next innocent words fell on Duncan's ears as though from miles off. 'I must tell Kirsten. She will be most interested to hear it. She was always such an admirer of yours, Uncle. She has just come back to Glasgow, you know.'

'She's back? Here?'

'Only yesterday. I heard from her mother, whom I met in town. She was involved in the London riots, bruised and injured when the police set about the crowd with their batons. Her mother hopes to keep her home for good.' She looked at him concernedly. 'Are you all right, Uncle?'

'Certainly. It's this heat.'

'I must go.' She smiled guardedly at them both, her eyes shadowed and thoughtful. 'Mama is sleeping. She'll be all right till I get back.'

She was glad when she stepped into the comparative cool of Miss Cranston's Tea-rooms, below Aitken's Hotel in Argyle Street. She threw Miss Cranston a timid smile when she saw the little restaurateur seated behind her cash-desk, as usual. Sandia had unbounded admiration for Miss Cranston who, she heard, had had to fight family opposition tooth and nail to set up this place on her own. But why shouldn't women run tea-rooms? They knew far more about providing a pleasant, relaxing atmosphere and attentive waitresses than any man could. She would not mind such a career herself . . .

Dandy Peel was seated there, in the corner, and her heart gave a great spontaneous leap of pleasure. How handsome he was, no longer the gangling youth who had first courted her, but a mature and prepossessing figure.

He had gone home to Belfast after he had taken his degree at Glasgow University, three years ago, and was now in the family shipping business. His work brought him sometimes to Glasgow, when they always met, but their chief contact now was by letter, and his latest one had made his attitude clear. He loved her, of course he would always love her, but he could no longer put up with her procrastination. Either she had to accept his proposal of marriage and come and set up home with him in Ireland, or they had to stop seeing each other and writing. And he means it, she thought, noting the firm and resolute set of his unguarded face before he saw her.

'How's Ould Mother Oireland?' she greeted him.

He rose and kissed her brow, took her parasol and settled her in her chair, signalling to the waitress to bring tea and cakes.

'Why don't you come over and see for yourself?' So he was going into the attack straight away.

'You know why.'

'No, I don't. You tell me.' He could be very brusque.

'There's Mama –'

'But there's always been Mama,' he mocked her. 'What Mama says, what Mama does. Mama's iron will.'

Her face had flushed a delicate pink. She said defensively, 'Her health isn't good, Dandy. And she misses the boys terribly – she can't understand why Andrew had to join the Highland Light Infantry so soon after George went into the Merchant Service.'

'Doesn't she see they do it to get away from her tentacles? She'll make a fine job of young Alisdair, now the other boys have gone. She spoils him enough as it is.'

'You have no right to criticize,' she protested.

'I have, when I see what she does to you. You'll end up

the old maid of the family, at everybody's beck and call.'

He could see she was near to tears, but he felt all the bitterness of a lost cause and went on vehemently, 'It seems you don't care anything about *me*. Anything at all.'

The look she gave him through glistening eyes made him feel a monster. 'You know that isn't so. But it's not as simple as that. I don't think I could settle in Ireland. It's so far away and such a restless country.'

'When the Home Rule issue arrives at Scotland's door, you may have some sympathy for us.'

'Scotland doesn't want Home Rule.'

'Some radicals do. Even Campbell-Bannerman is thinking about it; maybe being Irish Secretary gave him the notion. I hear he used to put "North Britain" on his letters but has changed it back to "Scotland".'

'You see, if we lived here, in Glasgow, I could be near Mama to help —'

'But my job is in Belfast. You know that.'

'You could find work here. We have no shortage of shipping lines.'

The angry knot grew deeper on his forehead. He said in a low, furious tone, 'You're being deliberately provocative. You know ours is a family firm. And you also know it is a wife's duty to be where her husband is.'

Her lips were trembling. 'I know that love doesn't lay down duties.' She lifted her cup to her mouth with a hand that shook.

'So, it is all over, then,' he said, defeated.

Her voice was very small. 'Do you have someone else in mind?' She could not look at him.

'No one.'

'Could we not still write to each other?'

'What's the point? That could go on till we're both a hundred years old. You won't break your mother's apron strings. Perhaps you can't. And there's an end to it.'

She knew there was no way of explaining how she felt. When she saw her mother's pale, exhausted face after one of her attacks, for example. That expression that said: 'I'm depending on you, Sandia.' It was as though in a very real and terrible sense her mother owned her. The others in the family felt it too. Was it true what Kirsten had once argued, that her mother manipulated their feelings to her own ends? If it was, could her mother help it? She seemed to need the constant reassurance of her family's presence and love. But she was blind to the emotional needs of others. Whenever Sandia tried to discuss her own dilemma, her mother's eyes filled with tears and she would gently say, 'You have plenty of time, dear.'

What was Dandy saying? 'I must make it plain. I don't intend to sit around waiting to hear from you. But if you change your mind, then write and tell me.'

He paid the bill with a hangman's face. They stood up together, each expression as set as the other, and he walked her along Buchanan Street in the grilling heat and saw her on to her tram. Afterwards, he remembered her white-gloved hand waving and her head turned partly towards him, but not all the way.

When Duncan walked away from his brother's house in Ashley Terrace, it seemed to him the heat was affecting his legs. They felt full of lead, while his head felt woolly. He shook himself mentally. Even the bailies in the courts were refusing to sentence Glasgow termagants for brawling in this weather. It affected everybody.

He took off the clean, decent jacket Jack had given him, folding it neatly over one arm, and rolling up his shirt-sleeves, showing scrawny arms. One thought pushed out all others in his mind: she was back in Glasgow. *His burnet rose.* So she'd been in the riots down South, had she? He felt obscurely glad of her show of spirit. It made up some-how for his own defeat.

He wanted to see her. Tell her he was quitting Scotland. Explain his reasons. The likelihood was she wouldn't be interested. Not after all this time. He could have seen her, on his trips to London. He never had. But now she was crowding into his imagination again, filling it everywhere with her presence, so that her scent and her smile and the shape of her hands were as real to him as though he had been with her only yesterday. It was like being struck by a sudden illness. He fought against it, yet it was invading him.

Gilmorehill. In the university grounds, he looked through shimmering heat and saw hundreds of red-gowned students. Wagons, led by milk-white horses. Kilted pipers. Crazily he thought: they're there to welcome her. Another spectator, a little grey man with a head like a tortoise, informed him that the election of the Lord Rector was in progress. The reds were for Lord Rosebery, the blues for Lord Lytton.

'It's all right for the privileged few,' muttered the little man, glaring at the flag-waving, high-spirited students in procession. 'But what about the rest of us?' And he stumped off without waiting for an answer.

She would say: you need an intellectual elite to lead the rest. He answered the old man in his mind. He was nearly at her parents' home. He was going to see her. Make sure she was all right. Pity he felt so fuzzy, but there was no going back on the decision. He lifted the door-knocker and swung it hard.

Her mother glared at him suspiciously before recognition dawned. 'Mr Fleming! You're a stranger.' He wondered whether she knew anything about that time seven years ago, but decided not, as she led him hospitably into the parlour.

'You know my husband is retired? But he's gone down to the university to see the fun.' She gestured to him to sit down. 'I'll get you some tea – '

'No, don't,' he pleaded. 'I came to see how – how Kirsten was. My niece has just told me she was hurt.'

'Oh, she'll soon be fine.' She looked at him, mild questioning and reproof in her eyes. Perhaps, after all, some rumour had reached her. Glasgow was a gossiping city. 'She's got a few bruises. But she's young and strong.' Had she emphasized the 'young' for his benefit? He was past caring.

'Will she see me, do you think?'

He was never to know her answer, for the door opened and Kirsten herself came in. She was wearing a long blue skirt and a cream blouse and her hair was piled high above her pale face. On one cheek a deep bruise was changing from purple to yellow.

'Duncan!' Her mother might not have existed. He said, 'What have you been doing to yourself, lass?'

'Getting myself knocked about. Stupidly.'

Her mother's voice broke in on them, a little strained and cool. 'I'll make some tea.' She went out of the room.

'I was just passing –'

'I didn't expect –'

They could not take their eyes from each other. She said, directly, softly, 'What have you done to yourself, Duncan? You look – ill.'

'Look who's talking!' he joked.

'I used to nag you about taking care of yourself. I can see I'll have to start again.'

'No point. I won't be here. I'm going to New York.'

She looked frail. Why hadn't he noticed it before? Her shoulders were thin, sharp, her posture a little stooped. Was that what study had done for her? She made the smallest sound in the world, 'Oh.'

'Is that all you can say?'

'What do you expect me to say?'

Her mother came bustling back in with the tea-tray, looking from one to the other and saying busily, 'She's come back for good, we hope, Mr Fleming. Has she told you? And not before time. It seems to me she's swallowed too many London notions as it is.'

He took the tea from her hand, saying cautiously, 'What notions? Do you mean palmistry? Horoscopes? Head bumps? That's what's all the rage just now, isn't it?'

Kirsten glared at him. 'Hardly that.'

'She's talking about this quack from Vienna, this Freud, who denies there is a God,' said Mrs Mackenzie bitterly. 'She's left the church –'

'Now, Mother.' Kirsten upbraided her parent firmly. 'I've merely said I don't want the formal constraints of religion any more.' She looked at Duncan. 'I've met Salvationists,

Spiritualists, all sorts, and I've begun to think there are many ways to God.'

'Or away from Him,' her mother interjected.

'What about Frank Smith, the Salvationist? He runs farm colonies on the Essex marshes, and city workshops for the poor? Is *he* un-Christian?'

'Perhaps not. But I don't like you dabbling in Spiritualism. All this talk about one incarnation before birth and another after death – '

'Mother!' Kirsten held up her hand. 'We'll continue our arguments later. Mr Fleming has come to tell us he is going away. To New York.'

The older woman looked at Duncan, then said gently, but with a hint of relief in her expression, 'Times very bad, are they?' She looked from one to the other and then seemed to make up her mind on something. She rose and said, with an unexpected directness, 'Then I'll leave you two to have a word together. I have matters to see to in the kitchen.'

When her mother had gone, Kirsten blurted out, 'When I came back, I had the wild hope of seeing you. And you came. I think it must have been thought transference.'

It was odd, he thought. As though she had never been away. The same feeling that was near to delirium. Maybe he was delirious? He certainly felt strange. Hot. And there was this piercing pain in his chest.

He smiled at her and said, 'They've filled your head with too much airy-fairy nonsense, down there in England. Was there someone in particular – ?' He had to know.

She shook her head. 'There were friends.' Her eyes met his. 'Never anyone like you.'

'What about all those young academicals at the university? You must have met trained and exalted minds – '

'I did.' She nodded. 'None you couldn't have measured up to. Besides, they are taught how to think, not how to feel. You could have shown them how to do both.'

He knew, if she didn't, the gap between them now intellectually. His reading, though wide-ranging and catholic, was no substitute for the meeting of like minds. He had always felt his intellectual isolation like a hair shirt. Never more so than now.

He said angrily, 'I hope you've not come back here to impose high-minded Liberal notions. *Here* we're moving on. Here a Labour party will be a reality, sooner than you think.'

'All right.' She met his anger with an almost joyful recognition. 'I concede that no one could live and work at Cambridge without being influenced in some way by the Liberal tradition there. But I never met anyone there who put it better than Burns: "A man's a man for a' that." It says it all. And we know it better here in Scotland than anywhere else.'

He felt the words sustain and nourish him like food from the gods. He had waited so long for this, while the world grew cold. No one knew, no one understood, as Kirsten did. He watched as her eyes filled with tears. His arms opened to hold her. He felt his chest rise in a great sigh of relief, as hers did. He kissed her, feeling his whole universe judder and shake back into its true proportions.

'Don't go to America. I'll help you make a go of things here.' She looked at him pleadingly.

'I've promised Josie I'll go. There's Carlie, with the soles hanging off her boots. I've no option.'

'Oh, you have,' she urged. She looked at him curiously. 'Are your teeth chattering? What's the matter?'

'I'm cold. I've felt like this all day. I'm coming down with a chill or something.'

She insisted on paying for a cab to take him to the station for the train home. She said nothing more about America. Perhaps he wouldn't have taken anything in, anyhow. His illness, whatever it was, had suddenly taken over. His eyes were bright in a feverish face and he walked and breathed with difficulty. She put some money in the pocket of his decent jacket. He did not even seem to notice.

'There.' Josie put her hand up the chimney and brought down more soot to smear over Carlie's already sooty features. 'You're a proper sight now.' Carlie wore an old, long skirt of her mother's, a tatty feather boa someone had given her and a old tile hat her Grannie Kate had donated. She gave a sigh of satisfaction. 'Do you think anybody'll know me?' she demanded.

Josie shook her head obligingly, then laid down the rules for Hallowe'en guisers.

'You've not to bang on old Mrs Hope's door – the old body'll be in her bed. Don't go to old Willie Dunsmuir – he wouldn't give the time of the day. And if folk give you anything, mind and say thank you very much.'

Carlie nodded dreamily. She had been thinking of this last day in October for weeks, preparing 'tumshie' lanterns and practising her 'turn', which might be her own version of the Highland Fling or maybe one of the several poems her father had taught her.

'Get Betty Grey to take you up to your Aunt Tansy's,' Josie reminded her. 'It's too dark to go up there on your own. And stay there till I come and fetch you.'

The spoils from the houses in the Rows were very gratifying. Carlie counted three apples, an orange, some nuts and fifteen conversation lozenges, plus two pennies and a ha'penny. She set off with Betty for Dounhead House, urging the older girl to ask there for her Hallowe'en. Betty, however, was incurably timid. She delivered Carlie to the front door then ran off, crunching her teeth into her fourth apple that night.

Carlie thought of Donald while she awaited entry. Poor Donald! While she, Carlie, had got over the scarlet fever quite quickly, and could now run and play as well as ever, Donald had nearly died and was still an invalid. Aunt Tansy had thought it would cheer him up if Carlie came in for an hour to 'dook' for apples and eat champit tatties with charms in them, although there would be none of the customary ghost stories as too much excitement would be bad for Donald's heart.

Carlie went up to the big house quite often these days to play with her cousin. Once Aunt Tansy had lifted her red curls and tut-tutted at the 'tidemark' she'd left on her neck (she couldn't be expected to wash her neck every day, could she?) and another time had asked her if she had ever had nits in her hair. But she'd asked quite nicely. And she'd said several times that Carlie was a good little nurse and play-mate, and cheered Donald up better than anyone.

The trouble was, he grew quickly tired and then he behaved like a big spoiled baby. The last time Carlie had visited him, he had told his mother he didn't like living in Dounhead House, and that it would be more fun living in the Rows.

Carlie found this hard to understand. He had everything, a rocking-horse, a fort and lead soldiers, a musical box and all the books he wanted. Certainly he couldn't run about the Rows, playing games like The Fiery Cross and rattling the snecks on people's doors with a piece of thread or string stretching away into the darkness. He missed a lot of fun. But Carlie had only to think of the silk fringe on his bed-spread, the soft feel of the woollen rug over his knees when he sat up on the sofa, the sugared plums he got on demand and the puddings which were such a rarity in her own life, and she couldn't see what he had to grumble at.

A maid admitted her and took her through to the parlour where Donald lay back listlessly on his sofa. Aunt Tansy greeted her with cries of pretended horror. There was another visitor there, Mr Macleish the painter. He said nothing. He was lying back on the big luggie chair by the fire, one leg over the side. Carlie decided that if he did not speak to her, she would not speak to him. That seemed best manners. She had seen him before and sometimes he was nice and jokey, at others preoccupied and quiet.

'What are you supposed to be?' Donald demanded grumpily.

'A tattie-bogle.' Carlie hopped around with her arms out-spread. 'To frighten the birds.'

'I don't think you're a good tattie-bogle,' Donald argued. 'You should have straw for hair, for one thing.'

She ignored his ill-temper. That was the best way. Instead,

she spread her Hallowe'en spoils in front of him. 'You can share,' she said generously. 'Except for the money. I'm saving that up.'

It seemed nothing she could do would improve Donald's mood, however. Even when they dropped a fork over the back of a chair into a big wooden bine full of water and apples, and he speared six apples to her four, he was still disconsolate and hard to please.

'What's the matter with you?' Carlie expostulated at last.

'He's been in trouble today,' said Aunt Tansy. 'He's been very naughty.'

Donald stuck his head underneath his plaid blanket. A rumble of angry, tearful sounds came out. 'I hate you! I hate everybody!'

Aunt Tansy looked down at the heaving blanket vexedly.

'Donald, behave. Play a quiet game with Carlie. I am going to see Mr Macleish off to catch his train.'

When the two grown-ups had left the room, Carlie folded the blanket back inch by inch till she saw Donald's rosy, angry face.

'What did you do? Were you very bad?'

'*Somebody* squeezed the paints all over his paintbox!'

'Was it you?' She was scandalized.

'It was *somebody*.' His dark eyes glittered with anger.

'You?'

'She says it must have been me. She didn't *see* me. I went in quiet as a mouse.'

'It was a bad thing to do, Donald.'

'I hate him.'

'Well, your mother doesn't. She speaks to him – different.' She couldn't quite explain what she meant.

'He gives her things.' Donald was stabbing the sofa with his heels.

'What sort of things?'

'Flowers and letters. Things.' He pointed to his toy-box in a corner. 'In there – the painted pencil-case. Fetch it,' he ordered imperiously.

Carlie did as she was told. He opened the box and took

a long envelope from it, half-hiding it with his blanket. 'He
sent her this. It's a letter. She doesn't know I've got it. I took
it from under her pillow, when she wasn't looking.'

His face looked triumphant and at the same time guilty.
It made Carlie uncomfortable to look at it.

'You shouldn't take things,' she said, subdued.

'It says, "My beloved darling, the days are long when I
don't see you. Tell me you will come away with me." '

Carlie wrestled with him and took it from him. She didn't
believe Donald when he said he'd read it. He wasn't as quick
at reading or writing as she was, and she still had difficulty
with grown-ups' handwriting. This, however, was remark-
ably clear writing, large and somehow – well, pretty was
the word for it. Innocently she read from the top of the
second page. 'Tell him you need a holiday. Tell him anything.' Then she put the sheets of paper back in their
envelope, feeling her face go red as it always did when she
wasn't sure a course of action was the right one.

'I think you should put it back,' she said quickly, but
Donald didn't answer. He was crying, in a furious, half-
ashamed way, and she pretended not to notice, for boys
weren't supposed to cry.

It was a very miserable sound. In a little he put his head
under the blanket again and pretended to be asleep. Carlie
was glad when her mother came for her and took her home.

Going down the drive in the dark, Josie catechized her.
'Was your Uncle Lachie there?'

'No.'

'But Mr Macleish was?'

'Yes.'

Josie made a clicking sound with her tongue. Carlie said
nothing to her about the letter. Instead she said, 'Aunt Tansy
gave me a banana. From the Colonial Exhibition.'

When they got home they examined it with interest. It
was the first either of them had ever seen. Carlie peeled it as
Aunt Tansy had shown her and gave her mother half.

When she lay in the recessed bed that night, behind the
snug curtains, Carlie thought of Donald. Now that no one

could see, it was all right for her to cry, too. Not understanding why just made it worse.

By the time he got back to Dounhead, after seeing Kirsten, Duncan had developed a raging fever. The doctor was called and diagnosed pneumonia, aggravated by undernourishment.

Josie nursed him through the crisis. She had fallen into a nagging, upbraiding way of talking to him, which her tender actions belied. He was grateful for her care and unmindful of her attitude. If she but knew where his thoughts so often lay, she would have full justification for her anger.

'Don't go to New York,' Kirsten had said. There was no question of him going anywhere, said Dr Pettigrew. It was going to take a long time to rebuild his strength and the basis of that was good, nourishing food.

Jack sent word that he was to keep the six guineas, lent for the trip to New York. Tansy dispatched her maid with calves' foot jelly and Kate brought brown eggs and rich barley broth in a little lidded canister.

But he ate little. When the illness had burned itself out, he lay as though washed up on some grey, sunless shore, detached from his own feelings, remote from the worst the world could do to him. Ivy Thompson, thinking herself out of earshot, had pronounced the verdict to Josie: 'He's just a rickle of bones.' His heavy bones lay under the hodden blankets; the rough wool scratched his papery skin. He was aware of the bright red head of his child, Carlie, playing her games; hearing her voice like pleasant music. Faces came and went in the kitchen, mouths urged him to get on his feet again.

When Josie built up the fire and got him up to sit by it with a blanket round his shoulders, he stared into the small, shooting flames, seeing Kirsten there. If he had any will, it was to see her again. Old Adam in that rickle of bones. Josie coaxed him to take some broth. Her kindness made him retch.

'Keir Hardie's standing at Mid-Lanark,' she said to him

one day. 'If he can go independent, so can you next time you get the chance.'

He laughed. 'You'll not see me standing again.'

She ignored this expression of self-pity.

'He's having a go at the Kirk and the Queen. Some of them at Lanark seem to like it.' She ticked Hardie's other campaign issues off on her fingers. 'Home rule, the eight-hour working day, temperance, electoral reform. Even those that don't agree with him say he's made his mark.'

She thought she detected a spark of interest, followed by a feeble but genuine irritation when she reported that Hardie had in the end polled less than ten per cent of the vote.

'I could have told him that,' said Duncan. But he took the paper from her hand to read about it.

A few days after Hardie's predictable defeat, Josie showed Jamie Pullar to Duncan's bedside. The ruddy-faced widower brought some black bun and what he averred was good news. He had been to Mid-Lanark and, he maintained, he had seen a Sign. Hardie might not have polled many votes, but he had focused attention on the genuine possibility of working-class representation. And all kinds of factions who had warred against each other before Mid-Lanark were now talking of getting together at last and starting up a Scottish Labour Party.

It was after this visit that Duncan pulled on his trousers for the first time in many weeks and, wrapped in all the scarves Josie could find, walked on tottery legs a few yards down the Rows. The warm spring air filtered into his lungs and brought colour to his cheeks. That night, he ate cheese toasted on soda scone. And when Carlie looked at him warily, still seeing the frail invalid father who wasn't to be bothered, he pulled her on to his knee and sang to her.

When April came, he was in Glasgow for the founding meeting of the Scottish Labour Party. As Jamie Pullar had shrewdly predicted, the time was ripe to gather together many shades of unrepresented opinion.

There were those who wanted the immediate nationalization of the banks, land, railways and mineral rights, and some, like the Harrow-educated Liberal MP for North-West Lanark, Robert Bontine Cunningham-Graham, who urged the abolition of Royalty and the House of Lords.

Land reform and home rule were the preoccupations of men like John Murdoch, the crofters' leader, and Dr G. B. Clark, Good Templar and radical freelance, while temperance and improving the immediate lot of the poor were the overriding concern of Keir Hardie and his fellow trade unionists.

When Duncan and Pullar came out of the meeting, they grinned at each other tentatively.

'What do you think?' demanded Duncan. 'Will it last any longer than the Miners' Federation?'

'Who's to say?' replied Jamie. 'It's a mixed bag of tricks we've got. But it's better than nothing.'

By the winter, he was again involved in political matters with the new Labour Party and New York was never again mentioned. The 'New Unionism' of the unskilled workers, the dockers' demands for 'a tanner an hour', and the strike of 'those filthy, haggard harridans', the Bryant and May matchgirls, had combined to bring about a new interest in his writings and meetings.

And he was seeing Kirsten again. She, too, joined the new party and helped him write, shape and sell his articles, determined he should make enough to live on.

Helplessly, he slipped back into the old infatuation for her. All the time he was ill, she had been helping an English friend, Mary Banks, in her mission offices in the East End, fitting out destitute families with cast-off clothing and boots, and living in Spartan rooms above the mission.

He was often there, in those rooms, part of the circle of friends the two girls drew about them who discussed the topics of the age. He would allow himself to be coaxed to stay behind to eat the nourishing cheap stews they made and to discuss the book on the new radicalism that Kirsten insisted he should be writing.

'No one but you can write this book,' she persuaded.

'You've got both the journalistic ability and the experience from life.' She helped him plan the book under chapter headings, putting new heart and resolution into him when she praised his sharp insights and straightforward, readable style.

One day, when it was sleety-cold outside, and he had just built up the fire in the shabby East End parlour, she came and sat on the edge of his chair and absently stroked his hair.

He looked round, sensing her mood was troubled. He caught her cold hand and held it. 'What is it?' he demanded.

She didn't answer him immediately. Instead she watched the burgeoning flames in the grate, her eyes deep and thoughtful.

'Kirsten,' he urged.

Slowly she said, 'I'm going to have a baby.'

'Kirsten! Is it true?'

'Of course it's true. Why shouldn't it be? We've behaved like two crazy children. Not taking care. I'm robbed of sense when I'm with you.'

'Don't say that.'

'Why shouldn't I? What are we going to do, Duncan? How could we have been so – so stupid and selfish?'

'We'll find an answer.' She gazed down at his face and saw that on top of the concern there was triumph. It shot through her worry like a warm, sweet, atavistic pain and she slid on to his lap and let his comforting arms go round her.

'You're *pleased*,' she accused.

'There are worse things than love bairns.'

'How can you be so – so casual? There's Josie, and your little girl, and your chance of getting in at Dounhead next time. If it gets out, it could ruin your career.'

'We'll find an answer.'

'There isn't one. Except that I should go away.'

'No, there's another. It's that I should leave Josie and be with you.'

'We've been through all that before. Josie doesn't believe in divorce. You told me. And even if she did, it's what she represents that matters. Josie *is* Dounhead. Leave her and you leave behind your chances of getting to Parliament.'

'There are other seats.'

'Your reputation would follow you around.'

He put her from him and stood up, his face kindling with a slow anger.

'I'm not ashamed of loving you. Let the world know it and do what it likes.' But she saw that she had got through to him.

'Wheesht!' She used the vernacular tenderly. Drawing her black crocheted shawl across her chest and holding it tightly under folded arms, she strode about the room.

'I've been thinking and thinking. Before I told you. In a way it's a kind of test of me as a free woman. I've loved you without strings. Part of me wants to disdain marriage. I'll go to London and have it, Duncan. When the time comes.'

'And afterwards?'

'Afterwards we'll see.'

'Kirsten.' He put his arms round her, holding her close. 'I can't let you go. I love you too much.'

'And I love you,' she said softly. 'That's why I'm going.'

After Christmas, when her slender figure began subtly to change its contours, Kirsten set off for Bloomsbury in London with her friend Mary Banks to await the birth of her baby.

She had meant it when she said to Duncan that she didn't know what would happen afterwards. She wanted the baby, because it was Duncan's, but she found it hard to envisage what motherhood would be like, especially in her single state.

After the initial shock of the news, which had registered only too plainly on her homely, dedicated features, Mary had been a true friend. She had arranged for the mission work to be taken over by someone else and committed herself to looking after Kirsten till the baby was born. This was partly on the urging of Kirsten's mother, who had been deeply shocked and grieved. For several weeks before Kirsten broke the news to her she had kept rejecting the scandalous suspicions that had entered her mind when she saw her daughter. It couldn't be . . . Not with Kirsten. But it was. She had pleaded with Mary to go with her daughter before the pregnancy became obvious to all, especially to Professor Mackenzie, who would almost certainly never get over the shame and the humiliation to someone in his elevated position in the city. The Professor must never know. London must swallow up his daughter and the pretext that she was on a study course must be maintained, even if in the private hours of her day Mrs Mackenzie brought out baby gowns to scallop and baby bibs to embroider and water with her anxious tears.

On a cold spring day when a harsh wind broomed the London streets to bone, Kirsten's baby was born. It was a protracted birth but in the end straightforward enough. Exhausted but triumphant, Kirsten gazed down at her son. He was a little like Duncan, a little like her father and, at the same time, chasteningly, his own baby entity, a totally new human being, glaring at her with the innocent aggression of the new-born. Mary was enchanted by him. 'What shall you call him?' she demanded.

'Wallace.' Kirsten smiled at her friend over the tufty baby head. 'It's got the right independent Scottish ring to it, don't you think? I want him to be brave and independent and free.'

Duncan did not possess the money for the fare south to see his son, but he wrote frequently, letters full of love and concern and loneliness.

'I am prepared to leave everything and come down to you,' he wrote. 'I am in a vacuum here. My work has begun to mean nothing. The road stretches south from Dounhead and how can I keep my feet from starting out on it? If I walked the whole way, it would take me but a week or two.'

Kirsten wrote back: 'Be patient. I won't let you throw away everything you've worked for. What would you do here? Besides, you must give me time to think out what is going to be best for baby. I want you to finish your book and be a good Stoic for a while.'

Although she scarcely admitted it to herself, Kirsten knew that she could never take the baby back to Scotland. There were her parents to think of – her mother assured her her father's heart would not withstand scandal. She didn't think people would necessarily connect any child of hers with Duncan, as they had always been circumspect in their affair, but some explanation would be necessary – that she had adopted the infant, perhaps. At the same time, motherhood was not proving something that came naturally or easily. The baby cried a lot and sometimes Mary came home from shopping to find her friend in tears of frustration and even desperation.

It was agreed when Wallace was six weeks old that a holiday with Mary's sister and brother-in-law in the country would be a good thing all round. Jill Banks had married a comfortable seedsman in Suffolk and after five years of childless marriage was prepared to lavish her attention on the new infant. In the fresh country air the colour came back into Kirsten's pale cheeks and her eyes regained their sparkle. For two weeks she and Mary walked the country lanes, argued about women's suffrage, which had caught up with them again in London, and arrived home to enormous country teas and a quiet and contented baby.

Towards the end of the holiday Mary began quietly to press Kirsten for a decision about the future. She had decided that she herself wished to remain in London, with a view to going out later to the mission field, perhaps, with luck, as the wife of a certain hesitant clergyman. Even so, she was prepared to remain in the rented Bloomsbury flat for a time, if that was what Kirsten wanted. 'But it's the baby's future that worries me,' she said gently.

'He is not your concern.'

Mary took a deep breath and said with sudden, firm resolution, 'Kirsten, do you mind if I suggest something?'

'Please do.'

'It was Jill's face that made me think of it. The other day when we came back from Aldeburgh and she had looked after Wallace all day. She looked so – so blissfully happy.

She was made to be a mother.'

'What are you saying?'

'Why don't you let Jill and Walter foster the baby? Look how he's thrived since he's been here –'

'I would never consider it.'

'I could broach the matter with Jill.'

'How could I give up my baby?'

'It wouldn't be giving him up. You could see him whenever you wished. Please think about it, Kirsten. I think it may be the way out for you.'

The idea, once Mary had brought it forth, seemed to have been lurking in everybody's mind, awaiting discussion. At first Kirsten refused to consider it. But when Jill and her husband, whether prompted by Mary or not, made a gentle, tentative offer to care for the baby one evening at supper, Kirsten's resolution wavered.

'Jill's taken to the little tyke,' said Walter. 'And he to her. We'd look after him like our own. London's no place for a little lad, no more is Glasgow, from what I hear of it.' He looked with loving concern at his wife. 'Jill likes hearth and home. She has no battles to fight like you, Kirsten, or our Mary here.'

It was a long speech for him and afterwards there was silence. Kirsten's chair scraped back on the polished wood floor. Without a word, she went up to the baby's room, looking down at his small, sleeping form in the handsome farm cradle.

They were never going to be a conventional family, Duncan, Wallace and herself. She could not see herself as the sacrificial mother, giving up all outside interests to be with her baby. In some ways, she saw clearly, she would be a poor mother.

And yet there was a wrenching pain inside her that was the worst thing she had ever had to bear. She wanted to be there to see whether the downy gold hair would darken to auburn like her own, or turn black like Duncan's. She wanted to watch the growing awareness in the dark-blue eyes, to see the little hands stretch out for rusks and flowers

132

and rattles, to be there when he took his first steps.

She drew the knitted blanket up over the curled fist. A soft wind swept through the tall trees surrounding the farmhouse. Sentinel trees. She knew then she would leave the baby here. She would go back to Duncan and there was comfort there. Already she could hear his soft Lanarkshire burr and already plans crowded into her mind for the work they had to do.

Chapter Seven

Alisdair Kilgour looked out from the windows of the house in Ashley Terrace on a cold day in 1894. Heavily looped and curtained, shutting out the world, these windows oppressed his spirit, like everything else in the house at the moment.

Mother was dying. It was strange to be a medical student yet know there was no part of your own experience you could use to save the person who had given you birth. How could he tell his father? The family doctor obviously thought it best to keep the truth to himself. He couldn't fool Alisdair. The signs were all there.

He turned his morose attention to the windows. Alexander 'Greek' Thomson, responsible for so much of the best of Glasgow's architecture, couldn't really have wanted these bow windows. They must have been forced on the classicist by people like Ruskin who, while in Edinburgh, had gone on about the 'delightfulness' of bows or bays or oriels. It was Alisdair's considered opinion that Glasgow and bow windows did not go together at all. Glasgow and trams; Glasgow and football; Glasgow and tea-rooms; Glasgow and slums, fights and drink, yes. Glasgow and the Greco-Egyptian churches built by the aforementioned 'Greek' Thomson, even. But bow windows were a southern conceit and had no place in a hard city like Glasgow.

Having arrived at this somewhat irrelevant decision, Alisdair felt marginally better. But only just. The problem of putting his father in the picture returned. The old man had already had one recent blow, in the death of his friend, the Irish-American, Joe O'Rourke. It had raised complications over the Dounhead-Boston Trust which he and Joe had started up together, with Uncle Paterson. To compound matters, there had been a run on gold reserves in America which had closed the nation's banks and brought the economy close to collapse. His father was deeply worried but refused to talk about financial matters at any length. Alisdair felt he was probably out of his depth.

There was Kitty, weepy and short-tempered ever since her best friend, Jean Wilson, had emigrated with her family to Canada to farm free acres. Jean's brother, Fred, had been starting to court Kitty in a clumsy, uninspired way, but perhaps she was missing his dog-eyed devotion and his strong arm for carrying her shopping parcels.

As for himself . . . Part of his present dark mood was tied up with the knowledge that he had not yet grown up and away from his mother. He had enjoyed being the youngest, the family pet, 'the clever one', for too long. Yet it was bred in him to please her. Why else did he go twice to church on Sunday?

Self-awareness came slowly, painfully. His fellow-students talked freely about women and drink, for example. In order not to upset his mother, he had not allowed himself to indulge in either.

He was going to have to grow up on his own and he had the wit to know it was going to be desperately difficult. Not his medical studies. His mother had pushed him into those but she had been right : he had found the vocation to involve him heart and soul. Now she would be gone before he qualified. And he would pass out top of the list. It wasn't conceit. His tutors already accepted it as hard fact.

It was going to be his own uneven nature that was going to be the problem. Still so desperate for commendation. Still so unsure of how far a good man – and he wanted to be good – should live in the world. How realistic was it to think you could live an aesthetic life? If *she* went . . . he found he was on the verge of blubbering like a child and stared hard out of the window again, at anything. Anything to focus the mind . . .

Someone was coming along the terrace, walking steadily and purposefully, swinging a gold-topped cane. His plaid

Ulster was just that bit louder than a Glasgow man would venture. American, possibly. Or an emigrant Scot, back from New York with some swagger in his step.

The man was crossing, making for the front door. The bell jangled importunately as Alisdair crossed to the first-floor landing, to listen to the visitor announce himself. His unequivocal tones brought Alisdair bounding downstairs, pushing the maid out of the way, extending his hand.

'It's never Cousin Finn! From Boston!' They all came crowding out then, his father, Sandia, Kitty, to see what the noise was about. They hustled the young caller into the front parlour, taking his coat, his cane, his hat, sitting him down, handing him a glass of Madeira, overwhelming him with questions.

The head was narrow, fine, long, topped with blond hair with a slight wave in it. The lips thin, firm, not readily smiling. The eyes were large, blue, calm, intelligent.

'You're the image of your father,' said Captain Jack. 'And you're welcome here, my boy. Are you on holiday, on business? How long – '

'I've come to see you,' said Finn Fleming composedly. 'It's a family visit, Uncle, but I also have business to discuss with you, on my father's behalf.'

Something serious in his tone made them look at him curiously. But Sandia said, 'We are never going to talk business tonight! I shall get your room ready, then we will eat and if Mama is well enough, you must come and see her, Finn. She'll want to hear about your parents, about Bertram and little Marie-Louise, who wasn't even born when you last visited us all those years ago!'

Finn's level, blue-eyed gaze met hers.

'I'm afraid, Cousin Sandia, I must talk to your father after we've eaten. It's really rather important.' There it was again, that serious note. Sandia's face fell and Kitty turned away, scarcely able to hide her disappointment. She had been hoping for talk, parlour games, music round the piano. The house was so moribund these days, revolving round Mama and the crises in her health. A handsome cousin with a

Yankee accent had seemed, for a moment, like a gift from heaven.

Captain Jack led Finn into his study after the evening meal, settling him into one of the two big leather armchairs with a small whisky and water.

'I want you to come straight to the point, laddie,' he urged. 'It's about the trust, isn't it? How bad a way are we in?'

'Bad as possible.' Now that it was out, Finn's face showed something like relief. He pinched his trouser-knees, cleared his throat nervously. 'This isn't easy for me to tell you, Uncle. But I must. My father wants to wind up the trust. He has to concentrate all his reserves on keeping up the railway. That is, and always has been, his first concern.'

'Can't we weather the storm? I've known things look black for us before, but the market always bounces back.'

Finn shook his head. 'I wish I didn't have to bring such news. But I said I wouldn't hold out false hopes. I promised my father.'

'It puts the kibosh on me.' Jack poured himself another whisky and drank it down, neat. 'The trust has been the backbone of all my financial operations. I'm not going to survive this one, Finn. Does your father realize that?'

'I hope you can salvage something,' said Finn in a low, careful voice which had all emotion ironed out of it. 'You must let me explain why my father has had to make these decisions.

'Joe O'Rourke's dying changed everything, Uncle. His affairs were incredibly complicated. I'm sure Joe was straight but Tammany Hall – you know that's what we call the kind of political graft that goes on in New York? – had a hold on some of the others we roped in.

'We went to New York together, my father and myself, after Joe died, to try and straighten things out. We took the best financial advice there we could. We thought we might be able to lift out the New York section like a bad apple but our advisers said the rot had spread through the whole box.'

'Can't you raise the wind over there, then?' Jack's body and neck were rigid, yet his hand holding the glass shook.

Finn's voice changed, taking on a note of desperation.

'Can't be done. Lord knows, we've tried. But I've never known a situation like the one in the States at the moment. Workers are pouring in from Europe, upsetting the labour market, and it's one violent strike after another. They're marching on Washington, fighting at the pithead and railway yard. Men get killed. My father says there could be battles soon as bad as any in the Civil War.'

'Your Aunt Clemmie mustn't be told any of this.' Jack looked like a man fighting his way out of a bad dream. 'The house at Helensburgh'll have to go. The yacht. I'll fight to keep this place and to see Alisdair finishes his studies. I don't know if it can be done. But I'll try.'

'I can tell you more,' said Finn. 'We've had a slump in farm prices and the suggestion is we give American farmers credit by coining free silver, in the ratio of sixteen to one. We've got this "Prairie Populism" to cope with, in addition to everything else.'

'We'll go into all that another day.' Jack raised his head tiredly. 'At the moment, all I can take in is the sound of my own business crashing about my ears.'

'I'm sorry,' said Finn. 'This hasn't been easy for me, Uncle. We could have sent somebody else – '

Jack patted his arm. 'It's none of your doing, boy. All I ask is that you keep quiet and let me break this to the family in my own way.'

Everyone's reaction on hearing the news was the same as Jack's: Clemmie mustn't be told. Alisdair faced his father and said categorically, 'You know her heart is giving out? I've been trying to tell you – '

'Your mother has pulled through bad times before, and she'll do it again.' It occurred to Alisdair that his father could not accept the finality of any verdict. But they all put on cheerful faces on entering the invalid's room and gave her no hint of the conferences that went on downstairs, nor of the procession of lawyers and accountants streaming through Jack's city offices and out again with pursed lips and angry expressions.

Then one afternoon Sandia answered the summons of her mother's bell to find Clemmie sitting up against her lace pillows looking bright-eyed and determined. She had always retained a certain girlishness in her appearance and this was enhanced now by the flounced nightdress and the fading though still pretty hair falling about her shoulders.

Sandia put a cobwebby Shetland shawl about her shoulders and perched on the edge of the bed with a questioning air.

'What can I get you, Mama? Some barley water?'

Clemmie waved a dismissive hand. 'Sandia, I have been thinking. Your father looks preoccupied these days. You, too. There's something going on I haven't been told about – '

Sandia issued an immediate denial, but Clemmie smiled. 'I want to see your father when he comes in. I've made up my mind to it. Tell him, will you?'

'There's nothing, Mama,' Sandia assured her, but Clemmie looked past her, determined not to waste strength in argument. When Jack came in and got Clemmie's message, he left his high tea uneaten and climbed the stairs to the bedroom, feeling his own heart pounding unevenly.

'Shall I light the gas mantle?' he offered.

'No,' Clemmie protested. 'I like the gloaming. Just come and sit by me.'

He took her hand. It was very light and dry.

'Now what is all this?' he protested gently.

'Something's up, Jack.' Her breath was coming very light and fast.

'There's nothing. I've just been very busy.'

He was conscious of her face turned towards him and knew what the expression would be, though it was too dark to see. Love and trust, that openness that was for him alone. She had been too frail for him to lie beside for a long time now, but he had a sudden overwhelming desire to be close to her. This highly-strung, volatile, demanding woman had been his Clemmie on Kenner Brae, wild as he. Wild as the heather. In an excess of grief he put his head on her bosom. He felt the right, dry hand stroke his hair.

'Finn brought bad news from America. About the trust.

That's it, isn't it?' He marvelled at her sharpness, even now. 'It's since he came that you've all been – different.'

'There's no cause for alarm.' He rose and lit the gas now, then clumsily straightened her sheets and shook out her top pillow. Looking down at her, he told the most convincing lie of his life. 'There's nothing that won't sort itself out. You'll see. Now rest. I'm going down to have my tea.' He made it sound as though he were annoyed and hungry, like any normal man home after a normal day's harassment at the office. On the way to the door he had to step carefully, for everything was blurred, the flowers on the carpet, the antimacassars she had embroidered, the silver-framed photographs of George and Andrew in their uniforms, all the careful, useless bric-à-brac of their life together.

Ten days later, the doctor who had become almost like a member of the family, but who had been called in hastily as consciousness slipped at last from Clemmie's grasp, came down the stairs towards Jack's waiting presence and parted his hands to show her life had gone.

Jack sat in the darkened bedroom for two hours, sometimes weeping, sometimes looking at the calm face he felt sure must awaken from such a serenity of dreams. At last he felt able to go down to his family. The girls were pale but composed, but then they had the saving grace of small household tasks to perform. Alisdair wept noisily, his eyes puffed and red. Finn took over practical tasks, such as sending cables to George, due to dock in Australia, and Andrew, now an officer and stationed with his regiment in Cawnpore.

But when the funeral service was over and the black-plumed horses had borne Clemmie away to lie by the ornate but comfortless white marble headstone, the calamitous state of the family finances was brought home to them.

The house at Helensburgh was quickly sold, then the boat, and the house in Ashley Terrace took on a skeletal air as anything likely to fetch a fair sum of money was sent for auction.

Sandia dismissed the maids and tried to get Mrs Jessup, the cook, to go, too. Unsuccessfully, as Mrs Jessup firmly said she would remain till the last, having no place else to go, and didn't care whether they paid her or not. It still did not look like being enough and Jack was being pushed nearer and ever more inexorably towards the decision to sell the house. He did not want to go. Clemmie's presence still haunted the denuded rooms. What would be left of her if they moved elsewhere?

In these conditions of flux and misery, Finn was an ever-present and practical help. Sandia found she was growing very fond of him. It was like having one of the absent brothers to mother. With Kitty, it went further. She appeared to admire everything about Finn – his clothes, his speech, his attitudes. She grew uncharacteristically clumsy when he was near her. And despite her grief for Mama, he could make her smile and perk up and discuss the lighter items in the newspapers, and forget about the earth moving so frighteningly beneath her feet.

As the time wore on towards the day of his return trip to America, Finn changed from helpful relative into taciturn, moody visitor. It was Kitty who probed, delicately but insistently.

'Is there something the matter, Finn?' They were sitting in the morning-room, so much cosier and friendlier than the parlours.

He looked at first as though he might turn her question aside, but then he changed his mind and came and sat beside her at the table, taking the piece of tatting she was doing from her hands, so that he could command her full attention.

'I feel badly about what has happened.'

'But we know it wasn't your fault. It was nobody's fault.'

'But you've all been through such a harrowing time. Aunt Clemmie's death and now the house threatened.' He scraped his chair back and stood up. 'Kitty, I'm staying. I want to, anyhow. I like Glasgow. I'll get a job and contribute to household expenses. I'll help your father sort out his affairs.'

'I would like you to stay.'

'Would you?' Down he went on the chair again, peering closely at her expression. She had long, sweeping lashes over dark-blue eyes and a distracting little chin with the hint of a cleft in it. He was staring at the chin as Sandia came in.

'Finn wants to stay in Scotland,' Kitty announced.

Before the questions reached Sandia's lips, Finn had launched into explanations. They had the sound of issues well fought over in the battleground of his mind.

'Look — first and foremost I'm an engineer. I've been caught up in all these negotiations over the trust, but I don't like juggling with figures. What I really want to do is make automobiles.'

They stared at him.

'Automobiles?' repeated Sandia.

'Horseless carriages. Motor-cars. There's a man named Ford making them in the States — '

'But wait a moment,' said Sandia. 'Surely your father depends upon you. He must expect you to go back home.'

Finn turned an unhappy face towards her.

'Ah, well, there's the rub.' He lapsed into broody silence, biting his nails, while the heavy lock of fair hair fell down over his eyes. Kitty put out a hand and pushed it back.

'Your father and you don't see eye to eye about the horse-less carriage?' she probed, with a sudden flash of insight.

'More than that.' Finn's voice was bitter. 'He won't even listen to anything I say. In less than six years, we'll be entering the twentieth century. It's got to be the century of the motor-car, just as this one has been the century of the steam train. But, of course, steam locomotives have been his life. He can't, or won't, see the freedom the motor-car will confer on people. His mind runs along a straight set of rails.'

'Father always told us that he was a first-class locomotive man,' Sandia put in. 'Even as a little boy, he was obsessed by steam engines, Father says.'

'Obsessed is the word,' said Finn glumly.

'I think you're two of a kind,' Sandia observed percipiently. 'Maybe it is good that you should break away on your own.'

Finn's face brightened at these words of encouragement.

'Glasgow's the home of engineering, isn't it? I could learn so much here. It isn't just ideas we fight about, you see. It's a question of dominance. Father wants me in his shadow – '

'I know,' said Sandia quietly. Who better than she understood the harsh demands of family loyalties?

Kitty began circling the room excitedly.

'How would you drive them – these cars?' she demanded.

Finn looked at her in surprise, then said, 'There are several possibilities. Steam, for example.'

'Too noisy.'

'Gasoline.'

'Too smelly.'

'All right, then.' He grinned at her. 'There are other ways, like electricity. Or compressed air. You could even combine two systems in one car.'

There was a wicked gleam in Kitty's eye. She said mischievously, 'Why not combine all four systems? You could have a steam engine at the back – '

'No, Kitty, don't tease!' interposed Sandia.

'It's all right.' Finn was not perturbed. 'When I meet her trudging home one of these days, I'll pass her in my elegant machine and call her peasant. You, on the other hand, Sandia, shall ride beside me like a lady.'

He wasn't looking at Sandia, however. His gaze was for Kitty and her flushed face. He grabbed her wrist with his left hand and began scoring out an imaginary diagram on the table with the forefinger of his right.

'Look, Kit! Gasoline would be best. Gasoline engines could be cooled, by air or water. You could have a two-stroke engine – like this – or a four-stroke, placed back or front. Or even centre, if you like.'

She gazed down where his finger traced as though the actual engine had assembled before their eyes.

'You haven't any money,' she said, mesmerized.

'All I need is a shed somewhere. The rest I'll get as I go along. But time's wearing on. I want to have my first machine on the road in a year.'

'You're not serious?'

'I've never been more so.' He looked at her exultantly. His grasp tightened on her wrist and he pulled her close to him. A quick check ensured that Sandia wasn't looking. He kissed Kitty quickly on the lips.

Sandia had something she wished to discuss with her father. It was his last day at the office. She knew that when he got in he would be sick at heart, dispirited, but she couldn't keep her idea to herself any longer. She wanted to open a tea-room.

She had to talk her father into giving his approval. For a start, he would be aghast as her even thinking of a career outside the home, a prejudice reinforced by Mama's firm notions in such matters. She might even have to go ahead without his support. But she would hate that. They were a family still and should operate like one, helping and encouraging each other.

The five hundred pounds Mama had left her was her trump card. He would argue she should keep it. She would argue that it could be put to work for them. It could save the house in Ashley Terrace, it could bring back some of the luxuries they had grown used to, it could furnish again the near-empty rooms.

In her own head, she extended the arguments. She was still young, she was strong, and she needed a new interest to help her forget the unhappy days that had gone before. It was strange how her idea for the tea-room had sprung, fully realized, almost on the day of Mama's death. As though it had been waiting there, desperate for consideration.

She had known exactly how she would decorate it, what the furniture would be like, what the waitresses would wear. (She had heard that her idol and predecessor, Miss Cranston, even inspected the waitresses' underwear to make sure it passed muster. She would not go so far as that.) She knew what Glasgow-made delft would grace the tables and what scones and cakes and tea-bread would seduce the hungry shopper across the threshold.

She would have to pick the site with care, for she wanted

it to be smart enough to attract the ladies from Kelvinside, but central enough for more ordinary folk. The first would lend style and elegance; the second the numbers necessary for survival.

Not for the first time, Sandia wished she had Dandy to turn to for advice. Although they had not been in touch since that fateful day in Miss Cranston's Tea-rooms, she often addressed his shadowy figure in her mind. In a strange way, he was still *hers* and the possibility of reconciliation something she had never let go. She knew in her heart the foolishness of this.

She had watched so much that was sensational and un-believable happen in his Ireland. Parnell involved in the scandal with Kitty O'Shea. Named in her divorce suit. And then after his marriage to her, howled down by the crowds who had once loved him and lime thrown in his face.

Poor man, within a year he was dead and now his old opponent, Randolph Churchill, was clouded in his mind, they said, and dying, too.

She had thought of Dandy a lot last year, when after Gladstone's second Home Rule for Ireland Bill had been thrown out by the Lords, there had been riots in Belfast and Catholic workers driven out of the shipyards. But she doubted if he ever thought of her . . . did he? *Dandy, Dandy.*

She was thirty now, quite the traditional old maid, as he had predicted. She had put on weight and had the set, mature look that came from household responsibilities and family cares. Yet, when she looked in the mirror, a fresh, milk-maid's face gazed back at her. Waiting for life to write something there, something more.

The clock in the hall struck up a sonorous din and she saw it was six o'clock. She pulled aside the parlour curtains, looking down the street for her father. At last he came. He climbed the front steps like an old man, hanging on to the iron railings. Her heart melted in love and concern.

'Papa.' She took his hat and cane. 'So it's all over?'

He nodded, giving her the ghost of an ironic smile. 'They tried to make a businessman out of me, lass. I should have stuck to my ships.'

'Can we still remain here?'

'If we make the strictest economies.'

She told him then of her idea. She had no notion she could be so persuasive. She even brought in Kitty, as a last-minute inspiration. Until Finn had arrived to distract her, Kitty's theme had been Canada, morning, noon and night. Might she not still want to emigrate there to be with the Wilsons, as she had often begged? A tea-room would take up the slack of Kitty's interest, provide a challenge and diversion.

She knew that Kitty was too taken up with Finn for this to be likely, but she had to put her case as strongly as she could.

The captain looked at his eldest daughter as though seeing her as a person in her own right for the first time.

'There's something of your Grannie Kate in you,' he mused. 'She was a great one for rolling up her sleeves when she got in a tight corner.'

'You mean you approve?' Sandia could not believe her ears. But it occurred to her later that her own life was not the only one to be circumscribed by the strength and tension of her late mother's will.

Once the decision was made, events moved with an almost terrifying turn of speed. Premises were found just off Sauchiehall Street and Sandia invested in dark green curtains with gold braid and loops, solid chairs and tables, napery that was not quite so fine as she would have liked, but was the best she could afford, and three-tiered cakestands to take the scones, crumpets and wide variety of cakes for which the city was justly famous.

Kitty was not very enthusiastic to begin with, having reservations about the propriety of going out to work. But she soon found the stir and bustle of setting up the tea-room irresistible. She helped Finn put up the flocked wallpaper and pestered her relatives to donate pictures for the walls.

She helped with the baking in the morning, set out the tables with a dainty touch, hired the waitresses, and still found time to go out to look round the shops or meet friends.

Once the place was opened, her many friends came in for tea, bringing with them all sorts of light-hearted fun and harmless gossip, and there were plenty of city blades who tipped their hats to her and indulged in the sort of discreet, flirtatious repartee that lent wings to the day.

As for Sandia, she felt a satisfaction she had never known in her life before, a liberation and a joy that made light of all the hard work. 'I want to be famous for comfort and cleanliness,' she told her small staff, and the motto was repeated in gilt lettering on her snowy lace-netted windows: 'Miss Kilgour's, For Comfort and Cleanliness.' City wags took up the claim and gave it a familiar ring. A regular clientele sang the praises of the establishment's French cakes and the fruit slices christened 'fly cemeteries' by whimsical young men. It wasn't long before Sandia found it prudent to employ two steady bakers and to start a selling counter displaying delicacies and treats to be taken home.

The Tea-room Movement was sweeping through Glasgow with an almost evangelical fervour and spreading to other cities in Scotland and England and abroad. Cheap and frequent trams brought customers into the city to sample and pass judgement on the wares of every new establishment. It was generally agreed that no tea-rooms in the world equalled those of the Second City of the Empire, where it had all begun. Sandia realized that she had a certain business acumen and that soon she would be able to branch out.

It was gratifying to take the worry of keeping up the house from her father's shoulders. And working in the heart of the city, with its changing kaleidoscope of people, its theatres, music-halls and concerts, its lively shops and clean, brightly-painted trams, was like living in a child's dream of cosmopolitas.

What she wished for now was that one day, when her tea-rooms were looking their best, and the tables freshly laid, with flowers in their silver vases and the sun striking her favourite picture, a sunny cornfield by Hamish Macleish, her Dandy would walk through the swing doors and give her that cheeky, confident smile and say 'How are you doing?' and she would sit down with him, with her best silver service, and tell him everything that had happened in between.

Chapter Eight

'Are you going to Glasgow to see Jamie Pullar?' Josie asked Duncan.

He wasn't home very often now, in Dounhead. Since he had brought out his two popular books, *A Newer Look at Radicalism* and *Politicians in the Wake of Christ*, he had been in great demand as a public speaker, not only on political or union platforms but wherever the livelier issues of the age were being discussed, whether it was free love or socialism, anarchy or humanism.

His books and journalism had brought in money. Josie had two fine Alhambra covers on her beds now and a bought rug before the fire. There were decent delft cups and saucers on the dresser and two china dogs she had bought in Glasgow, where they were made in their thousands to satisfy popular demand. She knew he had come into his own now. He no longer had to stuff newspaper down his boots to keep out the worst of the rain. He even had a suit to call his own.

But she knew the price she had paid. She personally. He had grown away from her, become the public figure, even at home. The door-knocker went continually with people seeking his advice or attention. When he spoke to her, sometimes, it was with the same almost impersonal kindness he gave these callers. And yet her pride in him was too great to admit criticism. After the lean years, did he not deserve all the attention and near-adulation that was paid him?

He nodded now in answer to her question.

'He says he has a matter of great interest to discuss with me.'

'Have you any idea what he's talking about?'

'Not the faintest. But he's got me intrigued.'

'I was going to say –' She paused, feeling strangely reticent.

'What is it?' He looked at her sharply, his mind on letters he was anxious to answer before he set out.

'Can I come with you?'

'To Glasgow?' They seldom went anywhere together now, her life being largely in and around the Rows, and taken up with the women's co-operative movement in Dounhead.

She backtracked hastily. 'Oh, never bother. It was just a notion –'

He looked at her skinny figure covered in an unbecoming print overall. Her red hair was fading now, and the curl gone from it. She had the big, swollen knuckles of the Rows housewife and she walked badly because of corns and bunions from years of ill-fitting boots and shoes. A chord of long-dormant tenderness was struck in him. He remembered the angular little girl, all jabs and elbows, he had played with years ago.

'Put your best bonnet on, lass. You're coming with me. I'll buy you your tea in our Sandia's tea-rooms – "Miss Kilgour's, For Comfort and Cleanliness". What do you say to that?'

She divested herself of overall and shabby brown dress and had a cold-water wash by the kitchen window. By keeping her head only above the net half-curtains she could conduct her toilet and keep an eye on who went up and down the Rows.

The brown dress had to go on again – it was the best she had, for she was careless in such matters. But she was glad her green coat with the darker velvet frogging on it was new and she had a small velvet hat to go with it. When she sat in the train with Duncan she felt he had no reason to be ashamed of her looks. The thought made her chatty and confidential.

Duncan's mind had been on other matters to start with, but for the latter part of the journey he allowed himself to be amused and taken up with Josie's chatter. Much of it was about the co-operative movement, which she was largely responsible for organizing in the Dounhead area. Since Parliament had exempted 'the Co-op' from income tax a year ago, providing goods were sold only to members, the Dounhead 'Co' had taken off in a big way and now had regular support from most of the miners' families, to the chagrin of the ageing Wylie, the master grocer.

'I think things are getting better,' Josie ventured. 'There's not so much unemployment about.' She was looking thoughtfully from the train windows at the tenements in Glasgow's outskirts, a sight that seldom cheered her, and her comment was almost by way of being a mental shove against despondency.

'Trade's reviving,' Duncan agreed. 'We'll maybe even see some decent houses built here now. God knows they're needed.'

Glasgow itself seemed to bear out the suggestion that times were on the upswing. The shops were full of delectable, well-made goods and the streets had their full quota of fashionable, leisurely folk. When they reached Sandia's tea-rooms they were full to overflowing and Sandia and Kitty were so busy they scarcely had time for more than the exchange of enquiries about family health. Sandia, however, loaded their table with exquisite cakes and would not take payment, no matter how Duncan protested.

'It's repayment for my tram fare,' said Sandia, joking about the time her uncle had saved her and Kirsten from the crowd in St Enoch Square. Her contact now with Kirsten was minimal. She knew she was back in Glasgow, but the conventional side of Sandia's nature had deepened with the years and she was not sure she could acknowledge a female agitator as a friend.

On the way to Jamie Pullar's house-cum-office, Josie dragged Duncan into a milliner's 'just to look' at the hats and, still in indulgent mood, he bought her one with veiling and flowers which she asserted was a rare bargain. She should have had such hats years ago, he reflected sombrely. They were for chits of lasses. But he said nothing. Josie deserved all the fal-lals that came her way.

Jamie welcomed them with the offer of whisky or tea.

'We neither of us drink,' Josie pointed out, with a certain sharpness. Putting on the kettle for tea, Jamie observed that there were plenty who said that in public, but weren't averse to a medicinal drop in private. Like himself.

'Have I got news for you!' he announced, when he'd provided them with cups of thick brew sweetened with condensed milk, and a spice biscuit each.

'Don't keep us waiting any longer,' Duncan pleaded.

'Well,' said Jamie, importantly, 'you know there's a series of exchange visits going on this year between American and British trade unions?'

Duncan nodded.

'Our brothers in New York have specifically asked for the author of *A Newer Look at Radicalism*.' He smirked at Duncan's astonishment, adding, 'And yours truly has been invited along to accompany him, on account of my brother being a railwaymen's leader and close to the great Eugene V. Debs.'

'Is this true?' Duncan demanded.

'It's only got to be ratified at our next meeting,' said Jamie, 'and the tickets are as good as booked. I'll tell you something else. That young friend of yours, Kirsten Mackenzie, the women's suffrage body, she's been invited along, too, to talk to her American sisters about out-of-doors meetings. It seems they haven't started those out there yet.'

Duncan looked briefly at Josie. Her face was set.

'Has Kirsten accepted yet?'

'I saw her only this morning, and she seems keen on the idea. Especially if you go, too.'

There was a clatter as Josie set down her cup and saucer.

'And what about me?' she demanded.

Jamie looked at her, nonplussed. 'The expenses'll not run to wives, lass,' he said kindly.

'If I can pay my own expenses?'

'Well, then, I would say it would be all right. It would be fine.'

'I can go as a representative of the women's co-operative

movement.' They looked at her in joint bewilderment. 'That's another thing our sisters in America want to hear about.' The penny had dropped with Jamie Pullar. Hadn't he just put his foot in it, mentioning the lassie Mackenzie? There were those who said she and Duncan had tig-togged in the past, though he was never astute in these matters, and had no way of knowing the truth. But a look at Josie's vinegary face made him realize something was up.

He said cautiously, 'That would be up to you.'

'I can organize it,' snapped Josie. 'I would only want my fare. I've a bit put by for other expenses. What do you say, Duncan? Carlie could stay with her Grannie Kate.'

Duncan's face was carefully without expression. This had been the last thing he had expected to happen. Non-committally he replied, 'We'll have to see, lass. I don't think the Co-op will agree.'

'I'll make them,' said Josie fiercely. 'I've worked hard for them and this is little enough to ask for.' She looked at their faces and burst out laughing at their discomfiture. 'My, a sea voyage would just set me up fine.'

. 'Aye. Well,' Jamie temporized, playing with a leaky pen on the table in front of him. 'There's something else, Duncan. Something else I have wind of. By the time you come back from America, you're going to have an election on your hands in Dounhead. And this time, we're going to make bloody sure you get it. Now we've got the Independent Labour Party boys behind us, we can bring up the big guns.'

He looked up with a pretence at a casual air, seeing the colour recede from Duncan's face.

'Do you tell me, man?' he exclaimed. 'What's happened to Scoular, the Liberal man, then?'

'He's been involved in some scandal with a Minister's wife. I haven't the full details. But I hear he has been given three months to wind up his affairs and then he has to fade quietly from the scene, no doubt they'll say for health reasons.'

Josie was clutching Duncan's arm. Now she shook it, her face alight.

'Your time has come at last.'

'We'll have to wait and see,' he said, half-apprehensive, half-euphoric.

She never took his arm as a rule but this time, on the way back to the station, she did: awkwardly, her fingers pinching his arm. The placards for the newspapers had brought out their tallest print: the newsboys, hoarse from yelling, could not keep up with the queues of would-be buyers.

One placard read: DUCHESS OF YORK: A SON. Another: WELSH PIT DISASTER: 251 DEAD.

Josie heard Duncan swear beneath his breath. He bought a paper and read it closely on the way home. She reflected that it was too much ever to expect untrammelled pleasure. The day had been a good one for them but seeing the pit headline had suddenly shut out the sun. When she closed her eyes, she could feel what it was like, having slurry fall on them, shutting them in for ever.

Going up the Rows, she held his arm again, her face grim enough to match his own.

'Is it true?' shouted an old man from an open door. 'Is it Blantyre all over again?' And, like Duncan, he swore in helplessness and rage.

A child of about three, from a house farther down the Rows, was playing on the step as Duncan and Josie reached home. A dirty, barefoot child, with scabs where she had picked at flea-bites. Josie scooped her up and carried her indoors.

'Would you like a piece, Annie?' She spread some bread with jam and handed it to the little girl, first wiping hands and face with a piece of damp rag. The gesture was automatic, second nature. The child sat quietly and companionably while Josie stirred the fire and put the kettle on for tea.

Later, she put the new hat Duncan had bought her on top of the dresser, carefully, in its paper bag. She was consumed with guilt. It had cost one shilling and elevenpence.

If Duncan had been apprehensive about Kirsten and Josie both travelling to New York, he was not the only one, but the opposition, when it came, was from an unexpected source. Jamie Pullar sought him out after a meeting and made an excuse to accompany him on his way. Duncan could feel that the union organizer had something on his mind, but he was unprepared for the blunt question out of the darkness:

'What does the wife think of Miss Mackenzie, then?'

'She has not said. Has she any need to think anything?'

'You tell me,' Jamie said.

No one knew better than he the draughty halls, the chill station platforms, the suffrage meetings and labour rallies that Kirsten Mackenzie had shared with Duncan since she came back to Glasgow after a brief stay in the South that must have been all of seven years ago. But now, with the election in the offing, Josie who had always been a figure in the background at Dounhead seemed suddenly determined to play a more prominent part. Well and good, Jamie thought. She had many friends and supporters in the co-operative movement. She was too valuable an ally to lose. If she had not been, he might not have put his next question, but it had been swimming around in his mind ever since Josie had shown her determination to accompany Duncan on his American trip.

'Have you been playing a double game, man?'

For answer, Duncan quickened his pace. Jamie followed him, dodging in and out of the pools of lamplight, protesting his lack of intention to offend.

When Duncan had won back a measure of composure, he turned and said evenly, 'I wouldn't have thought such prying part of your nature.'

Jamie refused to be put off. 'I'm going to see you win this election that's coming if it's the last thing I do. I believe in *you*, man. Now listen, for your political life depends on it. Don't be seen on too many platforms from now on with your friend Miss Mackenzie. And travel out on a different ship. It's Josie who must be beside you from now on. Do you think the Tories and Liberals alike won't be watching your every move? A breath of scandal can kill you stone dead. There's nothing more puritanical than the working-class vote.'

The face that Duncan turned towards him in the semi-darkness was strained and angry.

'There might be a limit to what I'll put up with for the working-class vote,' he said furiously. 'And that might just include you, Jamie.'

'She's a bonnie lass,' said Jamie, none too perturbed. 'I've seen the look she gives you, when you're up on some box, jawing.' He put a conciliatory hand on Duncan's arm. 'You can't take offence at me, laddie. We've been in this struggle too long together. Just remember where your greater loyalties lie – to the party, to me, and to the folk who believed in you when the arse was out of your trousers.'

When Jamie had gone his way, Duncan walked on unheeding, not caring that his steps were leading him in the direction of Kirsten's house. To be deprived of her now, when he had looked forward to the voyage, to seeing her daily, transformed the journey into exile. Without Kirsten, what was the New World to him? But the New World with Kirsten would indeed be a new world. Thousands of others had gone there to make a fresh start. He thought of Jamie's words: A breath of scandal can kill you stone dead. What sort of scandal would it be if he were seen by some of those watching Tories and Liberals, visiting her house late at night? Or even by some of his own party? Nothing so puritanical as the working-class vote.

Resolutely he lifted his hand and knocked.

When Kirsten appeared at the door she had her dressing-gown clutched about her, her hair hanging down over her shoulders.

'Can I come in?' he demanded shortly.

For answer she opened the door more widely.

'What's the matter?'

He sat down and buried his head in his hands.

'I've just had an exchange with Jamie Pullar. The thought of the election when we get back seems to have turned his brains. He claims I'm making too much of you in public.'

She brushed sleep from her eyes, amused in spite of her perturbation at his turn of phrase.

'Making too much of me?'

'He thinks it's obvious – what we are to each other. That it could jeopardize my chances.'

'How could that be?' She was as wide awake as he was now. 'Duncan, we've always taken care. Kept it formal in public.'

'It seems to even Jamie's untutored eye that you look at me in a certain way.'

She gave a strained little laugh. 'I can't be the only one.'

He pulled her down beside him. 'I'll not have you blackened. If there's any more talk of this sort, I'll tell them what to do with my nomination.' He kissed her on the lips. 'Kirsten, have you ever thought? We could stay in America, you know. I could tell Josie everything. She could say what she liked when she got back. You and I could make a new start –'

She pulled away from him.

'You're talking nonsense. It's a form of cold feet, that's all, because the election's getting nearer. I won't let you give up. I'll stay out of your campaign, if that's what Jamie wants. Someone else can tell them in America about women's suffrage. It doesn't have to be me.'

'No,' he said, protesting the enormity of her sacrifice half-heartedly because it was a measure of her love.

She turned towards him. 'Do you think I'd ever do anything to harm you? I'll keep out of your life altogether, if need be.'

He pulled her close and groaned in her ear, 'Don't say that. Tell me about our boy. Have you heard from him recently?'

'Yes,' she said. 'I had a letter. And one from Jill, saying he was using the surname Banks at school because they thought it would make life easier for him. They mentioned adoption again, but grateful as I am to them, it's one thing I'll never agree to.'

'I'm sorry, I'm sorry, I'm sorry,' he murmured into her hair.

'What for?'

'For this unholy mess. For loving you. For not making it possible for us to have Wallace with us.'

She stopped his protest with a fierce kiss. He pulled her hair down like curtains round his face, parted her gown and kissed her breasts. She went to him as easily as she had done the first time. But afterwards, when he had gone, she lay wide awake in the darkness, listening to the sounds of the night. Duncan would be away three months. Was she being given a chance to make their temporary parting permanent, to grow used to his absence from her life? Beyond the window the white brilliance of moon and stars reminded her that winter was approaching. She shivered, but not with cold. She had wanted to go to New York.

In the dark of the small cabin he shared with Josie aboard the SS *Northern Star* Duncan tossed and turned. The ship was rolling and pitching her way across the Atlantic, and an unaccustomed glass of whisky taken to ward off incipient sea-sickness had set his thoughts whirling like dervishes through his brain.

The American trip had been a success, but now he was exhausted. Lecturing, travelling as far afield as Chicago, talking – often far into the night; it had been stimulating while it lasted, but once on board ship the reaction had set in. Josie, by contrast, had spent the time in New York, staying with Jamie Pullar's brother Eric and his family on Lower East Side. Eric was a labour agitator who had served a prison sentence for his part in the riots during a recent railroad strike, but his wife was a pleasant Ayrshire girl with whom Josie had at once felt at ease. Even so, she had made it no secret that she was glad to be going home to Dounhead. Duncan too was glad to be going home, but to him home meant Kirsten. He whispered her name in the darkness. *Kirsten, my bonnie bird.*

He remembered the last time they had made love, that

night when he had thrown caution to the winds and gone late at night to her house. There had been a kind of aching desperation about it that had frightened them both. 'I'll keep out of your life,' she had said, but what was life without her? And yet a part of him knew that there was a truthful shrewdness in what Jamie Pullar had said. He had supposed they would always be able to go on working together, he and Kirsten, but if their closeness became too apparent, it would put an end to his election chances. He thought of Dounhead and the hold the Kirk had there, even on those who never attended a service. Nothing so puritanical as the working-class vote . . .

And Josie – did she suspect something? Her attitude throughout the trip had been one of aggressive comradeship, but sometimes when she stood beside him he had surprised a look almost of terror in her eyes. Was it over his own indecisions, the knowledge that behind the public man and his speeches he was being torn apart? For some reason he remembered the night she had lost her job with Tolley the draper and had stood at the end of the Rows, afraid to go in and face a beating from her father. From then on he had felt responsible for her. In its way it was as powerful a feeling as his love for Kirsten, because it was bound up with the way he felt about Dounhead and its poverty, its dirt, its narrowness, its lack of proper expectations – all the things he had set his heart on getting to Westminster to change.

And if he chose Kirsten, he would never achieve it. A strange dry sob burst from him. He felt as though his guts were being torn out, as though his head would burst from the conflict within it. Kirsten and Josie, Kirsten and Dounhead. The woman he loved and the woman he was bound to, and his duty to those who had nothing, which in a strange way bound him to them both. A shuddering he could not control went through him, and he gripped the sides of the bunk until he felt as though his knuckles would burst through his skin.

'Duncan!' Josie was sitting up in the bunk opposite, fumbling for the light. He saw her eyes wide with alarm.

'Duncan, what is it? Are you ill?'

He could not answer her at first. She took his hand and chafed it, brought him a drink of water and held it to his lips. 'You've been overdoing it. Too many meetings. Too much travel. I was afraid of something like this.'

'No, Josie, no. I've something to tell you.' He looked pleadingly up into her face.

'It'll wait till morning,' she said, suddenly defensive. 'I don't want to hear it now.'

'You must,' he said. 'I have lain with Kirsten Mackenzie and I am the father of her son. I have feelings for her such as I have never had for a living soul. I want my freedom, Josie. I can keep it from you no longer. Seven years is long enough.'

She said at last in a small, light voice, 'I knew there was something between you. I never knew it had gone that far. What do you expect me to say, Duncan? Go to her? Do you think it would be the answer?'

He said nothing, but he had stopped shivering. He felt weak, yet bathed in a kind of relief.

'You would have to give up the idea of standing for Dounhead,' Josie said. 'Give up all we've worked for, me as well as you. They would never stand for it. You know that.'

A breath of scandal can kill you stone dead . . .

'I could still be of use to the cause.'

She said then, with bitter vehemence, 'The cause? That's not what I've worked for. Nothing so airy-fairy as a cause. I've worked for my own folk. You've moved away from them, haven't you? And it's been through *her*. Well, when you led the miners out on strike for sixpence a week, I was behind you. When you fought the masters to start the union, and give the men a week's holiday, and look after their widows and orphans, I was behind you. I don't belong to the world of grand ideas and fancy words, but I know where the help is needed. I know where the bairns go hungry.'

'I'm sorry, Josie,' he said inadequately.

'I'll not let you do it!' she cried, and he was reminded poignantly of Kirsten, who had uttered a similar cry. 'I could never go back and face them if I had a man who let them down. I'd never hold my head up again.'

She swore at him then, Joakie Daly's daughter who had never been a stranger to words of violence. She broke down and wept, wiping her tears with her hair or her nightgown sleeve, it did not matter. 'I don't care if you go to your doxie,' she raged. 'Go to her when you like and where you like. But I'll not divorce you. You're my man and my man you'll remain. You hear me, Duncan Fleming? God, how I hate you! I could kill you.' She pummelled him with both fists.

He tried to hold her hands. 'Be quiet!' he pleaded, fearful that someone would hear above the creaking of the ship.

'You stayed away from my bed,' she spat at him. 'So be it. You'll never touch me again.' Her eyes burned their contempt and rage at him. 'Never mind the promises you made me, but at least I thought you were man enough to keep your promises to the folk in Dounhead.' He watched as her face crumpled and she flung herself down on her bunk and broke into uncontrollable weeping.

It was his turn now to stand over her, touch her shoulder. 'We'll go on together,' he said. 'Calm yourself and we'll go on.'

At last her weeping tapered off, and he got back into his bunk, pulling the blankets around him, listening to the unfamiliar sounds of the ship. The *Northern Star* was taking him nearer to Kirsten, but he could no longer picture her face. Pain blotted it out. Eventually, as the dawn came, he and Josie both fell into a spent sleep.

Duncan and Josie got back to a Britain held in the grip of snow and ice. Small steamers tried to break up the frozen surface of the Clyde so that their ship could berth, but it took two days and one of the little ships sank in the process, though fortunately no one drowned.

Josie handed the evening paper over to Duncan as they sat in the train on the final stage of the journey home. 'Read it,' she ordered. 'While we've been away, folk here have been dying like rats of the cold. Fifty-four to every thousand, it says.' She pointed to a particular headline. It declared: AUTHORITIES ALARMED, and underneath was a story carrying the civic admission that many people were too under-nourished and badly housed to withstand the bitter weather.

'Never mind,' said Josie, with a set face. 'I read that the out-of-work in London are finding employment sweeping the ice for skaters on the Thames.'

Prompted by her grandmother, Carlie had prepared a royal welcome home for her parents in the cottage in the Rows. She had brought her cousin Donald down from the big house to help her scrub, polish and shine and the two of them awaited the return of the travellers with ill-concealed impatience to see what New World presents would be theirs as reward.

On the very day of their return, Scoular, the farmer who had held Dounhead, announced his resignation as MP and Dounhead was plunged into the frantic preparations for a by-election.

Duncan had had no further discussion with Josie about whether he would stand. Now that his relationship with Kirsten was no longer a secret from his wife, the worst of an intolerable burden seemed to have rolled away from him. He wanted to see Kirsten, to agree on circumspection for as long as was necessary, but willy-nilly he was caught up in the political machine. It was as though his nomination carried him along on an irresistible tide.

A week went by while he made no attempt to get in touch with her. Then after he and Pullar had spent a long day canvassing and were on their way to a supporter's house to rest and eat, Jamie said with a certain truculence, 'I have words from the woman Mackenzie. She says to meet her in Miss Cranston's Tea-rooms on Friday, after the St Andrew's Hall meeting on land reform. I am instructed to tell you it's important. Six o'clock.' Jamie's expression closed down, indicating he had given the message but would brook no further discussion.

She came into Miss Cranston's wearing an amber-coloured

dress and jacket, with a fur muff and tippet. The colour
suited her, although she looked a little tired, and pale from
the cold. She smiled at him, taking a frozen hand from her
muff and putting it against his cheek briefly. 'This must be
the worst winter ever. I'm trying to organize the distribution
of food in Bridgeton. There's never enough. Can't you get
some of your rich relations to help?'

'I'll see what I can do.'

He poured tea for her as she seemed too chilled for action.
He thought her dark-fringed, harebell blue eyes were dulled,
with smudges under them as though she had not been sleeping well.

'You wanted to see me,' he prompted.

'Yes.' At last she brought the eyes round to his face. 'One
of us has to make a move, my darling, and I've decided it has
to be me.'

'I've been caught up, ever since we got back,' he said. 'It
doesn't mean you've been out of my thoughts.'

'Or you of mine,' she admitted. 'Duncan, I deliberately
arranged that we should meet like this. To keep it formal.
I'm going away. I've had an awful lot of time to think while
you were in America, and I've decided that I want to give
all my energies to the women's movement. That means
London. They want me to take over an administrative post
down there.'

He said nothing. Her hand clattered the teaspoon nervously on her saucer and she went on, 'It's Josie who's your
wife, who stands beside you in this election. Josie *is* Dounhead. And I don't see how you can ever, ever put me above
Dounhead. It would be like cutting your own throat. It's
part of you.'

'*You* should have been my wife.'

'In some ways, I've been more than that. Let's part kindly,
love.'

'What about the child?'

It was as though he had touched an unbearably raw nerve.
Her composure, which till then had been absolute, began to
break up. He saw a tear fall on to her muff.

'Not ours. Jill and Walter's. Really.'

'Don't,' he begged.

'Will you write to him? Promise?'

'Yes. Of course. *Don't go, lass.*'

'Duncan,' she said, almost like a schoolmistress, 'I have to. It has come to that. I can see what I'm doing to you. I am not blind.'

'Drink your tea before you go,' he said.

'No. I don't really want it.' She could not stop the slight, rhythmical chatter of her teeth.

She rose, pushing her hands into the muff and he noticed for the first time she had pinned some artificial violets on it, in a rare romantic gesture. She saw his gaze rest on the flowers and said with the lightest irony, 'Yes. The real things wouldn't stand up to the cold, would they? Let me go first, won't you? And I won't say goodbye.'

He had always liked the way she walked, straight-backed, with a slight unconscious swaying from the hips. She pushed her way through the swing doors and into the bitter, darkening street.

All day long, those who had the franchise had tramped in and out of the parish chambers, registering their votes. Carriages bearing the supporters of the Conservative man had rattled through frozen ruts to disgorge their passengers muffled to the eyebrows in capes and furs.

Josie had taken Carlie with her on her rounds to muster support. Exhorting, chaffing, encouraging, she had been tireless. The exhilaration and challenge had got through to Carlie, who had only one question for which she sought an answer. She handed her father a steaming mug of cocoa as he paced the committee rooms awaiting the count, and put it to him: 'Why haven't women got the vote, Daddy? If you get in, it's the first thing you must do.'

He looked at his red-haired daughter indulgently. She was still at that gangling, half-awkward stage between childhood and adulthood, but she had a lively, sharp intelligence that pleased him and was delicate balm to that other, secret, unacknowledged pain that was deep inside him.

'I'm hoping to be MP for Dounhead, not the Emperor,' he reminded her. 'But I'll do what I can. Why do you think women should have the vote?'

Jamie Pullar was watching with a smile.

'Because they have the children. And because they often have better brains than the men. They don't go getting drunk, or gambling –'

Duncan hugged her absently and she rose on tiptoe and kissed him.

'Will it be long till we know? Daddy, I'll die if you don't get in!'

'Not long now.' Josie had come into the room. The hems of her coat and dress were spattered from the thaw which had set in late in the day, then hardened again. Her face was pale from fatigue, but her eyes sparkled with expectation. 'Whatever happens, we've given them a run for their money.'

The returning officer mounted the platform in the parish chambers, his gold watch and chain gleaming importantly, a vagrant drop of clear liquid trembling on the tip of his nose from the long, chill wait. Duncan surreptitiously eyed his opponents – the burly, blond Conservative Menzies, public-school educated, rich from South African gold; the aesthetic Galston for the Liberals, from a family of lawyers and dominies. Had he really a chance against them? He had decided to go in under a totally independent Labour banner, a fact that had not pleased too many of his friends in the Independent Labour Party. He and Jamie between them had fought a hard battle.

As though to make up for his private troubles, things had gone well on the platform. He often reflected not without bitterness that he merely preached the same things he had always done, but it was only since he had 'made his name' that folks were prepared to listen.

He had been surprised, too, by the loyalty that Josie commanded now throughout Dounhead. If he made it, he knew his debt to her was incalculable. As if she read his thoughts, she gazed at him now and gave a nod of encouragement, a brief smile. He had a swift vision of her, labouring over the printing press at the *Clarion* in those early days, working at that intractable stove that only she had been able to coax into life.

'. . . and that the said candidate, Duncan Fleming, is duly elected MP for Dounhead – '

Ninety-eight votes. Galston's thin-lipped congratulations acknowledged the narrowness of the victory, Menzies's robust greeting acknowledged a lost cause. Duncan felt emotion rise in him like a jubilant rocket, as though he were about to take off for the stratosphere and not return. It was Josie's hand on his arm that brought him back to earth, that and Carlie's kiss and Jamie Pullar's slow, spreading smile that refused to go away.

'Speech! Speech!'

He looked around and saw that miners still black from the shift were grinning up at him with their pink lips, pounding their hands together, shuffling their feet in a rumbling, rattling dance of victory.

From the back of the hall where she had been brought by Tansy in the carriage from Dounhead House, his mother smiled at him and he noticed fresh beads of snow on her bonnet.

Young Donald had come, too, a gangling, spotty boy who now insisted on pumping his uncle's hand with great enthusiasm.

'I think I might be an MP some day,' said Donald. 'It must be a good thing to be liked by so many people.'

For a moment, Duncan was distracted from the hubbub of congratulation around him, the younster's words cutting through to him. *To be liked by so many people.* He hadn't let them down. That was something. He could feel their goodwill and trust around him, almost bearing him up.

And then they did bear him up, physically, on coaly shoulders that were somehow no longer tired and carried him down the main street in this town where he belonged.

Chapter Nine

'Another tea-room?' said Kitty. She disengaged her arm from that of Sandia and flopped down on the slatted seat on the deck of the *Isle of Arran*, looking flabbergasted.

'Yes, another tea-room,' Sandia said, smiling. She judged this was as good a time as any to put Kitty in the picture. They had indulged in the popular Glasgow pastime of a day's sail 'doon the watter', meaning down the Clyde. A whole day's sail, with dinner and plain tea, for 4s. 6d. They had had a good lunch, laughed at the antics of Glasgow clerks and their girls on an office outing, dancing strathspeys and reels on deck to a melodeon after a light smirr of rain had been and gone. And now, as the paddle steamer chugged homeward in the sunlit evening waters, had walked on deck, arm in arm, in happy, confidential mood, faces stinging pleasantly from sun and wind.

'Do you think it is a good idea?' demanded Kitty.

'Well, if the rest of us don't watch out, the Cranstons will take over all of Glasgow,' said Sandia severely. 'Since Kate Cranston got married to her Major Cochrane, she has gone from strength to strength.'

She gazed out over the dear, familiar Clyde scenery, seeing not the distant, green banks with their scattered cottages, but Kate Cranston's establishment at 114 Argyle Street, which had grown from a mere tea-room into something altogether more impressive and splendid. There city businessmen could gather for lunch and afterwards take their ease in lounge, smoking-room or billiards-room, while in the afternoon the place became a general rendezvous for anyone with money to spare. It wasn't just set up for the men, though; ladies had their own separate tea-room and reading-room where they could discuss important matters like feathers for a hat or how to stop their maids thieving from the larder. It all made her own efforts look homespun and amateurish.

'Now,' said Sandia, with some vexation, 'the latest is that she has caught up with some architect who is going to design further tea-rooms for her.'

'Charles Rennie Macintosh,' said Kitty promptly.

'You've heard of him?'

'You must have too, dear, unless you go around with your ears stopped up! He designed the new School of Art in Renfrew Street.'

'Oh, that's who he is!'

'Yes, that's who. He sounds quite interesting, I must say. You know they've just opened the first part of the school and nothing would do but he had to design a special key for the door and have it presented on a white satin cushion with a silver fringe. And do you know what he and his wife have in their Main Street flat? A *white* carpet. Can you think of anything less practical, Sandia? I think Miss Cranston may find he's a little too artistic even for her taste.'

'I wish I had her flair,' protested Sandia. She went off into a brown study, her eyes clouded with thought. Kitty surveyed her from under her lashes, astonished by the almost maternal tenderness she felt today for this older sister. Sandia had been restless recently – it showed in the way she ran the tea-rooms, changing the decor, badgering the waitresses; and now in this wish to open up a second place.

There was something else. Over lunch, in rare confidential mood, Sandia had confessed to her she was still in love with Dandy Peel. Kitty approved of this. One should always be in love with someone. She had never understood why Sandia had not married him, anyhow, and Sandia's confused explanations earlier had not really satisfied her.

Mother had been demanding, of course, but there was something soft, giving, in Sandia's nature, that almost asked for martyrdom to be laid on it. Kitty sighed. It wasn't easy to read into another's heart, even your own sister's. Perhaps especially your own sister's.

Sandia had revealed that Dandy had been so much in her mind recently she had taken up the cudgels and written to him – just a friendly letter, so that he should not mistake it for opportuning. Asking how he was, giving news of her venture into the tea-room business, and saying if he was ever in Glasgow she hoped he would be sure to look her up. Kitty had been astonished at this admission. It was very un-Sandia like. She was not sure of the wisdom of it, for their youthful romance had been over a long time. But she had shown Sandia none of this, merely made reassuring, confiding noises and squeezed her arm as they promenaded, to show sisterly concern and affection.

'You see,' said Sandia consideringly, breaking out of her rapt silence now, 'that's what it is to have a man at your back. Kate Cranston has the major. But I have no one. And middle-age is beckoning. I've been counting the grey hairs, and I have at least six!'

'There's always Mr Beltry,' said Kitty, with a mischievous smile that became a wholehearted laugh. Sandia flicked her a doubtful look. She was not altogether prepared to have Mr Beltry laughed at, although she knew what Kitty was getting at. Mr Beltry was a prosperous draper who dropped in at the tea-rooms most afternoons, making sheep's eyes at Sandia and calling her his 'dear young lady'. Well dressed, with a carnation in his buttonhole, his attempts at heavy-handed backchat had the waitresses raising patient eyes to heaven. And nothing could disguise the fact that, well-preserved widower though he might be, Mr Beltry was fast approaching sixty and getting a little short of wind. None the less, he was an admirer and at times good for one's morale.

Sandia eased herself along the seat till she was close to her sister.

'I'm deadly serious about branching out, Kitty,' she said. 'It's the money that's going to be the problem. I've ploughed most of what I've made back into the business up till now.' She looked away momentarily and said with face averted, 'How would you feel about putting some money into the new venture?'

Kitty did not answer at first. She got up and moved to the steamer rail, shading her eyes to look into the sunset. Sandia rose and followed her, consumed with curiosity over her reaction.

'What's the matter, Kit? Shouldn't I have said what I did? Forget it, then. I merely thought – '

Kitty's face was set as she turned.

'We're going to fall out over this, Sandia, and it's so hateful when we've had such a lovely day together.'

'Fall out? Why ever should we?'

'I want to give the five hundred pounds Mama left me to Finn. If I don't, I can't see how he will ever build his own motor-car.'

Sandia's mouth folded down grimly, fulfilling Kitty's worst fears. She marched off up the deck, serge skirt swaying with her annoyance, and after a moment Kitty followed her.

'I haven't absolutely decided,' lied Kitty.

'What's got into you over him?' Sandia demanded. 'It seems he just needs to crook his little finger and you'll do anything. I warn you, Kit, he doesn't take your feelings seriously. Cars are all he cares about. He'll take your money and you'll never see a penny back.'

'It wouldn't be like that at all,' Kitty faltered. 'I've been down to his workshop and he's got a machine half-way made. He's hamstrung because he has so little money – '

'You're a fool,' Sandia said bitterly. 'You're not getting any younger, either. You could have the choice between half a dozen well-doing men – '

'You exaggerate!'

'What about Hugh Fowler? His father has a house at Helensburgh, a place in London. If you went out with him just once he'd be over the moon.'

'Have you seen his chin?' enquired Kitty succinctly.

'At least, don't give Finn all your money.'

'I want to, Sandia. You can raise the money you need. Mr Beltry for one would help. Everyone knows you're a success.'

'I certainly won't ask you for a penny, ever again. To put Finn Fleming against your own sister – '

'It isn't like that.' Tears of vexation sprang to Kitty's eyes. She burst out, 'I love him, Sandia. You've talked about Dandy today, and how you feel about him. Well, that's how it is with me. I love Finn and I think he cares for me.'

'He certainly likes having you moon around him, catering to his every whim,' upbraided Sandia. 'But what makes you think he has marriage in mind? I think you're sadly mistaken if you take him seriously. What about the nights he's promised to take you to the theatre and then come in about ten o'clock, covered in oil, having forgotten all about you?'

'It may have happened once or twice – '

'It happens all the time. There's a selfish, single-minded side to Finn, and I can say that because I'm as fond of him as the next one.'

Kitty was weeping into a scrap of lace hankie.

Sandia went up to her and put her arm around her.

'Oh, come on! It's not as bad as all that. You'll get over him one day.'

'Just as you've got over Dandy?' returned Kitty fiercely. She said in a hard, low voice, 'I'm sorry, I'm going to give Finn my money. It *is* mine, after all, to do what I like with.'

'Very well,' said Sandia, with a terrible resignation. 'On your own head be it.'

With the money safely in an envelope inside the dainty velvet pouch that swung from her wrist, Kitty half-walked, half-ran to the tumbledown hut behind a friend's overgrown garden where Finn was working on the car.

In a way, telling Sandia her intentions had been the worst part. Opposition from Father and from Alisdair had been easier to take. In the end, she had talked them all down. Now all she had to do was get Finn to accept the money. Five hundred pounds. It had been intended as a sort of dowry. Well, that was what it would be, in effect. For she was determined to get Finn to ask her to marry him. She was coming up to twenty-five. With her slender girl's body and lively face she always passed for younger. But she wanted to be settled. She wanted a home of her own. She wanted Finn.

His friend, Alec Mackinlay, sometimes worked with him on the car, but recently he had got fed up with the slow development and was devoting more time to wooing a plump, laughing girl whose parents ran a dairy.

Picking her way over the tussocks of grass towards the workshop, Kitty had a sudden attack of nerves. What if she really was behaving with a total lack of sense or discretion? What if Finn never got the car beyond the blueprint stage, and all her money was lost? She only knew she had felt his frustration over the recent months almost like her own. He needed to pay for parts to be made at a local foundry and practically every penny he earned went towards this. Sometimes an expensive component would develop a fault under stress, and it was back to square one.

Although at first they had regarded his car-building enthusiasm with amusement, the family had to admit that the horseless buggy looked like being more than an overnight wonder. A man called George Johnston had started up the Mo-Car Syndicate and was producing the first all-Scottish car, based on the German Daimler. And as Glasgow was a city of engineers, Finn was by no means the only young enthusiast dreaming up the future in a draughty workshop with what looked like a pile of scrap for raw material. There were dozens of young zealots and they visited and encouraged each other, talking technicalities and arguing about first principles like prophets of some new religion.

'Finn.' She stepped over the sun-dappled floorboards, the peplum of her cream worsted suit sweeping a spanner off a low shelf, her eyes straining to pick him out after the glare of the sun outside. She realized then he was not alone. A tall, slender figure in a well-cut tweed suit, with lank dark hair, was bending over Finn's shoulder as they both perused a sheet of figures on the rough surface before them.

'Kitty!' There was a note of surprise mingled with a faint annoyance in Finn's voice.

'Am I interrupting?' she demanded swiftly.

Both men rose. The dark man said in a deep, cultured voice, 'My dear lady, would that all interruptions were as delightful!' He was smiling at her, but she thought he was being sardonic and returned the smile reservedly.

Finn took her hand and held it towards the other man.

'Frensham, I want you to meet Miss Kitty Kilgour. Kitty, this is Sir Peter Frensham. He is interested in my motor-car.' His eyebrows were signalling frantically at her that she should now go, that she had come at a critical time in negotiations. But resentfully she stood her ground. Why had he said nothing about Frensham to her? Finn could be so maddeningly close and secretive at times, she despaired of ever getting to know him.

'If you don't want me to stay, I suppose I can find something else to do,' she said bluntly, glaring at Finn.

'It's just that we're talking technicalities and figures,' he said embarrassedly.

Frensham laughed. 'We shall soon be finished. I heard of Finn in New York, you know. I met his father there, at a convention. I am another with faith in the future of the horseless carriage. Do you think we are all mad, Miss Kilgour?'

Kitty shook her head, already partly regretting her bad temper. 'Only a little, perhaps.' She looked guardedly at Finn. 'I shall see you later, then?'

He nodded absently and anger rose in her again as she walked away over the grass. She had built herself up to having an important talk with Finn, away from the house and Sandia's watchful eyes, and now she felt frustrated and unreasonably hurt.

A small shop at the corner of the street advertised ginger beer. She asked the shopkeeper to pour some from its cool, stone bottle into a tumbler and stood drinking gratefully, her nostrils assailed by spiced ham, currants sticky in the heat and strong yellow cheese.

She was undecided whether to go home again or wait about till Finn's visitor left. In the event, her mind was made

up for her, for as she finished the ginger beer she saw
Frensham's tall, droop-shouldered figure stride past the shop
and make for the main road beyond.

This time, Finn stood outside the workshop, straining his
eyes this way and that, as though looking for her, and he
came towards her almost at a run.

'Kit! Guess what? He's going to back me. We've been
invited down to his country place this weekend – you and I,
both – and I'm to meet some of his influential friends.'

She had never seen him so excited. His face was flushed
and his fair hair lay damp on his forehead. She put her hand
out with a tender gesture and pushed it away from his forehead. He backed away from her into the workshop, grinning
like a four-year-old, and when they had got within its
protective shade he swept her into his arms and swung her
round, so that her feet left the ground. Infected by his joy,
she began to laugh, crying for him to put her down, but
loving the sweet pressure of his arms. When he did put her
down, he would not let her go, but gazed with sudden fierceness into her eyes, then brought his lips down firmly on her
mouth and kissed her till her head buzzed.

She put her hand up to bruised lips and said faintly, 'Finn,
I've brought you some money.' She brought the envelope
from her velvet reticule and handed it to him. 'It's five
hundred pounds. My savings. I want you to have it.'

She didn't know what she had hoped for: an expression
of pleasure, perhaps; surprise, certainly. She wasn't looking
for gratitude, but she hadn't expected the look of hurt, of
embarrassment. Suddenly it was as though she had been
brought down to earth. She had made a terrible miscalcula-
tion, misjudged Finn's attitude completely.

He took the packet from her, looking down at it as though
it were some strange object he didn't recognize, and turned
away momentarily towards his work-bench, saying nothing.

'Finn?'

'I can't take this. What kind of person do you think I am?
The sort who'd take money from a woman – '

She cried out. 'It's not like that. It's because – '

'Yes?'

'Because we're special to each other.'

He said nothing.

'Are we not?' she persisted.

'What do you mean? Special?'

'Don't demean me,' she pleaded. Suddenly as angry as he was, she turned on him with rosy face and sparkling eyes. 'You kiss me. You take me out. You don't like me to have other friends. But where do we stand, Finn? Do you love me, or don't you?'

She watched the slow red creep up his neck. Still he said nothing. She could feel all the life and promise and vigour seeping away out through her button boots. Her head felt swimmy.

Well, she had staked everything, and lost everything. Somehow, she lifted her feet, which felt as though they were unaccountably glued to the dusty floorboards, and propelled herself away from him.

'Wait.'

She turned.

'Don't you know a man has to do it his way? *I* have to do the asking.' He was alarmed by the sullen stillness of her face and burst out, 'Dammit! I *was* going to ask you to marry me. But not until I've got the car on the road. I thought you understood that, Kitty? It has to come first –'

She was back in his arms, damping his shirt-front with her tears. Two small boys on their way to play football stopped to watch the scene with interest.

'Will you come to Willow House with me on Saturday?' Finn pleaded. 'I told Frensham you were my girl. You see? He thought you were lovely.'

'Did he?' She dabbed at a small, reddened nose.

'How could he not? Kit, if I can get him and his friends interested, our troubles are over.'

'You won't take my money?'

He shook his head.

'You keep it, sweetheart. You didn't really think I'd take it, did you?'

175

She said nothing. She was beginning to wonder how well she knew him. But she put the money back in her purse without argument. She was never going to be able to manipulate Finn as she had done most people in her life. Things would have to be done his way. And marriage would come in his time, not hers. She gave a barely audible sigh.

'Where is Willow House?' she asked.

'Near Loch Lomond. Frensham's given me careful instructions how to get there.' She saw from his expression he had something else he wanted to tell her. He drew her back into the workshop and took her right to the far end. There stood a small, neat vehicle which for once did not seem to be missing on any vital detail.

'Is it finished?' She looked at it apprehensively.

He nodded. 'As good as. That's how we travel on Saturday. Meet the Fleming Flyer!'

'For goodness' sake, be careful!'

Jack surveyed his daughter, perched on the Fleming Flyer, her flowered boater tied under her chin with a pale-blue veiling that matched her dress and jacket. She made him think of a young sapling, all slender willowy beauty. So Clemmie had been, when first he knew her. He felt the familiar, grieving need for his dead partner moisten his eyes and make his voice gruffer than need be.

Finn adjusted his goggles and smiled down at him.

'I'll take care of her, never fear! We're safe as houses.'

With a splutter and a roar, the little car took off. The sophisticated tenants of Ashley Terrace did not come out in the street to watch it, but observed its noisy progress with clicking tongues stilled between gaping jaws from behind their douce lace curtains. On the outskirts of Glasgow it was a different matter. Urchins stampeded from close-mouths and garden gates to race it till their breath gave out. Young men turned and grinningly tipped their hats to Kitty, while old wives, stunned out of a doze by open windows, shook their fists and talked of the Devil.

Kitty was being bumped up and down so much that even

the velvet cushion underneath scarcely prevented her bottom from feeling as it had done when she was spanked with the hairbrush when she was young.

'Suspension's the next thing I'll see to,' Finn promised cheerfully. 'Beats the train any day, doesn't it?'

Kitty reserved her opinion, but once they were out in the open country, at least where the road was good, she began to enjoy it more. Except for worrying what it would be like at Willow House.

'How did the Frenshams make their money?' she demanded.

'Steel!' shouted Finn, above the engine. 'Converting pig-iron through the Bessemer converter.'

'Are they very rich?'

'Filthy rich! So I'm told. Willow House is just one of their summer retreats. Mostly they live in London. There's Sir Peter's mother, Lady Pamela, and his sister, June. They have American family connections. Seems that's how he got to hear about me. Someone told him Paterson Fleming's son was building cars in Glasgow. Thinks a lot of my old man, it seems. Ironic, isn't it?'

'When you think about it,' Kitty agreed, 'it does. I think you are probably more like your father than you realize.' Finn's expression became forbidding, so she did not pursue the conversation.

Willow House stood a few miles from the banks of Loch Lomond in soft, lush countryside. Finn turned the car in at a long, wide drive lined with rhododendrons, and drew it up triumphantly in front of a sunny terrace where a number of people were having afternoon tea. There was a little scatter of applause as he and Kitty dismounted and Peter Frensham, followed by a fair, animated girl in a pink dress, whom Kitty took to be his sister June, ran down the terrace steps with hands outstretched in welcome.

Kitty was no stranger to luxury. In the old days before the Trust was broken up, and before her mother's health had shattered, the house in Ashley Terrace had known its share of parties and grand occasions.

But she quickly realized the Frenshams were rich on a scale she had not encountered before. Everything about Willow House, from the faintly reserved and languid guests to the servants who seemed to spring from nowhere to attend one's every whim, spoke not only of money but of people well used to deploying it to provide a constant cushion of luxury and ease in their lives. It made her feel uneasy and provincial. But she had a sudden, unaccountable vision of her Grannie Kate, unassailable in her dignity, though she lived in a humble little cottage in Dounhead, and she felt the family pride stiffen and straighten her backbone. She placed a wide smile on her face and softened the broader edges of her Glasgow accent into gentler consonants and more careful vowels. Every Glaswegian had to do that automatically, anyhow, when faced with a visitor from abroad or the South.

Of course, the talk after they had been plied with fresh tea and dainty sandwiches was of nothing but the Fleming Flyer. Peter Frensham could not wait to try it out, and drove it carefully along the drive to a volley of applause from the more sycophantic visitors.

June Frensham patted its radiator.

'This is the honeycomb sort,' she volunteered, 'isn't it?' Kitty watched Finn's mouth fall open in surprise and knew a jealous tug as he then went into a detailed technological description of the car for June and her brother which the girl seemed to have no difficulty in following. Unlike Kitty herself.

'What I think is so interesting,' Peter Frensham was saying, 'is that your design is more in line with the kind of small car I've seen in America than the looser efforts I've seen over here. The "gas buggy" formula, in fact.'

Finn gave him that grateful look he reserved for the mysterious brotherhood of the automobile fanatic; a look, Kitty thought with forbearing irony, he seldom bestowed on the rest of the human species.

'You see what I've done?' he explained. 'I've concentrated on a low-speed, centrally-mounted engine, with two cylinders, here and here – '

'Epicyclic gearing,' enthused Frensham, 'and drive by the central chain. It's a beaut. Don't you think so, June?'

'A beauty,' June agreed, in her high-pitched, cultivated tones.

'Well, she's the first,' Finn admitted modestly. 'There's so much I want to experiment with. I can see us doing thirty, even forty miles an hour one day. But I visualize pneumatic tyres for that. And we have to think of covering the driver and passenger from the rain.'

'We have to get away from the old phaeton and landaulet notion,' observed Frensham thoughtfully. 'The motor-car is not, in effect, simply a horseless carriage. She must have line and style that are her own.'

Kitty found she could not take any more car talk. She had sat in the thing for hours, after all, and could feel her spine stiffening and aching as a result. She went off with a shy but pleasant young man to admire the peacocks on Willow House lawn and then indulge in a gentle game of croquet.

She was almost glad when dinner was over that evening, for she was too tired to enjoy the succession of rich courses placed in front of her and then whipped away before she had done more than toy with them. The champagne gave her a tendency to giggle. She had a vast bedroom in the west wing of the house and didn't know whether to be amused or nauseated to see that the night table had been furnished with covered dishes of sandwiches and devilled chicken. Bottles of Vichy and Malvern water had been thoughtfully provided, and she sipped from one of these as she undressed. Although it was summer, a fire had been lit in the grate and a kettle purred on a brass trivet. The reading-lamps on either side of her bed had pink silk shades and there was a coverlet of white swansdown on the brocaded sofa.

Hopping into the vast bed, she felt her limbs relax but she could not sleep. All day long she had waited and hoped for some attention from Finn, but he had been too taken up with his new friends. Now she imagined his mouth kissing her, his hands moving along the languor of her body. It was all she could do to stop herself getting out of bed and running through the great house in search of him, but she had no idea where his room might be. She said his name, *Finn*, into the velvet darkness, and her limbs moved constantly, restlessly with the yearning of her body. This is what it's like to burn, she thought, seared with her own humiliation.

It was raining the next morning. A curtain of mist had come down between the rolling lawns of Willow House and the bonnie banks of Loch Lomond. In the great dining-room, servants were bringing porridge to silent, overhung males who ate it standing up while they watched the sparrows flutter in and out of the bird-baths in the Italian garden. The whole atmosphere was one of shivering ennui, scarcely overcome by the huge log fires that tongued up the chimneys at either end of the room.

Kitty smiled briefly at Finn who was eating porridge by himself and passed down between laden tables, not knowing where to begin. Her appetite was quite restored and now she peered under their covers to see what was in the silver dishes warmed by rows of little spirit lamps. Kidneys, beef, omelettes, fish. On another table were ham, tongue, cold grouse, pheasant and partridge (she judged) and hot or cold ptarmigan, which she felt pleased to recognize.

She wondered whether to have a little plain pressed beef, but settled instead for a slice of melon and a nectarine, after which she would have a scone or two, with honey. More decisions . . . should she have China tea (indicated by the yellow ribbon on the pots) or Indian, with the red? It seemed simpler to have the coffee instead.

'Do you mind going to church with the rest?' Finn hissed in her ear. 'I can't come. We have too much to talk about.'

'Shall I see nothing of you all day?' she demanded in alarm.

'We'll meet later,' he promised. 'But there's plenty to amuse you, isn't there?' His face was pleading, and she gave in and agreed.

But it was after tea before they met again. The egg and cucumber sandwiches, the chocolate, walnut and coffee cakes had been wasted on Kitty as she'd tried in vain to will Finn to her side. Everywhere he went, Frensham and a growing band of interested devotees seemed to surround him, and June Frensham was never far away either, her tinkling, affected laugh jarring Kitty like toothache.

He was wiping chocolate cake from his mouth as he strode over to her. She knew from his excited look that he had something to tell her and a prescience rose up in her, urging caution, caution.

'Kit, you'll never guess. I'm invited to go to London to meet connections of Peter's who're already manufacturing. And then he wants me to go to the States to see what this man Ford is doing.' His feet were tapping with impatience, he seemed raring to be off again. She felt as though her stomach was going down in a lift, down a pit shaft, down, down, down.

'I thought he was going to subsidize you in Glasgow, maybe find you a decent place to work,' she faltered.

'Oh no, it's going to be much bigger than that. Much bigger.' He scarcely seemed to be aware she was there; his gaze wandered almost feverishly about the room.

'When do we drive back?' she demanded, levelly.

'Eh? Oh, tomorrow. Tomorrow afternoon. You can keep yourself amused till then, can't you, Kitty? The rain's lifting. It's going to be a lovely evening.'

'Why won't she speak to me?' Finn asked Sandia. His bags were packed and strapped, waiting in the hall at Ashley Terrace to be taken to the station.

'I don't know,' responded Sandia, a little impatiently. 'She's so moody these days I can't make anything of her. She simply says she has a headache.'

'Well, tell her goodbye for me,' said Finn. 'I'll write to her from London.'

'There's nothing *really* amiss between you two, is there?'

Sandia demanded curiously.

Finn shook his head. 'I don't think so. We talked last night and I explained as best I could why I would be away for six weeks or so. I think she feels it is too long. But I have no option. I'm sure she'll see that for herself, when she has time to think about it.'

He suddenly dashed upstairs, knocked on Kitty's door and called: 'I am off, dear girl. Can I come in and say goodbye?'

The answer must have been in the negative for he came slowly downstairs again, his face clouded.

'I don't know what to make of her.'

'She's a bit spoiled, that's all,' Sandia assured him.

She fastened her fur tippet. 'Come on, Finn. You said I could share your cab. It's time I was down at the tea-rooms.'

Because she felt sorry for Finn, Sandia went into the station with him and waved him off. Some complicated emotional game was in progress between him and Kitty, but as an outsider she had no way of knowing the rules. She felt marginally sorrier for Finn, if anything, with so much concerning his future at stake, and Kitty behaving like a spoiled child. But then, Finn *had* had Kitty on a string ever since he arrived in Scotland and it was understandable that she wanted their relationship moved forward and properly defined.

Once at the tea-rooms, Sandia became so busy she had no more time to puzzle over her sister's affairs. Business was so brisk, both in shop and tea-rooms, that the staff scarcely had a moment to themselves. They were all good, reliable girls, willing to curtail their dinner-break when things were busy, clumsy at times but anxious to keep up the standards she had set them. But then she took no one without a recommendation from the minister of the church the girl attended.

She had, besides, decided that this would be the day she would approach Mr Beltry. They had become very friendly of late and she had taken to having tea with him, at her own special table near the cash-desk, when he came in

182

around four o'clock.

He was a lonely man. He told her how empty his house at Troon was, in the years since Mrs Beltry had died. His only child, a daughter, was married to an eye specialist in Edinburgh, and he saw little of her. The house at Troon was from all accounts a mansion, richly furnished with rare objects Mr Beltry had brought back from his travels. There was an elderly housekeeper who gave him scant comfort, dishing up eternal cold meats and watering the whisky.

Sandia knew well enough the road Mr Beltry was leading her along when he described such discomforts. 'These little tête-à-têtes we have, Miss Kilgour, are like an oasis in my day,' he said more than once. 'But it's the company that does it. You'd make a mausoleum like home, with your cheery smile.'

Would she be committing herself to anything deeper if she asked his financial help? Sandia pondered this all day as she sat behind the cash-desk, watching the constant trudge of Glasgow humanity to the tables. She knew it was probably risky. But she was suddenly tired of being cautious. Like Kitty, she wanted life to move on and even if it was in an uncharted direction, it was better than doing nothing.

She was still absorbed in her thoughts when the tea-room doors swung open and Kitty came in. The time for high tea was approaching, the aroma of hot mutton pies wafted from the kitchen and Kitty knew her help would be needed. She was wearing a deep-blue velvet costume trimmed with dark fur, and two bright spots of colour burned on her cheeks, making her look fiercely beautiful. She stopped in front of Sandia, who judged she had been crying, because there were two little puffy lumps under her eyes.

'Well, he got away, then, Finn, did he?' demanded Kitty.

'Yes.' Sandia looked at her musingly.

'That's that, then.' She tapped her toe.

'What do you mean?'

'It's all over. I told him so last night.'

'Oh, I wish the pair of you would grow up!' said Sandia impatiently.

'I have. At last.' There was something in her face that moved Sandia to sudden pity. 'You did warn me, Sandia. He's not in a hurry to marry, me or anyone else. Cars are his obsession.'

'He needs time. He's got a lot to think about – '

'He can have all the time in the world. I haven't. I can feel the days and weeks go by and I'm no farther forward. Sandia – ' Kitty impaled her with a hard look – 'I've made up my mind. I'm emigrating to Canada. You remember I wanted to go, before Mother died? The Wilsons still want me to go to Saskatchewan. I had a letter from Jean just the other day.'

'So you don't love Finn any more?'

Kitty looked away. 'What's the point? Seems he doesn't return the compliment.'

'You're being silly. Spoiled and silly.'

'You think so? You've changed your tune. Well, I've just been down to the shipping office to enquire about a passage.'

'What would you do?' Despite her alarm, Sandia almost laughed. Kitty's ploy, for surely that's all it was, seemed so implausible.

'The Wilsons have a livery and feed barn. They supply coach and horses to settlers who want to look over the land and provide stabling for the ranchers' horses.'

'Just your cup of tea,' said Sandia with heavy irony.

'Jean and her mother make lunches for the lodgers and ranchers. A dollar a week. I've had some experience, thanks to you – '

'Oh, you don't really mean it?' Sandia demanded wearily.

'I do,' Kitty said defiantly. 'See if I don't!'

Mr Beltry was sitting at the usual table, waiting for his tea and toasted bun. It had been Sandia's intention to sound him about the money today, but now she was too confused and upset to tackle him. She simply sat down opposite him in silence, and, sensing something was wrong, he tactfully waited till she felt like speaking.

'What a day!' she said at last.

He poured her tea from the silver pot, put in the sugar and milk, and stirred solicitously. She did not demur when he put his large, dry hand over her hot, tense one and squeezed it briefly but gently.

'Sandia!' She saw hope light up his ruddy face like a beacon. 'Tell me if I can be of help to you. I am here, at your service. You only have to ask.'

She looked at him speculatively, tiredly, trying to be as honest with herself as she could. Could she get used to the thinning hair, the somewhat blubbery skin, the reedy voice? Underneath was kindness, that she knew. But the years between seemed illimitable. Like the gap between Glasgow and Belfast. Between herself and Dandy, who had never written back.

'Maybe you can help, John,' she said, like him, using Christian names for the first time. 'And maybe you can't. I want to open another tea-room.'

PART
THREE

♦

Chapter Ten

Donald Balfour, son of Lachie and Tansy, was twenty-one
that year, the year of the old Queen's death and of The
Groveries, the biggest and best international exhibition
Glasgow had ever staged.

1901. Crowds half a mile deep had trampled the small
railings flat in Hyde Park during the Queen's London
funeral procession, before the doughty old lady was finally
laid to rest two days later at Frogmore.

The Boer War was still in progress, despite the victories
at Ladysmith and Mafeking which had had those same
crowds jigging for joy up and down Fleet Street and elsewhere, though there wasn't quite the same enthusiasm for it
now. Donald remembered the day it had started. Had there
ever been such heroes as the first hundred picked men of
the London-Scottish, fêted and petted and bought drinks by
strangers? Then in 'Black Week' two thousand British troops
had been slaughtered and that had emptied the theatres and
concert halls. Now everyone wanted it over, wondered how
much longer it would go on. Those who spoke up for the
Boers' case, like his Uncle Duncan, no longer went in direct

fear of their lives.

But sitting in the new electric tram, swaying towards his cousin Alisdair's consulting rooms in the West End, Donald decided ironically that, war or no war, the Empire had not exactly crumbled away during his sojourn in the clinic in Switzerland. Perhaps the worst most people had suffered was the sugar tax, to pay for the war. It was as though his absence enabled him to see everything very clearly and objectively. Wasn't there almost a smugness about the country, and Glasgow in particular? Or was it just his own heightened sensibility, his crushing wish to see his cousin Carlie again and the uncertainty about how she would react to his feelings for her?

Sometimes the concept of Empire overwhelmed him. Victoria, the papers pointed out, had acceded to one-sixth of the world's surface. Her profligate Eddie would reign over one-fourth. He decided he still wasn't strong enough to face up to the corollary to all that – the fact that someone, some day, was going to try and take it all away.

He'd been pretty ill when they'd decided to pack him off to Lucerne a year ago. He remembered the concern in Carlie's face when he'd told her. Although since starting at Glasgow University he'd had digs in the city, he had tried to get home at weekends to see her. They'd been going for walks together, their talk getting deeper and more intimate. He'd been getting serious about her. She was so easy to talk to and that face, with its wide mouth and grey eyes and gentle animation, had been so easy to look at.

Lying in his neat, hard bed in the sanatorium, he had got wound up about that face. They said TB increased the sex urges, didn't they? He'd wanted Carlie badly, but her letters had been friendly, informative and funny, in no way passionate like his. Was it that she was just too shy to put her real feelings on paper? She had a vein of reserve running through her make-up. Or didn't she really care for him at all?

He knew he had come to depend on her. When his parents' marriage had broken up and his mother started her continental travels with her paramour, Carlie had been the one fixed point in his shaken universe. Carlie laughing, joking, cajoling. How he wanted to see her again!

Well, he soon would. He had to report to Alisdair first of all. He was his doctor, a clever one, they all said. But then he was going to meet Carlie at The Groceries. He wondered how much she could have changed in a year.

To distract himself, he stared hard through the tram windows at the Glasgow streets, trying to reconcile what he saw with the ecstasies of some Americans he'd encountered abroad over this city.

Had he heard how *pure* the Clyde was, with its marvellous new methods of sewage disposal? Did he know how much they admired the Glasgow tramways system in Chicago? What about social advances, like municipal crèches and kindergartens for the children of Glasgow widows and widowers, and the model lodging-houses where the unmarried could find good food and accommodation for sixpence a night? And those marvellous Clyde ship-builders, fitting up new cargo steamers with fast *turbine* engines?

He had to admit there were prosperous-looking folk about. Ladies in velvet costumes with jade and ivory necklaces and hats trimmed in excess of anything he'd seen in Paris. But still plenty of poor-looking women, too, carrying infants in shawls. Still barefoot urchins and beggars with a permutation of missing limbs.

When his tram stopped outside a large dairy-cum-grocery store, he looked at the price tickets in the window. Milk a penny-ha'penny a pint, cheese sixpence a pound, sugar twopence, tea one shilling and fivepence and, in sacks by the door, potatoes at a ha'penny. Suppose you earned a pound a week and your rent was about an eighth of that, and you had six children to support, could you have any kind of a life?

He smiled to himself, thinking how Carlie would have an immediate answer to that. She was following in the parental, socialist tradition, but while she could make him feel guilty on occasion about privilege, he wasn't sure yet where his own opinions lay.

He had been sickened by the excesses of the very rich in Marienbad, for example, on his way home. He'd gone there to see his mother and her painter paramour – Macleish had any number of commissions from the wealthy, loose-living hordes who took coffee at the Café Rubezahl, or flocked to hear Yvette Guilbert, or Beethoven played in the woods. Everybody who was anybody went to Marienbad. The new King himself. And Campbell-Bannerman, who would be Prime Minister if the Liberals came to power – he went there year after year, stodgy Liberal haggis that he was, with his plain wife Charlotte whom he so doted on.

But on the other hand, what was the point of Carlie's father, his Uncle Duncan and his like, trying to set up their socialist paradise when it was plain that at the moment most folk were more or less content with what they had?

Alighting from the tram, he dodged one of the alarming new motor-taxicabs that had sprung up in his absence, ran up the steps to Alisdair Kilgour's consulting rooms and rang the bell.

'My dear fellow, you're better. Not all the way there. But better.'

Alisdair had given him a thorough going-over and now after helping Donald on with his velveteen jacket he patted his shoulder paternally. Alisdair had suddenly acquired middle-aged *gravitas* and self-importance along with a pretty wife and a practice.

'That chest of yours is a lot clearer. Switzerland has done the trick, as I said it would.'

'Can I take up my studies again?'

'I don't see why not. Though why you stick to law, I can't imagine.'

'I'm not harming anybody but myself,' countered Donald. 'You know what Grannie Kate says about doctors – they kill more than they cure!'

Alisdair smiled. 'She exempts me from her strictures. At least, I hope so. Now you've to watch your diet. Plenty of milk, butter, eggs. Build up your resistance. Don't smoke.'

He looked at Donald's nicotine-stained fingers and shook his head. 'I see my warnings haven't gone home. And don't overstrain yourself.'

'I've heard that all my life,' said Donald. He compared Alisdair's robust, stocky frame with his own narrow shoulders and concave chest.

' "We maun do as things do with us," ' quoted Alisdair. 'Another wise saw from our aged grandparent.'

'You should charge for them too,' Donald observed drily. 'You'd make a fortune!'

After the consultation Alisdair took Duncan through to the living quarters to meet his wife, Tina, and share a pot of tea with them. Tina was small, dark and rather nervous, with a smile that turned her from pretty to entrancingly beautiful. She moved and talked in little spurts, looking to Alisdair to confirm or qualify everything she said. Donald saw that this was probably what had attracted Alisdair to her in the first place. He had a certain affection for his cousin, but Alisdair had always had this tendency to pontificate and lay down the law. He was a kirk elder now, taking Tina twice to church on Sundays. And of course, he was also a snob. There was no getting away from that. Tina's father was a rich city landlord, with family properties going back to the days of the great tobacco barons in their scarlet cloaks, those same lords who'd thought so much of themselves they'd allowed no one else to walk on their plain-stanes at Glasgow Cross.

It was Tina who in her nervous, darting way brought Donald up-to-date with the rest of the family news, between plying him with sultana cake and shortbread.

Sandia seemed to be happy in her marriage to Mr Beltry. She had just opened her fifth shop and tea-room, so that her little chain stretched profitably right down into Ayrshire. Her style was carefully stamped on each establishment. Rich, dark-green carpeting; dark-green curtains with gold cord ties. And the motto, 'Miss Kilgour's, For Comfort and Cleanliness', above a mock coat-of-arms showing a milkmaid with snowy bosom and dainty feet.

Captain Jack and Finn Fleming still lived in the house at Ashley Terrace, looked after by Mrs Jessup. The only difference was that the bottom half of the house had been let off to a fashionable dentist.

And Kitty? Oh yes, they heard from her frequently, from Canada. She was the most reliable correspondent in the world.

'Not married yet?' enquired Donald.

Tina shook her head and smiled. 'No. But she's a pillar of the temperance union and she writes about literary evenings, where I'm sure she'll meet some nice young men.'

'Fred Wilson'll get round her in the end,' opined Alisdair. 'I note she mentions him often – Fred this and Fred that.'

Tina giggled. 'I sometimes wonder if Finn Fleming has got over her.'

'Of course he has.' Alisdair nodded decisively. 'Finn's a big, important car-manufacturer. A man of substance, with his own factory.'

'But it doesn't mean – '

Alisdair cut her off. 'He's had more things to think about, these past few years, than women – '

'Hold on!' cried Donald, obscurely needled by Alisdair's treatment of Tina. 'Finn's no different from the rest of us. He must need – well, love.'

'Money's the next best thing,' said Alisdair hardly.

'But it can't make up for affection,' Tina murmured.

Alisdair was glaring at her irately. Hastily, Donald rose to go, saying, 'I'm meeting Finn tonight. After I've been to the exhibition with Carlie. I did some business for him in Marienbad. Got the specifications from a very rich cotton man there for a custom-made automobile.'

At the door, Tina said, 'I'm glad you're seeing Finn. I think he works far too hard. Try and get him to enjoy himself for a change.'

He smiled at her. 'You have a kind heart, Tina.' Impetuously, he kissed her cheek.

On the grassy slopes outside the University, he stopped to take in the view of the exhibition. Some fanciful imaginations had been at work, filling the prospect with towers and gilded domes, glaring white palaces and stucco minarets. It was so unlike the sober, Presbyterian image of his native land that he couldn't restrain a smile. Venetian gondolas on the Kelvin! It seemed a most unlikely fancy.

In his anxiety to see Carlie, he was too early. He entered a turnstile at the University entrance and wandered up and down the avenues, keeping an eye on the Van Houten Pavilion which was where they had arranged to meet. It was all very pleasant and amusing, even the eldritch screeching of young ladies hanging on the rails of the switchback railway and the occasional frustrated infant wailing because he couldn't go on the water-chute.

He listened to the spirited Sousa band and the Edison talking-machine. He wondered idly if the day would ever come when they would marry moving pictures to sound. Now that *would* interest him. More than the motor-car or all this talk about getting a machine to fly through the air. He'd been singularly unmoved when, as a schoolboy, someone had told him an unmanned machine had flown half a mile along the Potomac in the USA.

'Hallo! Sorry if I'm late.' A breathless voice sounded behind him and he turned to see her standing there, in a brown pelisse and her hair done up like Vesta Victoria's, in little curls with a fringe, with a small saucy hat atop and velvet streamers behind.

He grinned at her foolishly. 'You're not late at all. Would you like some hot chocolate?' You could tell she wasn't used to crowds and was a bit in awe of everything around her. Probably that little hat had been a mistake. But it was Carlie, rioting red hair and all. He couldn't take his eyes off her, he was so pleased to see her.

She smiled back at him and, refusing the chocolate, said, 'Let's have tea later. First tell me how you are and everything you've seen and done.'

She wasn't joking, either. He had to give her a lengthy catalogue of his stay in the clinic, his holiday with his mother and Hamish Macleish, and Alisdair's verdict on his present state of health, and all the while she was dragging him into pavilions to enthuse over vulgar displays of furnishings and food or tapping her feet to the military band and looking as though she might take off up one of the avenues any moment in a solitary waltz.

Eventually they were both footsore and weary. He looked longingly at McKillop's Lager Bar, but she persuaded him they would be better to have a proper high tea at Prince's Restaurant nearby.

'Finnan haddie, poached egg, toast and tea.' Carlie read from the menu and looked at him doubtfully. 'It's one and sixpence, Donald.'

He dismissed her objections, ordering scones and cakes as well.

'A feast,' she pronounced gravely, watching the plump waitress inexpertly lay the table. 'Listen! I've got something I've been saving to tell you. Guess what?'

'Don't know.'

'I'm going to London.'

He didn't know what he'd expected her to say. Not this. Not when he'd looked forward so much to their being together again.

'On a visit?' he asked stupidly.

'No, silly. To work.'

'You can't.'

'Why can't I?'

'Because I don't want you to.'

She looked up at the hovering, interested waitress, blushed and waited till she saw the girl's retreating back, then said, 'What do you mean by that?'

It was his turn to shift about in his chair and look embarrassed. 'I've only just come back. That's what I mean. And I've missed you.' He grabbed her hand. 'Terribly.'

She pulled her hand away, but gently. 'Well, it was lonely for me when *you* were away. It's not been the same at home, since Mother took Nellie Daly in.' Nellie was her mother's unmarried sister, legs swollen to enormous size from some unspecified complaint. She'd brought with her a bevy of

Catholic plaster saints and a tendency to discuss her complaints in embarrassing detail. Josie was forbearing, but often Carlie was not.

Carlie went on, 'I've been taking shorthand and typing lessons. I thought I might be able to help my father in London, and perhaps other MPs as well. Those who could pay. But what I'd really like to do eventually is work on a magazine or be a reporter on a newspaper.'

'They'd never have that.'

'They might. Women are starting to do all sorts of things.'

He sat with his face growing more and more thundery, till he burst out:

'Isn't Glasgow good enough for you? What is it about London that's so special?'

'Opportunity.'

'Money, you mean.'

'You can afford to be superior. I can't. I'd get eight shillings in Glasgow as a typist, but twice that in London.'

'What about spiritual values, like loyalty to Scotland, being a companion to your mother?'

'How is it being disloyal to move around? You've done your share.' Her eyes shadowed at his second jibe. 'As for my mother – I've told you what it's like at home. I can't stand the boredom any longer. I must get out and stretch myself.'

He attacked from a different direction.

'You'll be no help to your father. You're a political idiot.'

'Donald!' Now he really had wounded her. She turned her face away, looking out over the restaurant's balcony at the Kelvin, faintly hearing the screams from the switchback railway.

'Well, politically naïve, at any rate,' he amended. 'It *is* naïve to think women, all women, should have the vote. Those shawlies down in Govan and the Gorbals wouldn't use it if they had it, any more than they do soap.'

She was too angry to answer. He felt a perverse pleasure in thus upsetting her.

'You don't even know about the Taff Vale business, do you?'

'It means unions can be penalized if they go on strike.'

She glared. 'It'll just bring *more* people into the unions, out of a desire for justice, that's all.' She rose to go. 'Are you coming?'

'Have another cake.'

'It would choke me.'

Outside, he said in conciliatory tones, 'Let's go somewhere quiet. I'll take you in the tram to some gardens I know. We can talk. Properly.'

In the tram they were both silent. He put his arm round the back of her seat, and she didn't object. When they got to the gardens, he sought out a sequestered spot where they would not be disturbed, then put his arms around her, staring into her face. Somewhere in the distance a band played. There seemed to be bands all over Glasgow that summer. The voices of children down by a pond wafted to them as though from another world.

'Kiss me, Carlie.' She kissed his cheek.

'No, like this.' He took her lips. He put his hand on her nape so that she could not move her head. His other hand moved up and down her slender back. At last she protested, 'No, Donald. Someone might *see*,' but he pulled her down on the grass and kissed her again. The little hat went askew on her hair, her hands struggled frailly to stop his wandering ones. At last he lay back, but holding one of her arms in a pinion lest she move a fraction from him.

'Carlie.' He looked up into the moving fretwork of a sycamore tree. 'You know what I want, don't you? I want you wholly. All of you.'

She sat up, fixing her hair, straightening her hat.

'You could give me a bairn, like my father did Kirsten Mackenzie.' Her voice was low, her look, scared and accusatory.

'There doesn't have to be a baby every time you do it. There are ways of avoiding it. I learned at the clinic. A lot of people were lovers there. It was quite accepted.'

He put his hand under her skirts, but she pushed him away, her face red with determination and fright.

'No, Donald. I'm scared. I don't want to get tied down with babies, not for a long time. I want to go to London and find out what I can do, first.'

'Will you come back to me?'

'I don't know. I think so.' She studied him, tenderly but objectively. She had always felt responsible for him, had always given in to him. But something in her at this moment resisted, would not be rushed or overwhelmed. She kissed him swiftly, stood up and said in a matter-of-fact voice, 'We must go. You're meeting Finn.' She refused to notice his dejection but made instead towards the gates.

'This is good,' said Finn. He was looking at the sketch Donald had done of the Marienbad cotton millionaire's specifications for his custom-built car. 'I could use you in the firm. You've got a natural flair.'

Donald looked suitably modest. '*He* knew exactly what he wanted. I just followed instructions. He wants it to be ready for Christmas, as a surprise for his wife.'

Finn nodded, tucking the paper away in an inside pocket. 'Any time you get fed up with your law studies, I'll give you a job. Mind you, you'd need to start on the shop floor, get your hands dirty.'

'Come to think of it,' said Donald, 'I've always liked machinery. I could be an engineer manqué.'

'Well, my offer's always open!' Finn grinned at him. 'What say we eat now? Talking business always makes me hungry.'

In the sober, businessman's restaurant, Finn disposed of mutton broth, steak pie and suet pudding, but Donald was restless and picked at his food.

'Tina says you work too hard,' he accused Finn. 'I've been instructed to make you enjoy yourself. I wish we could find a couple of women, have a few drinks, take in a theatre —'

Finn picked up the glass of water in front of him and drank abstemiously. 'I'm temperance myself. There's too much evidence of what drink can do to a man in Glasgow for me to lower my guard.'

Donald stared at him moodily. In his expensive tweed suit and hard collar, the faint odour of Euchrisma coming from slicked-down fair hair, Finn looked staid, confident and, it had to be admitted, faintly boring for someone generally regarded as an up-and-coming tycoon.

Testily, Donald said, 'What do you do with yourself when you're not working?'

'I go in for climbing.' His Boston accent overlaid with the broader West of Scotland vowels, Finn gazed keenly at his younger cousin. 'Scotland has such wonderful scenery. I like the loneliness of mountains. I can think and plan there, come back refreshed. Nature, unlike women, never lets you down.'

There was a faint note there of frailer passions and Donald looked at his cousin with a little more approbation.

'How about the music-hall? Would that corrupt your notions of propriety? I tell you, Finn, you mustn't let the terrible Scottish need for respectability get too great a hold on you! There's more to life than the kirk and suet pudding.' And he looked with distaste at the second helping of the latter which a matronly waitress was heaping on to his cousin's plate.

'Where do you suggest?' demanded Finn, looking apprehensive.

'The Britannia.'

'But that's a well-known rough house.'

'I know.' Donald grinned mischievously. 'What do you say we give it a try?'

Finn gave in, with what was really a feigned reluctance. He was actually quite amused by this younger cousin. After years of struggle, he felt he could turn his back on the factory for five minutes without problems arising. His friend Sir Peter Frensham, a great help in the beginning in rustling up financial support, had not always been the practical support he might have been. When business interfered with 'fun', wherever that was obtainable, he was woefully liable to let business look after itself. Or let Finn cope as best he could. Finn felt like someone whose head had been under water for a long time. Maybe it was time he came up for air.

On the way to the theatre he became a little more confidential. 'You see – ' side-stepping two quarrelling urchins – 'I read Thoreau. You should try him, Donald. He's very strong on solitude. "I never found the companion that was so companionable as solitude." That's what he says. And "You can't kill time, without injuring eternity." '

'Is eternity what you find on the mountains, then?' demanded Donald.

'Something like that. Although when I hear Handel played, or Bach, it's the same thing. An exaltation.'

'I don't think I should be taking you here,' Donald qualified, outside the music-hall. He looked longingly at a barrow where people were buying rotten eggs and bad fruit to throw at the turns they didn't like, deciding Finn wouldn't want any part of such direct criticism.

All the best seats were gone. They were obliged to sit at the back to watch the ragged chorus, the bosomy female singer, the eccentric dancer and the obligatory Glasgow comic, innocently ribald in his baggy suit, striped stockings and red nose. But in any case, the show that held their riveted attention went on in the aisles and the seats around them. Infants peeled oranges and threw the peel at one another. Men already well gone in their cups passed whisky flasks and beer bottles along the rows. One was spectacularly sick, emptying seats all around him at breakneck speed. And when the comic went flatly into a sentimental rendering of 'My Old Dutch' fruit and eggs whizzed indiscriminately through the air, splattering impartially against skin, clothes and stucco and adding their odours to an atmosphere already richly redolent.

When the curtain had dropped, Donald hopefully suggested a drink, and a bemused Finn, gamely declaring it was as well to know how the other half lived, found himself agreeing.

'It must only be a small glass of light beer,' he stipulated, but Donald had his hand on his arm and was indicating, with fierce forward jabs of the head, two young women leaving the theatre ahead of them. 'My landlady's daughter-in-law, Chrissie Macausland, and her friend Big Nellie,' he hissed. 'Come on, I'll introduce you.'

Finn suddenly bore an uncanny resemblance to his grand-father, the old minister James Galbraith. In tones of horror he objected. 'Mrs Jessup'll have my milk and biscuits await-ing me at home.' But he was too late. The crowds pushing their way out had held up the girls' progress and Chrissie had spotted Donald, falling upon him with loud, welcoming cries.

'This is *Mrs* Macausland.' Donald effected the introduc-tion. 'Her husband is away fighting the Boers – '

'And this is a Miss Nellie Byers, to a Mr Donald Balfour and – ' Chrissie interposed, then stopped questioningly.

'My cousin, Mr Finn Fleming,' Donald finished off.

Finn could see that Chrissie Macausland was, in fact, a decent and presentable young woman in well-pressed navy serge. Her friend, however, sowed seeds of grave doubt in his mind. She had one of those mouths that kept breaking into smiles despite its owner's efforts to stitch it up with decorum and probity. And Donald would never have referred to her as Big Nellie, in the low Glasgow fashion, had she not been known for a certain laxity of manners and possibly, even, of morals.

Uncomfortably, he began to make his excuses, but Donald would have none of it. He wanted to buy the ladies a drink, but there was no place suitable. It was agreed after much laughter and discussion that they should all go back to the Macausland home. Chrissie's mother-in-law was away on a visit to her other son, who had just become a father, and as Chrissie put it, 'We can have a wee bit of a baur and not disturb a soul.'

Trudging through the now rain-soaked Trongate towards the Macausland residence at Glasgow Cross, Finn hissed in Donald's ear, 'What, for heaven's sake, is a baur?'

'A bit of fun,' answered Donald easily. 'You'll like Chrissie, Finn. She can play the piano and sing like a lintie.' A little reassured, Finn walked on. He was seeing a side to Glasgow he had never known before and it intrigued him in spite of himself. Nellie Byers had an infectious laugh, big and sumptuous, like her bosom. Once in the cosy tenement kitchen, his gaze lingered on that bosom.

Decorously covered by a white lawn, pin-tucked blouse, it was decorated with a seed-pearl brooch, a fob watch on a velvet ribbon, a string of coral beads and a lace jabot, reminding him of one of those crammed shop windows in The Arcade in the city.

'What'll you have?' Efficiently Chrissie stirred the fire to life, removed a sleeping cat from the rocking-chair, brought forth bottles of whisky, port and ginger wine and cut black bun into fingers.

'Is the ginger-wine non-alcoholic?' demanded Finn. Chrissie nodded and the other two went into fits of laughter. Donald took over the pouring from Chrissie. Turning his back, he poured a measure of whisky into Finn's ginger wine, winking at the girls as he handed over the glass.

It was quite pleasant in this working-class home, Finn admitted. The gas mantle plopped, the fire blazed, the chenille curtains cosily shut out the damp night. Donald and Chrissie had gone off into the front room to play the piano and sing a duet, and he found himself talking to Nellie.

'Have you got a lassie?' she asked him teasingly. She sipped the dregs of his glass, playfully, then poured him another, this time putting in the whisky quite openly.

'I'm a businessman, you see,' he explained to her, carefully. 'I've been building up my business, and I haven't had much time for women.'

'But you had one, once?' she asked, percipiently.

'Oh yes.'

'What was her name?'

He grinned at her, a little foolishly. Then he wagged his finger. 'I'm not telling you that.'

'Go on. You got a photo of her? Let me see.'

'Nellie.' He was having difficulty getting his tongue round the simple syllables. The word came out more like Ne-ollie. Funny that. 'Don't pry, Ne-ollie.'

She began to tickle him. He fell about, gasping and help-less. She put her hand into his inner jacket pocket and brought out his wallet. Skilfully she riffled through it till she found what she was looking for, then put the rest back in his pocket.

'Give it me back.' He was serious now. Angry even.

She danced about the room keeping out of his reach, try-ing to look at the photograph more clearly. 'She's lovely, Finn. Honest. You love her, do you?' She placed it on the mantelpiece for all to see, but stood guard before it.

He sat down, suddenly boneless. He put his head in his hands. 'I'm dizzy,' he protested. She pulled his hands away, laying his head on her shop-window bosom, stroking his hair. 'You've got lovely hair, Finn. For a chap. You really have. I mean it.'

In the front room, Chrissie sang:

> 'The River Clyde is very wide
> Especially where it's narra.
> There's mony a chiel stands at the bar
> That couldnae wheel a barra.'

She slapped down the piano lid.

'Play more,' Donald pleaded. 'I love those Glasgow non-sense songs. Think of another.'

Chrissie slumped into one of the highly-polished horse-hair chairs placed round a solid mahogany table bearing a crystal bowl of realistic wax fruit. She had run out of songs.

'I once tried to eat the pear, when I was younger.' She mimed the act now. 'That's how I came by this broken tooth.'

He peered into her mouth. 'I like it broken. It gives you character.'

'I think I've had too much,' said Chrissie. Her face fell into remorseful lines. 'When I've had too much, that's when

I think of oor Jimmy.'

He stretched across the table and took her left hand, playing with the wedding ring. 'Do you miss him very much?'

She nodded without speaking. 'I dream that he's getting killed. Time after time. I see this Boer soldier with a rifle cocked and then I hear the bang and Jimmy's lying there. And another time I dreamt he had his – his you-know-what-I-mean blown off. That must be the very worst thing that could happen to a man.' She began to weep softly, plucking each tear away delicately with the tips of her fingers.

'Do you miss his love-making?' Donald persisted.

'You cheeky wee blighter!' She looked at him through her fingers, caught half-way between laughter and annoyance.

'No. The question's serious,' he protested. 'What do you do? I want to make love to my girl, and she won't let me.'

'Quite right, too.'

'I'd marry her.'

'Won't she have you?' She flicked his dark hair teasingly and then saw that he, too, was near to maudlin tears.

'Och, poor wee man. Here, here!' And she kissed him impetuously. He took her in his arms, kissing her back with interest. It was altogether different from Carlie. This woman was soft and giving.

'The bed!' She turned her head towards the decorously recessed bed along one wall, covered with an Indian silk spread, draped with curtains. He bundled her towards it, helping her to take off her skirt, untying the tapes that held up her striped bloomers. Gracelessly but successfully he straddled her. Her smile spread away on her face like milk.

In the kitchen, Finn slept with his head on the table, while Nellie donned her coat and hat and went home. The nerve! He had actually fallen asleep as she stroked his hair. She had had to lift his head from off the fob watch and the coral beads and lay it on his arms.

She left the photograph where she'd put it, on the mantelpiece. The girl had dark hair and a slight cleft in her chin. It was signed 'Fondest love – Kitty.'

Chapter Eleven

When Donald Balfour let himself in at the heavy front doors of Dounhead House the next evening, he realized it was so late the housekeeper must have retired to bed and in all likelihood his father also.

His first reaction was one of relief. They had been expecting him yesterday. He could always say he had been with Finn. But even if his excuses were accepted, there would then follow the over-anxious enquiries about his health and the interminable discussions about his future. At least these were postponed for a little longer.

And then he heard it. A sound between a groan and a shout. It came from his father's study on the ground floor. Donald hurried along the red-carpeted hall to the open door and saw his father spreadeagled across his reading-desk, a glass of water overturned and seeping into the blotting-paper.

'Father! What's happened?' With difficulty, he lifted Lachie back against his chair. The eyes fluttered. 'Are you ill? Shall I get the doctor?'

'No!' With an enormous effort, Lachie pulled himself upright. 'Where've you been? Waited for you. Get me some coffee. Best thing. Black coffee,' he stipulated.

Not very efficiently, Donald made a pot of black coffee and carried it back to the study with two cups and a bowl of sugar. He held the liquid to his father's lips, making him drink two cups before he was satisfied. Lachie got up, his movements still clumsy and swaying, and moved to his chair by the dying fire. Donald stirred the ashes and put on more coal.

'Sorry I didn't get back sooner,' he offered. 'I had some business with Finn in Glasgow, and stayed the night.'

'Well, you're here now,' said Lachie shortly. 'Are you better?'

'Much better. Don't worry about me. It's you I'm concerned about. Were you drinking, Father?'

'You know I don't drink.' Lachie picked up a small, dark-blue bottle from the sofa table and held it up. 'I take a few drops of this stuff from time to time, when the headaches get beyond bearing.'

Donald saw the label on the bottle. 'Laudanum! Isn't that addictive?'

'What isn't? Whisky's addictive, smoking's addictive. All I know is I have to have some relief from the pain. The doctor can do nothing.'

Donald stared at his parent, thinking how little he knew him. After Tansy had left, Lachie had spent long periods abroad and on the Isle of Arran with his painter friends. Painting had become his entire way of life. Donald remembered now coming on his father in the atelier he had built in the grounds of Dounhead House. It had been a warm, sunny evening and Lachie had been inspecting a picture he had just finished. It did not seem to Donald to be representational at all, although it was called 'Seascape and Sunset'. It was so incandescent with colour you felt it might burst, not into flames, but to reveal some ultimate beauty of nature beyond.

Lachie had scarcely seemed aware of the boy's presence at first. Then he had put an arm about his shoulder and they had looked at his handiwork together.

'Are you pleased with it?' Donald had asked.

'Yes. I think so.' Perhaps he had been hoping his father would talk about the picture, what it meant, what he'd been hoping to achieve in it. But he didn't. He seemed mesmerized by it. Donald slipped his arm and left him to it. He had felt a great anger against the picture, and the look of love his father had for it. Now the feeling of exclusion was always there. Funny. He had thought himself old enough to be immune to *that* kind of pain.

As though somehow he had detected the trend of his

204

thoughts, Lachie said, 'It's time you and I had a heart-to-heart. While you've been away I've thought a lot about us. I think I may have neglected you.'

Donald looked at him in surprise and Lachie gave a short, unamused laugh. 'Well, we're getting the chance to try again. Cards on the table. I wanted you to know about the laudanum. About the pain I've suffered. But you've had your share of ill-health, haven't you? Now you're better, I want you to tell me what you want out of life. Do you want to stick to your law studies?'

'I don't know.' To his surprise, Donald realized this was true. Over the past few days, a steady resistance to the thought of going back to the university had been building up in him.

'I've had a word with your teachers. They don't think you have the application for it.' As Donald started up in protest, Lachie silenced him with a raised hand. 'Even allowing for the decline in your health before you went to Switzerland, they felt there was a certain lack of dedication to your studies. In short, they'd as soon not have you back.'

'That suits me,' said Donald grimly.

His father looked at him in some exasperation, but for a few moments said nothing. Thoughtfully, he fed a meerchaum pipe and drew on it. From time to time, he passed a hand across his forehead, as though to clear his thoughts. But the effects of the laudanum seemed to have worn off.

'You have an alternative,' said Lachie slowly, 'now that you're of age. You can take over the management of Dounhead. You can marry and have the house. There's a cottage in Arran where I'd be more than content to spend the rest of my days.'

'You've hated it here, since Mother left.'

His father nodded.

'I don't think I want it either.' Donald let his words fall away into the waiting silence. The big clock in the corner ticked in rhythm with his heartbeat. If he could have brought Carlie here . . . But she would never come. She would laugh at the very idea of being the lady in the big house. How was he going to get her to listen to him? For despite what had happened with Chrissie, it was still Carlie who possessed his mind. She needn't think that going away to London was going to stop him loving her. And one day they were going to be together. He had even checked out the question of being cousins with Alisdair, who had said there was no reason they should not marry, as there were no inherited weaknesses on either side. If he had to turn into the kind of person Carlie would take seriously, so be it. She would never take him seriously in the role of county gentleman.

His expression as he looked at his father was more open than he realized. 'I don't want the big house, or what goes with it, either.' Lest his words were tainted with – could it be revenge? – he added slowly, 'I always felt there was something bogus about us living up here, away from the rest of Dounhead. Maybe it was because Mother came from the Rows –'

'And Carlie Fleming.' His father watched the effect of his words through a thick haze of tobacco smoke. 'I hear she's going to London. You're fond of her, aren't you?'

'Is it *us* talking like this?' Donald spread his hands in embarrassment and something more. Amazement. 'I've never felt before I could bring my problems to you –'

'A year's a long time. I realized that if you'd died I would have been faced with a lifetime of regret. I realized that fathering a son doesn't give you ownership of his life. I was trying to shape you for a life I had never wanted myself. Well, now I'm saying to you, Donald: tell me what you want to do. Does London come into your plans?'

'Do you think I should follow her?'

'With some, the harder you chase them the faster they run.' Lachie came near to smiling.

'Suddenly, I've too many options!' Donald cried. 'Finn's even talking about giving me a job –'

'Why don't you take it meantime?'

'Are you trying to tell me to stand on my own two feet?'

They smiled at each other. 'Could be,' said Lachie.

'Then I say to you: sell up this damned place, pit and all,

and run like hell for Arran. You'll have enough money to live like a king till the end of your days.'

'I want to make you an allowance – '

'I'll not take it, Father.'

'It's there if you need it.'

Donald shook his head. It was like being given a kind of freedom, but like all freedom, it was strangely alarming at first. For the first time, he felt the warm bond of kinship with his father and wished it might always have been like this. They sat talking long into the night, cronies who could say anything to one another.

It was a day made for the gods, that Saturday in April 1902. Coming up in the train from Ayrshire, Sandia looked through the carriage windows at fluffy cotton-wool clouds scudding for their lives across a brilliant blue sky. Even she felt some of the excitement and she knew nothing about football.

Her husband, John Beltry, was sitting opposite her with the expression of a schoolboy out on a treat. He would not, he told her many times, miss the International at Ibrox for all the tea in China. Today, England was bound to go down against Scotland. The Scots footballers had everything on their side – skill, speed, intelligence, grace. It was a wonder, she teased, that the feet of such exemplary creatures ever touched the ground, never mind the ball. It was daft nonsense, she averred, but it was nice to see him so happy.

'You've not to get too excited,' she scolded. But his high spirits were not to be dampened. Looking at her fondly, he said, 'I've never seen you look bonnier. That hat suits you.' And he gave her that intimate, cherishing look that always stripped the years from him in her eyes and made her wonder at the unexpectedness of human love.

She had gone into the marriage not loving but respecting him. Then together they had built up something that certainly approached the state of happiness. He never took her for granted. What she wanted, he saw that she got, and that did not merely apply to material things but to a listening ear when she was uncertain and a gentle but surprisingly passionate approach to love-making.

It was as though the marriage gradually cancelled out the years between them – he grew younger and sprightlier while she grew mature and ever more maternal, towards him and everyone else.

She had come to terms with her childless state – well, almost, and that was the only thing, the only sadness, she thought now.

John was going to the match with Finn, Alisdair and young Donald, who had all promised to shield him from the rougher excesses of the crowd. They expected a gate of 75,000. Sandia couldn't envisage that many people, but they'd be mostly on the terraces. John had paid the top price for all four tickets. It was his treat.

She had come in to supervise matters in her first and favourite tea-room, for Glasgow would be bursting at the seams today, its trams overflowing with the usual Saturday shoppers as well as the football supporters, and her poor girls rushed off their feet. Even if she didn't do much, it was good for morale for them to see her there.

At the station, she watched John go off with the others and then pushed her way through the touts and rosette-sellers to the comparative calm of her restaurant, half-wishing it were already time to return to the high-ceilinged mansion in Troon and their evening game of cards.

Her mind flicked back to Donald, and his pale, dark-eyed face as he'd greeted John. The family were worried about him. She permitted herself a small, inward smile. The family, John was fond of pointing out to her, meant as a rule Sandia herself. Now that Grannie Kate was getting on, she'd assumed the mantle of matriarch and was never content unless trying to smooth the path of life for some relative or other. He did not mind, she knew. He quite enjoyed the ramifications of family, having been an only child himself and undervalued and uncossetted by his daughter in Edinburgh.

Finn was concerned too, she knew. He had been pleased to take Donald into the factory, but was disappointed at his lack of ambition. He seemed quite content to remain on the shop-floor and to have his friends among the gambling, hard-drinking element and the young radicals who enjoyed nothing better in the lunch-hour than a good hard-hitting argument.

She had tried to persuade Donald to stay with Finn and her father at Ashley Terrace, where they could keep an eye on him. But he remained in what had been his student digs near Glasgow Cross, in a grey tenement up a musty close that smelled of urine. Once he had been seen at the theatre with Chrissie Macausland, whose husband had been invalided out of the Army, minus a leg. He'd explained that the poor girl needed taking out of herself, but Sandia did not feel he should be the one to do it.

When she'd said this to Finn, he had laughed and declared Donald was young and was working out a philosophy of living. She had then asked Finn what *his* philosophy was and he had given her a dry look. He knew she meant he was still giving too much time up to work. She had wondered sometimes if there had been anything between him and June Frensham, whom he had escorted to occasional social occasions and theatrical first-nights, but that had obviously petered out and she was now engaged to a peer's second son.

Afterwards, Sandia was to think it uncanny how the premonition that something had gone wrong at the match reached her before the actual news spread through the Glasgow streets. Maybe it was when she saw the first ambulance thread its way through the packed street outside. Or it might have been the second, since one was not all that remarkable.

Or maybe it was the ripple of disquiet running through the crowds, changing their sound somehow. But confirmation came when a distraught woman rushed through the tea-room swing-doors, catching her feather boa in them, and saying to anyone who would listen: 'There's been a disaster at the grounds. People killed . . .'

The floor, the walls, tilted away from Sandia momentarily. She grabbed the woman's arm and shook it. 'What's happened? What did you hear?'

'The ambulances,' the woman babbled. 'I've never seen so many. One of the terraces, I think that's what the man said –'

She didn't really take in any of the descriptions that began to flood in with the pale-faced crowds seeking the familiar comfort of a cup of tea. A corner kick. The mass of men surging and swaying to watch it being taken; the creaking and groaning as the structure gave way –

'John.' She said the name, thinking of the supper tray laid at home in Troon, with its white-on-white Ayrshire embroidery.

She knew, before they brought the news to her. She should never have let him go. But how could you stop a grown man? You couldn't say to him, 'Live like the old man you are.' He had never done that. He had wanted life, been greedy for it.

It was Alisdair who came to her later to explain: 'We didn't even know anything had gone wrong at first. The game went on, even after the terrace had collapsed. It was afterwards, the crowds and the crush. A kind of hysteria seemed to run through our section of the crowd, as word spread about the disaster. Everybody wanted out. We got pushed up against the barrier. We protected John as best we could but I could see what was happening, that the pain in his chest was overwhelming him. I did what I could, but it was inevitable, Sandia. It could have happened at any time.'

It had started out a day for the gods. It had left her rich, a widow of substance. Yet all she could think of then was his happy schoolboy face on the train and his words, 'I like you in that hat.' Afterwards, she could never wear navy with a veil. Somebody moved the tray set with the white-on-white embroidered cloth before she went back to the high-ceilinged parlour in Troon.

It was Captain Jack who suggested the trip to visit Kitty in Canada. He was convinced it was the only thing to shake

Sandia out of her depression following her husband's death. She had always been a soft-hearted girl, her father acknowledged, but he had not accurately gauged the depth of her feelings for her husband. She had a bee in her bonnet that she had not watched over him as she should : that she should never have let him go to the football international. They were all getting a little impatient over her frequent visits to poor John's grave, her refusal to have anything to do with the tea-rooms, her tendency to stay in the villa at Troon and do little but brood.

Finn had put the idea to her as they walked one calm day along the sands at Troon. Cunningly, knowing she could always be persuaded to do something for another's good, rather than her own, he had pointed out, 'It would be a great adventure for your father.' She had turned the tables on him. 'I'll go if you come too. You deserve a break.' He looked sharply at her, but read nothing in her face. In the end, he too agreed to come.

The South African war ended before they left. The sense of relief in Glasgow as elsewhere was palpable. Many of those who had set off in such high spirits with the London-Scottish would never see the bonnie Hills of Galloway again from a returning troopship. Six thousand men had died in action, three times as many had succumbed to disease, and now twenty-three thousand wanted nursing back to some kind of health. There was also some bad conscience over the concentration camps in which Kitchener had herded civilians, even children, and over the numbers, said to be 20,000, who had died there.

But it was over, that was the thing. And, once recovered from his appendicitis, the new king was due to take over the throne. Even if he was sixty-one, he was cheerful, lively and scandalous, which made a change after Victoria; and at fifty-eight his Queen, Alexandra, was glamorously youthful-looking, and the object of almost equal doses of commiseration and curiosity on the part of her subjects.

The hammering from the shipyards provided an incessant chorus on the hazy summer day when they set sail from the quay at Finnieston. Jack wanted to miss nothing. How it all had changed since the time when he'd stowed away, aged twelve, on the sailing-ship *Titania*. He thought of her mainly as a sailing ship because that was how he liked best to remember her, full-rigged, beautiful. But she had been sail-and-steam. And how bravely she had fought the ocean, then. But he remembered with photographic clarity the dreadful night when the captain and first mate had been swept over-board and the ship reduced to little more than a valiant matchbox. He'd seen some storms at sea since, but never anything to equal that. Steel boilers, steel ships, had changed everything. He looked up at the *Colintrae*'s three large dark funnels with respect, if without affection. A good ship, a sound ship. These hopeful emigrating souls milling around on deck in this day as in his, would be safe on board her, but beautiful, he decided, she was not.

'Papa.' It was Sandia beside him, breathless, excited. 'We're on our way at last.' He smiled at her, remembering how she had badgered him at Gourock, when she was about four, to be shown the big ships. Now he pointed them out to her again – that one there was bound for Montreal; this one was just back from Calcutta, and that one probably returned from Cape Town with a cargo of fruit. And the one with the lascar seamen, that would be from the Far East, probably China.

'The four-masters, Papa?' Sandia nodded in the direction of the windjammers, knowing full well her father's love was still reserved for them. His voice was gruff. 'They're still used on the grain routes from Australia. That one over there will be getting ready for New Zealand.' She marvelled at his intimate knowledge of ships and docks, as detailed and certain as her knowledge of her own kitchens.

'It's not beautiful, but it has a certain romance of its own,' opined Finn, coming up to join them and indicating the river banks strewn with the angular furniture of the shipyards, where the clatter of the riveters' hammers never stopped.

'Wait till we reach the Tail o' the Bank,' said Jack. How

could he describe to them that swelling moment once Gourock was passed and the firth opened up to the open sea? How describe the feeling when eventually there was no land visible and nothing but the great element of unpredictable water to sustain you till New York?

He was determined not to make an emotional fool of himself and busied himself needlessly pointing out landmarks like the Kilpatrick Hills and Dumbarton Rock, the craggy peaks beyond the Holy Loch and the hills of Arran as the firth inexorably widened. Not a puffer or coaster missed his interested gaze and he instructed his companions in the difference between them and the hoppers and dredgers keeping the river from silting up and the channel clear for ships.

In the summer air, they could hear the music from the paddle steamers taking trippers to Rothesay. Sandia thought the sound of piano, melodeon, fiddle peculiarly appropriate that day, for the liner was like some great stage-set, peopled as it was with emigrants all set to enact the biggest drama of their lives. Unlike themselves, most of these people would never return to Scotland. Somehow, the thought shrank her grief to proportion. Determinedly, with no more tears, she set her face to the west.

Canada imposed silence on them by its scale and grandeur. There were times when Sandia thought it looked very like Scotland only conceived on a much larger scale. The huge spaces emptied her mind, made her glad when they reached resting points and human contact was restored. Tuned to the rhythms of the transcontinental trains, she let the gentler griefs of her widowhood wash up on her consciousness like an outgoing tide rustling through sand and shingle. It was strange how John Beltry and Dandy seemed to be twinned in her mind, as though she had lost both. As though the more recent grief had revived the earlier, attenuated one of Dandy's going away. Sometimes, idly, she tried to picture him married, the father of children. She would not mind that, she thought. But they should have been hers.

Every other thought was put from their minds, however,

by the warmth of the welcome at the Wilson homestead, where it was quite clear that Kitty was regarded as one of the family. Great preparations had been put in hand and every Scots-born homesteader for miles around had been invited to a party and barn-dance to greet the newcomers. The livery business and lodging-house were booming and Kitty seemed to thrive on the hard work involved, for her slender figure had rounded into womanly curves and even seeing Finn did not apparently shake her cheerful, back-chatting equilibrium. Sandia took in right away the proprietorial attitude of Fred Wilson and Kitty's flirtatious response to it. A small thud of premonition jolted her stomach.

But that first night at the barn-dance everything went off like a firecracker. Melodeon and violin provided the music for reels, strathspeys and cotillions and the white-clothed trestle-tables groaned under their burden of plenty. Sandia noticed one or two dark-eyed, soulful creatures who joined lustily but inexpertly in the dancing and was told these were Doukhobors, a Russian sect arriving in the province in large numbers.

'Uncle Duncan would take to them,' said Kitty. 'They won't carry arms or fight. I don't know if he would approve of what they do when they're up against some kind of opposition from the authorities, though.'

'What's that?' demanded Sandia.

'They take off all their clothes,' said Kitty, with a mischievous smile.

Sandia gazed at the Russians curiously. Did they find it so much different from their Tsarist homeland? She thought again of the people coming over on the ship with them, Scots bound for America and Canada to make a new life, and it seemed to her as though half the world was uprooting itself and settling down somewhere else. Finn had volunteered the information that a million and a half Scots had emigrated in the last century. What did it do to the country thus denuded? Maybe her Uncle Duncan's internationalism would be thrust on them, whether they liked it or not.

What warmed her was that Kitty kept off the subject of her widowhood till they were alone in the latter's bedroom and then simply put her arms around her and hugged her close. It was better than words. It was kinship, it was sharing. And talk came then, slowly and naturally, part of the filling-in process about each other's lives since they had parted.

Then Kitty said unexpectedly, 'I wish Finn Fleming had not come,' and it came again, that thud of premonition. Sandia looked at her blankly, saying, 'Surely you can afford to be friends now, dear. You've made a happy life for yourself here.'

'Yes.' Kitty's face darkened. 'And it wasn't easy.'

'Will you marry Fred Wilson?'

'He wants me to.'

'There's a "but" in your voice.'

'But I don't love him.'

'In that case –'

'Does it make any difference?' Kitty challenged. 'Did you love John, to start with, at any rate? It seems to me that folk who marry for friendship, respect, that sort of thing, have just as good a life.'

'I think Finn has set a lot of store by coming here.'

'Then why didn't he come sooner?' Kitty demanded.

'Did you expect him to run after you?' asked Sandia, in amazement. 'Then it shows you don't know Finn. He's a very buttoned-up, inward-looking person. With a lot of pride. He's clever, Kit. It sets him apart from the herd.' She put a hand on her sister's arm. 'Don't be hard on him, dear. If you don't want to take up with him again, at least let him down gently.'

Kitty's mouth hardened, but she said nothing more.

On the third day of the visit, Kitty and Finn disappeared together for about three hours. Ostensibly they had merely gone for an exploration of the little township. Fred Wilson, handsome in a thickset, solid way, had been taking the local doctor to a homestead twenty miles away where the mother was sick, and after he had settled his horse on return he made anxious enquiries about Kitty's whereabouts. When Kitty and Finn did return, looking upset and, in Kitty's case, even tearful, Fred's expression became positively forbidding and Sandia waited fearfully for some kind of emotional storm.

Nothing happened that night, however, mainly because Kitty went out of her way to placate Fred and because Captain Jack embarked on some spellbinding stories about his seafaring days. His listeners had never heard of the famous Arran stowaway case, in which seven youngsters had stowed away at Greenock for Canada and been put out on the ice (save for one) on St George Bay, Newfoundland.

Sandia thought her father had something of the Ancient Mariner about him, sitting there in the snug timber house with his rapt audience about him. He described how the urchins, who'd been flogged and starved on the crossing, blundered about on the ice-floes till one drowned down an ice-hole and another was left behind to die, crying for his mother. The rest, temporarily blinded from the ice-fields, eventually reached the shore and were saved. Jack had had the full story from one of them, who had grown up to be a riveter at Greenock.

In the days to come, Kitty appeared to do her best to keep out of Finn's way, but Sandia noticed them occasionally engrossed in conversation, and once, in a corner, what seemed to be an angry exchange. Even so, she did not know everything that went on, for she and her father were invited to visit all over the place, sometimes quite a few miles out into the prairie.

The visit was to end, as it began, with a party. An even bigger affair than the barn dance, Sandia was assured, and it could go on till dawn. Everybody was coming, even the babies, who would be put to sleep in improvised cots. Provincial Canada was like that: friendly, extrovert, hard-working and fun-loving. Sandia began to see what Kitty liked about it.

The day of the party, Sandia found Kitty packing a wicker basket with goodies and covering it with a red and white checked gingham cloth.

'What's this?' she demanded curiously.

'At midnight, we have an auction lunch,' Kitty explained. 'It's the tradition. Your beau is supposed to outbid all comers for your lunch-basket. If he doesn't, it means he's cooling off.'

'I see,' said Sandia thoughtfully.

It was a nerve-tingling, rumbustious affair. Thin and vibrant, the fiddles whined out country music and red-necked boys straight from the fields whirled their girls into exhausting patterns of dance. Grannies smiled from the side-lines and babies fell asleep in the corners, huddled among their parents' coats and galoshes.

Sandia danced with an abstracted Finn, who answered her comments vaguely and monosyllabically. Captain Jack enjoyed popularity among the ladies, especially the older, widowed ones, as he stomped through the dances at his own pace, his broad back forbidding the frivolous passing of younger partners round the hall.

The auctioneer, a burly, middle-aged ex-Glaswegian called Alec Hardie, mounted the rostrum round about midnight to cat-calls and shouts of encouragement. All around him were the lunch-baskets of the young and eligible females, and some not so eligible, who stood adjusting their skirts decorously and putting hands up to fix combs or flowers in their hair.

When Kitty's basket went up, there were several bidders and much good-natured joshing, but soon to Sandia's mount-ing concern there were only two bidders left, Fred Wilson and Finn.

She moved to Finn's side to caution him, but he did not seem to be aware of her. His eyes were fixed on Kitty, on the other side of the room. In a blue and white dress she looked distraught and beautiful. As though she were a girl of eighteen, Sandia thought. Not a woman of almost thirty.

The bidding went up, cent by cent, dollar by dollar, till it had the dancers gasping and incredulous. At ten dollars, Fred Wilson turned and strode from the hall and Finn took possession of the basket and carried it to Kitty in triumph.

His eyes glittered down at her.

'Right,' he said decisively. 'Now they all know. You know what I'm asking you, Kitty.'

It seemed as though everyone in the hall waited for Kitty's answer. She stood for a moment, shaken and indecisive, not taking the basket from Finn's extended arms. Then, like Fred before her, she too turned on her heel and walked out.

Finn followed her. On the wooden balcony outside the hall he pulled her into the shadows, but she shook herself out of his arms.

'Why are you punishing me?'

'Because *you* punished *me*.'

'I don't understand.'

'You made me suffer. I swore you wouldn't get the chance to do so again.'

'I've been clumsy, Kit. I've been taken up with my work. But I love you. You know that – '

He wasn't able to finish his protestation. Fred Wilson had come up silently behind and caught him by the jacket collar, swinging him round so that his chin was neatly lined up for the punch Fred delivered.

Scrambling up from the porch floor, Finn bent his head and attacked Fred like a pile-driver. The two rolled over and over, grunting and struggling while Kitty screamed at them to stop.

Finn's right fist landed a blow that seemed to leave his opponent temporarily stunned. Rising groggily, he dragged his man to his feet also, holding him at arm's length so that Fred's hands circled like useless windmills, much to the amusement of the young men in the rapidly-gathering crowd.

'You can't marry this oaf.' His nose bleeding, his hair plastered over his eyes, Finn fixed Kitty with a grimly determined glare. Kitty covered her face as Fred at last tore himself free from his tormentor and with a bellow like an ox threw himself on top of Finn and began pummelling wildly at his head.

'He'll kill him!' Sandia screamed. One heavy blow had gone home and brought Finn to a dazed standstill, his eyes glazed and incredulous, while Fred at last stood back demanding: 'Have you had enough?'

Seeing the ugly turn of events, Hardie the auctioneer and another man took advantage of the lull to pinion Fred and lead him away. But shaking his head like a terrier with a rat, Finn staggered after him, taunting him to return to the fray: 'Come on, you yellow bastard! Let me finish you off!'

Fred cast off the two men like an old overcoat and sailed in towards his opponent with a massive right hook that missed. He had to swing round again in a half circle in order to renew the attack but meantime Finn's fist came up cleanly under his chin with a crack that some swore afterwards could be heard inside the hall. Fred fell with a thud like a railway sleeper and Finn stepped back with a smile and a gesture of primitive satisfaction. He put his pole-axing fist to his lips and kissed it.

There was a momentary hush before Bedlam broke. Helpers rushed to assist the unconscious Fred. They put a folded jacket under him and lifted his eyelids to see pupils rolled up into his head. Sandia, pink-faced and agitated, brought a sponge and trickled water on to his temples.

Kitty confronted Finn, her eyes flinty with rage.

'You – savage, you! You heathen and blackguard!'

He did not meet her eyes. 'It's what you wanted, isn't it? Proof of how I feel. I should bloody well have killed him.' He looked at his raw knuckles and then, despite what he had just said, with ill-concealed relief at Fred, who was at last sitting up and regaining consciousness.

The next day was departure time. Sandia could not find Finn all morning, but an hour before they were due to leave he turned up and got their luggage together, ready for the station, as though nothing had happened.

Kitty had gone about her essential duties in the lodging-house and then changed into her formal clothes for the goodbyes. She was quiet and subdued.

She hugged her father and Sandia warmly and after a pause extended a hand coolly to Finn, who as formally shook it. Sandia was convinced then that it was all over between the two.

But later, in the train, she wondered. Covertly looking at Finn, she tried to guess at the emotions behind his grim, silent mask. He crossed his legs, uncrossed them. He rustled papers open, then folded them to look out of the window. She had the feeling of emotion that would not contain itself. If Kitty had wanted to push Finn towards realization of his feelings, she had succeeded. But what would Kitty do now? Marry Fred Wilson? And could that possibly work? It seemed to Sandia there were nothing but raw nerve endings all over the place. She was about to speak to Finn when she saw her father indicate by a minimal shake of the head that it was best to leave things alone. She decided he knew best.

As the return Atlantic crossing grew to a close, Sandia was aware that she was putting an era in her life behind her. Her marriage to John Beltry seemed like something she had dreamed, except that after marriage there was this feeling of not being quite complete, of involuntarily turning for comfort and answer to someone who was no longer there. But she had come to terms with her widowhood and now she found herself thinking of the tea-rooms. She still loved them, loved the contribution they made to the life and bustle that was Glasgow. She began to plan an extension of the original tea-rooms; perhaps a wood-panelled smoking-room for the men and a pretty, light, airy restaurant mainly for the ladies . . .

All of it was put out of her head by the cablegram awaiting Finn at journey's end. It was from Kitty and it simply said: HAVE BURNED ALL MY BRIDGES AND AM COMING HOME. Instead of helping to draw up plans for the tea-room extension, Sandia found herself knee-deep in preparations for a wedding.

Kitty and Finn had a large church wedding with a splendid reception. Honoria and Marie-Lou made the crossing to attend, and Alisdair's wife Tina was the matron of honour.

All the Glasgow papers carried pictures of the wedding. Finn's name was becoming well known, and Kitty's family's influence in the city was not unacknowledged. The camera caught the bride and groom facing each other with happy, if slightly wary, smiles, and the captions said they would set up home in Kelvinside.

Sandia was not altogether sorry when it was all over. She felt Kitty and Finn needed time on their own after all the fuss. And going back to work, with all its problems, was almost soothing.

One of the waitresses remembered, when she had been back in harness for a couple of days, that during her overseas trip a man with a Northern Ireland accent had been asking after Sandia. A big, handsome, fairish man who had said he was a Mr Dandy Peel. He left his kind regards, and hoped to call again.

Chapter Twelve

Carlie Fleming thought briefly about her cousin Sandia as she made her way excitedly to the House of Commons with her friend from the East End, Aggie Fermoyle. Her mother had written that morning to say that Sandia was being courted again by Dandy Peel who, it seemed, had turned up in Glasgow some months before, following the sad death of his wife from tuberculosis.

It was a touching situation, Carlie felt, but at the same time, she considered that romance must come low on the list of female priorities, today of all days. For after eight years, and much pressure from Mrs Pankhurst and the Women's Social and Political Union (motto. 'Deeds, not words'), the original Women's Enfranchisement Bill was due to be presented once again to the House of Commons.

Supposing it were passed! This was, of course, its first reading. It would still have to go through the perils of a second reading, and then passage through the House of Lords, but supposing today the House at last took the women's cause to its heart, what a triumph that would be!

She grabbed Aggie's arm as they passed through St Stephen's Hall on their way to meet her father in the Central Lobby. Pale-faced and tense, Aggie smiled back at her. Together they had addressed many meetings in draughty East End halls and on windy street corners; with others of the 'Pankhurst lot', they'd gone north before Wakes Week to vie with the quacks and the Salvation Army for the attention of the crowds; and together been splattered with rotten tomatoes, knocked off their soap-boxes by angry males and kicked in the shins by vindictive children.

But today was a day to forget the indignities. Women of all shapes and sizes, all ages and classes, were converging on the House as she and Aggie were doing, the purple and green of their movement displayed on hat ribbons, rosettes and scarves.

She remembered now, as they entered the crush and swell of the Central Lobby, with its huge stained-glass windows of the patron saints, its stone arches, its didactic paintings and insistent sense of history in the making, how when her father had been elected the first thing she had said to him was, 'You must see that women get the vote.'

She smiled a little to herself, watching him come towards her now, people plucking at his sleeves as he passed, anxious to have a word with him. He had done what he could. At the same time, she had to be honest and admit that Labour supporters as a whole could have done more. Some felt that women could wait till all working-class men had the vote and that by supporting the Pankhursts they were helping only middle- and upper-class women. She knew well enough her father had to weigh open and patent support of the female suffrage against the conservative element among those who put him in Parliament. Politics, as she was discovering, were seldom a case of black and white, but many shades in between.

'I've secured your seats in the visitors' gallery,' said Duncan, kissing his daughter and shaking hands warmly with Aggie. 'Bamford Slack has been balloted to present the bill. I think he'll do a good job – always providing he gets the chance.'

'What do you mean, gets the chance?' demanded Carlie sharply.

'There's a lot of opposition,' answered Duncan, looking round the Lobby, which seemed to be full of chattering, laughing, excited women. 'I've never seen a turn-out of women like this, but it's one thing to find support in the Lobby, another thing altogether to sustain it in the House.'

Carlie looked at his face closely. Did he know something they did not? There was no possibility of further talk, for a policeman was clearing a way through the crowd for the Speaker's Procession with the cry of 'Hats off, strangers!'

and it was agreed that it was time she and Aggie took up their seats in the gallery.

Since coming to London, Carlie had often sat in the gallery, especially on those occasions when her father hoped to speak. She had heard him rise to make impassioned intervention on behalf of the unemployed, to urge caution in the Balkans and to plead for improved conditions in the 'sweated' industries. Now she wished with all her heart that it was he, not Bamford Slack, who was submitting the women's bill. But that perhaps was selfish and unreasonable. The important thing was that the bill, first drafted by Mrs Pankhurst's father and advanced as far as its second reading in 1870, was once again a live issue.

'What's happening now?' Aggie demanded in a stage whisper.

'It's the Roadway Lighting Bill first,' said Carlie informatively. 'Shouldn't take long. It's just to make sure that carts travelling along public roads at night carry a light behind as well as before.'

'Do they have to have a bill about that?' demanded Aggie. 'Seems only common sense to me.'

'Seems they do,' Carlie whispered. 'But sssh, or we'll be thrown out!'

The long-winded Parliamentary procedures had always irked Carlie and the speakers to this bill seemed even more given to circumlocution than any she'd heard before. Mentally she switched off and looked down at the floor of the House. As always, it thrilled her to see her father sitting there. He was looking as restless and fed-up as she felt. No wonder! Couldn't they stop going on about carts and roads and lights?

She gazed at the packed public seats. So many faces she had come to know, dedicated workers in the Women's Social and Political Union. She felt a stab of shock as she recognized Kirsten Mackenzie, listening intently. Of course, she would be here. Carlie had seen her at all the big WSPU meetings, though she had avoided meeting her face to face.

Even approaching middle-age, she was a vibrant and attractive woman and not short of admirers, so it was rumoured. Carlie's feelings towards her were ambivalent – half anger that she had once superseded her mother in her father's affections; half admiration that Kirsten Mackenzie could make the liberated woman look so admirable to the public eye.

A sharp kick on the ankle made her look at Aggie, who whispered vehemently, 'Something's happening. What's gone wrong?'

Turning her full attention back to the debate, Carlie saw that yet another Tory MP was on his feet. He was telling some complicated, silly story that went on and on. And when he sat down, another rose behind him to relate a feeble joke. Realization dawned, as the 'promoters' of the Roadway Lighting Bill filibustered like mad. They were determined to 'talk out' the franchise bill.

There was a great subdued roar of fury from the women when it became clear their bill had foundered. Carlie and Aggie rose, stiff-limbed, and found themselves carried into the Lobby on a furious tide.

Some women were weeping tears of open frustration. Others were gathering in angry groups to consult. Carlie pulled Aggie aside from the crowd to wait under the stained-glass window showing St Andrew for Scotland. It seemed an appropriate place to wait for her father.

When he appeared, Carlie burst out at him angrily: 'What happened in there? Can they do that in a democratic country?'

'Unfortunately they can,' admitted Duncan. 'Our late friend Parnell perfected the art of the filibuster. You have just seen it used to good effect tonight.'

'Why was there no intervention?' demanded Carlie.

Duncan shook his head. 'What you have seen,' he said slowly, 'is the expression of the view that women are unfitted by their physical nature for the exercise of political power. Most men still believe that.'

225

'Then most men had better watch out!' cried Aggie, unable to contain herself any longer. 'Look! Those women over there are trying to tell us something!'

A stout matron in a large, dipping hat broke away and approached them. 'There's to be a protest meeting in Broad Sanctuary, near the gates of Westminster Abbey. Come along, sisters! We'll show them whether we mean business or not.'

'Be careful,' Duncan advised. 'Militancy will only get you arrested.'

'And where has caution got us?' demanded the stout woman. 'From now on, it's going to be militancy all the way. And if we go to jail, so be it. Women should vote for the laws they obey and the taxes they pay!'

'There you have it, Duncan,' said a soft voice behind him, and they turned to see Kirsten Mackenzie, dressed in dove grey, surveying Duncan with a look of angry irony. 'Tonight the dam broke. There'll be no stopping us now. Tell all your friends in the House it is so.'

'Kirsten!' Duncan held out a hand to her, but with a set face she swept past him. Carlie could think of nothing to say to him either. She was choking with a sense of angry betrayal. It was turned on all men, even on her own father.

She took Aggie's arm and they marched with the rest to Broad Sanctuary. Kirsten Mackenzie was already there, addressing a section of the crowd. The night air was full of cries and agitation. Buttons glinting, London's constabulary advanced on the crowd. Facing them, Carlie found herself shouting at the top of her voice, 'Votes for women! Votes for women!' An old flower-seller carrying home her basket of fading violets looked at her and then spat in the gutter.

'You ought to be ashamed of yourself, my gel,' she advised her.

Lying in bed that night in the Fermoyle home in Albert Road, Bow, Carlie felt the sensations of anger creep over her skin like the bed-bugs she hoped she had got rid of.

226

When would the chance come again to put a bill before the House? And even supposing the Commons eventually accepted it, wasn't it more than likely the House of Lords would throw it out? She knew, from her travels about the country, how hard it was to make a dent in public opinion.

It would be easy to give in to despair, except for the certainty that tonight *something* had happened. As Kirsten Mackenzie had put it, tonight the dam had broken. Women's tentative plea for recognition and dignity had been ridiculed in the House. But the tactic would prove counter-productive. From now on, men too would be ridiculed, wherever there was an election. And that would be only part of a whole new campaign to make the world listen. Women had waited long enough.

She lay thinking of Kirsten Mackenzie and the sense of near-hostility between her and her father. Was that what a *grande affaire* could come to, in the end? Yet there had still been something between them, an electric awareness that had communicated itself to Carlie. She was sorry for Kirsten Mackenzie for the first time in her life. Coming to London had helped her to become more open-minded, less ready to divide human relations into good and bad.

Unable to sleep, she lay thinking of other ways in which coming to London had changed her. One thing was sure: she had been right to come. It hadn't been easy in the beginning, when she'd been so timid and raw, so aware of her Scottishness. She was often surprised, looking back, that she'd had the gumption to refute Donald's pleas and entreaties. Even now, she still missed him. There was a nexus of pain and responsibility somewhere in her thoughts that was labelled in his name.

Yet only by getting away had she been able to realize how stunted she was: by the rigid codes of behaviour at home, by the greater hypocrisies. London invested its comers with the almost overpowering gift of freedom: but it was a gift for adults only. She had been forced to grow up here and the extent of her adulthood was that she knew now how much farther she had to go.

Even so, she had been more sheltered than most. Her father had found her secretarial work and she had started to write for the Labour organ, *The Champion*, finding an easy editorial style that came naturally. In the beginning, she had found most of her friends through the Independent Labour Party, earnest young men and women who came to her father's apartments and sat till the small hours discussing how socialism could be made to work.

She'd joined the cycling corps which bicycled into Kent and Essex at the weekends, singing 'Jerusalem' on the village greens and sticking slogans urging the workers of the world to unite on gates and walls and once, in a facetious moment, on a cow's rump.

But there had been something less than satisfying about all this theory on the part of pipe-smoking clerks and adventurous lady teachers. She had gravitated to meetings in the End End, where she had met Aggie Fermoyle. And she had left her room in her father's flat and become a paying guest in the teeming household which made no secret that it needed her money. It was more cheerful and companionable than the Westminster apartments, for her father was often away on Parliamentary missions or sitting late at the House.

It had been a gesture, she saw now, coming to live in the East End, a reaction to the constant talk and posturing of the new wave of 'educated' radicals which had started in the colleges and crested in the comfortable London suburbs.

Perhaps unconsciously she had wanted back to the uncomplicated socialism of the Rows, arising out of need and not of theory. And certainly, here with the Fermoyles, she had found the dynamism she sought. For they lived on a level just above squalor, and then not always. And all around were the rope-makers, the stitchers of shirts, the biscuit-packers, waste-rubber cleaners and chicken-pluckers whose lowly-paid jobs barely kept body and soul together.

Carlie had not been able to believe it when Aggie told her what her own job was: making wooden seeds for raspberry jam. But it seemed it was so. And this restless, needle-sharp, warm-hearted Cockney was glad to have it for the money it brought in. But she wasn't prepared to leave it at that. She wanted the vote for women so that people like her mother, whom she adored, would have a say in the running of a better-organized society.

She modelled herself on Annie Kenney, the millgirl from the North who had succeeded in softening the upper-class image of 'the Pankhurst lot'. Except – and Carlie smiled in the dark – Aggie could be a lot funnier and more scurrilous when she addressed the East End crowds . . .

'You awake?' Carlie juddered to consciousness to see Aggie standing by the bedside, with a cup of tea in her extended hand. From downstairs came the squawks and shrieks of the younger Fermoyles getting ready for school. The sun poured into this bright front upper room that was the best in the house, something that never failed to tweak at Carlie's tender conscience.

'What d'you think?' Aggie demanded, watching critically as Carlie swallowed the tea. 'Now you've slept on it, what about last night, then? Are we going to let them get away with it?'

'I don't think so,' said Carlie slowly. 'Aggie, I'm going to see my father today. He *must* do something. So must Keir Hardie and any others with a vestige of humanity.'

'Gotta get to work,' said Aggie tersely. 'You do what you can, gel.'

The day was well advanced and the streets of Bow lively with horse-traffic and shoppers before Carlie set out. In Albert Road, a pre-school Fermoyle and her friends danced to the music of an organ-grinder with a singularly ugly little monkey holding out the cup for Carlie's penny. She had dashed off an angry article on the previous night's happenings for *The Champion*. Whether the editor would publish it was another matter, for she had pulled no punches.

The Central Lobby was quiet, reflective after the angry scenes of the night before. She sent in the customary Green Card to see if her father was available. In about half an hour he appeared, seeing off a deputation of men in cloth caps and rough clothes.

'A "Right to Work" deputation,' he told her. 'There's a million of them out there, Carlie, without jobs, and still the best we can offer them is soup kitchens and stone-breaking.' He looked tired and her resolution wavered slightly, but only for a moment.

They sat down on a leather bench in one of the stone alcoves. She came straight to the point.

'Paw – ' the old, childish nomenclature slipped out – 'you've got to help with the suffrage.' She could not keep the hurt from her expression. 'Last night it was as though we hadn't a friend in the House. But you believe in the female suffrage. You've always said so. Now you must come out and say it loudly. Rally support for us. Today we feel very let down.'

He seemed to be only half-listening to what she was saying, his gaze at some point beyond her right shoulder. But at last he looked at her, very directly, and said, 'Would you understand me, Carlie, if I said to you now that political dynamics are sometimes more important than political argument?'

'No, I wouldn't!' she cried hotly.

'I didn't think you would,' he said ruefully. 'Well, think of this. Think of how small and delicate a plant our Labour organization is today. A mere seedling. How can we feed it, nourish it? By getting more members in the House. How would you set about doing that, Carlie? Right. By public meetings, stirring the electorate. But you might also want to reach an accommodation with the Liberals over the seats you might contest – '

'You mean a secret pact?'

'If you like to call it that. And the Liberals in their turn might ask you not to rock the boat by pushing the female suffrage – '

She gazed at him in dismay and disbelief.

'I didn't think you were that sort of politician,' she said at last.

He stood up then, in front of her, and she had never seen him look so angry.

'There is only one sort of politician, Carlie, worth his salt. The one who thinks of the common good. And while the women's vote is important, it's more important that the starving be fed, the sick looked after and the out-of-work found jobs.'

He began to walk off up the corridor, but changed his mind and returned, to add: 'There's a time of great social upheaval coming. If we have a small but stable Labour Party in the House, we may be able to keep the balance. And I must give that aim my first priority. I expect you to understand that.'

'It's dishonest,' she said slowly.

He was very angry indeed now. She could see a little vein stand out on his left temple and she was frightened as well as angry.

'Dishonest? When have I ever been dishonest?'

'You were dishonest with my mother over Kirsten Mackenzie.' There, it was out, the other resentment that had been simmering somewhere in her mind since last night, when for the first time she had fully realized the bond between Kirsten and her father.

She was sorry the moment she'd said it. Dreadfully sorry. There were some pains no civilized human being should ever inflict on another, some territories no daughter, however privileged, should invade. It would never have surfaced had she not felt unbearably let down over the women's vote.

Her father's face had changed. It looked pinched and withdrawn, as though he were in physical pain.

'I am glad you think you have the right to judge me.' His voice shook over the ironic words. 'But I would have expected something kinder from you, Carlie.'

'I'm sorry,' she faltered.

'It is no matter,' he said coldly. 'Now let me get back to my work.'

'Even if you're not speaking to your father, can't we go

231

down to the Horticultural Hall at Westminster and join in the celebrations?' Aggie demanded.

She looked at Carlie's stubborn, freckled face and sighed impatiently. Sometimes the Scots with their slow-burning tempers, their broody silences, their insistence on working a moral issue to the bone, really infuriated her. At least, this specimen Scot, the only one she knew, did. She tried again. 'We've got twenty-nine Labour MPs now!' she exulted. 'Think of that, gel! Twenty-nine! And twenty-five Lib-Labs and it means the working-class have fifty-four representatives in Parliament now. Oh, come on! They'll have the champagne out down there. You gotta celebrate. Even me mum is, downstairs. She's sent out for eel pie and stout. It's a poor heart that never rejoices.' She punched Carlie's arm, but gently. 'Come on, gel. Put on your best bloomers and join the fun!'

Carlie gave a reluctant smile, but agreed. In the omnibus going towards Westminster, she observed: 'My father isn't the whole Labour movement, after all. I'm glad for the workers. Glad for people like my mother, who works so hard, away from all the excitement and adulation. *She* got my father in again at Dounhead, as much as his efforts.'

'I still think you should have swallowed your pride and gone up there to help him fight the election.'

'If he'd wanted me, he could have asked.' Carlie's tone was stiff.

'What I can't understand,' said Aggie, 'is your ma never coming down to London.'

'There isn't the money. MPs get nothing from the electors, you know, and Labour MPs have to depend on what they get from the compulsory fund. My mother never asks for anything above mere subsistence. She lives her life for and through my father. That's why –' Carlie's mouth worked and Aggie saw she was near to tears – 'that's why I hate what my father did to her through Kirsten Mackenzie.'

'We've been through all this,' said Aggie patiently. 'You think people should be bloody saints. That's because you've never fallen for nobody –'

'I was fond of Donald – '

'I mean real go-to-bed stuff,' said Aggie roughly. 'You're not like that, gel. You're a bit frigid and stand-offish, tell the truth.'

'Aggie!'

'Bit sure as death you are!'

'Have you done more than – kiss a man, then?'

'Naow, give over,' said Aggie. 'Last thing I want is to end up in the family way.'

'There! That makes two of us!' said Carlie, smiling and in better humour.

The Horticultural Hall was full of Labour people in a near-ecstasy of jubilation. Carlie did not see her father at first and half-hoped he had still not returned from Dounhead. She knew she would have to speak to him and yet there were hurts and contradictions inside her she had still not resolved. She vacillated between the wish to talk to him in private and the instinct that a rapprochement might be easier in public.

A young Nonconformist preacher who had been one of the earnest band of debaters at her father's flat came up to her now, beaming all over his innocent, well-scrubbed face, full of rumours as to who would get which office in the new government.

'John Burns is to look after the unemployed, I'm told,' he confided. 'And Beatrice Webb says he is pleased as a child.'

'He's the one who got fed-up with "working-class boots, working-class trains, working-class houses and working-class margarine," ain't he?' demanded Aggie. 'Good job they've given him the unemployed.'

Her irony was lost on the young preacher, who went on: 'Keir Hardie's in at Merthyr, of course, and he's tipped to lead Labour. Campbell-Bannerman will be the Liberal Prime Minister. So Scotland will be well represented, Miss Fleming, and justly so!'

Carlie scarcely heard him. She left Aggie in his clutches and made her way through the crowd to where she had just spotted her father.

'Well, daughter?' he greeted her. She was still close enough to him to know how much he might have wanted the job of looking after the unemployed.

'Well, father. 'Twas a famous victory.' She did not kiss him.

'Will you be coming to the opening of Parliament?'

'Will Mother be coming?'

'You know she never comes to London.'

'Then I fear I shall not be there either.'

'Cor! What a bunch of raggle-taggle gipsies we are!' sighed Aggie. She surveyed the little procession of women with an air of comical disillusion. 'We're supposed to be the very first suffrage procession in London, ain't we? Can't you get your end of the banner higher, Vera? Sylvia Pankhurst herself embroidered it, you should think a lot of it.'

Vera's riposte was sufficiently lively to send a nervous titter through the ranks, but the uneven procession at last set off, possibly four hundred in all and nearly all East Enders. Carlie joined step with Aggie while they raised a smaller banner, this one largely the work of the Fermoyle family even, Aggie boasted with a grin, down to the stout mark in the corner.

Perhaps raggle-taggle wasn't a bad description of them. Certainly by the time they reached Caxton Hall, a few hems of cheap skirts were beginning to dip and boots which had started out well-shined betrayed their age by the dust in their cracks. The police had made them furl their banners, in deference to the pomp and ceremony at Westminster, where Black Rod was on his way to signal the start of the new Parliament.

While Annie Kenney addressed them, they waited to hear if the King's Speech had mentioned women's suffrage. Perhaps Mrs Pankhurst knew already that it would not. When the news came, she suggested they should move to the House of Commons, where only twenty of them were

234

allowed in at a time to beard their MPs.

Neither Carlie nor Aggie was lucky in the ballot. They remained outside in the increasingly dispirited crowd.

Carlie knew the outcome, anyhow. Not one single member of the brave new regime could be persuaded to take up the cause.

'I feel I'm getting to know him,' said Aggie. She was standing in Central Lobby with Carlie, the banner disguised to look like a parasol over her arm and gazing up at the stained-glass, unresponsive features of St Andrew.

'Won't be long now,' said Carlie. She shivered a little.

'Any way I can help you young ladies?' The policeman's voice was excessively bland, his small brown eyes shrewd and suspicious.

'We are waiting to hear the result of the Plural Voting Bill,' Carlie told him, more crisply than she felt.

'You know,' put in Aggie irrepressibly, 'the one what will allow qualified women to be registered, and put you men in your place at last.'

'Been thrown out, it has,' said the constable. 'That I *can* tell you. So why wait around any longer?'

For answer, Aggie stripped the cover from the banner and she and Carlie hoisted it between them. It bore the legend: 'Women should vote for the laws they obey and the taxes they pay.'

Together they walked quickly through the Lobby, the policeman behind them. While he caught Aggie and confiscated the banner, Carlie mounted a bench and with her arm raised cried: 'Will the Liberal Government give justice to working women? Will Campbell-Bannerman give women the vote?'

A second policeman made a hasty appearance and dragged her from her perch. She kicked his ankle and watched him grimace in pain. Twisting nimbly from his grasp, she sprinted into St Stephen's Hall and on to the pavement outside. There she began again. A thin-faced, patrician girl in the movement's colours provided her with a soap-box to stand on. A crowd gathered round her, by no means all of it sympathetic, and a stone struck her a glancing blow on the head. Reeling, she saw the constable she had kicked so resoundingly cleave his way through the people like an axe.

Once in the cell, the shaking stopped. Carlie looked around her. There was a plank bed, a skilly and some prison clothes the wardress had left behind, with the instruction that she was to change into them. She had no intention of doing so. On top of the clothes was a yellow cloth number. Number Eighteen. She managed a grim smile.

She tried to remember the other instructions the woman had given her, not looking at her. You washed in that unbelievably tiny basin. In the morning, you were expected to empty your slops. Roll your bed. Clean your tins with three pieces of rag and a bath brick. Make sure they were really clean.

You would be given a pail of water in order to scrub the stool, bed, table, shelves and floor. Well, if they expected to break her spirit with that, they were up a gum tree. She didn't mind scrubbing. She had learned in the Rows, for Josie had always maintained a healthy contempt for housework.

The wardress came in the morning, bearing a pint pot filled with gruel.

'I don't think I can eat that,' said Carlie.

The woman ignored her words. 'You get that and six ounces of bread a day,' she intoned. 'You'll eat it, all right. I'll bring your sheets.'

'Sheets?'

'You're expected to sew at least fifteen a week.'

'I won't be here that long.'

The woman smiled at last. 'Thirty days, wasn't it? Four weeks. Sixty sheets.'

It was the sewing that was the worst. At school, she had been strapped with the tawse because she had never been able to make small, even stitches, and now it was as though the nervous embarrassment of these days came back, making her clumsy and reluctant. She watered the sheets with her tears.

The time passed slowly. She speculated on the shouts from other parts of the prison. Once she thought she heard Aggie's voice shouting, 'Don't give in.' In the beginning, anger and righteous indignation sustained her. But she couldn't eat the gruel and after four days she began to feel weak in the legs. Her thoughts tended to wander away from her. She lay on the bed, thinking of the games she and Donald had played in Dounhead House, the fat grapes and cold, creamy milk they had had from Aunt Tansy.

In a weak and silly way, she longed for Donald. It was foolish, because he would have forgotten about her by now. And she thought how she did not really like London, with its seductive air of knowing everything, its brassy restaurants and jangling cars. Only Aggie and the Fermoyles made it tolerable. Now that her father did not care about her any more. But she wouldn't think of him. She wouldn't. She wouldn't.

On the sixth day, the cell keys jangled and the door opened to reveal him. She flew into his arms and he patted her gently, telling her she would be released and so would Aggie. He had pulled strings, there was no doubt of that. But she accepted the means of escape, for there was nothing you could do for the others as long as you were locked up. And, in any case, when a by-election loomed, everyone was released as a matter of vote-catching. The Government had to accept the unpalatable truth that the Suffragettes – as the *Daily Mail* called them – were gaining support.

Back at his rooms, he served her with coffee and scones, inexpertly and clumsily. All around was the evidence of his 'bachelor' existence – dusty surfaces, unwashed cups and unfinished sandwiches. She knew none of this mattered to him.

'Well, Carlie,' he said at last, 'are we friends again?'

237

She hung her head. 'I'm sorry. If it's any consolation, I've been very unhappy.'

He patted her shoulder. 'You've suffered because I am what I am. I've taken a lot for granted in my life – your love and your mother's support.'

She looked at him in surprise. 'I never thought to hear you say it.'

He smiled at her. 'Well, perhaps it's time we were more open about things. I want to talk to you about Kirsten Mackenzie.'

Her mouth set in a line. 'Not her. Please.'

'Yes,' he insisted. 'Now you know all about – what happened between us, so I won't be mealy-mouthed. Your half-brother, Wallace, is completing his education in Grenoble. When he comes back, I want you to get to know him, to be friends. We are all adults now. And I want you to go and see Kirsten.'

'Why do you ask me to do this?' she demanded.

'Because she came to see me about you, while you were in Holloway. She was very concerned for you and very impressed by your courage.'

She made a protesting sound.

'She thinks you ought to be in Scotland, in Glasgow, strengthening the women's movement there. They need the campaign skills you've learned.'

'Go back to Glasgow?'

'Yes. But first see Kirsten. It would please me very much.'

'So you're Duncan's daughter.'

She had imagined that this would be Kirsten's greeting and had thought of her rejoinder : 'And Josie's.' Only it came out less seriously than intended and they both smiled. The resistance Carlie had felt towards Kirsten melted in her presence. She was gentle, warm, responsive.

'Carlie, I don't know what you think about me,' Kirsten began boldly, 'but I want you to know that, whatever it is, it doesn't matter. What matters is that we force this government into the realization that women must have the vote.'

She sighed. 'It's been a long struggle. You know that Emily Davies, who is still with us, handed the first petition for suffrage to John Stuart Mill in 1866? We sent a memorial to Gladstone in '84. The answer's always been the same. No, no and no.'

'They've got to crack some time,' said Carlie grimly.

'They'll crack before we do. It's got to be all-out war. Carlie. Intervention at every by-election. Meetings, rallies, deputations. And if these fail, attacks on property. Other symbolic acts that will draw attention to our case.'

'I'm ready for anything.'

'You'll find plenty of support in Glasgow. The Sunday-night street-corner meetings are well established. We've got teachers and nurses behind us, but we need to rally support from every quarter.'

A plain-faced girl brought a tray of tea and biscuits into Kirsten's office and laid it on the desk. Kirsten poured the tea and handed Carlie a cup. There was a somewhat constrained silence as they both sipped.

'How is your mother?' It was Kirsten who spoke first.

'Very well. When I say very well, I mean slowed down a bit with rheumatism. But the front room at home is still as full of strangers as ever. All wanting her time, her signature, her help.'

'Funny thing was,' said Kirsten, 'we got on rather well, your mother and I.' She did not look in Carlie's direction, but out through the window to the dusty London square. She threw down the pencil she was toying with and said, more briskly, 'People who question convention get into painful situations sometimes. We might find in the future that the convention of marriage will be outgrown. Especially when families are limited or some women choose not to have children at all.'

Carlie said nothing. She wanted to put her mother's case, her own case, for that matter, but it was suddenly irrelevant.

'When I first met your father,' Kirsten was saying, 'he was like a man in pain. Not physical pain. That's not the worst sort, in any case. He wanted to do so much, but he

239

had lost his religion and he didn't know how. I helped. It did not seem frivolous or evil at the time, and it doesn't seem so now.' She paused, then said gently, 'I sense you're at some sort of crossroads, too, Carlie. Am I right?'

Carlie nodded dumbly.

'Then go back to Glasgow. I think you will find work to do there.'

Chapter Thirteen

Kate was standing on a hillside looking out towards water and islands. It was a beautiful day. No mist. Just golden sunshine, bathing the pale strip of shore below, the little knots of dark green forest, the white farm cottages dotted here and there. These were the Western Isles, the beautiful, fabled places of song and legend, whence her forebears had sprung. It was right she should be here. Soon the silence would tell her why. Or the shadowy figure by her side.

'Findlay,' she said. She could not see the shadow's face, but he held out something she recognized as a clatch-iron. Little children went down into the dark on one of those. Findlay and his brother Tam.

'I had to wash them and put them to bed. They fell asleep as soon as they came up the pit.' Grannie Fleming? Had she spoken? Did she know the pit had taken Findlay as well as little Tam?

'Listen! Listen!' Kate cried. But there were so many voices. Her children playing down the burn. And Jack? Young Jack? 'Don't cry,' she told him. He had never wanted to leave Greenock. He had wanted his ships, his lovely ships. 'God will take away all pain,' she told him. *Shall I see my ships in heaven?* 'Yes, yes. And Clemmie too.'

'She's wandering,' said Tansy. She moved over to the set-in bed where Kate lay, propped up by half a dozen pillows, her old, veined hands plucking at the patchwork quilt. How pretty her hair looked, thought Tansy irrelevantly, the snow-white strands tumbling down over the clean cambric night-gown, curling and waving like a young girl's. It moved her as nothing else had. She gentled one of the roving, plucking hands in her own.

'Can I get you something, Mother?'

Kate's eyes opened and she stared.

'Who are you?'

'Tansy, Mother. Could you take a little broth?'

Kate's eyes closed again and she lapsed into sleep. Carefully, not to wake her, Tansy picked her way to the fireside and sat down on the rocking-chair. They'd bought this when her father was alive. It had been in the front room then. You were only allowed to sit in it with reverence, rocking it gently. Her mother had polished the arms till they glittered, and crocheted a white and crimson cover for the back. She'd taught them to take care of her treasured pieces. Poor mother! They were few enough.

'Would you like a cup of tea?' Josie whispered from the chair opposite. Tansy felt Josie's presence was the only one she could have borne. There had always been goodwill between them. Strange, when they were so different.

Tansy shook her head.

'I came as soon as I could, Josie.'

'I know.'

'You've been good to her. Better than a daughter.'

'I've been here,' responded Josie simply. 'And she never failed me. Are you sure you won't lie down? You must be exhausted. What was the crossing like from France?'

'Rough, but I don't get sick. Josie,' she burst out, 'she didn't know me. I wanted to come sooner. But Hamish needed me, too. He has cancer, Josie. He's in the hospital in Paris.'

'She's old and confused. Don't take on.' Josie rose and put a hand on Tansy's shoulder. 'Come into the front room. We can talk there.'

'It seems strange, coming back to Dounhead now,' said Tansy, staring round the little front parlour. Dounhead House was a convalescent home now, an annexe to one of the county hospitals. She had never found out what Lachie sold it for; he had refused to tell her. The faded print of 'The Light of the World' caught her eye and she did not see it now as she once had, artistically in bad taste, but as a sort of icon that had sustained her mother in her widowhood and old age.

'She wants you to have that picture,' Josie nodded, 'and her cameo brooch. The Apostle spoons have to be sent out to Jean in New Zealand and Isa gets her wedding-ring and châtelaine.'

'She said all this?' asked Tansy, dumbfounded.

Josie smiled. 'Not once, but many times. In the winter when we had a chat by the fire, she liked to portion out her bits and pieces. Jack's to get the family Bible, Duncan poor old Findlay's few bits of books, and Paterson the wag-at-the-wa' clock, if he wants it.'

'What about you?'

'There's a tea-cloth with Ayrshire embroidery I've always admired. And the rocking-chair. She says I've to take care of it.' Josie dabbed her eyes. 'She'll make a lady of me yet.'

Kate felt as though she stayed out of her body for longer and longer spells. The spirit had to get used to its new freedoms. Oh yes, she believed in the spirit. What else was it dragged you through the days when the flesh was tired and unresponsive? It was tugging now, like a ship from its mooring.

'There, Kate. Do you see it? The steamship *Comet*. First ever built. Built in Scotland.' There was pride in her father's voice. 'Never forget you saw it. Tell your children.' Her feet had been bare on the gorse and heather, the skin of the soles so hardened she could run as fast as the red deer. She saw them leap now, the red deer, against the waterfall. Was there ever sight so lovely? No wonder she came back to look.

Voices saying 'Mother.' Was that Jack? And that Duncan? Faces hovered. Other young faces. Too many. She sat up suddenly and looked around the room. The faces turned towards her. Was her Duncan's beard grey, like that of an old man?

She held out her arms to them. There were things she wanted to say. Don't grieve. I want to go. But they receded so fast they became a blur, caught up in whirling sky and sea and sunlight. She saw the Land of the Apple Trees, Tir-Nan-Og, the beautiful land of the leaping deer. And she cried as loudly as she could, 'Findlay!' for she wanted him there, too, and in an instant she saw him.

Josie folded back the snow-white sheet over the lifeless face, put the pennies on the eyes. There was nothing to fear. This was a state of peace. And she had seen it many times in the Rows. These tears that fell from her own eyes were immaterial, and soon would dry.

Carlie saw her Aunt Tansy off on the train after the funeral. Nearly all the family had attended, but Donald had not been there, a fact that grieved his mother. She and Donald had become totally estranged as the years went by and he had even refused to meet her in Glasgow for a brief talk. His relations with his father Lachie were a little better, but Lachie seldom left Arran now and had not come for the funeral.

Carlie had at one time shared Donald's resentment against his parents, particularly Tansy because of the extravagant way she and Hamish Macleish appeared to live on the Continent. But she had come to understand that there were always two sides to a story. Josie pointed out that it was Lachie who had let down the marriage in the first place, by his absences: Tansy was an open-hearted if ambitious woman who needed to give and receive love, and if she was fashionably and, yes, extravagantly dressed, it had to be remembered that Macleish was younger and the worry of losing his devotion surely would be always present . . .

When Tansy had pleaded with her, 'Try to see him, Carlie. Keep an eye on him for me,' Carlie had not resisted. Ever since she had returned to Glasgow, she had hoped Donald would get in touch. There had been times when she had been too busy to think of him – when she had been moving into her apartments and going the rounds of the newspapers to line up some freelance journalism. All this and her work for the suffrage kept her busy enough, but at the back of her mind were always the wish and the hope to see Donald.

She knew, of course, that he worked for Finn. It was on the shop floor, too, although he'd been offered something better. It was as though, Sandia had told her, he wanted to defy the family at every turn. Sandia had warned her that Donald had changed out of all recognition, half-hinting that Carlie would be well advised to have nothing more to do with him.

But the need to reassert herself with him was strong in her. She was curious and proprietary. He could not have changed so much she would not be able to re-establish some kind of relationship.

Rather than write to him, she decided she would simply go to the factory one evening and wait till he came out. It did not seem such a good idea when she got there, because the men looked so much alike in their grimy overalls. But she spotted him, in the middle of a group, and waved tentatively, calling his name.

'Carlie!' He was, she realized, embarrassed at being accosted in front of his work-mates. He scraped the gutter with the toe of his boot, keeping his hands in his pockets and his head low. 'What are you doing *here*?'

'Sorry,' she said immediately. 'I just wanted to see you. Didn't you know I'd come back?' They began to walk slowly up the street.

'I'd heard.'

'But you didn't get in touch?'

'That was your prerogative. You were the one who went away.'

She said nothing, deciding that it had been a mistake, after all, to see him. What Sandia had said was true. Even his voice had changed and was rough, gibing, goading, bitter, the aggressive weapon of the Glasgow proletariat. Once he had spoken carefully, without accent, and once his hands with their clubbed, tubercular nails had been as white as a woman's. Now they were filthy with oil. His hair was long and unkempt. Worst of all was the expression on his face, hard, defensive, giving nothing away. But she tried again.

'Your mother asked me to try and see you. Couldn't we meet somewhere, when you've had time to change? What about the Ca'doro? We could have tea – high tea.'

'Who's paying?' He gave her an amused, speculative glance, but there was a glimpse of the old, affectionate spirit and her heart rose.

'I will, if I have to,' she retorted. 'Shall we say seven, then?'

She did not go home to her own place, but bought an evening paper and read it in the restaurant. Lord Kelvin, the former Sir William Thomson, had died and was to be buried next to Sir Isaac Newton in Westminster Abbey. She felt a twinge of chauvinism, wondering why he could not have been laid to rest in his own city. His distinctions and honours, one hundred and eighty of them, took up a full column of print.

Donald appeared on the stroke of seven, cleaned up and wearing a good tweed overcoat she recognized from the old days. But she was shocked all over again at his thinness and the stoop of his back. The resentment she had shared with Tansy had dissipated. She was back on his side again, whatever he'd done, however he'd behaved. He was simply Donald.

'So London couldn't hold you?'

'Why didn't you ever write?'

They faced each other like jousting knights.

'I knew you wouldn't stay there.'

'I suppose it was your way of getting back at me. You always were a spoiled child.'

A buxom waitress staring down at them, thinking they were involved in argument, was surprised to see the smiles break on their faces. She took their order and retired in confusion.

'So you didn't find yourself another man, then?'

'What happened to you? Opted out, have you?'

She suddenly grabbed his oil-grimed right hand and stared at the orange-tipped fingers. 'Nicotine. That must do your chest a lot of good.'

'I take a drink as well. And go about with women.' The tone was joking, but his stare was steady, challenging.

She dropped his hand, suddenly frightened. 'What's happened to you?' she demanded. 'I don't know you.'

He took a battered tin case from an inner pocket, offered her a cigarette, which she refused, and lit up.

'I was a big, soft lump of a laddie when you went away,' he said, 'and now I'm a man. It's as simple as that.'

'That's not what we're talking about.'

'Isn't it?'

'We're talking about standards. Aren't you doing a job beneath your ability? And why don't you take care of your health?'

He smoked furiously for several seconds, tapping non-existent ash from the tip of his cigarette. His nostrils were white, which always happened when he got angry. The waitress placed two plates of sole and chips in front of them and Carlie began to pick at the food, while he ignored his.

At last he said in a low, bitter voice: 'What sort of standards are we on about? My mother's? Gad about Europe and take all you can from any mug who'll stand it? My father's? Talk about improving the lot of your pitmen and then go away and paint pictures?'

'I just mean ordinary, decent standards,' she protested.

'Well, I wasn't taught ordinary, decent standards,' he gibed. 'So I've had to make my own.' He lit a second cigarette from the first.

'You remember when you went away to London? It took me a while to forgive you for that, but it was a good thing for me, in the end. I was too dependent on you. A bad thing, that. But I was a mess. I didn't know where I stood with anything – my health, my work, my parents, you, life.'

'I had my problems, too,' she protested. 'We've all got to grow up.'

'Yes.' He gave her a brooding look. 'Well, I made a great discovery. I discovered I wanted to do a very ordinary job and be with very ordinary folk. I discovered I had no ambition, in the ordinary sense, except to live from day to day.'

'I see.' But she did not.

He shook his head at her. 'You don't see. I wanted – I suppose I wanted the solidarity of being ordinary. Let me put it this way. I remember, when we lived in the big house and you came up from the Rows to play with me, I envied you because you were going back there. Where lives were lived. Not played at. Lived.' He gave a rueful laugh. 'I suppose I've ended up more of a socialist than you or even your father.'

She said, 'I think it's just a way of getting back at your parents. Particularly your mother.'

He spread his hands. 'Could be. Who's to understand the springs of his own nature? But there, that's the way it is.'

'What about the women you spoke of?' she asked, quickly.

'I don't need to tell you that sort of thing,' he responded moodily. 'Shall we say I haven't been all I should be, and leave it at that?'

'I'm not your moral arbiter.'

'Exactly.'

'I'd just like to know the facts, that's all.'

'I'm not particularly proud that I found out what it was all about from a married woman.'

'Who?' she demanded, pale-faced.

'My landlady's daughter-in-law. Her man's no good to her. Lost a leg in the Boer War.'

'I see.'

'There've been others. You asked for the truth. I even see Alisdair's wife sometimes. Not *con amore*, however. She's another kettle of fish entirely.'

'Alisdair's wife? You mean Tina?'

He nodded. 'Their marriage is a total disaster. She can't live with him, and she can't make up her mind to leave him.'

'So she comes to you?'

'Not exactly. I look in on them from time to time. He prescribes for me, you know. She started writing to me – '

'What sort of letters?'

'Pitiful. Saying she thought she was falling in love with me.'

Carlie looked grim. 'Did you encourage her?'

'What do you take me for? Of course not. I can listen, though. And she has to talk to somebody. Their marriage has never been consummated.'

Stunned, Carlie questioned, 'Whose fault is it?'

'Hers to begin with, she says. Then his. Now it's blurred. All I know is her life's a torment.'

She said slowly, 'She probably sees you as a vulnerable person, like herself. You are, you know. You've got a skin too few.'

He shook his head. 'Not any more. Not me. You're the vulnerable one at the moment, Carlie. Am I not right?'

Sudden tears shot into her eyes at his perception.

'I'm missing my political friends, like Aggie Fermoyle.'

'Glasgow will soon fold its hospitable wings about you,' he said, a gentle note in his voice for the first time. 'This is where you belong, after all.' She stared at him to see if the warmth was false. Apparently it wasn't. 'I love this place. You know the Yanks think it's a copybook city? They send folk over to see how our trams are run and to praise our councillors! I can see what's underneath, but I still love it.'

Afterwards, they dodged the clattering, swaying trams and he walked with her back to her rooms.

'You must take care of yourself,' she warned him as they parted. 'You're too thin for my liking.'

'I'm tougher than I look,' he promised her. He touched her chin with his forefinger, but did not kiss her. 'I'll be seeing you.'

The smart little donkey clattered along the edge of the tram rails in Sauchiehall Street, led by a page-boy in a green uniform and drawing a cart laden with flowers.

Sandia drew Dandy Peel's attention to it.

'It's going to the Willow Tea-room. Miss Cranston does the flowers herself, although they say the architect Macintosh has the final say,' she told him. He looked covertly at her face, smiling a little, knowing how she longed to pattern herself on the stylish Kate Cranston, yet not having the latter's totally elegant touch nor her disdain for public opinion, which on occasion found the Cranston élan too much for the Glasgow decorum.

'Your tea-rooms have more – more warmth and genuine homeliness,' he told her. 'I prefer them, myself. But if you want to eat at the Willow Tea-room, let's go there and I'll help you criticize.'

Kate looked up at the white façade of 'The Willow' as they approached. She sniffed. Never mind what visiting pundits from abroad said about it, or the raptures the papers went into over its modernity, she thought this brainchild of the famous Charles Rennie Macintosh was on the plain side, too severe and simple to linger in the mind. Climbing the winding stairway to the Room de luxe, however, and seated on a Macintosh-designed ladderback chair, she could not restrain a vexatious sigh of admiration for the three red camellias and their dark-green glossy leaves, so discriminatingly arranged by Kate Cranston herself on a tiny willow-pattern soup plate at the centre of the table.

'Drips and dangles,' commented Dandy, grinning as he took in the hanging lights, drips of pink glass, in the centre of the room. The lights in particular had come in for some gentle newspaper satire. Neil Munro had written about his coalman Duffy, a beloved contemporary fictional figure, being shown round the Willow and asking what all those 'drips and dangles' were. 'Airt, that's Airt,' he'd been informed, and Dandy's look of smirking enjoyment showed it was an attitude he shared, however Philistine.

But Sandia handed the palm to the Willow. The lights, she thought, were exquisite. The waitresses wore white dresses, chokers of white or pink pearls and even if some of them looked like glossy bolsters, the whole atmosphere breathed luxury, gentility, taste. She looked not without a faint wistfulness at Dandy and said, 'It's funny. Coming here has helped me to make up my mind.'

Heedless of the interested matrons seated at the tables nearby, he took her gloved hands between his and said tenderly, 'About what, my love?'

'About us marrying quickly. I think we should. I have got the tea-room business out of my system.' She gave a quick, half-rueful smile. 'I think.'

'I'll make you forget all about it,' he promised. He had grown very solid and handsome with the years, his complexion ruddy and fresh, his greying hair crisp and distinguished. He had made a comfortable small fortune in Belfast and was prepared now to hand the business there over to his younger brother, while he would set up a subsidiary firm in Glasgow.

This was what he had come to Glasgow to tell her, those months ago when she had returned from her trip to Canada. He had not come tentatively, but with the plans of a man who has given the matter a great deal of thought.

He still carried that letter she had sent him, asking to see him again. It was in his wallet, its edges torn and tattered from all the times it had been abstracted and looked at. He had not answered because his wife, Phidelma, had been dying. But afterwards, he had seen the only way to any kind of happiness was to return to Glasgow. To offer to stay there, in the city Sandia loved, if she would marry him.

She knew Dandy's determination that they should marry was something she could never resist. Did not want to resist. But there had been details. Such as her tea-rooms. And now, sitting in the Room de luxe, she knew this was a part of her life she could afford to let go. She wanted time with Dandy and they had wasted too much of it already.

'I'll give up the management of the tea-rooms,' she said, with finality. 'You'll have to look after the financial side for me, Dandy. My job is going to be staying at home and looking after you.'

'Your job is to go on looking as beautiful as you do today.'

Dandy's tribute was no empty one. In her thirties, Sandia had looked handsome, middle-aged and verging on the dowdy. Now in a flowing pale grey dress, a wide-brimmed hat lavishly trimmed with lace flowers, her parasol resting on the chair beside her, she looked like an Edwardian rose that had suddenly opened its petals to the sun. He felt desire for her swamp him almost to the point of disorientation.

She smiled at him. 'Hadn't we better get down to Wylie and Lochhead's? We've got to choose some furniture if we're taking that house in Pollokshaws.'

He escorted her back down the winding staircase and into the street, clumsy in his adoration.

'I wish we were marrying this very afternoon,' he whispered in her ear. 'I can't wait much longer!'

She laughed at him from under the big brim of her flowery hat, suddenly remembering the boy who'd brought violets to her in the West End Park and the sweet summer kisses behind the rhododendron bushes. It seemed impossible so much lay between then and now. She gripped his hand hard, like pinching herself to make sure it was all true.

By the time Sandia and Dandy had inspected most of the stock of Wylie and Lochhead's large emporium, and decided on a number of items they wanted, they had also somehow reached agreement on the wedding date: five weeks forward, if all the arrangements could be made in time. It would be a quiet wedding, after all, but Sandia wanted it to be as perfect in its way as she could organize. A ninon dress in café-au-lait, a Paris hat with pale pink silk roses, a wedding breakfast in the first tea-room, the one dearest to her heart . . . all these had to be arranged.

They decided they would ask Alisdair to be best man, and thought there was no time like the present for dropping in on Tina and Alisdair to acquaint them of their plans.

'Imposing,' said Dandy. It was his first visit to Alisdair's house and consulting rooms in the West End. Sandia pulled the bell again, remembering it was probably the parlour maid's afternoon off and that Tina's old cook, in the basement, could not manage the stairs. If there was no reply, it must mean Tina was out. Sandia made a little moue of disappointment at Dandy.

But the door opened abruptly, and Tina stood there looking at them, almost as though she had never seen them
before. The greeting died on Sandia's lips as she saw her
sister-in-law had been weeping. Her hair was dishevelled and
her eyes were puffy. What was more, a large red area stood
out like an angry birthmark on one cheek.

Sandia stepped quickly into the hall, dragging Dandy
behind her and closing the door discreetly. She rather than
Tina led the way to the sitting-room, where Sandia put her
arms round the girl and sat her down on the sofa. A snuffly
Pekingese peered curiously up at the trio from a hearthrug
at the dying fire.

'Where's Alisdair?' demanded Sandia. It was outside his
consulting hours and she suddenly had the feeling he was in
the house somewhere.

'Upstairs,' said Tina.

'Have you two been having words?'

Tina seemed to pull herself together, with an effort. She
tucked her hair up off her neck, wiped her eyes with the
back of one hand and tried to smile at Dandy.

'What makes you think that? I – I knocked my – my
cheek on the corner of a cupboard in the kitchen. It brought
tears to my eyes. Sorry! It's lovely to see you. Can I offer
you some tea?'

'Tell them!' The harsh command came from the doorway.
Alisdair stood there, in shirt-sleeves and waistcoat, his fists
balled and his expression alarming in its intensity. He came
forward, not taking his eyes from his wife, and shouted,
'Tell them! Tell them about this mockery we call a
marriage! Tell them who struck you –'

'I won't tell them!' cried Tina. 'If anything's to be told,
it must come from you.'

He looked down at her as though he despised her, as
though, in fact, he was going to strike her once more. Dandy
rose in alarm and restrained him, saying, 'Calm down, man.
This is none of our business. Do you want us to go?'

Suddenly the fight had all gone out of Alisdair and he
collapsed into a chair, weeping.

Sandia said, appalled and helpless, 'What is this terrible thing all about?' Alisdair threw up his arms and began to protest, 'Beat me! Whip me! Cur that I am. I struck a woman. I struck my wife –'

Sandia said, 'Dandy will get you some brandy. Pull yourself together.' She tugged Alisdair's head back gently by the forelock, looking down at him compassionately. 'I'll take Tina up to her bedroom, till you've got a grip on yourself. Unburden yourself to Dandy. He's a man of the world. He will understand.'

Upstairs, she tried desperately to get Tina to tell her what was the matter. The girl's mouth set mutinously. 'It is nothing I can talk about.'

'Are you not suited to each other, as lovers?' probed Sandia gently. 'Is that what it is?'

'I did love him!' Tina burst out passionately. 'I couldn't show it at first. I was brought up to think – that sort of thing was – well, disgusting.'

'Oh, not between husband and wife!' Sandia sighed, discomfited.

'He doesn't want *me*! That's the root of it. If he had come to me, been patient with me, it could have been all right. But we live like strangers. I would leave him, but he would never survive the disgrace. It would affect his practice. And he's a kirk elder –'

'They can be the biggest sinners of the lot.'

' "Thou shalt not be found out," ' quoted Tina bitterly. 'He reads the lesson on Sunday: "The greatest of these is charity," but it's hypocrisy that keeps him going. Keeps both of us going.' She dissolved into broken, heart-rending weeping. Sandia let her cry for a little, then said in a brisk, sharp voice, 'Come on, now, Tina. This will get you nowhere. Wash your face, tidy your hair, and we'll go back downstairs again.'

The girl did as she was bid. Sandia saw that she was desperately thin and highly-strung, nervous in her movements, and her heart moved with a strange sorrow, knowing she was looking on suffering that was genuine and possibly incurable.

When she had finished her toilette, Tina gave her a shaky smile and they went back downstairs. Alisdair had put on his jacket and rose as they entered, his face pale and expressionless.

'If you are both so unhappy, perhaps the best thing to do is part.'

It was Dandy who spoke. The three others looked at him, but said nothing at first. Then Alisdair, looking tentatively at his wife, said in a low voice, 'Is that what you want? Do you want to go back to your father?'

She shook her head.

'That old man.' There was a volume of bitterness in Tina's voice. 'He has love for nothing but his money.'

'You have no other relatives you'd like to live with? Aunts? Cousins?'

Bright-eyed, Tina answered, 'None.'

'You are welcome to remain here.' Alisdair spoke to her directly. 'What happened today will not happen again. You have my word on that.'

'I believe you.' She gazed back at him quiveringly, but dry-eyed.

'Shall we try again? I shall respect your privacy.' He turned to the others, changing once again before their eyes into the weighty, ponderous young doctor. 'She runs my household well, you know. I owe her a debt of gratitude for that.'

'You owe me nothing.' Tina rose wearily. 'Sandia and Dandy are here to testify to my words: I'll not desert you, husband. Not yet. I have nowhere else to go.'

When they were back in the street later, Sandia said to Dandy, 'We forgot to ask Alisdair. To be best man.'

'In the circumstances, maybe it had better be Finn,' suggested Dandy.

Sandia nodded. They had chosen Alisdair in the first place because Kitty's time for her first confinement was near. Now they would have to persuade Finn to come to the wedding without her, as she refused to be seen out-of-doors in her advanced state of pregnancy.

'Just so long as he doesn't try to persuade us to buy his new model car,' said Sandia.

'Maybe we should have one?'

'What? At fifty miles an hour? You won't get me risking my neck as Kitty does. She actually drives one of these machines, you know.'

After this brief exchange, they lapsed into silence. They were both stunned by the misery of the atmosphere they had just left. The way Tina had said 'Husband' when she promised Alisdair she would not leave him had struck an icy chord in Sandia's mind. She was about to say, 'Alisdair was very close to Mother,' but did not see what that had to do with the present impasse, or why she should think it now. Except that Clemmie's emotional chains had been cast-iron and that Alisdair had been the youngest, the most cherished, the one of whom so much had been expected in terms of loving response.

The thoughts were too inchoate for her to express them to Dandy. Instead, she looked at him wordlessly and saw her own bewilderment reflected in his face. They floundered in a morass of pity and perplexity.

PART
FOUR

♦

Chapter Fourteen

Finn Fleming drove his car into the yard behind the factory, parked in lonely isolation and began the walk towards his office with the air of a man with something on his mind.

Kitty had told him that morning she was pregnant again. She had been a little tearful. With the younger of their two infant daughters, Mairi, still not 'shortened' from the long gowns into the little frocks that indicated the toddler stage, it was no wonder. He felt a cad and yet another part of him looked forward to the joyful possibility of a son.

These had been productive years for the sisters. Sandia, to Dandy Peel's unabated delight, had produced a 'late bloom', a daughter named Catriona. But it was clear Kitty would have welcomed a rest before trying for the son she and Finn both wanted. And, Finn thought grimly, he could have done without the morning sickness and the evening frailty of a reproachful spouse, when the factory seemed set for yet another period of financial crisis and technical upset.

'Mornin', sur,' said the old man sweeping the yard, touching his cap respectfully.

'Morning, Willie,' Finn responded. For a moment, he envied the other the simple satisfaction of his job. But then the works caught up with him again. There was a smell, a sound and a purpose that entered into him each morning so that he knew all over again no way of life could have any meaning for him but this one. He was prepared to give it everything, every last ounce of inspiration, dedication, energy, guile. It was his in a way not even Kitty was his. He had built it up from that crazy, erratic first 'Fleming Flyer' into one of the few concerns to survive in the West of Scotland after the initial, lunatic burst of enthusiasm for the new mode of transport had waned.

His partner, Peter Frensham, had been one of those determined to bring the car-manufacturing industry to Scotland, but he and Finn had clashed over the vexed question of whether they should buy component parts from specialist manufacturers, or make their own. 'We are car *makers*,' Finn had argued, 'not assemblers.' But when they had changed from making bi-bloc engines to mono-bloc, the plant installation had been heavily expensive and, angry over the massive retooling, Frensham was now sulking over the gambling tables in the South of France, leaving Finn to get on with it.

It was difficult, trying to keep up in technical sophistication while preparing to meet the demand for more cars that would surely come when the roads of Scotland were at last improved; difficult to produce the sort of solid, hard-working, dependable car that would appeal to the solid, hard-working middle-class buyer, while providing the refinements that one's *amour-propre* as designer demanded.

But hardest of all was coping with the labour problems that had suddenly intensified over the last year. It would have been optimistic to think he would escape them altogether, when industrial unrest was sweeping the country in a sprawling, untidy wave that crept and eddied into small and unexpected quarters.

But his original workers had been enthusiasts like himself, not unmindful of the rate for the job but prepared to waive the importance of a rise when times were tough. Not so the recent influx of workers needed to operate the new plant. And the final irony was that it was his cousin Donald who was organizing them in their demands and he had given Donald the job and therefore the power.

Donald was waiting for him now in his office, as he had requested last night before going home. Accurately, Finn tossed his Fedora on to the hat-rack and turned to meet Donald's saturnine gaze.

'You wanted me?' Donald's tone was deliberately laconic.

'Is it all right for you to be here, without your committee, then?' Finn decided to try some broad Glasgow satire.

'It's all right.' Donald acknowledged the broadside with a faint grin and nod.

'I didn't think you could go to the bathroom without them.' Finn's tone had hardened.

'Look here –'

'No, you look here. I'm fed up with all the circumlocutions and hedging of the real issue. I'm fed up with being shouted down by shop-floor bullies –'

'You'd better get used to it.' Donald's retort was abrasive. 'These men out there are your partners and you can't go on making cars without them. Come down off your high horse and listen to them.'

'I know what they're saying.' Finn's voice dropped and softened. 'They want more money and I can't do it, Donald. Not now. I'm over-extended as it is. I went into hock to get that plant, but if I hadn't the factory would have faded away. There would have been no future, no future at all for these men out there.'

'I don't believe Frensham can't raise more capital,' said Donald. His brows were down and he was glaring truculently at Finn. 'Leo Chiozza Money says that half the national income goes to one-nine of the population, and Frensham and his family are part of that one-ninth.'

'I've read *Riches and Poverty*, too,' said Finn drily. 'I'm not half as impressed by it as you seem to be.'

'Why have we seen so little of Frensham recently?' Donald ignored the gibe about Money's book and went straight to the heart of the question.

'I can't tell you that.' Finn had considered taking Donald into his confidence over Frensham's present ambivalent attitude, but had decided it would serve no purpose. 'But I got you here, on your own, so that I can put the rest of my cards on the table. If you insist on a wage increase, I shall have to lay men off. Part of the new plant will be inoperable. I shall have to go back to buying certain components from abroad. And how long we could keep going on such a basis, I don't know. Possibly six months.'

'How am I to put this to men whose wages can't keep up with the cost of living?' demanded Donald. 'What cost a pound in 1900 costs twenty-five shillings now.'

'Can't you try?' Finn was conscious of pleading.

Donald laughed, an expostulatory sound that had no mirth in it. 'Can't you see that with all this talk of syndicalism, they've glimpsed a workers' paradise? It started with the industrial workers in New York, after all. Your country.'

'Are you telling me that if they strike, it's not just the money that's behind it?'

'Certainly. The harder nuts want nothing less than the take-over of the factory. After they've softened you up with strike after strike.'

Finn gave an incredulous laugh. 'Some of them can barely write their names! They couldn't run a go-cart, never mind a factory. Come on, Donald. Let's stop talking fairy-tales and get down to brass tacks.'

'I'm sorry.' Donald's eyes refused to meet his cousin's. 'I don't think anything I can say now will avert a strike.'

Finn swore. His face was taut and strained. 'Then do your bloody worst,' he said shortly.

He watched Donald walk away along the works corridor, then on an impulse called him back.

'I hear you're seeing quite a lot of Carlie.' His gaze was savage. 'Does she know you're still going around with Chrissie Macausland?'

On her way towards the train for Dounhead, Carlie saw

the parade of strikers from Finn's factory marching towards a demonstration in George Square, Donald at their head. He saw her hovering on the pavement and gave her a brief, preoccupied smile. Something twisted inside her at the sight of him, so thin, shabby and febrile. What had he said? 'I'm tougher than I look.' She begged leave to doubt it. He looked barely strong enough to hold up his end of the home-made banner.

Still, she had to leave him to his fate, today at least. She had other things to worry her. She had to try and tell her mother she was seeing her half-brother, Kirsten's son Wallace, who had turned up in Glasgow to carry out some research work on wireless telegraphy. Not only seeing him, but liking what she saw. Her father had written to her, explaining that Wallace had been brought up in the country and was somewhat shy of meeting people. He felt sure Carlie would help him to make some contacts.

It seemed like a sort of treachery to her mother, that was the trouble, yet if she had refused to meet Wallace it would have upset her father. Why did she have to have such complicated family relationships? There was the further complication that she liked Wallace for his own sake.

She hadn't known what to expect. An anarchist show-off, perhaps, or an intellectual high-flyer. In the event, the result of her father's grand passion was a quiet, conventional young man, greatly taken up with the niceties of removing his hat, pulling out restaurant chairs and opening doors for her.

She had recognized some element of herself in him, a sort of quiet, amused balance. He had her father's gaze, direct and questioning, and Kirsten's rounded chin. He was obviously dedicated to his scientific career, impressed by being in the city where the great Lord Kelvin had lived and worked.

'He started it all, you know,' he told her, 'with the result he published in 1853.'

'What result was that?'

'If I mentioned things like square roots and electrical circuits and oscillation, would they mean anything to you?'

'Not a great deal!'

'I thought not. The old man's search was to relate electricity to ponderable matter and he admitted at the end of his days he knew little more than when he started out. There's humility for you. If politicians had that kind of humility, we should all be much better off.'

Startled, she had led him on about politics but found he had a great resistance to them. He was suspicious of Lloyd George, disliked Asquith and would not talk about the Labour Party.

'My foster-parents didn't bring me up to take an interest,' he explained. 'I don't see any reason to question their values.' He had met her curious gaze blandly and Carlie had decided there and then he was a lot more complex than she'd at first realized.

The Rows at Dounhead hadn't changed all that much, even if Blériot *had* just flown the Channel, thought Carlie. There were still the communal privies, still the smelly middens with pig bins alongside where householders dumped their potato peelings for the pig farmers to collect. Someone had told her about Keir Hardie bringing a Government minister out to see such houses and keeping him standing near the middens as long as he could, in the hope he would pass out from the smell. On the other hand, the little houses of the Rows themselves sparkled with self-respect and elbow-grease, their windows bright with pot plants and plaster ornaments, clean lace curtains looped back with gleaming brass.

The sour-milk cart passed her as she turned into the Rows, and farther along she saw children clustered round a great, grave, Russian dancing bear, gyrating with immense offended dignity on its hind legs. It was difficult to describe the feelings aroused in her by these familiar sights. About equal parts outrage and identification. It was home. Warm, rough, hospitable. It was not at all difficult to understand why Josie wanted to stay here. It had a dimension not to be found elsewhere.

She clicked up the sneck of her mother's door and surprised Josie by the sink, peeling potatoes. Her aunt, Nellie

Daly of the swollen legs, had died two years before, and Josie lived alone except for those times when Duncan came back from London, having refused Carlie's invitation to live with her in Glasgow.

Pictures of Duncan were everywhere, on mantelpiece and dusty dresser. Duncan with Keir Hardie, Ramsay Macdonald. Duncan with Bernard Shaw and the Webbs. Duncan with his friends from the Socialist International – the Belgian Camille Huysmans, the Frenchmen Vaillant and Jaurès. Duncan in America, outside Jane Addams's settlement houses for the poor in New York. Duncan with the roustabout Socialist Tom Mann, when he'd preached syndicalism in New Zealand . . . He doesn't belong to us, Carlie thought all over again. All she has are his pictures.

It made her specially warm in her greeting. She had brought a box of cakes from Glasgow and handed these to Josie now, expressing the wish for a good, strong cup of tea. While Josie made the tea, she kept up a stream of gossip – about Kitty's babies, Sandia's little girl, the freelance work she did for the Glasgow newspapers, her weekends working for the Suffragettes, mostly nice girls from Hillhead and Langside, she told her mother, but too few from the poorer districts.

Josie toasted her knees under the big print pinny and fed the grate with lumps of shiny coal while she listened. At last Carlie found the courage to bring up the subject of Wallace. She did it as matter-of-factly as she could, then turned to Josie with a vulnerable face and said, 'You don't mind my seeing him, Maw, do you?'

Josie studied her feet for what seemed like an interminable age. Then she looked up and with a slow, unconvincing smile said, 'I can't see the harm to it.' But two fat tears fell on to her hands.

'Then I won't see him again,' Carlie cried. 'Not if it upsets you.'

Josie found her composure. 'Poor boy,' she said. 'What would he think if you turned against him? He's done nothing wrong.'

'Maw,' Carlie lied, 'Kirsten Mackenzie means nothing to my father now. It was all a very long time ago.'

Josie gave her daughter a very clear-sighted, direct look.

'Learn not to give too much of yourself to any man, Carlie,' she advised cryptically. 'If I had my time again, I would be my own woman and campaign for women in Parliament. I would like to see women far less dependent on men.'

'You could have been Dounhead's answer to Mrs Pankhurst,' Carlie teased. She was glad to have got the Wallace business over and prepared to forget the uncharacteristic tinge of bitterness in her mother's last words. As for not giving too much of yourself to any man, she remembered Donald walking in the Glasgow street, his restlessness and discontent, and wondered if it was already too late for her.

The rain pelted down on the Glasgow cobbles and washed the bright colour of the trams even brighter as they sped along their water-logged grooves like so many drunken dowagers. In Pettigrew and Stephens they waited in vain for customers and in the Room de luxe at the Willow Tearooms the waitresses had no one to serve till the downpour was over. August, and Glasgow steamed like a tropical city in the grip of the monsoon while the rain impartially washed Kelvinside mansion and Gorbals slum.

'Lovely holiday weather.' Carlie had just stepped outside the newspaper office and put up her umbrella when someone nudged under its shelter and uttered the customary banality.

'Donald! Look at you! You're soaked!' she scolded.

He steered her in the direction of the Ca'doro. 'Then join me in a cup of tea while I dry off.'

Seated in the tea-room, she said, 'I can't stay long. I've got to meet Kirsten Mackenzie in an hour. She's coming up from London for the big political meeting tonight in St Andrew's Hall. Adela Pankhurst, Lucy Burns, Margaret Smith, Alice Paul – they're all coming.'

'Why do you bother?' he demanded moodily. 'The

women's vote is such a small part of the political packet.'

'You mean I should join your revolution in the streets?'

'Why not?'

'Because I believe in socialism by evolution, not revolution. I'm a pacifist, like my father.'

'You can't be a pacifist and a Suffragette.'

'Yes, I can. We never set out to hurt anyone. But I'm not getting involved in argument this afternoon. Is it true the men are going back at Finn's place? I heard a rumour in the *News* office.'

He nodded grudgingly. 'We've negotiated a settlement.'

'For more money?'

'We've had to concede that under present circumstances there will be no increase. It's the only way we could avoid sackings –'

'So you've put the whole firm in jeopardy and gained precisely nothing?'

'No. We've strengthened our negotiating position. For the future.'

She was silent. She could not escape the feeling that Donald used the factory as a focus for a deeper discontent in his own nature. It seemed he simply had to be at odds with someone. She longed to help him understand this, to come to terms with himself. He looked up now with that restless, challenging stare of his and said, 'I've something else to tell you. I've got Tina away from that man of hers.'

She looked at him in total astonishment. 'You've done *what?*'

'No help for it.' He spread his hands. 'She can't take any more. She's got a job in Pettigrew and Stephens in Sauchiehall Street. A nice refined saleslady's job. And a room in a clean tenement, with an old widow who makes her meals. I spent yesterday helping her move out.'

'What about Alisdair?'

'He's making all the customary noises. Doesn't make a scrap of difference. She won't go back.'

She said, stiff-lipped, 'Will you see much of her?' Instantly

265

she regretted the question. There was a smirk of satisfaction on his features, as if he derived a perverse pleasure from upsetting her.

'I'm the only one she trusts. She hates her father. I have to give the poor girl what support I can.'

Suddenly it was important that the meeting that night should be an immense success. 'I must go,' she said coldly, rising to her feet.

'You want to be careful.'

She glared at him. 'What do you mean?'

'Throwing stones. Sending yourselves as human letters to Downing Street. And the Lytton woman scratching Votes for Women over her heart with a hatpin. You lose public support when you do daft things like that.'

'Losing support?' she demanded furiously. 'On the contrary. We are gaining support all the time in Scotland.'

'I don't like to see women losing their dignity, that's all.'

She could cheerfully have struck him. He knew it. His thin, dark, goading face waited for it. Trembling, she picked up her umbrella from the stand by the door and welcomed the onslaught of the rain in the street.

'I think the world is going off its head,' said the middle-aged man in pince-nez, watching Miss Alice Paul being brought down from the roof of St Andrew's Hall. 'Suffragettes lying in wait to assault Cabinet ministers. Strikes everywhere. The country's changing and not for the better.'

Standing beside him, Carlie and Kirsten exchanged smiles.

'If *he* had no vote, perhaps he too would be prepared to lie on a roof and get wet, waiting for Lord Crewe,' said Kirsten, *sotto voce*. She watched the rebellious Suffragette being led away by the police. The workman who had spotted her watched too. 'I didnae want to give her game away,' he told anyone who would listen, 'but I thought she needed help.'

'You know,' Kirsten said, 'I believe the people here are on our side.'

'Try to look as though you're not a Suffragette,' Carlie

advised, as they moved towards the hall entrance. 'The police will try to keep us out.'

The queue stood patiently in the rain. Miss Alice Paul's exploits had set up an expectant hum of speculation. If she had been prepared to wait for hours up on the roof, in a deluge, what further surprises might her sisterhood have in store for the meeting inside?

'I heard your father speak in the House the other evening,' said Kirsten. She clung to Carlie's arm while the rain pattered down noisily on the silk drum of the umbrella above their heads. 'He was speaking against the money spent on Dreadnoughts, to keep up with the German Navy. But the spirit of the House was against him. I think I am with the man in the pince-nez we have just heard. The country is changing. There is aggression everywhere. Unions, workers, government. I don't like it, Carlie. I don't like it a bit.'

Carlie looked at the other woman's face, darkly illumined by the street lamp. It was a face burned on the public imagination by Kirsten's exploits in pursuit of the vote. Three times now, Kirsten had been in prison, for offences ranging from breaking windows to chaining herself to railings. The last time she had gone on hunger-strike and been forcibly fed. No doubt that accounted for the flaccid look of her skin, the boney frailty of her hands.

Feeling something that was much more painful than anger, Carlie said lightly, 'Perhaps we should not say too much about aggression, in view of the dust we are kicking up ourselves!'

'But we hurt no one!' protested Kirsten, echoing her own defence to Donald. 'It is only ourselves we hurt, our own lives we offer.'

They were nearly at the great doors to the hall. Carlie tried to keep her face averted from the large policeman, but a warm glow of self-satisfaction was spreading across his ruddy features as he recognized her.

'Ah! Miss Fleming, isn't it? Well, I'm afraid we can't have you in the hall tonight, miss.'

'Why not?' demanded Kirsten.

'And Miss Mackenzie, isn't it? Thought I knew you, from the papers.'

Carlie was about to argue when there was a sudden sharp surge from the people behind. Voices demanded, 'Let them in!'; others cried, 'It's a free country,' and some even, 'Votes for women.' In the good-natured but determined jostling the policeman's protesting face was gradually carried out of sight and Carlie and Kirsten swept into the hall. Carlie began to laugh. Inside there were still plenty of seats.

Suddenly she heard a small sound, like a moan, and felt Kirsten's grip at first tighten then slacken on her arm. Turning, she was just in time to catch the older woman as she slumped against her, face ashen, eyes closed.

With the help of a man who had jumped up from a nearby row, Carlie fought to get Kirsten back out through the crowds and into the entrance hall for air. The irony of it was killing, after their luck in getting inside. Someone thoughtfully provided a chair and a woman offered smelling salts. Kirsten's head jerked up and her eyes opened, but as though they had weights on them.

'You're ill,' Carlie accused her. 'Why didn't you tell me?'

'No.' Kirsten's tongue ran round her dry lips. 'I'm all right. Go back in, Carlie. You may be needed.'

'Certainly not. I'm taking you to my house and calling a doctor.'

In the dark of the cab going out towards Queen's Park Kirsten said in a weak but firm voice, 'I shall be all right. And there is no point in calling a doctor. I will not see him.'

As it was getting late, Carlie decided she could leave the decision about calling the doctor till the morning. She helped Kirsten undress and put her in her own bed. She would sleep on the settee. She made Kirsten some hot milk and saw that she looked better. But even so, she lay wakeful through the night, listening in case the other called.

The lemony Glasgow sunshine was filtering through the cream lace curtains when she woke to realize that her fitful night had ended in a last hour of deep, drugging sleep. Noises told her that Kirsten had risen and was moving about in the kitchen.

'You shouldn't be up.'

'I'm better.' Pale-faced and sunken-eyed, Kirsten scarcely looked it. But her smile was defiant. She had made tea and toast and they sat down together.

'What did they do to you, in that prison?' Carlie demanded. 'It looks to me as though they have half-killed you.'

She had said the words unthinkingly, not even looking for an answer. She was certainly unprepared for the effect they had on Kirsten, who rose, making retching noises, and fled to the kitchen sink.

After a few minutes, she returned and sat down, her hands pressed against her left side. She was deathly pale.

'They make your mouth into a pouch, you know.' The words tumbled out. 'They pour brandy and milk into it and make you swallow. And when that doesn't work, they put a tube up your nostril and pour egg and milk into it, through a funnel.'

'No, don't,' Carlie protested, white-lipped.

'The pain is excruciating, the worst pain ever. You have it here, in your breast, and you think your ears are going to burst. And when that doesn't work, they put you into a rubber cell and place a steel gag in your mouth and try it all over again.'

Suddenly, with a moan, Kirsten vomited again and again. Tears were running down her face and her grey-streaked auburn hair had escaped from its pins and fell down her back. Carlie led her into the parlour and sat with her till she was feeling better. Then she brought her water and a towel and, after she had washed, helped her pin up her hair.

'Don't talk,' she pleaded. She covered Kirsten with a shawl and left her to rest, wondering if she should send for Wallace. She felt a strange indecision. Kirsten's powerful will had prevailed in the matter of the doctor. Perhaps she should do nothing till she had spoken to Kirsten again.

In a little while she went back into the parlour and it was as though Kirsten had read her mind. 'Don't tell your father about this. Or Wallace. It is merely the reaction to what I have been through and I am determined to fight it on my own.' She smiled, and patted the settee beside her for Carlie to sit down.

'Do you know what I thought of, when I was at my weakest? The cakes in Sandia's tea-rooms! Scottish cakes. Glasgow cakes. Even Hazlitt praised them. I could see them so clearly, in all their glory. And this time I haven't been able to eat a single one!'

'You should be taking a long rest,' said Carlie helplessly. 'And I should make you see a doctor.'

'Where's your Scottish spirit, Duncan's daughter?' Kirsten teased, but gently. 'I must show them all. I am not done for yet.'

Chapter Fifteen

Finn had arranged to meet Kitty in the Japanese Tea-room of La Scala picture-house in Sauchiehall Street, and let her know the result of his meeting with Peter Frensham.

In this, her third pregnancy, she did not mind so much being seen in public, although she carried this baby neatly and a pretty, loose jacket hid her condition well. When he teased her about her modesty, she said her mother had dragged them indoors at the sight of a pregnant woman and it was no use expecting her to change her ideas entirely.

'Darling, how pretty you look!' He pulled up a chair beside her. 'Have you had your lemon tea?' This was something she had demanded from her second month.

'Yes. Don't worry about me. How did the meeting go?' She gave him her warm, dimpled smile but her eyes were shadowed with concern.

He knew there was no point in concealing anything from her. He swore she sometimes knew what was in his mind before it got there.

'He wants out. He says the signs are that Glasgow's on the wane. He cites coal, iron, cotton, marine engineering. He says it can't support a car industry and that if I had any sense I'd go with him to America.'

'Did you give him the figures?'

'He says 55,000 cars don't represent a British motor industry and that we haven't the roads to put them on anyway. He's right, he's right, but there must be a way we can keep going.'

'Did you suggest branching out into agricultural machinery and rolling stock?'

'I don't think he was listening to me. The truth is, he has gambled heavily in the casinos and I think the family want

271

him out of Europe for a while.'

'What will you do, Finn?' Her voice, though fearful, still carried the note of her total trust in him.

'Do?' He shook his head as though he could not believe the position he was in. 'What can I do? Rationalize. What's that saying of yours? – "Draw in my horns." I may have to diversify, take in jobs I would have considered beneath me a year ago.'

'Couldn't we sell the house? I don't mind where I live. I'll do without servants – '

'No, you won't. Come on, drink up your tea and we'll go out and buy you a new hat.'

Denial was on her lips but in time she saw, obliquely, what he was getting at. The hat was a flag, and the flag was still flying.

'One with egret feathers?' she suggested. She held his arm lightly as they walked out of the tea-room and her head was very high. She knew they made a handsome couple.

When they had picked the hat, in midnight blue velvet with ruby beads securing the grey feathers, and bought some wide satin ribbon to make dress sashes for the girls, she said consideringly, 'Finn, I think you had better take me home.'

'Are you all right?'

She nodded. 'I think so. It can't be the baby. He's not due for a month.' But her face increasingly told him she could be wrong.

He had parked his car in a quiet side street and now he got her into it and drove as fast as the engine permitted for home, while she made strange little squeaking noises as the contractions increased in frequency.

'There'll be no one at home. I told Cook she could take the maids to pick Beenie's wedding present' – Beenie being a former parlour-maid. 'Thank goodness the babies are at Sandia's. You'll have to call the midwife. And the doctor.' Between gasps and squeaks, Kitty was being intensely practical.

Finn swore as an elderly lady in shawl and mutch took

272

her time crossing the road in front of him. He pushed the lock of fair hair from his eyes as once again he let in the clutch. Cold sweat ran down his back and a kind of primal terror robbed him of straightforward, rational thought. He lifted Kitty down at the doorsteps, unable to look at the stress in her face.

'Phone the doctor.' She pointed to the instrument in the hall, as though addressing a dullard child, and painstakingly began the climb to her bedroom upstairs. When she got to the top, she felt she had climbed Ben Nevis. But in an orderly fashion, though unable to stifle her groans, she removed her outdoor clothes, climbed into a clean nightdress and began to prepare the bed for the birth with thick brown paper and sterile sheets.

'He's coming – she's coming. I mean they both are – the doctor and the midwife.' In shirt-sleeves, his hair on end, his tie awry, Finn made Kitty think of nothing so much as the mad scientist in a living picture she'd seen recently. She began to laugh weakly, and the laugh turned into a primitive sound that was half-shout, half-scream.

'Finn, you have to help me.' Kitty had gained momentary control over the pains. 'Hold my hand. Let me push against you when I bear down.' She smiled at him, her face damp with the perspiration of effort. 'It's all right. You won't die, you know.'

At the critical moment, Finn looked anywhere but at the bed. He could feel his head spin round and thought he was going to faint. There was a whooshing sound, a sound he was never to forget, and then unbelievably, a thin, mewing wail.

He fought back from the edge of panic and looked down. A small, blue-tinged creature lay between his wife's legs. Undeniably alive. Undeniably a boy.

'It's – it's a he,' he stammered, taking in Kitty's look of joyous achievement. He kissed her brow and her lips. 'You wonderful darling, you.' Just then, the midwife's urgent ring came imperatively from downstairs. Kitty's hand clung momentarily to his; they knew a moment of mystical union. Despite everything else the day had held, he felt touched by a near-unbearable bliss.

When the letter came for Carlie, she recognized Aggie Fermoyle's writing at once. Who else used loops and curls with such a flourish? She opened it, amused to note from the jammy pink stain on the bottom left-hand corner that Aggie still conducted her correspondence from an edge of the kitchen table. But the contents took the smile from her face.

> Dear Friend [wrote Aggie],
> I thought you ought to know the news about Kirsten Mackenzie, as I know you know her quite well. She is in a public ward at the London Hospital and I do not think she will ever come out again. Do you think something should be done about her? She has done a lot for our movement but folk have short memories. Write and tell me what you think. Your sincere friend, Aggie Fermoyle.

Carlie gave the matter much thought before she took action. Should she tell Wallace? Or perhaps, first of all, her father? Impulsively she decided on the latter, caught the train to London and then was pulled up short to discover her father had gone down into Wales.

'Why?' she asked the young man who helped her father with his secretarial work.

'Because of the trouble at Tonypandy,' he replied.

She decided on the spur of the moment that she might as well follow him. She was moved by the urgency of letting her father know how desperate was Kirsten's condition, the conviction that it was important he should know. She had read about Tonypandy, of course. Striking miners had gone on an orgy of window-smashing, angry at the import of blackleg labour, and the Home Secretary Winston Churchill had sent in the troops. An ugly situation had escalated into something worse and a miner had been killed.

The general opinion was that Churchill had over-reacted, partly because colliery managers had exaggerated in their reports of 'rioting'. But it wasn't as simple as that. A black spirit was abroad in the valleys. Twenty-six thousand men, ostensibly seeking better conditions and a minimum wage, were claiming back something more – the debt of thirty thousand lives paid to the Great God Coal in the past twenty-five years.

Carlie tracked her father down to a meeting in a miners' hall in the Rhondda. She had never heard working-men so articulate as here and most articulate of all was a young man who was calling for a 'fighting brigade' to meet what he alleged was the violence of the police towards the strikers.

When her father joined her after making his speech, Carlie found her legs were shaking. He had not been listened to patiently. There had been cries of 'Old Phlegm' – Fleming the Phlegmatic – a nickname he hated, and foot-stamping and shouts when he had tried to catalogue what the Labour Party sought to achieve in Parliament.

She had never seen him so shaken. His hosts tried to smooth him down but he shook off their arms and said to her with a gruff, uncharacteristic impatience, 'What brings you here, lass? Have you come to see democracy buried?' His mouth set in a furious line. 'They wouldn't listen to me out there tonight and I'm on their side. No one has fought harder for the miners than I have.'

She took his arm and walked him out into the calm Welsh night. She did not know how to be less brutal about it. She said simply, 'Father, Kirsten Mackenzie is dying. She has no funds. Everything has gone towards the Suffragettes. She's in a bare hospital ward – '

She could not go on. The emotionalism of the occasion clogged her throat. She took his arm and moved him still farther away from the knots of angry, arguing miners. They held up their faces to the evening wind. It was blessedly cool.

'You were right to tell me.' The breathing space had calmed him. He said in a low, resolute voice, 'We'll go back to London straight away.'

In the train she told him what little she knew of Kirsten's condition. 'I didn't know what to do,' she admitted. 'It seemed all wrong that she should be left there, as if no one cared.' She gave him a careful look. 'Mother needn't know any of this.' He looked up at her, his expression sombre but admitting her to full adult status, and full of gratitude and love.

He went alone to the hospital. An old crone without teeth, obviously a patient well enough to be allowed up, was holding a glass of water to Kirsten's lips as he went in. The old woman first stared at him curiously, then moved slowly back to her own bed. Kirsten's eyes were closed. He took her hand and waited. After what seemed like an eternity her eyes opened and slowly focused on him. She said through stiff lips, 'Is that you? Duncan? I didn't think you would come.'

'She has been given something for the pain,' said the little nurse who had accompanied him to the bedside. 'Don't let her talk too much. She needs to rest.'

'I came,' he said simply. Even in her drugged state, she was holding on to his hand as though she would never let it go. 'Carlie told me, and I came as quickly as I could.'

She smiled, then something which could have been present pain or past misery clouded her face and she said, turning her head away, 'You're too late, you know. You shouldn't have troubled.'

He felt a constriction in his throat, unmanning him.

He said gruffly, 'Did you think I would leave you here, facing up to pain on your own? I'm here to share whatever it is that ails you. Would you like to come and stay at my flat? I could look after you – get a woman body in to nurse you, if you like. What do you say to that, bonnie bird? You need a bit of feeding up and looking after, that's all.'

She turned her beautiful, ironic gaze on him, at once naked and candid, and he found himself urging, 'Say you'll come. I want to do this for you, Kirsten.'

She did not answer. All the while, her grip on his hand had never lessened, but her eyes closed again and he began to think the medication was sending her to sleep. The pause lengthened, while he took in the chill, white tiles of the hospital walls, the still, silent figures on the other beds. Then her eyes opened once again, this time carrying a different expression, one that sent his heart beating wildly with a daft, irrepressible hope. She nodded, almost imperceptibly. 'I'll arrange it,' he said. 'It shall be done.'

He gave up his bedroom to Kirsten. It offered a brief glimpse of the Thames and caught the morning sun. He carried her from the hospital bed into the carriage and from the carriage into his home. She was light in his arms. Carlie helped to settle her in the big brass bed, then excused herself to go and visit Aggie before catching the train back home.

He had spoken to the doctor at the hospital and been told there was nothing more they could do. But once he had her settled in the cosy, firelit room, he permitted himself more idiot optimism. Nothing was irreversible, people recovered from the brink of death, Kirsten had the strong constitution of her Highland ancestors. He put more coal on the fire and set a tray for tea, his hands trembling over the unaccustomed effort to make things look dainty.

He cut sponge cake into minute portions and fed it to her as he had once fed Carlie. She refused any more after the second mouthful, but took a sip or two of milky tea. He brought a chipped bowl from the kitchen, poured hot water into it from the spirit kettle and with the end of his rough towel sponged her hand and forehead, gentle as a girl.

'That's better, isn't it?' he coaxed. He lifted a wisp of dark hair off her forehead and said, 'No more campaigning for you, lass. Plenty of rest and good care from now on. I know of a girl with nursing experience. I'll arrange for her to come in. But mostly I'll be here. It'll be just like old times.'

He saw that the small effort he had demanded from her had exhausted her and so he left her to sleep. When he went in a couple of hours later, she was lying awake, her expression tranquil. He went over to her and she took his hand. 'It's so peaceful here,' she said.

'Is there anything you want?'

'Just to talk. Shall we talk of old times?'

He took the pace from her. Sometimes she recalled the winter nights in Glasgow when they had first started meeting. The trams, the snow, the skaters on the Clyde. Sometimes it was the Rows, when times had been so hard they'd crawled all over the bings for coal or pinched turnips from the fields.

Just as he was thinking he'd tired her enough, she said, 'There *is* something I want, Duncan. I would like to see Wallace once more. I wouldn't let him know I was in the hospital. Here is different.'

'I'll telegraph him,' he said. 'You know he's been seeing Carlie while he's been in Glasgow? They get on well together.'

'Yes. That's good. Tell him to come quickly, Duncan.'

When Wallace arrived off the late train the next evening, he strode into his mother's bedroom with an expression of acute concern. Without saying anything, he sat down beside her and took her hand. The look on Kirsten's face, one of hunger and gentle entreaty, was enough to make Duncan turn away.

'Mother.' Wallace's voice was low. 'I'm glad you asked me to come. What can I do? I want to help.'

Kirsten indicated Duncan with a nod of her head. 'Your father has been taking care of me beautifully.' She smiled at her son then. 'It's good that the three of us are together.' She rubbed his hand. 'I wish it could have happened more often. But you've been happy, haven't you? You've had a good life with Walter and Jill. Tell me you have, dear. I need to know.'

'You need have no regrets.' He kissed her brow clumsily. 'I understand. Jill helped me. She always said I was luckier than most, with two mothers and fathers.'

Duncan left them to talk and made a simple meal in the kitchen, which they shared. Despite the fact that Kirsten was sometimes in pain, the evening was one of strange, heightened happiness and fulfilment. Duncan watched his son covertly. He had the gentleness of the large and strong and his sensitivity to his mother's needs was something that moved Duncan profoundly.

Before Kirsten settled to sleep she looked from one to the other, her expression unreadable. Then she said, with total unpredictability, 'Wallace, take his name. Take your father's name, now that you're a man.'

'Kirsten!' It was Duncan who burst out. 'You didn't tell me you wanted this.'

'Will you?' Kirsten persisted, looking beseechingly at her son.

'I don't think I can.' Wallace looked from one to the other.

'Banks isn't your true name,' Kirsten protested. 'It was just to protect you while you were at school. You are *our* son –'

'Let me tell you why I can't,' said Wallace abruptly. 'I've been using the name Mackenzie since I've gone to live in Glasgow. It's your name, after all. It's how I've always thought of myself since I was a very little boy. I knew Banks was only a temporary convenience. Won't that do for you, Mother?' Seeing her look of distress, he rushed on, 'Why shouldn't I bear your name? As an emancipated woman, I thought you would understand.'

'I wanted you to do it for Duncan.'

Duncan stepped forward now with a raised hand, forbidding further discussion.

'Mackenzie will do for me,' he said. 'You have a brave and independent woman for a mother, Wallace. I would like you to carry her name.'

Kirsten looked as though she would like to argue further but he straightened her top sheet, smiling down at her. 'You must submit to the democratic vote. Two out of three are for Mackenzie.' Wallace was still looking at her anxiously, wondering if he had upset her. She gave in. 'All right. Mackenzie will do.'

Wallace's visit, though only one night, seemed to have done her good. She brooded happily over his good looks, manly figure and straightforward manner rather like a miser poring over his hoard of gold.

The next day, Duncan went down to the House of Commons after first seeing a young Cockney woman, Vera, installed as nurse. He knew that a debate on the trouble in the coalfields was coming up the day after and there were people he wanted to see before getting down to the draft of the speech he was determined to make.

To his astonishment, he returned home to find Kirsten seated by the bedroom window, fully dressed. Vera made an apologetic grimace. 'She wanted to get up, sir. Nothing I said would stop her.'

'Now you're not to blame Vera.' Kirsten put on her most wheedling tones. 'I want us to have a meal together. Vera's prepared some fish. I'm feeling so much better I thought it would be like a party.'

He pushed down the surge of disquiet he felt on seeing the hectic flush on her cheeks, and humoured her.

'All right. We'll have the little table by your chair there and a party it shall be.' He gave Vera a reassuring smile. 'It's all right. You get home now, lass. I'll take over.'

When the girl had gone, Kirsten said almost truculently, 'I won't give in, you know. If I can get back to eating properly, my strength will come back. Now let's talk about your speech. Let me help you with it, the way I did with the books in the old days.'

He placed a small portion of the creamed fish in front of her, urging her to eat. 'What I have to get over,' he explained, 'is the explosive nature of the ideas some miners have nowadays. Marxism, de Leonism, Sorelism – they flash about the valleys like wild electric storms. Somehow I have to convince both sides of the need for caution combined with open-hearted discussion of the grievances. I'll be called weak, I'll be called traitor, because I want conciliation, not bloodshed. But they'll not shift me. I'll not set man against man, class against class. It goes against everything that wise old man, my father, taught me.'

'No, don't give in,' she said softly. 'Your kind of politics is based on love, not hatred. Keep saying it. One day they'll have to listen, when all else has failed.'

She did not eat much. When they had finished, he carried her nearer the fire and they watched the flames for a time in companionable silence. In the cheerful glow from the coals, he thought she looked as though she might be gaining in strength, but knew it might be wishful thinking.

'Duncan.' She fished in her handbag and handed him something. He saw it was the small volume of Burns's poems he had given her years ago. When he opened it, inside was the same pressed burnet rose. 'I want you to keep it,' she ordered.

He smiled and nodded, speechless.

'I have been reading *Ae Fond Kiss* again,' she said. She quoted, ' "Had we never loved sae kindly, had we never loved sae blindly – " '

He finished it for her : ' "Never met and never parted, we had ne'er been broken-hearted." '

'Do you think,' she asked, not looking at him, 'that we Scots are too sentimental for our own good?'

'Undoubtedly,' he agreed. 'Like Rabbie, we wrap up our pain in bonnie parcels. Maybe because we can think of nothing else to do with it.'

'It's a fault in a practical people,' she opined.

'More of a paradox, I would say.' He smiled at her. 'Now you must go to bed and rest.'

She gave him a bright smile the next morning as he left for the House. 'Come for me if you ever need me,' he told Vera. 'It will take only minutes to fetch me.' But his mind was more at rest than at any time since he had brought Kirsten to the flat.

He had read his notes for his speech to Kirsten and her eyes had kindled with love and approbation. Watching him dress in his best serge suit, she had said, 'You look very – dignified.' Walking through Palace Yard, he thought of the word she had selected with such obvious care. Dignified. They had both always wanted dignity so much – not for themselves, but for those who had it snatched from them by hunger, poverty, degradation.

It wasn't the dignity conferred by rank or even achievement he wanted, but the dignity that should be common to all humanity. Maybe only someone who had worn his brother's cast-off jacket, or eaten his neighbour's ill-spared bread, could know how he felt. But the sensation was real to him still, as real as in his childhood in the Rows, when a handful of oatmeal had fed them during his father's drinking bouts and a scone from the farmer's wife had been halved, then quartered, with ravenous, meticulous care.

When he finally rose to speak, he was conscious that the House was prepared to give him all their attention. In his long career he had learned a thing or two: how to subjugate the irreverent and frivolous, how to wait for that moment of deep, attentive silence when there was the best chance of getting your message across.

He didn't spare them now. He painted a vivid, intimate picture of the unrest in the Welsh valleys and the danger of it spreading throughout the country, not only in the pits but to the other industries. And then he became conscious that he was saying things that weren't in his notes, that his spirit was taking over in a way it had not done since his youth at the pithead.

'I ask this House to take warning. Cynical old men must not be allowed to manipulate our lives. Young lions who have had not time to test their theories must not be allowed to plunge us into an armed struggle. If we become a nation divided, divided into those who want power without responsibility and those who cry "Send in the troops," then our future becomes too terrible to contemplate. We could have civil war. We could have revolution. Brother against brother. But to those of my own Party I say: none of this need happen if the centre holds firm.'

He became conscious of a young Welsh MP waving his papers at him, his face brindled with hostility and anger. 'Go home, old man!' shouted the young Welshman. 'Do you think the poor can wait for ever?'

Duncan deliberately ignored him, keeping his voice steady and strong as he went on: 'Blessed are the meek. You may think these are strange words to utter at a time like this. But we need them. We need to be meek in the face of so much certainty by so many that *they* know what is good for us.'

The House rumbled with laughter, but Duncan drew himself up for the peroration: 'Let me tell my young friend I have sacrificed much – I will not tell you how much – for a life of service in this House. I have worked for peaceful advancement of our people. *Peaceful*. For I would remind him that life, no matter how circumscribed or narrow, how painful or frustrated, is a sacred gift and a mystery above politics. Do not let us now sacrifice peace and life for sectarian advantage.'

There was a moment of silence and then they cheered him. Something in his demeanour this day had reached across party barriers and touched almost all of them. He saw affection on their faces and even though he knew it was tinged in many cases with an amused tolerance for his pacifism, he was touched by it almost to the point of tears.

Going out into Central Lobby afterwards, someone tugged at his arm. He turned to see a Commons messenger with Vera at his side. Instantly, he forgot everything except the look on the girl's face.

'Tell me! Something's happened?' He grabbed her arm so hard he saw her wince.

'It's Miss Mackenzie, sir. I had to get the doctor, the pain was so bad. He's given her something and he's staying with her, but I thought I'd better fetch you, like you said.'

Outside, the sky above the Thames was laden with clouds and the pavements flecked with rain. Everything seemed to take on a starker, harsher reality in his panic and urgency.

The doctor gave him a measured, warning look as he went into the bedroom, but Duncan ignored him and went straight to Kirsten's side. She was propped up against her pillows, her head with its mass of hair heavy on the frail stalk of neck.

He gazed down at her without speaking for a moment – a moment that seemed as long as his life. *Kirsten, my bonnie bird.*

'Are you in pain?' he demanded. 'Why didn't you tell me?'

'Not any more.' She patted the bed. 'Come and sit by me,

do. I want to hear how it went.'

He looked to the doctor for guidance. The man nodded, his look indicating 'Humour her,' as snapping shut his Gladstone bag, he left, saying he had another urgent call to make, but would return later.

Duncan sat down and covered both Kirsten's hands with his own.

'It went all right. But I want to know from you that what I did was worthwhile.'

'You mean, going into Parliament?'

'I mean the sacrifices we made. Both of us.'

She said in a gentle, girlish voice, 'I never had any doubt of it. I wouldn't have made them, otherwise.'

He smiled then. 'You are a very great comfort to me.'

The drugs the doctor had administered began to take effect and she slept, but in a little she roused and began to talk quite rationally. 'I am quite content to die for it, Duncan,' she said. 'For the vote. No one said it at the hospital, but something happened when they fed me forcibly, that time in prison. When they have killed a few more of us off, perhaps they will see the barbarity of it.'

He gazed down at her, his face inscrutable. ' "An affair of the heart," ' he quoted. 'You remember Keir Hardie saying that about Socialism? That's what your Suffragettism is, isn't it?'

'Not altogether.'

'It took the place of what you and I might have meant, had we been together,' he insisted. 'Nobody knows that better than I.'

She took his hand and said with infinite kindness, 'Don't fret.' She tried to smile at him, but something was darkening her eyes. He felt her hands clench spasmodically and knew her gasp of pain as though it had left his own lungs.

She seemed to recede from him then, to some half-world that was not quite sleep. At six o'clock the doctor came, beckoned him into the hall and told him that the end could not be far off.

She looked at him once more before she died. 'Do you remember?' she whispered. He put his ear close to her mouth to hear what else she wanted to say. He heard her give a little gasp, but it took him several moments to realize she was gone.

Do you remember? He wanted to tell her he had forgotten nothing. But he had. He had forgotten great patches of days and years when she had not been paramount in his life. All he could remember now were the cold days, the early days, a thin jacket that let the wind tingle his bones, her hands counting his ribs.

He touched her hair, where it curled at the temple, hearing Vera's sharp cry of pain and protest as she entered the room.

The Peels' house in Pollokshaws was of red stone, massive and solid, with stone lions on either side of its impressive front steps and a rolling lawn sweeping down to immaculate yew hedges.

On Hogmanay, the last day of the year 1910, a small servant was scrubbing the steps, her bare arms purple from the cold, while a senior girl polished the brass nameplate, knocker and door-handles. This morning they did not mind the chores, for the house was ringing with Ne'erday excitement and with preparations for the big party to be held that night. And Cook had promised them ginger wine and shortbread if their work passed muster.

The girls watched round-eyed as a motor lorry drew up on the drive and ashet after ashet of traditional New Year steak pie was carried round to the tradesmen's door. (They would have their own pie in the kitchen, they knew, and the pastry would be golden and melting, the well-peppered steak and kidney and sausages floating in a gravy of indescribable richness.) The water ran into their mouths in anticipation.

In the morning-room, a very small, plump girl in buttoned kid boots and a red dress pushed the *Glasgow Herald* down from her father's face and climbed precipitately on to his knee. This was Catriona, Sandia's baby, now aged two and well aware already of her autocratic powers over her father Dandy.

'Song,' she demanded, and he dandled her obediently up and down on his knee, singing 'Boiled Beef and Carrots'. With her arms full of napery, Sandia came in, gave the baby an abstracted glance, and pleaded with Dandy: 'Keep her out of the way, dear. She's into everything and I'm never going to get it all ready in time.'

'I warned you not to overdo it,' Dandy grumbled. 'Who's all coming? From the family, I mean.'

Sandia counted on her fingers. 'Father. Kitty and Finn. Then there's Carlie, Donald and Tina. And Wallace Fleming.'

'Seems funny. Having Tina without Alisdair.'

'He won't come. I've asked him, but he's determined to sulk and suffer and stay away from the family. So I thought I might as well ask Tina – I don't like to think of her on her own in those awful lodgings when the clock strikes New Year. And I've asked Carlie to bring Wallace. I know we've never met him but he sounds a nice young man.'

Catriona heaved herself farther up her father's knee and delivered a smacking kiss on his balding forehead. Sandia ruffled her hair. 'Do you love Mama, too?' 'Love Mama too,' said Catriona impartially. And Sandia's eyes met Dandy's in a deep, unspoken satisfaction. 'Come on, old girl,' he urged gently. 'You said you'd a thousand things to do.'

By the time the guests arrived, late in the evening, the house had been scrubbed, polished and decorated until the warmth of the Hogmanay welcome sparkled from every corner. The hall was hung with evergreen and in the reception rooms great yellow chrysanthemums held their dignified heads above a froth of maidenhead fern. The sideboards, laid with fine lace-trimmed linen, all but groaned under their burdens of cake, shortbread, black bun and other dainties, while the dining-room was laid with heavy silver cutlery, pyramids of fruit and sprays of spicy carnations.

Crunching up the path towards the house, Kitty held fast to Finn's arm to keep from toppling in her new hobble skirt.

'I won't be sorry to see this year go,' she said into the dark. 'Nothing but strikes and elections and the worry at the factory.'

Finn pinched her arm and said, 'We've hung on. And we've got Paterson, as well as the girls.'

She stopped and rose on her tiptoes to kiss him, suddenly overcome by his staunchness. 'Yes, we've got the baby. We've done something right!'

'Maybe,' said Finn, his mouth smiling against hers, 'in 1911, every big pot in Glasgow and the West will want a Fleming Flyer. But then again, maybe not.'

'We won't think about it tonight,' she said gamely. 'Tonight we'll have fun.'

A taxicab decanted more guests on the pavement – Belfast friends of Dandy's, from their accents – and a second brought Carlie and Wallace. Throwing open the front door, Sandia and Dandy greeted each arrival with a kiss and a hug. No one came empty-handed: the gifts were of china, linen, spirits or yet more black bun. Upstairs, perplexed by the comings and goings and the undercurrent of adult excitement, Catriona had sobbed herself robustly to sleep.

The little maids staggered up and down from the kitchen with the soup, the steak pies, the creamed swede and mashed potato, the trifles, the jellies, the blancmanges, the tea and coffee and petit-fours.

Tina, dark hair brushed up in a becoming top-knot, sat beside Wallace, unable to think of a single thing to say to this shy young man. At last he said, red-faced, 'What sort of work do you do?'

'I sell coats.' With an unexpected glint of mischief, she added, 'It doesn't fit me for talking to young scientists.' But once the ice was broken he found himself telling her about electrons and declaring that the atom would be shown to be mainly empty space. Heartened by her quiet, encouraging look, he decided she was brighter than she would have him believe.

The weary servants cleared away the tables before midnight struck. They dipped plates into the water in the sink automatically, as automatically dried them and put them away in their cabinets and presses. Their faces were colourless with fatigue. 'Like dish-cloots,' said Cook, who by midnight was herself asleep with her head on the table.

Sandia led her father, Captain Jack, into the hall, to stand beside herself and Dandy for the midnight rituals. The grandfather clock began to grind out the first strokes of the New Year. They threw the front door open and the night air reverberated with the sound of church bells and hooters, even the deep thrilling sound of ships' sirens far down the river.

At Glasgow Cross the crowds would be gathered to listen to the carillon of bells from the Tolbooth Tower. It seemed to Sandia she almost felt the Old Year rush out from the house like a presence, and the New One step boldly across the threshold, glittering with promise, some of it surely false.

Who would come and who would go in 1911? She felt the frailty, the mystery, the pain of existence crush her chest as she looked around at those she knew and loved. She cried out, throwing wide her arms, 'Happy New Year, everybody,' and felt her tears rub against Dandy's cheek as he swept her into an embrace smelling of tweed and shaving soap. She stood back from him, then kissed him carefully on the lips. 'Happy New Year, Dandy, my love.' His arms crushed her ribs.

As they raised their glasses, something vulnerable in her father's face sent Sandia to his side.

'Absent friends,' she toasted. 'And the last of the windjammers.'

'To Clyde-built,' said the old man. They smiled at him approvingly. 'Clyde-built,' they toasted.

Carlie muttered to Wallace, 'It's warships they're building on the Clyde now.' She peered, seer-like, into her sherry.

Someone struck up 'A Guid New Year to Ane and A'' and Kitty passed among the guests with small portions of black bun.

'What's in it?' demanded Wallace suspiciously.

'Currants, raisins, almonds, ginger, cinnamon, Jamaica pepper. And so on,' smiled Kitty. 'Quite harmless really.' But he shook his head. The glasses were filled up again. Someone suggested dancing and a lone male guest in a corner sang 'Dark Lochnagar' slightly off-key and with maudlin feeling. Mildly uneasy, Carlie wondered what had happened to Donald. Just then there was a crashing knock on the front door.

'First-footers!' murmured Sandia. It had to be a dark man or bad luck would follow. On the doorstep stood Donald, swaying slightly and looking somewhat pleased with himself, and by his side Alisdair, also smiling, but a little sheepishly.

Sandia drew them both in, with hugs and kisses, and took their proffered gifts. Small packets of more black bun. She patted Alisdair's cheek a little anxiously. 'I really didn't expect to see you but it's all the nicer surprise.' She added, 'Tina's here.'

'Told you,' said Alisdair, turning owlishly to Donald.

Expansively, an arm round both Sandia and Dandy, Donald explained: 'I was having a half-and-a-half in this pub and who should I see but Alisdair here. Like a fish out of water! Hogmanay's no time for a man to be on his own, is it? We've been drinking,' he added unnecessarily. 'Then I said to him, come and see your sister, I said. And here he is!'

Donald moved off into the crowd with that slight weaving movement which characterized most first-footers in the city that night, shaking hands with a bonhomie and vigour that made Carlie smile in spite of herself. Why were her feelings towards him always so twin-headed? The pleasure of seeing him always mixed up with an obscure, unidentifiable feeling that was almost – what? Anger? Reproach?

Still in the hall, Sandia hesitated. 'Tina's here,' she said again to Alisdair. 'Will it be all right?'

Alisdair raised and lowered his eyelids several times to indicate the soundness of his judgement.

'Far as I'm concerned, 's all right,' he intoned. 'Donald said you would be pleased to see me. Are you, Sandia?

Pleased to see me?'

'Daft thing!' she said affectionately. 'You shouldn't have got yourself in such a state. Come and sit by me and Kitty. We can watch the dancing.'

His sisters observed Alisdair surreptitiously as he sat beside them, lapsing into a morose silence. It tore at Sandia to see him, still dressed in his neat, dark, professional clothes, with immaculate collar and tie, trying to cope with the untidy emotionalism the whisky had forced on him. Every few seconds he would draw himself upright, casting his eyes coldly and defiantly around the room. If Tina had seen him, she gave no sign. Wallace had pulled his chair round almost in front of her and was talking to her entertainingly. Her hand went to her mouth as she stifled little gasps of delicate laughter.

'You've done it now, haven't you?' demanded Carlie, swinging Donald round to confront her.

'Happy New Year, my lovely one!' He tried to kiss her, but she dodged him and shook him by the arm.

'You didn't need to bring Alisdair tonight.'

'Found him in a pub. Very depressed.'

'You should have left him there,' she said crisply.

'Now! Now!' He waved an ineffectual finger. 'Don't be heartless. He could have ended up in a shop door, minus his trousers.'

'Well, take a look what's happening now,' said Carlie apprehensively. Alisdair was walking towards Tina, knocking chairs aside and bumping into other guests indiscriminately.

'Take yourself off,' he said to Wallace.

'Now just a minute –'

'I wish to speak to my wife.'

'Don't go,' said Tina. She put out a hand towards Wallace. Carefully Alisdair removed his jacket and laid it on a chair. As carefully, as though he were about to conduct a medical examination, he rolled up his shirt-sleeves. He pushed a white-faced Sandia away from him without ceremony and caught Wallace by his waistcoat.

'I am going to demolish you, you understand,' he said

deliberately. 'I am going to teach you to leave my property alone.'

'Is that how you see your wife?' Wallace demanded contemptuously. 'I don't wonder she wants nothing to do with you.'

'You bloody upstart!' Alisdair grabbed the younger man round the middle of his body and began a bout of wild wrestling. A woman guest gave a high-pitched, excited scream. His face scarlet from his efforts, Alisdair kept pounding a fist into Wallace's groin. After one such blow, the young man straightened in sudden agony and in a reflex of rage sent his fist crashing into Alisdair's face, so that he fell down on all fours, swearing and sobbing.

Finn pulled Wallace away then and Dandy heaved Alisdair on to his feet, using all his strength to restrain him when it looked as though he would lumber after Wallace and start it all again. They got Alisdair down to the kitchen, where he put his head on his arms and indulged in a bout of maudlin weeping. Kitty made hot, strong coffee and stood over him till he drank two cups.

Upstairs, Sandia faced Wallace apologetically. 'I don't know what got into him,' she said.

'Several whiskies too many,' said Wallace grimly.

'Yes. I'm afraid so. He isn't used to it. Maybe, Wallace, it would be better if you went, before he surfaces again.'

Wallace adjusted his shirt and tie. His face was sheet-white, bruised beneath one eye but animated by a dark and dangerous glint of temper. He looked at Tina. 'Would you like me to take you home, Mrs Kilgour? I would deem it a pleasure.'

As Tina nodded and took her leave with her protector, Carlie knuckled Donald between the shoulder-blades.

'Did you not see this would happen?' she demanded. She saw the incident had amused him and glared at him. 'You have a talent for mischief, you Iago, you.'

The city in the small hours was criss-crossed by drunken first-footers like dancers in a haunted ballet. They had been unable to get a taxicab and Wallace kept his arm about Tina as they walked towards her digs. Her landlady, a strict Rechabite who loathed the Hogmanay excesses of the city, would have gone to bed.

Tina explained that for once she had been given the front-door key so that she could let herself in, silently, without, it was hoped, waking either landlady or acrimonious dog.

Strange things were happening to Wallace Mackenzie – he had never taken his father's surname – as he experienced his first Scottish Ne'erday. He had his arm round a woman for the first time in his life and it was an experience both delicate and disturbing. She was fine-boned, soft, frail, different, giving off mystery as her hair gave off the smell of soap and oil. Yet wholly flesh. Human. Womankind.

Leading her through the streets away from the merry-making and the music, he felt as though senses were being brought into play he had never known he possessed. Something was watering his bones, changing his make-up.

Alisdair Kilgour could make all the threatening noises he wanted. He didn't own Tina, did he? Who did own her, then? It seemed that part of her existence was already mingling with his own and he wanted the process to continue.

He began to want to know urgently what had gone wrong between them. He stopped Tina in their tracks and, not relinquishing his hold on her, said abruptly, 'Why did you leave him, Tina?' In the dark he could use her Christian name.

'It's a long story.'

'Please tell me. I want to know.'

Her tongue was loosened, too, by the dark and by what had gone before. She told him all she understood. It seemed as though someone else took over, delivered this long, detailed monologue in an urgent, monotonous voice. Detail upon detail. Almost as though in terror that he would go away before she had made him understand.

She was not specific about the sexual details, but she was about the bruisings, the arguments, the painful emotions, living through them all over again, and sobbing as she spoke.

As they entered the close-mouth of her tenement, he pulled her against his chest and held her in his arms, unable to say anything, unable to move away from her.

He felt her fingers move on his face.

'Wallace,' she said, in a small, weak voice. 'I should never have told you all that.'

'Oh, I am glad you did. You wouldn't tell anyone else, would you? It brings us close.'

'Close?'

'Oh God, what's happening?' he appealed. He brought his lips down on her and pushed his body against hers. Her hands fluttered above his shoulders, then went helplessly round his neck. Her mouth opened to his tongue.

Gasping, at last she pushed him away. 'Oh, Wallace, I have to go.'

'Please don't. I've just found you. Stay a little.'

She sagged against him. 'It is very wrong,' she said, almost reflectively, speculatively. 'I am still married. I'm older than you.'

'None of it matters.' She heard the desperation in his voice and something in her gave up resistance. His untutored hands wandered over her at will and in the total dark of the tiled close-mouth they were in a green country and a little out of their heads.

Chapter Sixteen

They met all through that hot summer of 1911. The ferocious social unheavals of strikes, lock-outs, riots and demonstrations with which the class war came to a head touched them scarcely at all.

She came from her job selling coats bearing him small, unimportant gifts she had picked up during her lunch-hour – a silk handkerchief for his breast pocket, yellow gloves, a mother-of-pearl pocket-knife.

On his way from the university he stopped to choose ear-rings for her, or a brooch, or flowers. And they went to have tea in the Palm Court at the picture house in Sauchiehall Street, or to La Scala, where you could eat and watch the film at the same time. When she laughed at the inanities of serials like *Who Will Marry Mary?* the sound washed over him like sunlit, crystal water. When her hand lay in his he felt a tenderness that enveloped the universe.

In the hottest summer for seventy years, when the tempers of statesmen and strikers rose to dangerous levels, when the arteries of trade and transport choked and silted, when services trickled away to nothing, all that existed for either of them was this hothouse love. It blazed and flowered like the roses and pelargoniums, the dahlias and the red-hot poker that flamed in the city parks and gardens from dry roots in a relentless sun.

When Carlie met Donald, she reproached him: 'It is all your fault. By bringing Alisdair to that party, you threw them together. He sees himself as her Sir Galahad. He's that sort of boy.'

The strikes had thrown Donald out of work at Finn's embattled factory and he was in no mood to be placatory.

'Tina would have latched on to somebody. She was ripe

for the picking.'

She glared at him in distaste. 'I hate your crude metaphor. They adore each other. She wants a divorce but Alisdair won't give her one.'

'Then let Alisdair hang on, then. The other thing will burn itself out.'

They were sitting in her shade-cool parlour at Queen's Park. She had drawn the fringed and tasselled dark-green blinds against the glare and he could smell the watered earth round the aspidistra by the window and the softened wax of the fruit on the sofa table.

'You are a cynic,' she said lividly.

'On the contrary.' He gazed at her with maddening amusement. 'I speak from experience. I got over you, didn't I?'

He looked away quickly from the expression on her face then. He didn't know what had made him say it, except that, idle and purposeless at the moment, he found his only pleasure in needling others. Maybe it had been only an emotional scratch-wound, but he shouldn't have taken his frustrations out on Carlie, who had lent him money for the odd bet and the odd drink when no one else would.

She sat where she could stare out under the blind on to the sun-washed pavement. She was perfectly still, pensive. In her early thirties she had achieved an elusive distinction.

The red hair had darkened, changed from wild curls into deep waves worn in a large bun at the nape of her neck. The freckles on her white skin had faded and the bone structure, the fine grey eyes she had inherited from Josie, had come into their own. Momentarily, he let his feelings for her simmer in his veins like a sweet, bubbly wine.

Even so, the words when he spoke were defensive, rather than propitiatory: 'It's bordering on the lunatic to talk about personal feelings when the country could be on the verge of civil war.'

She flashed him a proud, angry look. 'That's just wishful thinking.'

'No, it isn't,' he argued. 'How can you say that when there's a national rail strike and nearly sixty thousand military, horse and foot, standing at the ready?'

'It'll never come to revolution here.'

He got up and strode restlessly about the room.

'It's either going to be that, or working-class blood spilt anyhow, in a war with Germany.'

'My father believes we can change by peaceful, democratic means.'

'Your father lives with his head in the clouds.'

'He would say it is you who do that.'

'Ach.' He made the noise of dismissal in his throat. 'It's too hot to argue. All I know is, I'm out of work and thousands like me. It's a good job it's summer or the poor in Glasgow would be dying like flies.'

She pushed some silver coins towards him.

'I don't want you to starve. But use it for food, not gambling.'

He picked the money up, and examined it ruefully as it lay on his palm.

'You should have been somebody's mother, Carlie,' he said softly.

She said in a careful, joking voice, 'But all my lovers get over loving me. Like you.'

'I didn't mean it like that. You know I'm fond of you.'

'Fond?' She perpetuated the joke, smiling dangerously.

He said with a calculated boldness, 'I once loved you well enough and it got me nowhere. Do you want me to talk about how I feel?'

She looked flustered. Looked away from him. Said in a low voice, 'No, I don't think so.'

'Then don't joke. Touch-me-not is not a funny attitude.'

'I am not touch-me-not.'

'You are. All Suffragettes have that – that sort of fierceness that repels males. Why don't you give it up, Carlie?'

She picked up a small silver pennant lying on her desk.

'I carried that in our last suffrage procession in London. All of us who'd been in prison had them. I've got Kirsten Mackenzie's too. The one she would have had, had she survived.' She gave him a small, forgiving smile. 'How can you talk about giving up, after what happened to her? No, the fight goes on.' She looked away. 'We've got plans that will *force* the Government to listen.'

He came to her and put a tentative hand on her shoulder. He felt her quiver slightly. She looked up and for a long moment their gaze held. Hers was the first to waver and break.

'I have some tickets for Will Fyfe,' she said brightly. As a freelance journalist, she often had theatre tickets and took him along. 'Want to come?'

He nodded, and began to sing the song that Fyfe had written originally for Harry Lauder, but had now appropriated for himself:

'I belong to Glasgow —'

She let him out into the hot street. A middle-aged Italian, the ends of his moustache waxed and curled, his face above the stiff white collar beaded with sweat, pushed his yellow ice-cream barrow dejectedly alongside the deserted pavement. On an impulse she bought a slider, ice-cream between two wafers, and carried it, already melting, indoors. She ate it quickly as if for comfort or to stifle sensation, feeling her rooms stuffy and oppressive and suddenly the place she didn't want to be.

Sandia held the door of the drawing-room open with a nervous smile and, with a gallows expression, Wallace walked inside.

A three-tiered what-not stood, laden with seed-cake, buttered scones and thin bread and butter. Sandia rang and a pink-faced little maid brought in a silver tray bearing a teapot and hot water for replenishment. Solicitously, Sandia plied her guest with food, talking about the weather and Catriona. Anything except the matter she had asked him there to talk about.

When she was satisfied he had had enough to eat, she swallowed and took the plunge. 'Wallace, I think you know how fond we are of you in the family. So I hope you won't take what I have to say amiss.'

A dark red rose on his face. He swallowed the last of his tea, but said nothing.

'Some might say it is none of my business, but I'm the eldest of the family and Alisdair matters to me. Do you think it wise – to say the least – for you to be seen going about with Tina?'

'You mean, if we met in corners it would be different?'

'No, no.' Her tone was gentle. She took her time before her next words, weighing them carefully. 'Seen or unseen, I simply mean that what you are doing is wrong. Tina is a married woman. You are destroying her reputation and that of Alisdair, too. He is making his name in the medical profession. There isn't anyone in Britain, never mind Scotland, who can do more for pulmonary cases than he can. Yet his strength and peace of mind are being ruined because of what is happening.'

'You know what he did to her?' His gaze was steady and, despite her agitation, Sandia felt a quiver of reluctant admiration. She dropped her head. 'Yes, I do know. I think she married him, in the first place, to get away from her demanding old father, and did not love him. So the fault in the first instance was hers – '

'No, I won't have Tina blamed,' said Wallace hotly. 'She told me she tried, but he wouldn't be patient with her. It's indefensible for a man to strike a woman – '

'But he was tried beyond endurance. He wanted a wife to comfort him when he was going through a difficult time in his profession. All he got was nervous weeping – '

'I don't see the point of my being here,' Wallace said abruptly. 'You are setting yourself up in judgement of a situation you do not understand. Tina and I love each other and she will never go back to your brother.'

Agitatedly, Sandia brushed invisible crumbs from her skirt.

'Wait. Let me speak.' She went over and in a disarming gesture took one of his large, bony hands between her soft, padded ones. 'I was your mother's best friend, you know. We knew Glasgow in the days of the first big steamships made of steel, when it was like New York is today, but without the skyscrapers. We thought we were very daring when we came in to drink tea in one of Stuart Cranston's new tea-rooms! We were, too. I got into fearful trouble!

'But Kirsten taught me not to be too hide-bound, Wallace. The kirk has had a very repressive influence on us all, on me as much as the next person. But I do see that it's inevitable that some marriages should end. I ask you to believe me.'

Her face was so earnest he relaxed a little and even smiled. 'All right. I do.'

'But not easily,' she pressed on. 'Not till everything possible has been tried to save them. So I'm going to suggest something to you. It's this. You should go away from Glasgow, so that everybody concerned can have time to sort out their feelings.

'It will give gossip a chance to die down. You're very young, you know. Younger than Tina. You should have a chance to see the world before committing yourself to one woman.'

She shrank away from the naked misery on his face.

'You're asking the impossible.'

'Even if Tina agreed?'

He laughed shortly. 'I don't think that's likely.'

She pressed her joined hands into her lap. 'She *has* agreed, Wallace. I've had a long talk with her. Pointed out to her what the gossip is doing to Alisdair. Tried to get her to see what she is doing to you – '

'What is she doing to me?' He jumped up, his eyes blazing, looking as though he were about to fly apart. Sandia knew a moment of fear that was purely physical, thinking he was about to strike her.

'She is leading you on – '

He stood above her, with both fists raised theatrically. Then he said in a low, powerful voice, 'You meddling bitch! How did my mother ever come to have you as a friend, with your narrow little notions of morality? You destroy

299

life – don't you see that? Don't you know that Tina and I have something genuine and good? She never loved Alisdair – '

'She cares for his good name. That's loving.'

He stared at her as though her words had ceased to make sense. Then he put his sleeve up to his eyes and began to sob. The grating, despairing sound filled the room. It disturbed Sandia profoundly, so that she wished everything about the whole episode undone. Not that she had gone into it without much heart-searching.

She said, as calmly as she could, 'If money is any problem, I can help. Couldn't you find work in London? For a while? Tina needs to be left in peace. She has had as much as she can take.'

'I'll do what she wishes,' he said tonelessly. He wouldn't look at her. 'I hope you're proud of what you've done, Sandia.'

'You may thank me, one day,' she said.

Finn saw the headline 'SUFFRAGETTES BURN GRANDSTAND AT AYR RACES', and felt a momentary irritation as he put the paper down and turned to his morning mail. What there was of it.

The truth was, he had little sympathy for any predicament but his own just now. It had been a year of major strikes all over the country. Miners, transport workers, railwaymen. And the smaller strikes had added their quota of petty irritation. At first he had thought he would be able to ride out the storm. His own workers had twice been out on partial strike but had not entirely crippled production. It was the spares that could not be delivered that had done that. And now orders had died away to a trickle and the mail this morning contained nothing but bills. He had begun to rehearse in his head what he would say to Kitty if he had to close the factory down. He could not put the words together. It did not seem to be part of his nature to admit failure.

The telephone shrilled beside him and he picked it up in an automatic gesture.

'Finn? This is Cousin Carlie here. Can you get a message to Donald for me?'

'I've had to lay him off, Carlie. With a dozen others.'

'I know, Finn. But can you send a boy with a message? His digs are near you, aren't they? Ask him to come to me. It's urgent.'

Unease broke over Donald all over again as he rang Carlie's bell, later that morning. He had been unable to extract much from Finn other than the simple urgency of the command. 'She sounded strange,' Finn had said. 'As though she didn't want to be questioned.'

The door opened slowly and she stood there, her right arm and hand in some clumsy sort of bandage. There was something wrong with her eyebrows and a large, angry patch on her forehead, shining with something like Vaseline. He stepped quickly into the narrow lobby.

'What's happened?'

'Thank goodness you've come.' He could feel her small free hand on his, damp with perspiration.

She led him into the best room with its dark-green chenille cover on the table, its green plush chairs, turkey-red carpet and flourishing aspidistra. Her large typewriter stood on a solid oak desk by the window.

As she sat down he saw that she was trembling.

'For God's sake, tell me!'

'I called for you, because you're the only person I can trust. I can't be seen out of doors like this. I'll need food –'

The penny dropped for him.

'It didn't happen here, did it?'

She shook her head.

'What were you doing?'

'I can't tell you. I don't want you incriminated.'

Donald laughed. 'Come clean, Carlie. I won't help if you don't.'

'It was Aggie Fermoyle. She came up from London, specially to brief me.'

'To get you involved in arson. That's what it is, isn't it? It wasn't a bomb, was it?'

'Of course not.' Her teeth were chattering. 'I wouldn't get involved in anything like that.'

'That woman chemist did. Black Jennie. She got five years. Only a woman would make a bomb in a marmalade jar –'

'Aggie wanted to burn down Dounhead House.'

His face was grim. 'You talked her out of it?'

'Yes. It was just a sports pavilion, in the end. I put too much petrol on the cotton-wool fuse. It licked back, caught my arm and face.'

She began to weep, tears of reaction and shock. He put his arm round her, making soothing noises. 'Where's the Fermoyle woman now?'

'She had to get back. We couldn't be seen together, Donald, it was foggy and cold and I was so frightened –'

'Let it be a lesson to you.' He mopped her face ineffectually with his handkerchief. 'Come on, now. Let me look at the burns. Do they hurt? What about a doctor?'

'No doctor.'

'You could say you pulled some boiling water over you, accidentally –'

'Can't risk it.'

He stayed with her till she was calm. She sent him round the corner to a little town dairy where he could hear the lowing of the cows at the evening milking, and he brought back milk, butter, eggs, bread and scones. He cooked her an omelette and cut up her bread and butter.

'You know what they are saying now?' he argued, over the meal. 'That your movement has undone all the good because of its excesses. You are put down as hysterical females. Look at some of the things you've done!' He listed them on his fingers. 'Blown up fuse boxes. Cut communication between Glasgow and London. Burnt the grandstand at Ayr races. Sent envelopes of red pepper and snuff to the Cabinet. Cut up a bowling green here in Glasgow, ruined the turf at Duthie Park in Aberdeen –'

'It's out of desperation. They withdrew the Franchise Bill. After all the starvation and imprisonment, how *can* we give

302

up? Don't forget I've been to jail, too. I still have nightmares about it.'

'But putting pebbles down railway carriage windows!'

'It stops the sash from working.'

'Slashing works of art.'

'I don't agree with that.' She touched her burnt arm. 'I don't think I'm in favour of arson, either. After this. Aggie talked me into it. But it's too destructive.'

'Thank God for a glimmer of sense!' said Donald.

Each night that week he brought in food and the evening paper. The patch on her face healed and faded and was scarcely discernible when she had lightly powdered over it with a swansdown powder-puff. She had singed her eyebrows and the front of her hair, but adopted a frizzy fringe that he quite approved of, to hide the fact.

Her arm was a different matter. He bathed it gently and put on fresh dressings, but for several days she was in considerable pain from it. What frustrated her most of all was that she could neither write nor type. By the end of the week the pain was less. She was pale, but had stopped the periodic shivering and weeping which were the result of delayed shock.

He had taken to sitting with his arm round her while they talked. It was a protective gesture she seemed to need. On the Friday he said gently, 'Let me help you off with your clothes. You should sleep in your bed tonight.' She had been lying each night, fully clothed, under a quilt on the sofa.

She lifted her chin so that he could undo her dress buttons. He saw a little pulse beating in her throat and it somehow disarmed him. He stared into her face and was not sure what he saw there – a waiting, an invitation, a question. He put his lips quickly to the pulse then drew back, placing a hand on either side of her face and drawing her to him to kiss her full on the lips.

'No,' she said feebly.

'Why not, Carlie?'

'I don't want things to change.' Her shaking left-hand

303

fingers were undoing the buttons on the clumsy combinations. He turned away delicately while she climbed out of them and into the starched cambric night-dress with its blue ribbons and drawn-thread work round the neckline.

'Here, let me.' He rolled off the grey, hand-knitted stockings. 'Is that better?'

'My arm hurts abominably.'

She put her head back against the settee, suddenly devoid of energy. He lifted her feet gently on to a petit-point footstool and covered her legs with a shawl. He sat down close beside her and her head sagged on to his shoulder. She seemed heavy with passivity.

'Stay with me tonight,' she said. Her teeth chattered slightly.

He watched her face closely.

'Carlie, do you know what you are saying?'

'Yes.' She nodded. 'I know.'

'Is it what you want?' He kissed her neck, under the ear. 'My love, is it?'

'Don't go. Don't leave me.'

Later, in her bed, he said to her, 'Have you ever slept with anyone before?' She shook her head, her eyes glistening.

'Then I promise to be gentle. I want it to be good for you, Carlie.'

In the morning, before he went out, she leaned against him, her eyes closed.

'It changes everything. You knew it would, didn't you?'

'I knew how it would be, making love to you.' He turned her round in his arms, so that she had to look at him. 'When I was with anyone else, I always wanted it to be you.'

'Don't.'

'You knew there had been others.'

'Yes.' She sighed. 'I knew. Everything is known between us now, isn't it? But this morning I feel as though I've peeled off a skin in the night and everything has the power to hurt and touch me.' She shivered, but forced herself to smile. 'I'm not sure I wanted to give so much.'

'Don't say that.'

'All right. Consider it unsaid.'

Kitty Fleming ran an expert finger along the dusty stair ledge as with her other arm she carried young Paterson downstairs for his breakfast.

One servant, and that one peaky and undernourished, subject to colds and earache, wasn't enough to help her keep up this place. She was almost resigned to leaving it, except for seeing Finn's dream crumble. They would have to talk about it soon. She had to get him to understand they would survive, no matter how humble the place. They had each other. But she knew instinctively that although this would be enough for her, if Finn's factory went part of him, made up of will and skill and imagination and masculine pride, would be destroyed also. She was very much afraid.

The girls were dawdling over their porridge as she went in.

'There are lumps in it!' Helen complained.

'Eat it up. Think of the starving children in Africa!' Kitty upbraided her.

'They can have mine,' Mairi offered generously.

Kitty looked hopefully towards her husband, willing him to smile.

'Finn, what is it?' she demanded quickly. He was sitting with an opened letter in his hand and a strange expression on his face.

'They want to come back to Scotland,' he said, dreamlike.

'Who?'

'Mother and Father. For good. Mother has been feeling very homesick and they want to see the children growing up. They want me to find a property for them, possibly a small farm or estate. Marie-Lou is going to the Argentine with her husband so they can hope to see little of her. And Bertram travels the world on business.'

'Well, there's a turn-up for the book!' Kitty sat down, scanning her husband's face carefully for his reaction.

'Mother says,' Finn went on, with slow deliberation, 'that Father also wants to go into ways of helping me with the business, as he is convinced the automobile is now established

305

as the best means of private transport and he commends my wish to extend into rolling stock and farm machinery as well – '

They gazed at each other.

'Dear God,' said Finn. 'I have prayed for deliverance, but this – '

'Can you stand it if he tries to dictate to you?' demanded Kitty. 'You know how you struck sparks off each other when you were young.'

She saw that the ink on the letter was spreading and that Finn, for the first time ever in her experience, had been shedding tears.

'Oh, my dear, you can make it work!' she said in a rush of tenderness.

Finn struck the letter with his free hand and said simply, 'This is our lifeline, Kitty. I don't think the old man will be unreasonable. I can handle him, now.'

The three children had come to stand near their parents, wide-eyed, puzzled, knowing something was afoot. Suddenly with a war-whoop Finn scooped them to him. 'Gramps and Gran'ma are coming from America to see you,' he informed them. 'You will have to be very nice to them, and sing them your songs, and tell them your stories.' The girls began to sing in unison now. They all held hands and trudged in a circle, round and round:

'Ring-a-ring-a-roses
A pocket full of posies,
'Tishoo, 'tishoo,
We all fall down.'

The little maid came in to see if it was time to clear the table. The master and mistress were lying on the floor, with the children shrieking and climbing over them. Sniffing, she retreated to the scullery till sanity was restored.

Later that evening, Kitty said reflectively, 'Finn, I remember reading in the *Herald* that Dounhead House is

306

up for sale again. Would it not be perfect for the grand-
parents? I remember it when Aunt Tansy and Uncle Lachie
had it – the grapes in the hothouses, the beautiful lawns, the
lovely rooms.'

Finn thought about it and then agreed. 'He'd like to go
back to Dounhead, I think. Have them raising their hats to
him in the Rows. The prodigal returned. Yes, let's try and
get it for them.'

While negotiations went on for the purchase of the house,
Paterson and Honoria were busy packing up the house in
Boston. Honoria's feelings were mixed, because so much of
her life was bound up now with the local church and com-
munity and she still remembered the thrill of belonging she'd
felt that day long ago when Paterson had brought her here.

But their longing to see Scotland again, and especially
their newest grandchild, the little boy named after his grandfather, had become almost painfully obsessive. Once they
had started talking about going back, nostalgia had taken
over. Now it seemed to them it had always been there, at
the back of their minds, the wish to go back to Scotland and
spend their last days there.

Honoria was nervous about the crossing. The sinking of
the brand-new White Star liner, the *Titanic*, on her maiden
voyage, was still fresh in everybody's mind. Despite the
fact that wireless had brought a fleet of vessels to the rescue
after the collision with an iceberg, only 732 lives had been
saved out of 2367. The image of husbands and wives dying
in each other's arms haunted Honoria, so much so that she
almost pleaded with Paterson to change his mind. But their
plans were too far advanced and, in the event, they had a
calm and easy crossing and a welcome that exceeded all their
expectations.

Dounhead House was having bathrooms installed and
other modernization work done on it, so Paterson and
Honoria moved for the time being into the house at Kelvinside. There the little boy took over his grandfather almost
entirely, mimicking his speech, his walk, his mannerisms

and even, with that lock of straight, fair hair falling over the eyes, managing to look at times almost comically like him.

'It's as though he's had a new lease of life,' Honoria marvelled. She took to life in Glasgow like a duck to water, loving the bands, the parks, the theatres, and taking Kitty and the little girls on lavish shopping expeditions to Sauchiehall Street, buying them tea in the Room de luxe and enjoying the serials at the pictures.

Finn took his father down to the factory in his own car, waiting for the inevitable comments on its modern bodywork, which he himself felt was possibly less attractive than the art nouveau, curvilinear styles of earlier days.

'In Scotland,' he explained, 'you must have a roof over your head. For the rain! And a windshield in front. Eventually I aim for a totally enclosed framework, with windows that will go up and down and even some form of heating for the interior of the machine, in the winter.'

'I don't know why you didn't go in for the steam cars,' the old man grumbled. 'The Stanley steamers are still contenders in the States. They're quieter, no fumes, easy accelerators. And easy to start.'

Finn hid a smile. No doubt it would please his father if automobiles were more like railway engines!

'One answer to that, Father, is that Leland's Cadillacs have an electric self-starter now. Soon we'll all have it and starting will be no problem.'

The old man's eyes were gleaming with interest as Finn took him round the shop-floor. Finn found he did not have to explain quite complicated matters – Paterson had the quick, instinctive grasp of the true engineer and it was at first chastening and then rewarding for Finn to realize how much he and his father had in common. Paterson felt it, too, that rapport between experts. It had already taken years off him.

'We have to build a solid car for Scottish roads,' Finn explained. 'They're not cheap, but they're hand-crafted and they go for ever. Trouble is, when we have to retool – as we did when we went over from bi-bloc to mono-bloc engines – the expense is crippling. I have come round to thinking that it would be better to buy some components from the specialist manufacturers and go into the assembly business ourselves. Though I had to learn it the hard way.'

The old man was decisive. 'Fine. But we'll do some casting too. Get in the best metal experts we can find. I always go on hunches and if the States are anything to go by, the market's going to rise one of these days for the mass-produced car. We should tool up for a long run. And we can diversify. Make other machinery. We'll have to find the premises to expand.'

'You want to know the costs?' demanded Finn.

His father slumped down gratefully in an office chair. He had been talking with all the enthusiasm of the old days, but he was suddenly reminded that bodies grew tired even if minds and imaginations did not. He said very deliberately and with a kindness Finn had not found in him before: 'You've shown the mettle, laddie. Now I'll put up the cash.'

Chapter Seventeen

Josie stood at the door of the house in the Rows, waiting for Duncan. It was Friday night and her house, like almost every other, shone and sparkled with cleanliness and smelled of lavender polish and rubbing-stone drying on the step. Not that she had done the work. Carlie paid for a willing girl to come in twice a week. Josie thought with wry humour: I'm not going to change now. Housework had always been beyond her.

Friday night. Pay night. It had a feeling all its own. In the shops, children would be standing by their mothers' skirts, tugging at their shawls, waiting for the free poke of sweeties that came with the groceries.

The lucky women would get their pay packets unopened. The less lucky, what was left after the pubs closed. But at least last year's long dragging strike was over. Asquith had intervened and promised a minimum wage in the pits.

Through the dark came the rumble of a taxicab and one or two wild laddies running after it, trying to jump on the running-board. Duncan stepped out while the engine kept running and felt in his pockets for coppers for the children. She brought him into the warmth and the firelight, turning up the gas mantle at last to display a table set with a cloth of Darvel lace, a cut-glass cruet and his favourite soda scones, with mutton pies from the Co-op sending up their peppery, cold-water paste aroma from a plate on the hob.

She officiated over the big brown teapot, stirring his tea, buttering his bread; loosing his boot-laces when at last he had eaten enough and was sitting in his mother's rocking-chair by the bright, warm fire. Just as she had done when they were first married and they'd come home from a stint selling the *Miners' Clarion*. He looked different now. He was stamped as a man of affairs. The beard was distinguished. The watch and chain stretched across the dark-blue waist-coat looked as though it belonged there, not like those which the miners wore on Sundays and holidays with a stiff self-consciousness.

He looked bone-tired but comfortable, his knitted grey socks singeing. 'It's good to be home,' he said.

'It's not for long.' She couldn't smother the protest.

'I sometimes wish –'

'What do you sometimes wish?'

'That I didn't have to go away again. That the only travels I had to take were to the Rows' end to see old Baxter's canary birds, or down to the river to sit in the sun.'

'Has the day not come yet?' she asked carefully.

'If I had any sense, it would.' He gave her a shamefaced smile. 'The trouble is, Josie, I've never had any sense. I never know when I'm beaten.'

'Do you have to go to Ireland?' she pleaded. 'What with Carson gun-running in the north and Connolly matching him up in the south –'

'We have to show solidarity with the transport workers and Larkin in Dublin. If we can get a negotiated peace in the strike there, it'll do more to stabilize Ireland than all the wild talkers.'

Josie sighed. 'Does there not come a time when a man says "I've done enough," and lives for himself?'

'It's not like you to talk like that.'

'How do you know what is "like me"?' she demanded, but without bitterness.

He did not answer her directly, but lay back in his chair for a long time, staring into the small hissing flames of the coal topped up with tea-leaves and potato-peelings. At last he said reflectively, deliberately using the vernacular for effect, 'Do you mind on the days we worked in the *Clarion*? And the time you told me our Carlie was on the way? These were good days, Josie. And you have been a good woman. Forgiven me much.'

Her face wore a stillness that contrasted with her agitated

and clumsy movements as she rose and began to clear the table.

'Sit down, woman,' he said, gently. She put the chenille cover over the table, then picked up the sock she was knitting before she obeyed him.

He said quietly, 'I would like to think I had brought you some happiness.' He looked at her. 'But I fear I haven't.'

She stopped knitting and placed the work on the table in front of her, her hands resting on it, her face unreadable. Then she said, 'I got what I asked for. I knew how it would be.'

'Did you?' He stretched a hand across the table and caught hers. She tried to pull it away but he wouldn't allow her. He looked down at it. It was a large hand, disproportionately, perhaps. The broad band of the wedding-ring had sunk deep into the flesh of the third finger. The veins stood up like purple pathways on the white skin of the back of the hand, the skin itself mottled with the pigmentation of old age, like freckles. The wrist-bone was big, too, protruding like a door-knob, and the wrist thick, not delicate.

She said, 'It's all rough. From doing the fire.'

'It's a good hand, Josie.'

'Away with you.' She snatched it back. 'Rabbie Burns isn't in it, with you.' She picked up the sock again, but her face was bright.

They had few more moments of rest or reflection during his visit home. The Glasgow papers sent their reporters out to interview him; vehement young Labour men knocked on the door, anxious for argument; constituents brought their problems; neighbours dropped in to bask in the reflected glory of the local celebrity.

The papers wanted to know what he thought of the anti-German hysteria, started by the British-German naval rivalry in 1909 and escalated by the recent Balkan Wars.

The party zealots wanted to know what the Socialist International would do in the event of war breaking out – would they carry out their promise of a general strike?

'If we don't know what the diplomats are up to, we're

powerless,' he told them. Josie read in his face something that disturbed her deeply – a disillusion, almost a desperation, as though events and emotions were tugging him ever more deeply into an irresistible, fatal current.

She looked at him when sometimes he sank into sleep by the fire. For a man not far off seventy, his resilience was remarkable, but in his sleep his face moved her by its near-total exhaustion. It was strange in a man so set on peace and reconciliation, but in these unguarded moments she thought of him as a soldier whose pack grew heavier with each campaign.

Her heart was gripped with terror and love and with the same desperate resignation as a soldier's wife's.

Finn edged his car through the crowded centre of Bridgeton, in the East End of Glasgow. Extreme care was necessary for no one here was prepared to give the car precedence: they contested its right to be there by stepping in front of it, standing in front of it, even having conversations in front of it, if it so suited them. He placed his hand on the horn and kept it there. Despite his leather coat, his gauntlets and his cap with the ear-flaps, he was frozen to the marrow and worried about his father, seated beside him, catching a chill.

With a thick plaid rug over his knees and his chin sunk in a huge knitted muffler, Paterson did not share his son's frustration.

'I don't know what we'd have done if we hadn't got the train for him,' he declared. He was referring to his grandson. 'I said he should have it for Christmas, and a promise is a promise.' He patted the large parcel on his knee.

They had been forced to come all the way out here to an outlying shop, the Sassenach celebration of Christmas having permeated the large central stores to such an extent that toy departments were all but sold out. Finn looked at the tinsel gaiety of the East End shops: garish mechanical toys from Germany, nuts and apples in the naphtha-lit fruit stalls, tea-caddies and hams in the Lipton windows. In the front of one window, a large tin trunk for emigrating. And, gleaming above the now wet-shiny cobbles, the pawn-broker's sign, where the Sunday suit and the Apostle spoons of the indigent poor found a place of rest five days out of seven. From a side street came a rattle of tambourines, voices raised in a Christmas hymn and the heavy thump of a big Salvation Army drum.

'It does nothing but rain in this infernal country,' Finn grumbled. The smirring wet, turning to ice, infiltrated the folding hood and windscreen. Glancing sideways, he saw women in bedraggled shawls, children in sloppy, gaping boots, or even barefoot, tattered clothes plastered to their bodies with the seeping, relentless rain. He thought of his own in Kelvinside, cinnamon toast for their tea, stone piggies warming their clean beds. There was a kind of indecency about safety and warmth when so many went without; but he could see no way of changing the lot of the poor unless they gave up their big families and drink.

'I see what's holding us up,' said Paterson suddenly. 'There's a meeting of some kind on the corner there ahead.'

As they rode past they saw a huge maroon banner with the letters PEACE in gold raised above a small makeshift platform, where a man was addressing the Saturday-night shoppers through a megaphone.

'Did you see who that was?' Finn demanded. 'It was Donald Balfour.' His lips narrowed. 'He's on a hiding to nothing there. I don't think there's going to be peace, Father. Do you?'

Paterson peered at his son, puzzled by the note in his voice.

'The big names of the Socialist International Bureau are having a peace conference in London, aren't they? I read it in the *Herald*. Jaurès, Molkebühr, Vandervelde, Adler, Anatole France.' Finn recited the names like a litany. 'But it's all too late. I think something savage and terrible will happen in the New Year.'

'Come on,' said the old man. 'Don't join the prophets of doom. We've found Junior his train set, against the odds. And there'll be a great roaring fire waiting us at home.'

Finn's face was set, almost gloomy. 'I can't help wondering what someone like Donald would do, if we had a war. I've given him his job back. Carlie asked me to and he's family, after all. But I think he could be a very disruptive element.'

'There won't be a war,' Paterson insisted.

'I didn't want to tell you till after Christmas,' said Finn, 'but I've had a visit from Whitehall. They want my help in drawing up certain plans for the factory. We may have to go over to munitions.'

Donald had not seen the car with his relatives in it drive past. He was too busy painting a picture of the future to his restless, heckling yet strangely hypnotized audience.

'If the workers do not stick together and make it clear to their governments there will be no war, then Armageddon will be upon us.

'We shall be in unholy alliance with the Tsar of Russia, against the Germans. Our ally will be this man who persecutes and murders his people, sends his parliamentarians and editors to prison and maintains his authority through spies and assassins. We shall put our own progress back by a hundred years. So, fellow-workers, I say to you, be prepared to strike if they try to drag this country into war. Join your fellow-workers on the Continent. Tell the rulers they must settle their differences by other means than killing.'

Donald lowered the megaphone and stepped down into the crowd. His ungloved hands were so cold they had no feeling left in them. His fellow socialists folded up the PEACE banner and by common consent they dispersed. The rain was set to win all arguments that night.

Donald pushed his way through the shopping crowds, watching the shop windows for something to take to Carlie. Some small offering, for although he was working again he had betting debts to pay off and new boots would soon be a necessity.

He settled for some scented soap, anticipating the look of her face when she got it. She accepted gifts with the elated delight of someone who never expected to get them.

'Hey! Donald!' said a voice beside him. He turned to see Albie Macausland, Chrissie's brother. Another man he didn't recognize had taken up position on his other side.

'Saw youse at the meeting,' said Albie roughly. He was an out-of-work carter, a man constantly in search of a dram and petpetually scrounging from his sister.

'Thought you might have the price of a pint on you,' said the other man.

'Sorry. I've nothing,' said Donald.

'What if I said you'd been two-timing my sister?' insisted Albie Macausland. 'Would you have the price of a dram on you then?'

'What is this?' Donald protested.

The men moved in, jostling him.

'I don't like to see oor Chrissie getting bad treatment from the likes of you,' said Albie. 'She was greetin', see? Me and my friend here thought we would teach you a wee lesson.'

Donald tried to move away as they approached the next close-mouth, but it was impossible. The two men hustled him into the dark, tiled corridor and Albie held back his arms while the other man smashed his fist into his face repeatedly.

When Albie released him, he staggered to the ground and they kicked him, none too effectively in the dark.

A woman in a shawl turned into the dark close to mount the stairs to her house.

'What are you villains doing in here?' she shrieked. 'I'll get the polis to you.' Albie and his partner fled into the night. The woman stepped delicately over Donald. 'Away hame, son,' she advised him. If he was in serious trouble, she did not want to know.

He managed to stagger to his feet. He was bleeding from a cut eye and from the nose. When he managed to get on a tram eventually, he drew only the most cursory of glances from the other passengers. Drunks and fights and bloody noses were common, acceptable fare for a Saturday night. You were lucky not to suffer worse.

The woman in the shawl found the scented soap in the close-mouth the next morning on her way to mass. She gave it to the girl at the baker's and got some black bun in return.

'Dear Aggie,' Carlie wrote to her Suffragette friend in London. 'You must have heard what happened to Mrs Pankhurst when she came to Glasgow. Arrested again! But the police had everything thrown in their way – flower-pots, tables, chairs. St Andrew's Hall was a shambles. We're not a lot for'arder, are we? I think you're right to join Sylvia Pankhurst and her East London Federation. It will show the politicians our movement is democratic, not autocratic as many say it is under Mrs Pankhurst herself. You know I've always had that reservation about Emmeline – '

The bell jangled and Carlie moved slowly along the lobby to answer it. She was totally unprepared for what she saw when she opened the door. Her cousin, Alisdair Kilgour, in an Army officer's uniform. He stood smiling at her uncertainly.

'Come in!' she invited. 'What is all this? The best kept secret of the year?'

'Hadn't you heard about me joining up?'

She shook her head. 'I haven't seen Sandia or Kitty for some time.'

'All done on the spur of the moment, anyhow,' he said. He stood, cane between his hands, in the sunshine of the parlour. She thought how well the uniform suited his ruddy, earnest looks and bristly moustache.

She poured him a glass of Madeira.

'Might you be sent to Ireland?'

'To enforce Home Rule? It's a possibility.'

'I hope it doesn't come to war there. Or anywhere else, for that matter.'

'Inevitable. We'll be in Europe before the year's out. I wouldn't have joined the Army, had I not thought so.'

She sipped her own glass and gazed at him consideringly. 'People generally join up to get away from something. Themselves, perhaps?'

His expression set up a barrier of reserve. No one was better at self-conscious dignity than Alisdair, she thought.

'It will be good medical experience for me. Broaden my horizons.'

'I know you don't want to talk about Tina,' she offered gently.

His blue gaze turned away from her. 'What is there to say about her? She doesn't see your half-brother any more.' His gaze returned, probing. 'Does she?'

'Wallace is in London,' Carlie said quietly. 'He was terribly cut up, but he went. No, I should think that's all over. Tina has her job, and we all see her from time to time. Have tea with her. Go to the pictures.' She gave him a swift, covert glance. 'Will you ever divorce her, do you think?'

He stared into his glass. 'Things might take care of themselves, without divorce.'

'What do you mean?' she demanded, shocked.

'Bullets find their target.' He smiled at her bleakly. 'Well, you never know.' Seeing she was upset, he said, 'It was a *joke*, Carlie.'

'Did you come here to ask me about Wallace?' she asked shrewdly.

'Not just that. To say goodbye. Be cousinly.' He rose. 'Aren't you going to marry Donald, then? I thought a year ago there was the distant jingle of wedding bells?'

It was her turn to look embarrassed. She hedged.

'Thanks for the job you did on him, when he was beaten up by those – those thugs last Christmas.'

'Yes, I did some fancy stitchery on his eyebrows.'

'He had been seeing Chrissie Macausland, you know. Not just casually.'

Her face had changed. It was as though past misery and tears puffed out the tissues, making her look worn, older.

He decided the best way to show sympathy was to say nothing. To let her talk if she wanted to. It was a strategy that worked, as it did with his patients.

'I wanted to get married. I wasn't blind to his faults. I've more or less grown up with him, after all. I could take the gambling, the occasional heavy drinking, because underneath it all, there's a good person who wants to help his fellow men.' She lifted her head and looked steadfastly at Alisdair. 'And I've always been – fond of him.' She blinked at tears. 'More than that, really.'

'Well then?' he prompted.

'I have to find a way to trust him. He says it's over and done with, as regards Chrissie. That she chased him up. But there have been others in the past and how do I know – '

'There won't be others in the future?' he finished for her. 'It's not very good for your self-esteem, is it?'

Carlie smiled again, the tight-lipped, tremulous smile that was more of a grimace. 'We sometimes don't have much option whom we love. I can't help my feelings for him. But marriage . . . no, I pause there. We'll wait and see.'

He said slowly, 'I'm glad you've told me. We all bottle up far too much. We can't bear to face up to our imperfections. Why do you think it's so?'

'I don't know,' she pondered. 'Perhaps it's got something to do with the kirk. It seems to me our religion wears an awful, unforgiving face. Can that be right?'

'I don't think so.' She saw he was becoming more relaxed, but it was still difficult for him. Touched by his awkwardness, she invited, 'Stay to supper.' He accepted eagerly.

'I can talk to you more readily than the sisters,' he admitted. 'They do tend to judge one.' They exchanged cousinly smiles of trust and amity.

Sandia had met Kitty in Buchanan Street so that they could spend the afternoon picking ribbons for the children's new Sunday hats. Usually the prospect of a leisurely trip into town pleased her, but today she was low-spirited. Before she had left home, she and Dandy had been discussing the Sarajevo business again. He'd always taken a reassuring line when she'd worried that the assassination could spark off a war. Hadn't there been trouble in the Balkans for as long as anyone could remember? But now all Army leave was cancelled and there were rumours that the Home Fleet was moving north up the Channel. Even Dandy was finding it hard to sustain an optimistic attitude.

Sandia flopped in the tea-room chair, absently buttering a scone and only half-listening to Kitty's account of little Paterson's precocious sayings. Irritated by her lack of attentiveness, Kitty demanded: 'What's up, Sandia? You're miles away.'

She wondered if she should tell Kitty. 'I dreamt last night of crosses, Kit. Fields and fields of them. Rows and rows. White ones. I had gone to look for flowers but there were none. Only crosses. They made me feel so sad. I began to cry in the dream and I woke myself crying.'

'What did you have for supper?' Kitty said.

Sandia smiled wanly. 'It wasn't that kind of dream. It was more a Grannie Kate kind. You remember she used to say I was fey? Highland nonsense, of course.' Her eyes seemed heavy-lidded. 'But if I believed in such things, I would say it was a premonition.'

'Don't.' Kitty shivered. 'I have enough gloomy forebodings from Finn these days. They're tooling up for something quite different at the works. He won't tell me what but I'm sure it's munitions.'

The sisters walked out to the street, where arm-in-arm they forced themselves towards more cheerful conversation. In some way, the familiar shops and trams, even the match-sellers and flower-girls, had become fresh and precious to them again. There was something, the scent of change and disorder in the air, and they didn't want to acknowledge it. They held it off with their quick smiles and laughter, the trifles bought in the haberdashery and the exchange of polite and gracious formalities between themselves and the trades-people.

Going home in the tram, it seemed to Sandia she had never seen her city look so seductively beautiful. A well-ordered place. She felt a quick twinge of conscience. Of course, there was poverty. She hated when she saw its evil manifestations. She gave generously to the many societies which sought to alleviate it. But she did not know how to be a rebel, a leader, a reformer. She knew only how to look after her own. She felt she had possibly been narrow, even selfish, but she could not change now. She was in her mould.

Deep in reflection, she was jolted back to reality by a shout from a man sitting behind her.

'Did you see that?' He was pointing excitedly out of the tram window at a newspaper placard, his wife on her feet the better to follow his gaze. 'It says "Jaurès Assassinated," ' he cried. The news ran through the tramcar in a ripple of excited conversation.

Sandia thought at first: jauries, that's the game of marbles that children play. Then her mind focused properly and she realized they were talking about the French Socialist leader, friend of her Uncle Duncan. Murdered? The bright day was shot once again with shadows.

Two days later, Dandy brought in the evening paper with a picture of her Uncle Duncan on the front page, attending a demonstration in Trafalgar Square in London, calling for a general strike by British workers 'to stop the war'. The Labour Party had issued a manifesto to the same effect.

'There can't be a war.' Sandia found herself saying the words over and over again. She could settle to nothing.

But four days after the Jaurès affair, the newsboys of Glasgow filled the streets with their clamour. War had been declared on Germany by Britain, her Dominions and her Empire. Sandia was no different from the other women in the city. Between the urgent conversations, the bursts of anger against the Kaiser, she withdrew blank-faced into herself, thinking of the men who would have to go and fight.

There was George in the Mercantile Marine. Alisdair, already in uniform. She was glad that her other brother, Andrew, had retired from the Army and was tea-planting in India.

'It'll all be over by Christmas,' she told Dandy. 'That's what everyone is saying.'

Her beloved Glasgow, which had expanded since her girlhood to encompass a million souls, seemed to jerk like a bad reel in a moving picture into urgent, febrile animation. The easy-going days of shopping, football, tea-rooms, picture-going, music in the park, faded into limbo.

Kitchener appealed to the country for 200,000 volunteers and in Glasgow the trades and professions conducted their own recruiting campaigns. Illuminated tramcars bumped their way round the city, persuading the wavering to join the Tramway Battalion, which was to be the 15th Highland Light Infantry, while the Chamber of Commerce summoned enough volunteers to make up the 17th Battalion.

Khaki-clad figures streamed in and out of the stations. The paper-sellers bawled out the heavy headlines with incoherent dramatics. Women seeing their sons or husbands off on service wandered the streets blankly, sat in tea-rooms sipping cups of tea they did not taste.

Butter went up by threepence a pound and bread was dearer. A woman wrote to the papers that perhaps war was necessary, as the population was increasing at too fast a rate. Sandia remembered Kirsten and what she had said about birth control, that night more than thirty years ago when they had intrepidly paid their first visit to a tea-room and the glamour of the Empire's second city had ensnared her heart for good.

She wished Kirsten had lived to see the new status women were at last achieving, even if it had taken the outbreak of war to do it. Those in prison for Suffragette activity were released to work in munitions and special services. Would Kirsten perhaps have stood out against the war? Sandia wondered. Sylvia Pankhurst did. But Emmeline, her mother, was wholeheartedly in support of it and handed out white feathers to young men who would not volunteer.

Far from being over by Christmas, the war had escalated by then and German warships had shelled Scarborough, Hartlepool and Whitby, killing over a hundred people. In January, the first Zeppelin raid took place on Yarmouth, Cromer and King's Lynn. By May, the name Ypres had entered everybody's vocabulary, the Germans had used chlorine gas for the first time and America, shocked by the callous sinking of the *Lusitania*, with 1100 drowned, was no longer talking with quite the same passion about the necessity of remaining neutral.

Sandia heard that Paterson and Honoria had given up all claim to Dounhead House for the time being that it might be used as a hospital. She herself began collecting linen for Red Cross bandages and organized knitting parties to make comforts for the troops.

Soon after, Alisdair came to say goodbye.

'Mother would have been so proud of you,' she told him, holding him close. She could not judge the look on his face exactly: it might have been relief or expectation. He kissed her and put her away from him firmly. 'Keep an eye on Tina,' he asked her.

She nodded. She didn't cry when she waved him off. Women were learning to put a brave face on it. Besides, when would the weeping end, once started, when every door and gate that opened was for another, and another, and another, leaving Blighty to put the Kaiser in his place?

Chapter Eighteen

Tina Kilgour had been to church and heard the minister pray for the boys at the Front. You could see the change in the congregation now – fewer young men and even the fathers of families missing. Since breaking up with Wallace, she had started church-going again because it helped to fill the terrible blank of Sundays. It was part of her weekly programme, like washing her hair on Fridays, visiting Sandia on Tuesdays, which helped to give some kind of shape and meaning to her days.

In church today she had thought of her husband, Alisdair. Each week, her wife's allowance came and she put it away, untouched. The fact that she was able to work and support herself was sustaining to her pride. As a separated wife, she had little enough status. But her work made her feel useful and she had recently earned some promotion. It was important to put on a show of managing, of being someone to whom respect, if not admiration, was due. There were some in the congregation who still refused to nod or speak to her, because of Wallace. But if they expected her to cringe, then they did not understand her character. God knew what she had given up, on relinquishing Wallace, and if God forgave her, then those whose lives were narrow and unfulfilled did not matter.

It was strange: sometimes how she couldn't remember what Alisdair looked like. His body had always been alien to her. She realized this now. She had married him without knowing in the least what it was to love someone, thinking it would be enough to run a man's house for him, and cook his meals and use his name in store accounts.

She had wanted to be married. Her shyness and nervousness had not made her popular with the brasher types of young men and when she had met Alisdair at a church soirée he had seemed sensible, undemanding, the first and only way out of the dull, unhappy existence she lived with her silent, evil-tempered father. She had liked the idea, too, of being a doctor's wife, when some of her more confident girl-friends had done less well in the marriage stakes, and married clerks or artisans.

So in church she had remembered Alisdair, not what he looked like, but his baffled, angry spirit, and had prayed that her foolish, selfish ineptitude in their marriage be forgiven. She had tried to picture him mending the broken bodies of wounded men : that somehow unformed boy's face that gave away so little of the intelligence beneath hovering above stretchers and makeshift operating tables. But he escaped her. She could feel humbled by his task, but untouched by the memory of their days together. There had been blows and cruelty, after all. Maybe forgiveness was best served by turning the mind, deliberately, to something else.

She had a word with the minister at the church door about helping to collect for the fund for wives and children of serving men, many of whom were in dire straits on the Government's twelve shillings and sixpence a week. And she promised the minister's wife that she would knit some more socks and balaclavas.

After the stone chill of the kirk it was pleasant to walk along the flower-bordered paths, past the quiet of the little kirkyard, just breathing in the soft air and letting her thoughts wander.

On Sundays, her landlady made a plain and wholesome dinner of broth, mutton and a pudding and they ate it together in the spotless tenement kitchen. Afterwards, refusing even to knit or sew on the Sabbath, her landlady read the Bible and in her own room Tina pressed and mended her clothes ready for the new week. She was in no hurry to get back to the pre-ordained ennui of such a programme. She stared at the lichen-covered stones in the older part of the kirkyard – here Eliza, Jane or Mary; there a week-old babe or a servant of the Lord buried in the fullness of his days.

'Tina.'

She thought at first she had plucked the sound out of the quiet air. Imagined it. Even that was enough to spin her round on her heel so that, facing him, she knew it was no chimera.

'Wallace!' she cried. He put out a hand to steady her. Her face had gone daisy-white.

He began to speak quietly and urgently to her. 'I thought you might be at church. I just came to say goodbye. I've been training in Scotland. Joined the Highland Light Infantry, as you can see. Thought with a name like Mackenzie, it was only right.' He stood looking down at her as though drinking her in, his face alight with pleasure while his eyes held wariness of her censure.

'They've made you an officer,' she said. She was beginning to tremble, and her lips felt stiff.

'God knows why,' he said lightly. 'I showed them how to de-louse our billets by running a blow-lamp along the seams of the floor-boards. Obviously thought I could be a leader of men.'

'You're too young,' she said slowly.

'Not as young as all that.'

'To me, you're young,' she persisted. 'You are seven years younger than I am, after all.'

'It never mattered to us, Tina, did it?' he demanded. 'To me, you've always been just right. In age, in beauty, in everything. My Tina. My girl.'

Her breath began to catch and she realized she was sobbing.

'You shouldn't have come here. It was all over.'

'I had to.' She felt his hand tighten on her arm to the point of pain. 'I couldn't go away and not see you. It didn't make sense. I came up here to join up because I thought: *I might see her.* Even in the street. It's not all over, Tina, and now I see you again, I don't think it ever will be.'

His pain overwhelmed her own. She said gently, almost

cajolingly, 'My dear, I never want to hurt you. You look so well in your uniform. Let's walk a little here, where no one sees us. Tell me – when is it you go?'

'Day after tomorrow.'

Now that she saw him again, nothing about him had changed. Eyes, mouth, hands. That concentration of expression, that earnestness that had been one of the first things to attract her. The straight back in its immaculate officer's uniform set up powerful reverberations in her mind. He should be wearing the old Norfolk jacket of brown tweed, the one that brought back now its own smell and texture . . .

She said stupidly, 'They can't take you so soon.'

'Come out with me tomorrow night. It's all I ask.'

There was no way she could refuse him. It was as though her emotions were hurling her down a great hill at a breakneck speed, too fast for her to analyse any of them.

'Yes,' she said. 'All right. Where shall we meet?'

'At the Ca'doro? At five. I'll book tickets for a show. Something cheerful.'

She would have to find some way of leaving work early. Plead a headache. Anything. It didn't matter. Her fingers were laced up in his, their steps matched, her legs were functioning properly once again.

'I wish we could have met tonight,' he said. 'But I'm on duty.'

'Tomorrow will soon come.'

'Will you think of me every minute till then?'

She laughed, all unconscious of the pretty sound she made and how beautiful laughter made her.

'I don't suppose there'll be any help for it,' she said.

She had to go home and eat the stolid Sunday lunch as though nothing had happened. The next morning, she had to explain why she had suddenly decided to wear her best things to work – she had just felt like it, she said, to cheer herself up.

They had a pleasant meal together and then in the theatre they sat among other Army couples, singing 'Joshua' and 'Hold Your Hand out, Naughty Boy!' They had gone to the first house of a variety show so that they would have a little time together, just to walk and talk, before he caught the last tram back to the barracks.

In the dark close-mouth, they said their farewells. It was where it had all begun, in the dark. She had been determined that if he kissed her, it would stop at that. But it was hopeless, just as it had always been. She forgot everything, the scruples about vulgarity, Alisdair, what They might think.

In the end, she wanted him as much as he wanted her and it did not matter that it was a close-mouth coupling or even that someone might pass them and curse. As it had been the first time, they were in a green country and again a little out of their heads.

Wallace Mackenzie went to France with a picture of Tina in his pocket-book. As he route-marched his men through the boiling French landscape that summer of 1916, her memory was seldom far from his mind.

He often thought that it was Tina he was fighting for: not his father, Duncan, to whom he would never feel close. Not even his foster-parents, who had been so proud of him for volunteering, but who seemed to have faded into a childhood image of their silent, Suffolk background. It was Tina who had given him the greatest moments of happiness in his life. And when this lot was over, he was determined he would find some way for them to be together. If she could not face up to divorce, he would take her away to Australia or Canada and they would simply live together. He knew his stronger will would eventually prevail.

He never brought the photograph out in his billets. His brother officers regarded him as a bit of an unknown quantity. When they talked about girls, he was silent, a small, secretive smile playing on his lips. He let them think what they liked.

Sometimes the married men under him queued in the French towns for 'a bit of grumble and grunt', paying two francs for the very real possibility of getting a dose of the clap. He thought they were beneath contempt. He struggled to compose poems to send home to Tina. Poems full of passion and high ideals that brought her bright-eyed and palpable into his mind's eye.

There was Tina and there was the war. He had joked to her about being 'officer material', but he had a steadiness and at times an almost inhuman ability to endure that brought him respect as well as abuse from his men. The war was teaching him, too, whose son he was. Not the son of quiet Jill and Walter, but the son of Kirsten who had been force-fed for her beliefs, and of Duncan who stood like a rock while the muddy waters of Westminster poured over and round him.

He could take men on route marches that had the weak ones falling like flies. When they fell out, groaning, he could encourage them to get up again and continue, building up the muscle and the will that would make fighters of them when the moment came. And two days later he could get them to do it all over again.

In the summer heat and rain, the shelling began. 'Coal-boxes' and 'Jack Johnsons' landed on the trenches and the men he had known as Big Tam and Snowy and Grunter turned into the first dead men he had seen. The unluckiest of all got hung on the barbed wire with their kilts thrown back over their dead heads and their buttocks obscenely bare.

He led his men in charge after charge. He was a loner who found no camaraderie in battle, but going 'over the top' to the skirl of the pipes he sometimes felt a wild, atavistic shriek breaking from him and knew the men who shouted 'Madman' after him would follow him to the last gasp.

Picking the ticks from his blanket during the lulls, he read the mud-spattered mail that came belatedly up the lines. From Tina, the protestations of love and the little pictures she painted from her memory: 'Do you remember the time we went to Rothesay and my shoe fell in the water?' 'I thought of the day we spent at Rouken Glen and a spider fell from a tree into my hair!'

'Only you,' he wrote back, his eyes closing from fatigue, the pencil slipping in the rain, 'only you keep me going in

329

this hell that living has become. I tell you, my darling, when all this is over we must make sure it never happens again.'

They had lost four hundred and twenty-one, all ranks, at High Wood, but they fought on for another six weeks until there were twice that number dead.

'We are still here,' he wrote her, with bitter irony. They had, in fact, been almost wiped out, but reinforcements from other Scottish regiments were arriving. Somewhat over three hundred and fifty men, some scarcely blooded, some old, some recovering from wounds.

'I have something to tell you,' she wrote, 'and I don't know if I should. But it is your right to know and you must remember I am safe and well and will be properly looked after. I am having our baby. Oh, my dearest, dearest love, be glad for me, as I am to be given this precious part of you. Now we can say we truly belong to each other, for ever and ever.'

They had to move through a sea of mud that swallowed up the moving animals and the dead men. He tried to envisage how this child would look when it was born in the spring. He wiped the tears from his eyes.

'God guard you,' he wrote. 'The autumn rains here are turning to sleet and snow. Last night it was so cold the oranges someone had from Blighty froze as hard as cricket balls and the ginger ale went solid in its bottle.

'I wish you had told me sooner about the baby. I hope it is a girl who looks like you.'

The Battle of the Ancre had begun in November. Once there had been no way back into the trench except over the snow-shrouded body of a brother officer. He had heard the dead lungs groan and grasp. Struggling on through the snow and sleet, the Glasgow Highlanders, the 16th and 17th High-land Light Infantry together, advanced against the Redan Ridge at dawn on November 18.

He felt the bullets rattle and whizz around him with an almost merry sound and knew the Germans had been nesting their machine-guns and rifles like hornets all over the area. Men fell like ninepins. Presenting bayonets, he led the survivors on. Something hit his shoulder like a hearty, companionable clap and he fell face downwards. His blood spread neatly in the snow.

'I am better,' he wrote in the New Year. 'I thought I merited a trip home to Blighty, but it seems I was wrong. I was lucky they picked me up in time. The stretcher-bearers were Quakers, noncombatants, but braver men you never saw. How is little bumpkins? Tell him/her I send my fondest love.'

In the spring he could look up from the trenches at hills covered in buttercups. 'It seems a tender blasphemy,' he wrote. 'And why is it that the sight moves me so, when I've wiped the tears from dead men's eyes and shed none of my own?'

'It is a little boy,' she wrote. 'Philip Wallace Mackenzie he shall be. I can't begin to tell you how splendid he is! Eight pounds and four ounces! What do you think of that? And every pound and every ounce resembling his father. I am so happy and proud.'

Carlie and Donald had just been together to see the baby, with gifts of a silver mug and an ivory teething-ring. Before the birth, Tina had settled into a housekeeping position with an elderly retired minister, who took little exception to Philip Wallace Mackenzie, just so long as he did not hear his cries or see his washing.

'Shades of Grannie Kate,' mused Carlie in the tram going back into town. 'That was what she did, all those years ago, when she had Uncle Jack out of wedlock.'

'Poor little devil,' said Donald of the baby. 'Let's hope the world is kind to him.'

'Tina's besotted with him, anyhow,' said Carlie. 'And as his aunt, I won't let the wind blow on him, either.' She gave Donald a lop-sided, wistful grin. 'It's nice to have a baby in the family. Even a little – what shall we say?'

'By-blow?' he suggested.

Donald handed the tram conductress their fares. As her broad beam waggled off up the car, Carlie said, 'I'm not sure that long tartan skirts are the right uniform for the Glasgow female figure.'

'Are you never satisfied, woman?' demanded Donald. 'Think yourself lucky we've allowed women on the trams at last. And that it's only the conductresses who are in the tartan. In the old days it was the trams – well, the horse buses. They used to be painted in their owners' colours, the Menzies and Macgregor tartans.'

She reined in his mood of gentle frivolity.

'I wonder why Finn and Kitty have asked us to tea?'

'To show what good friends we are nowadays,' Donald answered, lightly sardonic.

Carlie peered moodily through the tram window, unconvinced. In the early days of the war, Donald had brought the workers at Finn's factory out on strike, because American workers brought in to help what turned out to be aeroplanes had been getting a pound a week more than their Scottish counterparts. Donald had organized the hiding of tools and dismantling of machines that had finally brought about an offer of an extra penny an hour for the Glasgow men.

Like other engineering strikes endemic in the city at the time, it had stirred up public anger and for a while had soured relationships between Finn and Donald. But the factory had been on an even keel for a long time. Industrial relations were excellent and production high. Finn's brilliant stewardship had made him a very rich man.

Coolness in the family, however, had prevailed. Kitty persisted in criticism of Donald whenever she and Carlie met, and Carlie in her turn felt Kitty had grown somewhat high and mighty over her husband's success.

She said now, 'I wouldn't come with you, except that I like to see the children.'

'You're a proper broody hen today.' He grinned at her. 'If you're feeling like that, why don't we get married and have some of our own, before it's too late?'

She stiffened. For a long time, there had been no talk of marriage between them. Working hard, she had been content to leave it at that. But with his usual sharp perception as far as she was concerned, Donald had spotted the train of yearning thoughts set up in her by the sight of Tina's baby.

Their eyes met, trying to read what lay in the other's mind. She gave a gasping laugh.

'Should we give it a try?'

'I will, if you will.'

He held out his arms theatrically as she got off the tram and she jumped into them. To the amusement of the remaining passengers, he hugged and kissed her.

'What will folk *think*?' she demanded, but they linked arms and walked towards Finn's imposing mansion like two people oblivious of the world.

Donald announced it as Finn brought them into the parlour where Kitty was playing a board game with the children: 'Guess what? Carlie says she's going to marry me!'

They made a great fuss. Finn brought out his special sherry, Kitty kissed Donald with the first seal of approval for a long time and the children clambered over Carlie, the girls demanding to be bridesmaids in fairy-like dresses and Paterson announcing he would only attend if there was cake to eat, and ginger wine.

High tea was a spirited affair, though as wartime had brought its stringencies and shortages, not so grand as it might once have been.

Then, afterwards, while Carlie was led away by the children to hear them play the piano and recite, Finn said with a sudden gravity: 'Come into the study, Donald. I have something I have to say to you.'

'Out with it.' Donald's dark eyes sparkled with curiosity. His cousin was circling the room as though beset by last-minute misgivings. If it was to be an offer of promotion, Donald felt bound to accept it. It would show he was ready to accept responsibility. It couldn't come at a better time, with Carlie's acceptance giving a new edge, a new thrust to life's purpose.

'What do you know about Russia, Donald?' Finn's head was bent, he was cutting the end of a cigar, studiously avoiding Donald's first reaction to his question.

'Russia? I've seen Pavlova dance the *Dying Swan*.' Donald smiled, thinking it was some kind of joke.

'Well – ' The word came out like some kind of report. 'You're going to need to know more than that, because we're sending you there.'

'Sending me where?'

'Petrograd.' At last he looked straight at Donald. 'I'm sorry. The idea came from higher up. They need someone there who will pass on our know-how for the Russian war effort. They've taken a terrible battering on the Eastern Front, as you know. It has to be someone literate, good at explaining things. You know how complex our work can be. If there was someone else I thought could do the job, I'd send him. But it has to be you. I've thought and thought about it and the answer always comes out the same.'

'I see.'

'Will you go?'

'I didn't want it, but now we've got it, I suppose we may as well see this blasted war through. You know no doctor would pass me grade four, never mind grade one?'

'They're not too fussy about the half-mended men they send back to the Somme, either.' Finn's hand landed suddenly on Donald's shoulder. 'Look, it's important. I'd go myself.' As Donald looked up, he insisted, 'Yes, I would. It would be nice to make a big, heroic gesture. There are times I envy those in uniform, strange as it may seem. So what do you say?'

'If Carlie'll marry me before I go, I say yes.'

Finn shook his hand. 'I should think there'll be just about time for that,' he said.

The wedding was in the register office and Carlie had new shoes and handbag but no new outfit as she couldn't track down what she wanted in time. Josie was there, of course, shedding a few tears, but Duncan couldn't get away from Westminster. Sandia somehow contrived to make a wedding-cake and the little nieces, cheated out of being bridesmaids,

334

had to be content with throwing confetti and picking up coppers when the bride and groom threw coins from the window of the departing honeymoon car.

They were going to live in Carlie's flat at Queen's Park. There, they had one night of married life before Donald sailed on a munition ship to Archangel.

Carlie threw herself into her journalistic work. With so many men away, there were new opportunities for women there, as elsewhere, and her signed articles, serious in theme but with a light touch, were widely read.

She tried to imagine what the great continent where Donald had gone was like. The map showed Archangel straggling along the River Dvina. To get there, he would have sailed round the coast of Norway to the White Sea.

It was a pity, she thought, he had not been sent to Moscow. From her reading, she had this mind-picture of sumptuous Moscow cafés and the Mariinsky Theatre, where little ballerinas stretched their gauzy wings towards the candle-flame of fortune.

Or Tolstoy's Russia – would it be like that? Long, dreamy sleigh-rides through the snow, with a portable stove and fiery vodka for company, and feather bolsters in the sky opening their soft contents on the wandering entertainers, the *skomorokhi*, with their drums and their dancing bears?

She knew it would not be like any of that, of course. From all accounts, Imperial Russia was starving and desperate. After the resources of the Western Allies had been drained at Ypres, Loos and the Somme, the Russians had valiantly challenged Germany's might all along the Eastern Front. And then, when winter had intervened, the reports were that maybe a million frozen, starving Russian troops had deserted and begun a long, thieving, pillaging trek back across the icy wastes of their homeland.

The Allies were doing their best, in their turn, to stiffen Russian morale. There was a joint delegation in Moscow and commercial firms had sent in their workers, as Finn had done with Donald.

But as new reports came in of broken ranks and dispirited

troops and there was still no word from Donald, Carlie became desperately uneasy. She had known communication might be bad, but even Finn had heard nothing from the Russian firm he was offering aid. Finn was always calm and optimistic when Carlie sought reassurance, but his eyes gave away his concern. They began a grim game of mutual propping-up. Trust old Donald, they said. He would be in there, demanding an extra kopek an hour or whatever for the workers. *Of course* they would hear soon. British workers would be taken care of and respected. Wouldn't they?

Carlie could keep up the pretence no longer when the papers began to speak of revolution. The Don Cossacks, who had always been the strongest supporters of the Tsar, were reported to be joining the peasants and industrial workers in their demands for food and the other necessities of survival.

One day there was a hollow-eyed man sitting on the other side of Finn when she called to ask for news. Finn's face was pale.

'This man has been in Russia,' he explained. 'He tells me things are a little – difficult.'

She knew Finn had dared the man to tell her the true circumstances, but she waited for him afterwards and made him tell the truth. He had been working in a timber works in the Russian countryside. One night a band of desperadoes had attacked the stockade where foreign workers lived. They had battered down doors and fences with axes and murdered a dozen people, chopping off heads and sticking them on poles outside the sleeping quarters. He had hidden under a bunk – the one time in his life when being a bantam-weight was an advantage. And eventually he had escaped. But he was in no doubt of the carnage to come. Russia was in the grip of something separate from the war in Europe. She was on the edge of the abyss.

Carlie didn't know how she made the journey home. Once there, she retched and was sick, her mind filled with the terrible images the man had passed on to her. Afterwards, she found herself wailing into the silence, calling Donald's name. She saw the woollen dressing-gown she had bought him as a wedding-present hanging behind the bedroom door, and she held it and wept into it.

She had known all along, in some terrified recess of her being, that this was what Russia was all about. Donald was lost to her in its infinity of chaos, perhaps a prisoner in hiding. Or perhaps already dead.

'If Mrs Pankhurst is going to Russia, then I don't see why I shouldn't go, too.'

Carlie stared defiantly at her father. When she had read about the Suffragette leader's projected visit to Russia, to take the salute of the Women's Battalion, she had been filled with a wild, crazy hope and a steely determination. She would be able to find out something about Donald if she got to Petrograd. Two months had elapsed since her conversation with the man who got back and even Finn had admitted there was nothing more they could do here. Official British enquiries about the fate of Donald and other Glasgow workers had drawn a blank.

'How can you ask me to use my influence?' demanded Duncan helplessly. 'You know what it's like there. Murder, rape, looting. Even the journey by sea is dangerous.'

She had grown so thin that her clothes were hanging on her. But on her drawn and anxious face she pinned a wheedling smile.

'Do you think Mrs P. would be going, with the other top brass, if there was real danger? We'll go in convoy. And Petrograd is settling down again. Really it is. Kerensky wants to heal the wounds of the revolution, to make a gradual transition to socialism. It should be very interesting – good copy.' Her voice hardened. 'I *will* go, you know, Father. Whether you help me or not.'

They were sitting on the terrace at the House of Commons, watching the peaceful Thames. She had come to a London bristling with soldiers on leave, some recovering from wounds, taking their girls to see *Chu Chin Chow* at His Majesty's or tango-ing at the *thé dansant*.

337

'I love him,' she went on, in the same low, determined voice. 'When you were away when I was little, and Aunt Tansy bolted and left *him*, we were each other's family. He's my other half. I really don't want to live without him.'

He gave in then.

'I'll see what I can do,' he prompted. 'But you must stick with the official party. Not do anything silly. That's if I can bring it off.'

The journey to Petrograd was almost uneventful. Whatever they said about the stability of the Kerensky government, it did seem to be a reconciliatory one. The troops who had defected from the German front were being persuaded by platform appeals to return to the struggle. If that did not work, it seemed there would be no coercion: that a separate peace might well be negotiated with Germany.

But meanwhile there was the Women's Battalion – the Women's Battalion of Death. Watching Mrs Pankhurst take the salute, Carlie felt the whole idea a transgression of the idea of female emancipation. Did some of these women have children, and if so, what would happen to them if their mothers died in battle? She loathed the whole notion of women masquerading as men, and especially in man's last defensible role, that of soldier and killer.

Following the review of the women, Carlie was invited to a reception for journalists and other visitors. She went back to her hotel room to get ready, feeling the excitement rise at this first chance to circulate and put out cautious feelers about foreign residents in the city.

Her hotel room was scarcely salubrious. In the days of rioting and insurrection, raiders had taken most of the furniture, and she had to get by now with a jute bag filled with straw as a bed. She suspected the straw was infested with bugs. But with the state Petrograd was in, she supposed she was lucky to have a roof over her head.

She performed a sketchy toilet, grimacing at her skinniness, and entered the reception with her heart knocking loudly against her uncushioned ribs. The soirée was in a miniature ballroom which must once have been beautiful.

Now chandeliers had been wrenched from the ceilings, the walls desecrated with slogans and worse.

She was beginning to think her task was hopeless: all the faces were strange, filled with suspicion and sometimes even hostility. She remembered what a member of the Suffragette party had said to her: 'This is a city of spies and secret agents.'

But then a Russian woman who had been talking to someone near her suddenly turned and said, 'You are from Glasgow, no? I have been there. I am singer.'

Carlie allowed her to explain how she had travelled most of the world, singing arias from the famous operas, and then when she had engineered her into a quiet corner, said almost conversationally, 'Do you know of any other Glasgow people living here in Petrograd?'

'I do not know –' the woman began, then stopped. She turned her back quickly on the rest of the room and said urgently, 'I will come to your hotel tonight. Talk now of other things.'

'It's the Hotel Tatiana, room six,' said Carlie quietly. The woman's eyes dilated with panic-stricken warning, so she said no more.

She didn't know when her visitor might come so she retired to her room early on the pretext of having a headache, and sat there on her straw bed, heart beating unevenly at the possibility of at last having news of Donald.

She had almost dropped off to sleep, despite her vigilance, when there was a timid knock at her door, barely more than a rustle. She opened it and the woman, whose name was Anya, stepped in. She wore a black shawl over her hair and half-concealing her face.

'I know concierge,' she said. 'He will not say I come here.'

'Thank you for coming.' Carlie laid her hand on the woman's arm. 'I am looking for my husband. His name is Donald Balfour. He is a dark, thin man, about medium height –' She stopped. Anya's eyes were on her watch and ring. Carlie removed them without demur, handing them over. 'You can have them. Gladly.'

339

'For food,' said Anya. 'For my child. Now listen. I take you now to house where foreigners are. I do not know if your husband may be there. If he is, you must go with him on train to Bjelo-Ostrow. It is your only chance. Past there, you will be safe. Understand?'

Carlie nodded. She was already pushing everything she had into her carpet-bag, thinking how wise she had been to travel light. Anya asked her to give her some money to pay to the concierge on the way out.

Once in the street, they flew through the dark protective night, hugging the buildings. Anya's grasp never slackened on Carlie's wrist. All the while in a curious, hoarse accent she related what it had been like in the city since the revolution.

'The Tsar tried to come here. But the people stopped his train. He thought the Petrograd Garrison, the Cossacks, would save him, but they would not turn against the people. It was very bad here. The people had to queue all night for food and they were angry because it went to strangers with money, while old people died with the blood turning to ice in their veins. If you were stranger, you must hide, or you would be killed.' Her voice softened in pity. 'It is possible your husband die. I do not like to say it, but it might be so.'

Two soldiers came down the centre of the roadway, smoking and swaying slightly, possibly drunk. Anya pulled Carlie into a doorway till they passed. Then they were running again, two fluttering shadows, till at last Anya turned down a small shabby side-street and stopped at a large decrepit building. Carlie saw a dull red chink coming from a blind in the basement.

'I have sent word you come,' said Anya. 'Go down and tap on the window. They will let you in.'

'How can I thank you?' Carlie whispered. Anya's mouth brushed her cheek. 'One day I come back to Glasgow and see you. I will sing there. It is friendly city.'

'Yes, please come,' said Carlie. In a moment, there was a void in the dark where Anya had been.

It was the loneliest moment Carlie had ever experienced.

But fear lent her an unthinking courage. She tapped on the window and almost fell down the last of the basement steps as the door opened and a shaggy head peered out.

The next thing she knew she was in a large kitchen, with warm, yeasty smells. An elderly woman was sitting by a wood fire, watching her unsmilingly. There was the thickset man who had let her in and two men in ragged clothes, sitting at a table and looking at her with mixed wariness and curiosity.

One of the men rose and came towards her.

'You are the woman from Glasgow, then?' His accent was purest Geordie. His hand went out. 'My name is Harry Macready. From Newcastle.'

The other man rose slowly also and held out his hand. 'Peter Macbride, from Musselburgh,' he pronounced.

'I'm looking for Donald Balfour, a Glasgow engineer, who is my husband,' said Carlie, almost formally. 'If you have been working here, you must have some news of him. A dark man, slender build, medium height – '

Harry Macready took her arm and led her to a chair. She saw that he was filthy and emaciated, but his eyes, warm and sane, reassured her.

'Yes, we know Donald,' he said. 'He's been in this with us. He's been sick, Mrs Balfour. We've all been starving. These good people here – ' he indicated the man and old woman – 'have given us shelter, out of Christian charity. They even share their food, but there's hardly anything of it.'

'Donald,' she said. The words had dried up in her throat. She began to sob, not knowing she was doing it. 'Where is he? Tell me.'

Harry took her over to a corner of the room and drew aside some curtains. 'There,' he said, without preamble. The dark head was turned to the wall, the figure covered with mangy fur skins and ragged knitted blankets. 'He sleeps a lot,' said Harry.

She dropped to her knees and said his name. The figure stirred sluggishly, slowly, as though from a dream. He was thinner and dirtier than even Harry or Peter. His eyes

341

opened and he looked at her without recognition at first. Then his pink tongue began to work around cracked lips. 'Carlie,' he said.

She put her arms around the bundle of filthy rags.

'I've come to take you home. It's all right. I'm here.'

'Carlie?' he said again.

She wiped the tears away carelessly from her face. 'Can you stand, darling? Can you walk?'

He got up, like a stiff old dog. She saw that all the flesh had fallen away from his bones, so that he looked like the Christ-figure in some medieval icon. She cried out in protest and horror. She felt as though reason was about to desert her, as though she saw humanity being crucified everywhere, sickening and dying and rotting into bones and rags.

'Steady,' said Harry Macready. 'Would you have a tot of anything on you?'

She brought Donald forward to the table and rummaged through her bag to bring out a flask of brandy. She held it tenderly to Donald's lips, then everyone else in the room had a few sips.

'Carlie,' he said at last, in a more normal voice. 'How did you get here?'

'On a number ten tram,' she responded.

Through the night they went over the plans for getting away to the Finnish frontier. Bjelo-Ostrow. Carlie tried to persuade Harry and Peter to come with them, but they obviously had some plan of their own almost ready to put into action. She insisted on giving them her gold bar brooch which they could exchange for money or food.

'If you're prepared to pay over the odds for tickets, you'll get on the train,' Harry explained. 'The difficult part is when you get to the frontier. Sometimes you get passed through without any trouble. At other times, they question every single person on the train.'

Carlie looked at Donald. 'It's a risk we have to take,' she said.

They spent the rest of the night preparing for the journey.

With a pair of nail-scissors, Carlie cut Donald's hair. The house had no water but there was a cupful in a small wooden bowl with which they cleaned his hands and face. The old Russian brought a jacket from a cupboard to replace the rags on Donald's back and the woman gave Carlie a shawl so that she would look more like the other women passengers next day.

They had schooled her how to ask for two tickets for Bjelo-Ostrow in Russian. When she passed the money across the counter the next morning, the clerk said officiously there were no seats. Calmly she pushed more money towards him. The tickets were hers.

Fear. It was a kind of infection you caught in the streets. But it was outweighed by her concern for Donald. He looked so deathly ill she was afraid he would drop in his tracks. Yet once they were on the train, and it had started, he caught her eye with a glint of triumph that made her feel as if the sun were being poured over her.

They were stopped at Bjelo-Ostrow. Everyone was made to get out on the frozen platform. Horrified, she saw that the people ahead were subjected to the most rigorous searching. A woman screamed as an official ripped the hem of her skirt and gold coins fell out on to the snow.

She took Donald's arm as they shuffled forward, trying to weigh up the temper of the officials and glad when they got the youngest and, it seemed to her, the one who spent least time on the formalities.

Covertly and swiftly she pushed the tiny packet into his right hand. It contained her seed pearls and gold locket set with turquoise. Without flinching, she looked straight at him in total, naked supplication. If he arrested her, there was nothing more she could do. But, expertly, he palmed the small package into his own inside pocket. She felt his eyes rake over her figure with a certain amount of lustful interest. He muttered something in Russian that made a woman ahead turn and gaze at Carlie in open contempt. But he let them pass through. She was sure, as they stepped forward, that he

343

would change his mind and call them back. Second by second she waited. But it was growing dark. He let the night swallow them up.

As the train began its journey through Finland, she seemed to catch images and distortions of her own unholy terror in the darkling windows. Yet gradually the realization of what they had accomplished took over. She felt Donald relax into sleep next to her. She snuggled against him. The train wheels sang an insistent song of freedom and joy.

At the Casualty Station, that July, there were times when Alisdair Kilgour could hear the nightingales. He listened for them at the edge of the woods, when the quiet came after the bombardment. Their sound emptied and purified his tired mind.

You had to keep going on the small things of immense value. A clean pair of socks. A cloud shape. Flowers the cook had grown. A sycamore leaf lying in the palm of your hand. Its shape. Its veins. Only the small things made any sense.

When it came to the third battle of Ypres, he began to feel mortally weary. On the Messines ridge, where Haig was 'straightening out' the Ypres salient, he had to cope with the casualties of gas warfare as well as those who were wounded.

Passing down rows of stretchers, with barely room to stand or kneel between, he saw men gasping for air like landed fish, green stuff oozing from their lips. Some he could treat, especially if the type of gas could be identified; some he had to send back to Blighty, and some, too far gone, he could not help.

It was worse for him when the casualty was some pit lad from Lanarkshire or 'prentice from the Bridgeton slums. The sense of superiority he had once felt because of his background and university education had forsaken him once and for all and he could feel only rage that these stubborn, invincible men, some of whom had been fighting now for three years, had been hungry, lousy, wet and cold for most of that time.

Life had given them little enough before they came here, and nearly ten thousand from the Glasgow battalions had left their bones on the battlefield. The survivors should have had half a loaf a day. Often it was no more than one slice, with hard biscuits for tea. The nearer you got to battle, the more food was lost, stolen or sold.

Yet when they lay gasping through gassed lungs, or groaning from amputated limbs, they often managed to reassure him that they were 'all right'. He had brought the padre to one Govan boy dying of wounds, who had rounded on him, saying, 'I'm no' as bad as all that, Doctor. I'm going back to my wife,' and then turned his face to the wall and died.

As the main attack at Ypres gave way to the swamps of Passchendaele, he heard the nightingales no more. He felt as though all his life-energy was being sucked down into the damned, impenetrable mud. It was then he found he was thinking with a curious, hallucinatory persistence about Tina. He could see her so very clearly in his mind's eye, as he had first met her. A little quiet dark girl, whose smile always changed her utterly.

He had been in love with her. Not she with him. And he was someone who had always had women doting upon him. His mother. The sisters. He had thought love and submission and total dedication every man's due.

When the letter had come from Sandia to tell him about Tina's baby, he had been too busy with heavy casualties to let it sink in. It had done, after a time. He had felt jealousy and betrayal and anger and yearning ache through his bones like a destroying fever. Sandia had not wanted him to hear about it second-hand.

Well, now it did not matter. There had been the false euphoria after Byng's Third Army took Cambrai and they had pealed victory bells out over London. There had been no reserves to back up the advance of the tanks and he had had to patch up the men who had fought so hard for such a hollow victory. 'Green' men, just out from Blighty, without the resistance or the experience of 'Kitchener's Army'.

He was too weary for it to matter. The Germans were advancing once again. Both sides were throwing everything they had into the desperate fighting – tanks, cavalry, planes and men.

There were never enough beds or stretchers or nurses or medicine or bandages or hours to sleep. *Now it did not matter.* Let her flit in and out of his mind, like a flower or a butterfly. There was a foolish, secret comfort in it. He felt a fatal ennui most of the time. He was most probably going to die. Most of the men he had set out with had died. Every day he walked in the company of the dead.

But then, through the sensation of attenuated nightmare there threaded something they were calling victory. It had started when the twelve American battalions arrived. It grew stronger as Foch belaboured the Hindenberg Line and the Allied armies in Salonika reduced Bulgaria to collapse.

What would they do with it, when it arrived? The broken men, who would never walk or see again. Those who hopped on one leg or tied laces with their teeth and one arm. The skinny, pimpled, valiant lads who'd survived bombardment and come out the other side as men. What would *he* do with it?

Did they realize at home, he wondered, those who talked so facilely of victory, that it was still being paid for, in what they alleged were these last days of the struggle? He knew he was not alone in these angry resentments. There was a great void between those who had slogged the brutal days out on the battlefield and those who had remained at home.

On a day of torrential rain and thunderstorm the General sent for him to tell him he had been recommended for decoration.

'Nearly four years' service, Captain,' said the white-moustached dignitary. 'We're very proud of you. You've been a lucky man to survive, what?'

He agreed that he had been lucky. When the rain stopped, he sat on an upturned bucket outside the doctors' tents and listened in vain for the nightingales. In the distance, the bombardment began again.

The General had refused to go inside the Moribund Ward. He had gone green at the gills and pleaded lack of time. Soon, Alisdair knew, he himself would have to go back inside the two large tents, laced together and packed with dying officers and men. The last instalment?

They were waiting for supplies of morphia. If he could go into the tent with the means of easing agony, he did not mind so much. He went to look for the padre, knowing he could not go in there again alone.

The padre took one side, and he walked down the other. A young nurse not long out from Blighty, her eyes cupped with purple, accompanied him.

'Could you look at this one, Doctor?' she pleaded. 'He was brought in five minutes ago. A stomach wound.'

There was nothing he could have done. Nothing in all the world could have saved this one. A shot of morphia could have eased him into Eternity with dignity. But the morphia had not come. He had been making noises but now they were quietening. His face held that dreadful grey porridgy pallor that heralded death.

Alisdair looked down at Wallace Mackenzie.

He was never to know if Wallace recognized him, if some stab of recognition penetrated his agony.

'Put me away, doc,' he pleaded. His voice rose above the groans and tore at the air like a savage beast. 'Put – me – out – of – it.'

Alisdair took his hand. The young nurse took the other. Together they tried to make him a little easier. They put water to his lips. At last his eyes closed, A look that was almost of ease spread across his features. They did not have to sit with him for long. Life ebbed away peacefully, and after the rain the nightingales began to sing again. Deep in the wood they sang.

Tina's baby woke in his cot to a sound he had never heard before. It was a lone piper making his way down the street past the minister's house, playing 'The Flo'ers o' the Forest'.

People came to their gates and close-mouths, laughing, crying, sometimes both.

Testing to see first if the ink was dry, someone put a poster in the *Glasgow Herald* office window. It bore the Union Jack and the one word – VICTORY!

At Kelvinside, Kitty and the children heard the university chimes strike through the November air. Mairi and Helen rummaged like Furies through drawer and press to find flags to put out.

At Finn's factory, the men put down their tools. A woman sounded the hooter and smiled as though she'd forgotten how to stop.

Incomprehensible as ever, a hundred newsboys fled on to the streets with special editions, shouting above the cornet players and melodeon men.

Sandia took Catriona out into the street to point to the aeroplanes flying over the city in a victory salute.

In the evening, the students at the university joined in a torchlight procession. The Lord Provost climbed on the back of a lorry in George Square to communicate his civic joy to the dancers in the dark.

'Listen,' said Carlie to Donald as they sat by the window of their house in Queen's Park. Someone had dragged a piano into the street and was playing a ragtime tune. Flames from a bonfire nearby illumined their watching faces.

'Can you believe it's all over?' Carlie demanded. Donald shook his head. He was still very frail from his Russian experience, but earlier in the day they had gone by tram to see the celebrations in the centre of the city, and he had been none the worse.

With her head averted, she said, 'Poor Wallace. I have thought of him all day.'

He drew her towards him, to sit on the arm of his chair. 'There's only one way we can make sense of the Wallaces.'

'No,' she denied harshly. 'There's no way to make sense of a young man dying.'

'Your father wouldn't agree. He'd say you must go on

348

and improve things for the generation to come.' He stroked her hair. 'Carlie, I've been thinking. If your father doesn't stand at the next election – and he says he won't – what would you say if I tried for the nomination?'

'I would say no. Think of your health.'

He made a small, testy sound. 'I don't propose to let this ramshackle body of mine dictate my life.' As she began to protest further, he turned her head into his shoulder to silence her, kissed her ear and went on: 'You don't propose to leave the suffrage situation as it is, do you? Votes for women over thirty only?'

'It's better than nothing. It's a beginning.'

'Vote for me,' he joked, 'and I'll extend the vote to all women over twenty-one.'

'What else would you do?'

He thought for a moment, then said, 'I'd fight for Glasgow and the West. We could become an industrial backwater, if we're not careful. Do you remember what it was like when we were young, Carlie? This was a great city then, at the height of its power. Remember the Groveries Exhibition? The food, the clothes, the shops, the certainty it would all go on for ever?'

She nodded. 'On a Saturday night it was like a fairy-tale.'

'It's not going to be like that in future. English firms are taking over wholesale and we don't lead in things like marine engineering any more. We made the rest of the world rich with our money and our men, but what have we done for Scotland?'

'I've seen my father give his life to politics,' she said. 'Do I have to sacrifice you too?'

A firework going off in the street suddenly and briefly illuminated his face for her: a face full of questions and concern. She remembered the room in Petrograd where she had found him, his life on the point of extinction. Perhaps he had been spared for a reason. She had the sense of things taken out of their hands, pre-ordained. Only momentarily. But it shook her.

He looked at her and saw there was no need for an answer.

'For Wallace,' he said, his cheek against hers. Someone was playing a bugle outside and a woman's loud, screaming laughter echoed above it. For a moment, Wallace was almost palpable: his stubborn young face listening and waiting, as though to judge all they did from now on.